THE CHALKY SEA

CLARE FLYNN

CRANBROOK PRESS

The Chalky Sea. Copyright © 2017 by Clare Flynn

978-0-9933324-3-2

Cranbrook Press, London

For Jenn, Jane, Joan, Hilary, Bub, Pip and Wendy and our enduring friendship forged in Eastbourne.

THE CHALKY SEA

Clare Flynn

Cranbrook Press

PART I
1940

I never 'worry' about action, but only about inaction.

Winston Churchill, 1940

PARTING

JULY 1940, EASTBOURNE

*T*he sea was pearl grey and sparkled like the scales on a fish. Gwen stood at the window staring at it, as she often did. A few miles away in France, armies of German soldiers were probably staring back across the Channel wondering what lay ahead of them. Since the terrible events of Dunkirk the previous month, Gwen had been oscillating between fear and hopelessness. The German invasion was coming and defeat was an inevitability. Belgium, Holland and France had fallen, crushed under the onward thrust of German panzers, so what chance did Britain have?

She sensed Roger as he came up behind her. He placed his hands on her hips, then she felt the touch of his lips on the back of her neck. She stiffened and took a half step forward.

'Time to go, old thing,' he said.

Gwen turned to face him, her mouth forming an artificial smile to reflect her husband's real one. 'All set.' She dangled the car keys in front of him.

Roger reached for her hands, gripping them tightly as she resisted. 'Look, darling, I want you to promise you'll go across to Somerset to stay with Mother. I don't want you staying here. Things are going to get nasty.'

Meeting his eyes she smiled. 'I've told you. The moment the house is empty they'll requisition it. I don't want a lot of airmen in hobnail boots scratching the surface off my parquet floors. Half the road has already been taken over by the RAF.'

Roger moved his hands up to her shoulders. 'Once the war gets going properly – which will be any time now – we'll have more than scratched floors to worry about. Hitler won't bother to requisition the place. He'll just rain bombs down on it.'

'On Eastbourne? Don't be silly, Roger. He's not going to bother with a little seaside town. He'll want to flatten big cities, docks, factories. I can't imagine him sitting down with the Luftwaffe and targeting the pier and the Winter Garden.'

Roger let his hands fall. 'I wish you were right.'

'Of course I'm right. Don't you worry.'

'Gwennie, you know as well as I do that the invasion will happen here or near here. You can't possibly stay. The whole south coast is pitted with tank traps and covered in barbed wire.'

'Well that will keep the Germans out,' she said brightly. 'I promise you, at the first sign of an invasion, I'll drop everything and leave. Meanwhile I've things to do. There's the WVS. I can't let them down. So many have already left the town. Someone has to keep the flag flying. I want to move things into the cellar and the attic, out of harm's way in case they do requisition the house. As soon as I've done that I can go to Somerset.' She spoke the words and hoped he wouldn't know she was lying.

Roger sighed but said nothing more.

They passed the ten-minute drive to the station in silence, each conscious that this morning marked an indefinite period apart. It might be months, years even. He might never return but neither wanted to acknowledge the fact. After his escape from Dunkirk Gwen thought they may have used up all their good fortune.

The station concourse was crowded. There were young men setting off to join their regiments for the first time, women and children belatedly evacuating the coast where plans were advanced to counter the German invasion. Not so long ago the traffic had been in the other direction, when the town had opened its doors to give a rather grudging welcome to thousands of evacuees from London. They had all returned home or gone elsewhere as Eastbourne transformed into a frontline town, ready to stand hard against the German invasion that was expected imminently. Now the station, which used to be adorned with colourful hanging baskets, was lined with sandbags. Propaganda posters were plastered over walls that once advertised the attractions of pleasure boats and the programme of entertainment at the Royal Hippodrome and the Devonshire Park Theatre.

A month ago the first sign of German aggression had been witnessed by the town when a merchant ship, laden with food supplies, was bombed off Beachy Head. Gwen had watched the burning vessel from the balcony of her bedroom. It seemed unreal. Like watching a newsreel at the cinema. The war was no longer something happening on the other side of the Channel or flickering in black and white across the big screen.

A small group of uniformed officers were waiting apart from the crowd at the far end of the platform. Roger nodded at them then turned to say goodbye to his wife. He bent his face to kiss her, but she turned her head slightly so his lips met the hard edge of her jawbone rather than her mouth. She gave him another tight smile and said, 'Buck up, darling.

Don't let's get all soppy. The war will be over before too long, then things will get back to normal.'

Roger glanced towards the colleagues who were watching curiously. He swallowed and ran his hand through his hair. 'Look, Gwen, I'm not supposed to say this, but you need to understand. This war isn't going to end quickly and it's going to get very ugly. I can't even tell you where I'm going – I don't know yet myself, or when I'm going to see you again if I make it out the other end. I might be sent somewhere where I can't get word to you, but, Gwen, wherever I am, I will try and get in touch. If you don't hear, it won't be because I didn't try. I love you and I'll miss you every second I'm away.' He pulled her towards him, crushing her against his chest.

Gwen breathed in the familiar smell of him, felt the rough scratch of his uniform jacket against her cheek. She felt small and fragile when he held her, trapped, captive, like a caged bird. She stood rigid, willing him to release her and for the moments to pass until she could leave him to his colleagues and take herself outside the noisy station and away from him. Away from the possibility that he might see her mask slipping. That he might notice that her lip was trembling, that she was fighting back tears.

At last Roger drew back. He held her shoulders and looked down into her eyes. 'Gwennie, old thing. I love you so much but I know I've been a disappointment to you as a husband. I'm sorry.'

Panic rose in her when she saw his eyes were damp. She reached up and planted a quick kiss, square on his mouth. 'You are a silly sentimental thing. You know I hate that kind of talk. And it's not true anyway.' She tried to make herself say the words he wanted to hear, but they wouldn't come. Instead, she said, 'I'll miss you too, but the time will pass quickly. Now it looks like those chaps over there are waiting for you to join them, so I'll head off.' She gave him another tight, hard-lipped smile and turned and half ran out of the station.

There was a Local Defence Volunteer standing guard over her car when she emerged onto Terminus Road. 'You can't park a vehicle here, Madam, it's an exclusion zone.' He swaggered up to her, shifting his weight so that the rifle casually slung over his shoulder would be evident.

Gwen threw her handbag and gas mask carelessly onto the passenger seat, settled herself into the driver's, and fired up the engine. The LDV man stepped in front of the car, blocking her path. She engaged the reverse gear, then realised her retreat was blocked by a heap of sandbags. The man banged loudly on the roof of the car.

'What do you want?' she said. 'I'm moving the damned car.' As she looked him in the face for the first time she thought he looked familiar.

He drew himself up to his full height then bent down and leaned through the open window. 'I'm only trying to keep everybody safe, Madam. I was about to tell you that you can park across the road there.'

She remembered where she'd seen him before. He was a pump attendant at the petrol station. Always ready with a cheery greeting and an offer to wash her windscreen when she stopped by. Ashamed, Gwen gushed excessive apologies then put her foot down. Damn the bloody war. After a few hundred yards she realised she was crying. She pulled over and dabbed at her face with a handkerchief. For God's sake, Gwen, pull yourself together, woman.

Jerking her handbag open, she took out her compact and powdered her nose. After applying lipstick, she inspected herself in the mirror. No evidence of the tears. She snapped the compact shut, put her hands back on the steering wheel and took a few deep breaths.

Roger's departure had hit her harder than expected. She would be rattling around that big house on her own, no one to eat with, no one to share a sherry. And no one to share her bed. Not that Roger was unreasonable in that respect. When children had not resulted after several years of marriage, Gwen was grateful that he had not brought the subject up. It was as if he had sensed that it was a topic she wanted to avoid. Too painful to be confronted. Once it was tacitly agreed there wasn't going to be a baby, Roger didn't expect her to let him make love to her so much. Maybe once a month, unless he'd had a few drinks – that always made him amorous. Otherwise he left her alone, to her relief. No, she couldn't complain. She was grateful. Roger was a decent man. Yet that morning he'd said he thought he'd been a disappointment to her.

Gwen couldn't imagine what he meant by that. Lack of children aside, their marriage was probably no different from the other couples in their circle. They rarely argued. They muddled along fine. She certainly wasn't disappointed in him. Leaning back in the seat she sighed. Disappointed in life though. In marriage as an institution. In her lot.

Endless dull days when nothing happened. Her world contained by the house. Her purpose to plan meals, brief the cook, oversee the housekeeping. Her recreation the odd round of golf, tennis in summer, the weekly bridge game. She had never got round to telling Roger she didn't even like playing bridge. What was the point? At least it occupied an evening every week.

She envied Roger. He'd had his legal work with the Foreign Office to occupy his days. He'd travelled a lot with the work, often abroad, and, since the advent of war, he'd been involved in something top secret that meant he spent most of his time in London and closeted away in meetings at destinations to which she was not privy. If she had been frustrated with her lack of purpose before the war, now she felt more so. Roger wanted her to run away and wall herself up in a cottage in Somerset with his mother. There was nothing wrong with Maud. Gwen liked her, but she didn't want to spend the duration of the war with her, filling her days with knitting squares for refugees and growing vegetables.

The town was deserted. On a whim she parked the car and decided to walk the mile and a half up the steep incline back to her home in the district of Meads. She needed to work off her nervous energy. After a few minutes she removed her jacket. The day was already getting hot despite the still early hour. She wiped her brow. You're out of condition, woman, she told herself. That's what comes of a life of idleness.

~

THE FOLLOWING SUNDAY soon after eleven, Gwen was sitting on the terrace drinking tea. In front of her the sea was the colour of pale peppermint and milky with chalk washed from the cliffs.

She sipped the weak tea and grimaced. It was like dishwater. She would never get used to rationing. She would never get used to the war. At first she had thought, guiltily, that it might at last bring some meaning into her life, give her something to think about, something to distract her from the emptiness inside. She'd joined the WVS and supervised the dispersal of evacuees around the town, mended soldiers' socks for the war effort, and made endless pots of tea. But it was window-dressing. Inside she believed the war was already lost and the disaster that was Dunkirk had reinforced that. Gwen wasn't going to let herself be afraid. She had a plan. As soon as the invasion began she was going to down the contents of a bottle of codeine she'd set aside for the purpose and fall into a grateful sleep. Death was not to be feared. She had no idea what life under a Nazi occupation would hold and no wish to find out. If she were honest, she was using the invasion as an excuse.

In the distance, the faint sound of anti-aircraft fire grew louder. The low buzzing thrum of planes – ours or theirs? Was the invasion starting now? As the questions were forming in her head they were interrupted by the boom-boom-boom of a series of rapid explosions.

She spilled her tea on her dress as she jumped to her feet. Behind her the windows were rattling in their frames. The house faced south so she couldn't see the town, but already a plume of smoke was moving out over the sea. The war had come to Eastbourne. There had been no warning.

THE DISCOVERY

JULY 1940, ONTARIO, CANADA

*T*he sun was sliding low in the sky, a rosy glow spreading over the distant horizon behind acres of ripe wheat. Jim Armstrong rubbed the back of his neck where the sun had caught it. He'd forgotten his hat again. He reached down and grabbed a handful of ears of wheat, rubbing them together in his hand then blowing off the chaff to leave the plump grains. It was ready. The combine would be arriving tomorrow and it would take them a week to harvest the crop if they put their backs into it.

Jim loved this part of the day. Work over. Supper soon to be on the table. A chance to slake his thirst with a cool beer after a long, hot day, and now a leisurely stroll back to the house with the dog by his side, alone with his thoughts. Over the past months since war was declared, the news reports and the recruitment posters all over town had made him ashamed to be still here on the farm. So many of the men he'd grown up with and gone to school with had left for Europe as soon as Prime Minister Mackenzie King announced that Canada was at war.

Europe was thousands of miles away and their war wasn't

his, but he couldn't help feeling he ought to be playing his part. After all, Canada was part of the British Empire. His father had been involved in the last war and had a boxful of medals to prove it. There was a legacy to live up to. The old man had done his bit and now it should be the turn of Jim and his brother Walt to do theirs. But every time he'd tried to talk to his father, Donald Armstrong changed the subject. He hated any mention of his time in the trenches and always brushed off attempts by his sons to draw him on his wartime experiences. As for Jim's mother, whenever he or Walt broached the idea of joining up, she burst into tears.

Jim's dog, Swee'Pea, was sleeping under a tree at the far edge of the field. The dog was getting old and these days seemed to sleep more than he was awake. Jim had rescued him years ago as a puppy, when he found him floating in a sack in the creek, abandoned, presumably the runt of the litter. He'd christened him after Popeye's foundling baby in the cartoons. Swee'Pea wouldn't be much longer for this world. Jim couldn't imagine life without him.

He made his way slowly back towards the distant buildings, Swee'Pea trailing behind him. No sign of Walt, but that wasn't unusual. Probably fishing in the creek along the edge of the farm. Any opportunity to duck work and Walt took it. It annoyed their father but Jim always indulged his younger brother.

There was plenty of time to take a bath before supper. While meals were usually informal in the Armstrong household, he was going to make a special effort tonight as Alice was coming over to join them. He wanted to talk to her again about his dilemma over whether or not to join up – although he guessed what her opinion would be. She'd prick his bubble, remind him that it was someone else's war, halfway across the world, and that they had plans to marry next summer. He smiled as he pictured her narrowing her eyes and frowning at him in mock disapproval – she was always good at bringing him down to earth. He couldn't wait for next year to come, when at last he could have her to himself, when at last she would be his completely.

Spruced up, shaved and wearing a clean shirt, Jim sat down at the kitchen table. His father was already seated.

'Wheat's ready. I ordered the combine for tomorrow,' Jim said.

'Didn't you say Alice was coming to supper tonight?' his mother asked, as she carried a pot from the stove. 'I've made butter pies. Not like her to be late.'

Jim shrugged. 'I expect she got held up at the library. She'll be here soon.' He nodded towards another empty chair. 'Where's Walt?'

'Went to check on the cow,' said Donald. 'Maybe she's started. Not due for a few days but you never know. Why don't you go and see if he needs a hand?'

Helga Armstrong sighed. 'Dinner will be spoiled if you have to sort that cow out.'

'Cows don't care about mealtimes. When a calf's coming it's got to come.' Jim pushed his chair back and got up from the table.

The porch door opened and Walt came into the kitchen. He pulled out his chair and sat down. 'I've a right appetite tonight, Ma,' he said. 'What's for supper?'

'Nothing for you until you've scrubbed yourself up. We've company tonight. Alice is joining us.'

Walt sighed, got up and left the room.

His mother called out behind him, 'And a clean shirt mightn't hurt if you've been messing around those cows.'

A few minutes later the porch door rattled and Alice came into the kitchen. 'I'm so sorry I'm late,' she said, her face flushed and her voice breathless. 'I got here as fast as I could but that old bike was hard work tonight. Seems the whole town brought their books back today.' She gave Jim a quick kiss on the cheek and sat down.

Jim waited until everyone was tucking into the peameal pork and baked beans, then said, 'I saw Petey Howardson this afternoon when I went into town to book the combine. He's had letters from his boys.'

Walt looked up. 'And?'

'They haven't seen any action yet. Seem to be stuck at training camp. Nine months now. You don't go to war to spend all your time on exercises.' Jim shook his head.

'Better not to go to war at all,' their father barked.

'Thank God, is what I say,' said Helga. 'I feel for those Howardsons. Three boys and all of them joined up and overseas. I pray their poor mother will get them all back safely when it's over.'

'The war to end all wars. What a joke that was. Barely twenty years later and they're expecting more men to throw their lives away.' Donald shovelled a spoonful of beans into his mouth.

Alice tried to steer the conversation onto safer ground. 'How are the Howardsons coping without the boys? Must be hard work for Petey.'

'Mrs Howardson and the two girls are working hard and there are half a dozen kids who come by at the weekends and after school to lend a hand. The school has organised it that the older kids get off an hour early. Petey says they're coping fine.'

Donald raised his eyes from his dinner. 'I know where this is heading, son, and that's an end to it. Easy enough for Petey to get by with women and children – he's only growing vegetables and keeping cows. And two of those boys of his were worse than useless, specially that no-good Tip. It's a different matter here. We can't get by without you two.'

Helga wiped her hands on her apron and stood at the end

of the table behind her husband. 'What happens over in Europe is nothing to do with us, son. You're not expected to go and fight. You're needed here. The Prime Minister made it clear that fighting this war was voluntary. If Canadians were really needed they would be conscripted. Those Howardson boys were always work shy. Anything to get off the farm.'

Jim looked across the table at his brother, waiting for him to say something, but Walt stayed silent.

'Every time I go into town I feel people looking at me. I know what they're thinking. That I'm chicken. Afraid to defend my country.' Jim turned towards Alice but she was looking down at her barely touched plate.

'Defend your country?' Donald slammed his fist onto the table. 'No one's attacking your country. If Hitler invades Canada then you can join up. Until then you're staying here. No son of mine is going to go through what I went through. Not while I've breath in my body.'

Jim looked over at Walt who was frowning and scraping at the surface of the tablecloth, where one of the threads in the cloth was fatter than the others. He ran his fingernail over it repeatedly, as though trying to scratch it down to match the size of the other threads. Why wasn't he jumping in to support Jim?

'It's not about defending our borders – Mr Mackenzie King said it was about defending all that makes life worth living.' As Jim said the words he felt embarrassed. They sounded hollow coming from him whereas over the radio when the Prime Minister declared the country to be at war they had sounded noble, inspiring, compelling.

Eventually Walt looked up. 'If Jim wants to go, then maybe he should. I can stay and help Pa with the farm.'

Jim's mouth fell open. It was not what they'd talked about. How many times had they walked on the banks of the creek discussing joining up together? Walt had, if anything, been the prime mover. Right from last September, when Mackenzie King declared the country was following Britain into war against Germany, he had wanted them both to defy their father and volunteer.

Donald leaned back in his chair. 'This is the last time I want to hear about this. You're a grown man, Jim. I can't stop you, but if you do go, then don't bother coming back here afterwards. If you think risking your life for strangers is more important than supporting your own family, I've raised you wrong.'

Helga put a restraining hand on her husband's shoulder. 'That's enough of that kind of talk, Don.' She turned to Jim. 'Don't you be paying attention to what other people say. Your responsibilities are here. And talking of running off to war when you've a wedding to plan – shame on you, Jim Armstrong. Staying right here growing wheat and corn to feed the troops and send to those poor folk in England is what will make the biggest contribution to this war.' She smoothed down her apron. 'And I don't want you over there killing Germans. Remember your own grandmother was German. I was brought up German. Hitler may be a bad man, but all those German soldiers are young men like you and Walt. I don't want any son of mine killing anyone. That's the end of it. Now, who wants one of my butter pies? I made them specially for you, Alice.'

'You're spoiling me again, Mrs Armstrong,' said Alice.

'If I can't spoil my future daughter-in-law, who can I spoil?'

Alice tucked an escaping strand of hair behind her ear and blushed. Jim looked at her and wondered, as he often did, how he'd managed to persuade the best-looking girl in the district to marry him. Her hair was pale blonde, shot through with the colour of ripe corn when the sunlight was on it. He had to fight the urge to run his hands through it whenever he saw her. When she smiled she lit up the room, her eyes as blue as cornflowers and her lips full, revealing a slight gap between her front teeth. His heart pounded as he looked at her. It almost killed him not touching her whenever she was close: it was like a child being left alone with a piece of candy and being told he mustn't eat it. When he looked at her, the thought of joining up was less appealing. How he could he bear to be parted from her?

'Stop that.' His mother was addressing his brother. 'You'll tear a hole in my best tablecloth.' She slapped him lightly on the arm.

Walt got up from the table. 'I'm going to check on that cow again.'

'You'll go nowhere. We have a guest. Have you no manners?' Helga reached out to grab her son's arm, but he was too quick for her and left the room, the door slamming behind him.

'What's got into him?' Helga shook her head.

'I'll go after him,' said Jim half rising from the table.

'Leave him be,' their father growled.

The tension in the room was palpable. After a few minutes Alice looked at Jim, then got up and said it was time she was going.

'I'll walk you home.' Jim was on his feet.

Alice laid a hand on his arm. 'No, Jim, I came on my bicycle. I'll be fine. Thank you so much, Mrs Armstrong. It was delicious, especially those butter pies.' She waved at Donald and went out of the door, Jim following.

On the porch he pulled her towards him. 'Shall we walk down by the creek for a while? We haven't had a minute alone.' He bent to kiss her.

She eased herself away from him before their lips touched. 'I have a summer cold coming on and I don't want to give it to you,' she said. 'I don't feel too great so I think I'll head on home. You go inside. It's getting chilly.' Before Jim could respond, she had stepped off the porch and was running towards the fence where her bicycle was leaning. He watched as she mounted the bike and pedalled away down the track.

Jim had no wish to sit in the kitchen with his parents and open the argument again. He wished them goodnight and told them he was going upstairs to read a book. In the room he had shared with Walt since they were small children, he lay on the bed and stared at the ceiling, thinking of Alice.

She had been in Walt's class at school. Alice was a little kid with pigtails. He hadn't noticed her, until one day when he saw her in the school yard surrounded by boys who were trying to persuade her to kiss them for five cents a go. It was then he really saw her. Alice was up against the wall, like a trapped animal. When he approached, her eyes fixed on him, uncertain whether he was about to add to her troubles or be her rescuer. He looked at the gang of boys and saw Walt was one of her persecutors. Jim had gripped his brother by the collar and shoved him away. 'Leave her alone, you're a bunch of bullies,' he'd shouted and was rewarded with a smile from Alice that melted his indifference. She was thirteen and he was fifteen and from that point on she was devoted to him and he would have done anything for her. They started going steady the year Jim left school and had been together ever since, to Walt's initial disgust and eventual silent resentment.

Jim tried to read his book but tonight he was immune to the call of Jack London. Putting the book aside he got up and went in search of Walt. Maybe that cow was calving.

Swee'Pea followed him as Jim headed into the barn. He blinked as his eyes adjusted to the dark and shivered in the cool interior. There was no sign of Walt. The heavily pregnant cow gave a soft lowing as he approached then went back to munching hay. He ran his hands along her flank. Not ready yet. Maybe not until tomorrow. He was about to go outside and head back to the farmhouse when he heard a soft moaning. He looked about him. Apart from the cow the barn was empty. Another moan, louder this time and the sound of rustling straw. He looked up. It was coming from the hayloft.

Jim's heart began to thump in his chest with a sudden unaccountable fear. For some reason he didn't want to find out what was up there but felt compelled. It wouldn't be the first time he'd found hobos sleeping in the hayloft. A flicker of pain touched his right temple. He put his foot on the ladder and began to climb up.

Standing at the top of the steps he didn't see them at first. It was almost entirely dark up there but the loose roof panel that Donald had been nagging him and Walt to fix, allowed a narrow stream of light to penetrate the gloom at the rear of the loft. Walt, his overalls at half mast, was on top of a girl whose legs were wrapped around his back.

Walt had shown no apparent interest in girls. In fact Jim had begun to wonder if he might be inclined the other way and now here he was, doing the dirty with some loose woman. The sly dog. None of that lengthy courtship, waiting and holding back that he and Alice had undergone – were still undergoing. He'd too much respect for Alice to ever push her to go all the way before they were married, much as it nearly killed him, he wanted her so much. No such discretion for little brother – he'd gone right out there and rolled some girl in the hay. You had to hand it to him. Walt didn't believe in doing things by halves.

Jim was about to retreat discreetly, a smile on his face. He'd get some mileage out of what he'd seen – enough ammunition to tease Walt all winter – when the girl cried out. 'Oh God, Walt, what are you doing to me? I don't think I can take any more!'

At the top of the ladder Jim froze, his hands gripping the wooden struts so tightly his fingers were white.

Then her voice again. 'I didn't mean it! Don't stop! If you do I'll kill you.' Another groan.

The pain in his head grew, carving a path through his skull, blinding him. He swayed and clutched the ladder and the barn began to spin around him. Let this be a dream. Let me wake up. It's not true. How could it be true? Not Alice. Not Walt. They couldn't. They wouldn't.

Then they were looking at him, their eyes reflecting their horror back at him. Their shame. Guilt. They looked at each other and in that moment Jim knew his whole life was a lost cause. Seeing the look they exchanged was worse than witnessing what their bodies had done. It was a look of complicity, of shared understanding, of love.

He didn't wait while they scrambled to adjust their clothes. He slid down the wooden ladder, barely touching the rungs and began to run. As the twilight descended the sound of Swee'Pea's plaintive barking grew quieter as he ran until his lungs were bursting.

THE FIRST BOMBING

EASTBOURNE

*T*he phone rang and Gwen went inside to answer it. It was Brenda Robson, the coordinator for the Women's Voluntary Service.

'Did you hear the bombs?' Brenda sounded as though this were an adventure, a jolly jape. 'Here in Eastbourne. Whitley Road. Ten of them apparently. Can you get there as fast as possible? I'm heading there now. All hands on deck.'

Gwen changed into her WVS uniform and was opening the front door before she remembered she'd left the car in town. Dashing into the garage, she grabbed her bicycle, noticing that Roger had cleaned and polished it and pumped up the tyres before he'd left. So typical of him to think of doing this without even letting her know. She felt a stab of guilt as she wheeled the bike down the path. Her husband was so thoughtful, whereas she rarely did anything out of the ordinary for him. She didn't deserve a man like him. And now she had no idea when she would see him again. *If* she would see him again. Maybe he'd never come back from wherever the War Office, or the Foreign Office or the Inter-Services Bureau or whichever mysterious and unidentifiable section of Special Operations, had sent him. Her mouth twitched and the tears threatened again. Come on. Don't be daft. Get on with it. That's what we all have to do while this bloody war's on.

She smelled the bomb damage before she saw it. The stench of burning wood, plaster and brick dust, escaping gas. When she turned into Whitley Road, the fire engines were already there and a crowd had gathered in the street – bombed-out residents, ARP workers, LDVs, ambulance drivers, firefighters. Where there had once been a row of houses, a yawning gap was piled high with debris, nothing left standing but a lone chimney stack. Beside the hole, the next building appeared relatively unscathed, criss-crossed bomb tape over the still intact upper windows but the lower ones gone. Further down the street a shop had been blasted apart, the roof collapsed, windows blown out and an advertising sign for Senior Service hanging from the crossbar of a lamp post where it had landed. The road was covered in a carpet of rubble and glass. Choking dust filled the air and Gwen struggled to breathe. Nothing had prepared her for this. It was real. It was raw. It was happening here in this sleepy seaside town.

These were homes, not military targets: humble terraced houses where ordinary people had been going about their ordinary lives. What had they done to deserve the firepower of the Luftwaffe?

She looked up the street to where the residents of the ruined houses were huddled under blankets, in shock, and shivering despite the heat of the day. They were clustered together – a motley crew of women, the elderly, and one or two children. One of her fellow WVS workers was busy dispensing tea from a mobile canteen.

She hurried over to the WVS tea van where Brenda Robson thrust a clipboard into her hands. 'Good girl. You got here quickly. Go and collect people's names and house numbers and find out who's missing. And check if they've anyone to stay with. The school down the road is the rest centre – they'll be billeted there until we can find something more suitable.'

Gwen worked her way through the now homeless occupants, astonished at the calm with which people accepted the total destruction of their homes and possessions. She tried to imagine what it would be like if her house and everything she owned were reduced to a heap of smoking rubble. Ashamed at her reluctance to open her doors for the billeting of troops, she moved among the people, noting their details on her clipboard.

Five hours later, exhausted and covered in grime, Gwen headed home on her bicycle. The fractured gas mains in Whitley Road had delayed setting up the rest centre. She had to wait until field stoves for a makeshift kitchen were delivered, to see them through until the mains could be repaired. While most of her WVS colleagues went along with the homeless to the rest centre, Gwen stayed, making endless cups of tea while the fire wardens and stretcher party dug out more wounded from the rubble of their homes. Among the crowd of helpers Gwen recognised the LDV man she had met outside the station on Friday morning. That seemed like weeks ago instead of the day before yesterday. Feeling ashamed of her rudeness at the time, she gave him a huge smile and, ignoring rationing, added an extra spoonful of sugar to his tea. When he muttered his gratitude, she said, 'You deserve it after all your hard work today.'

'We're all in it together, Madam. Got to get on and do our duty, haven't we?'

He smiled at her and she realised that something had changed with this war, with this bombing. They were indeed all in it together. Where once she would have handed him a sixpence for wiping her windscreen and never given him a second glance, now she was serving him tea as though they were equals. Funny old world – but Gwen was beginning to think she liked it better.

She poured herself a large whisky as soon as she got inside the house. One dead and twenty injured. Nine houses destroyed, blasted into oblivion, and sixty more damaged. It was a wonder the death toll was so low, it being a Sunday morning and after the church services had finished. Thankfully many families and most children had been evacuated from the town weeks earlier. There had been no advance warning, as the War Office instructions precluded use of sirens for single raiders. What a stupid rule – all it took was one plane.

The stench of charred wood and plaster dust still haunted her. She slugged back her scotch, feeling it burn her throat. Gwen was not used to drinking, but if the war went on at this rate she could get accustomed to it – as long as Roger's supplies held out. Anything to dull the pain of what she had witnessed. The stoicism of the people of Whitley Road had made her feel selfish and self-centred. So far the war had asked so little of her and had barely touched her. Gwen resolved that all that would change from now on.

Her musings were interrupted by the door opening. Mrs Woods, her cook-housekeeper put her head around. 'May I have a word, Mrs Collingwood?' She didn't wait for Gwen's answer. 'I'm sorry but I've decided to go and stay with my son and his wife in Hailsham. They've been on at me for months. I didn't want to let you down, Madam, but these bombs dropping has made a difference. I'm not scared, but if I'm going to go I'd rather go with my own kith and kin.'

Gwen's heart sank.

Mrs Woods avoided Gwen's eyes. 'I'm sorry to let you down and leave you here on your own, but Mr Collingwood did say as you were planning to go to stay in Somerset with his mother.'

Gwen stifled her irritation. 'I'll be fine, Mrs Woods. When are you planning to leave?'

'First thing tomorrow if it's all right with you.'

Damn. How the hell was she going to manage without the woman? Gwen could barely boil an egg. Making tea and toast was the summit of her culinary skill. She forced a smile. 'I'll miss having you around, Mrs Woods. And I'll certainly miss your cooking.'

'Let's hope it won't be for long, Madam.'

DROWNING HIS SORROWS

ONTARIO

Jim ran until he was too tired to run any more, then, exhausted, he walked the rest of the five miles or so into town and spent the night on a bench in the park waiting for morning. He was in too much turmoil to sleep.

He couldn't rid himself of the memory of Walt and Alice making love – his brain imprinted with her moaning, their conspiratorial glance burned into his retinas. If he lived to be a hundred he'd never be able to forget this night. His stomach heaved and he dry retched. He was hollowed out, flayed, his nerves exposed and raw. Betrayed by the two people he loved most in the world. The two people he'd believed until tonight loved him best. He'd never been so wretched, so alone, so utterly defeated.

He watched Alice arrive at the library for work and as soon as he saw her walking slowly up the steps he knew he couldn't face confronting her. What was the point? The look that had passed between her and Walt was enough to know that he would never get her back. Accusing her of betrayal would make her miserable but would make no difference to the final outcome. Wouldn't it be better for him to fade away?

He clenched his fists. How long had it been going on? How had they managed to keep it from him? If Walt were to come by now he couldn't answer for the consequences. His own brother. Jim wanted to pulverise him. He let himself picture landing punches on Walt's face; smashing his fists into that smug expression; feeling the bones crunch as he beat him relentlessly; his brother's handsome face reduced to blood and pulp.

But the image brought no satisfaction. Why had they betrayed him? He had a right to know. Alice owed him that much.

Decision made, he ran up the steps two at a time and burst into the library. Alice looked up from the pile of books she was sorting and had the grace to appear embarrassed. She whispered something to the woman beside her and, signalling to Jim to follow her, went outside. They walked across to the park in silence and sat down on the bench he'd vacated. They'd sat on this same bench only a week or so ago when Jim had stopped by during her lunch break. How different that day had been. She'd been pleased to see him. Or pretended to be. Waves of nausea rose in his throat. Was she cheating on him then? How long had they been lying to him?

Eventually Alice spoke. 'It just happened, Jim. I'm sorry. We couldn't help ourselves. I was going to tell you last night before supper but I was late and there wasn't time. Then I was going to tell you after supper but—'

'But you thought you'd go out to the barn instead and make whoopee with Walt.'

'It wasn't like that.' She looked up at him with her soulful eyes and his stomach clenched with desire for her. Then he remembered her tanned legs wrapped around his brother's waist and he turned his head away.

'No? Looked that way to me.'

'Walt was angry because I'd promised I'd tell you about us, and when your mother kept on about you and me getting married I could see he was like a pressure cooker about to blow. That's why I went to the barn. I wanted to calm him down.'

'And calming him down meant letting him do what we've never done.' Jim slammed his fist into the bench with such force that the painted wood surface cracked. He raised his hand to his mouth and sucked away the blood.

Alice hung her head. 'I don't know what to say, Jim. I never meant to hurt you. Neither did Walt. But we couldn't help it. We couldn't stop ourselves.'

'And little brother was happy for you to be the one to tell me what's been going on? Too gutless to tell me himself. How long have you been sleeping with him? How long?' He leaned back on the bench, and looked up at the cloudless sky, struggling to contain his emotions.

'He wanted to tell you – or at least for us to do it together, but I thought it was better coming from me. I was going to break it off with you and we were going to wait a while before telling anyone about us. You know… to make it easier on you.'

'Easier on me? How the hell would that be easier for me? We're not at school. It isn't some teenage crush. We were going to get married next year. You agreed to be my wife. You told me you loved me. We were going to have a family together.' Jim's voice trembled with emotion. He jerked forward on the bench, holding his head in his hands.

Alice stretched a hand out and laid it on his arm. He shrugged her off as though she were contaminated.

'I did love you, Jim. I still do, but it's not the same as the love I feel for Walt. The feelings for him exploded in me. When it happened we both knew.'

Listening to her was torture but Jim forced himself. It was like lancing a boil. You had to get all the poison out before it could heal. But he doubted he would ever heal.

'It began three weeks back. I came over to talk wedding plans with your ma and when we were done she asked me to take some lemonade out to you and your pa and Walt. It was a really hot day. Remember?' She paused, her voice trembling. 'You and your pa were up in the top field and Walt was cutting hay down by the creek so after I saw you, I went down to him.'

Alice paused, closed her eyes and took a deep breath. 'He asked me to stay and sit with him while he drank, so I could take the cup and pitcher back. We shared the lemonade and got talking.'

She looked up at Jim, her eyes welling. 'You know how it was with Walt. He never seemed to like me. I thought he was angry you spent so much time with me instead of with him.' She looked down, eyes fixed on her knees. 'And then he leaned over and kissed me. I didn't expect it. I didn't mean for it to happen. I don't think he did either.' She looked up at him. 'I'm so sorry, Jim. Walt and I knew right away that we had feelings for each other. Perhaps we always had – we'd just hidden them. Tried to pretend they weren't there. Even to ourselves.' Her voice broke and she began to cry. 'It's all such a mess.'

Jim's voice was cold and he felt detached from his body, floating above it, looking down on himself, a thing apart. 'So you've been meeting him every night in the barn then? Lying down in the hay and letting him use you like a cheap whore.' He felt her tense beside him and heard her sob. He went on, his anger relishing her pain. 'You'd always told me you wanted us to wait until we were married. I respected you.'

She turned to look at him, her cheeks wet with tears. 'It only happened once before last night. We didn't plan to do it again until we'd cleared things up with you. But Walt was angry that I hadn't told you. We started to argue and then we were... well... we kissed and one thing led to another and we couldn't stop. It was me too. Don't blame him. It's... it's passion... between us. It's so strong. We can't help ourselves. Maybe that was the problem, Jim. You had me on a pedestal. Walt treated me like a woman.'

Jim jumped up from the bench. He couldn't bear to look at her, to hear the unconscious cruelty of her words. Alice reached for his arm but he jerked away and began to run. He didn't look back. He would never look back.

After drawing his pitifully small savings from the bank, Jim walked into a diner and asked if anyone was heading to Toronto and could give him a ride. He was going to sign up for the army. A smiling waitress offered him coffee on the house and he had three offers of transport. He chose the man who looked least likely to want to talk.

THEY REACHED Toronto too late in the evening for Jim to get to the recruiting office. Signing up would have to wait until morning. This was his last night as a free man before the army told him what to do. He couldn't wait to be in uniform – obeying orders without having to think would be a blessed relief. With a bit of luck he might even get himself killed and he wouldn't have to worry about what to do when the war was over. One thing was clear. He would never go back to the farm. It would be hard to leave his parents and knew it would be harder still on them but he had no choice.

He made his way to one of the city's beverage rooms – the only public places where one could drink beer. The interior was shabby and the atmosphere was fuggy and smelled of stale beer and cigarette smoke. Men leaned against the bar and sat around at tables. There were no women – they were not permitted in beer parlours. There was little talking, apart from placing orders at the counter. The place was intentionally uninviting. Jim didn't care. The miserable surroundings suited his mood.

He paid for his drink and sat down at an empty table, quaffing the beer quickly and returning to the bar for another. He drank, hoping to numb the pain, wipe out the memory of Walt with Alice's legs wrapped around him and forget that his dream of marrying and having children with her was gone.

He'd lost count of how many beers he'd drunk, when a man approached his table. Tall and wearing a suit that might once have been considered smart, but now looked as though it needed a good brushing, the man nodded and asked if he could join him. Jim shrugged.

While they drank, the stranger, whose name was Miller, regaled Jim with the story of his life, a familiar tale of declining fortunes, characteristic of many men since the Depression.

'Then they took the house. That was the last straw. She walked out on me. Said she never wanted to see me again. Took my little girl with her and went back to Calgary. What became of standing by your man? What about all those vows she made in church? Might as well have said "until death or repossession do us part". I had a good job when we married. Chief teller in a bank. As soon as they foreclosed on the bank and I was thrown on the scrap heap, she didn't want to know. Ran home to Daddy. Since then I have to get by on whatever casual work I can get.'

'Why don't you join up?' Jim spoke at last, aware that he was slurring his words.

'Won't have me. Don't think I didn't try. Failed the fitness test.' Miller paused and looked at Jim. 'That's what you're doing then?'

Jim nodded as he stared into the bottom of his beer glass.

'Stand me a beer, mate, and then you can tell me your story,' said Miller.

Jim slid a bill across the table. 'You line them up then.'

When the man returned, he clinked glasses. 'So, what brings you here drowning your sorrows, farm boy?'

Jim decided he was beyond caring about his pride. Self-esteem was a thing of the past and he was grateful that someone was prepared to listen, so he told Miller his story. When he finished, he expected jeers, ready to be the butt of the stranger's jokes.

Instead Miller flung an arm around his shoulder. 'Tell you what you need, farm boy. You need a woman. Fastest way to forget a woman is in the arms of another one. Drink up and let's go.'

Before Jim had time to protest, they were outside the beer parlour and moving down the street. He felt unsteady. What was he agreeing to? What had he come to? Then he told himself Miller was right. He needed to forget Alice by replacing the memory of her with that of another woman. He was done with respecting himself.

The brothel was as seedy as the beverage room had been, but this time there were women. In fact that's all there were – half a dozen of them in varying degrees of undress. Miller was evidently a regular. Several of the girls called to him and one jumped up and grabbed him by the tie, leading him out of the room. He looked over his shoulder and called out to Jim, 'Enjoy, farm boy! You could be dead before the year's out.' Then he was gone.

Jim stood in the middle of the room, uncertain what to do

next. An older woman, her face caked in make-up, appeared from behind a curtain.

She winked at Jim and said, 'Any friend of Mickie Miller is welcome in this house.'

It dawned on him that procuring clients for the brothel was probably a lucrative solution to Miller's employment problems – or at least a guarantee of preferential rates for himself. The madam snapped her fingers and nodded at one of her girls. 'Make sure our guest gets everything he needs, Penny.'

A pretty redhead took him by the hand and led him from the room.

Once inside the bedroom, Jim's head began to spin and his mouth tasted sour after all the beers. Penny ran her hands over his chest and murmured, 'Cash first, handsome. Two dollars. On the nightstand, please.'

Jim reached into his back pocket and pulled out the bills, dropping them onto the table. His heart pounded against his ribs under the light pressure of her fingers. Then her hand moved lower and cupped him through the fabric of his trousers and he felt himself harden.

'Mmm, nice,' she said.

She pushed him back onto the bed and straddled him, her fingers rapidly working at the buttons of his shirt and pants. Miller was right. The best way to forget Alice was in the arms of another woman. All that frustration caused by Alice's reluctance to do more than the most elementary sexual activity would soon be eased. But don't think about Alice. Focus on Penny who had now managed to open his shirt and pull off his trousers. He closed his eyes but it made it impossible not to imagine it was Alice touching him instead of the hooker.

He couldn't go through with it. As the girl's hands moved to release him from his shorts, an overpowering need to be sick overwhelmed Jim and he pushed her off and flung himself across the small room to a washbasin in the corner where he vomited copiously. He'd drunk more beer tonight than in his whole life and on an empty stomach.

'What the–' Penny cried, now sitting on her haunches on the bed. 'What the hell you think you're doing, mister? No refunds,' she added. 'And it's extra for messing up the basin.' She moved behind him and laid a hand on his shoulder. 'You're a first-timer? Had to drink to get your courage up, did you, mister?' She handed him a towel. 'Don't worry. You'll be safe with me. I'll give you a good time.' She moved her hand around him and slipped it into the front of his shorts.

Jim pulled away from her and grabbed his pants from the floor beside the bed. He pulled them on and reaching into his pocket, threw another couple of bills on the bed. 'I'm sorry, Penny. Nothing to do with you. You're a lovely looking woman.'

Then he was out of the room, running down the stairs, through the back door and onto the street.

He hadn't held back all those months with Alice to let his first sexual experience be with someone who had to be paid to do it. Making love was meant to be special, not sordid, not a financial transaction, like buying a beer. All of a sudden he was sober. Now he needed to find his way back to the YMCA.

STAYING PUT

EASTBOURNE

*I*t was always the same dream: blood diffusing in water. While it was happening Gwen was aware it was a dream – but knowing that didn't make it any less terrifying. Was there a name for dreams that replayed things that had actually happened? She would have been able to cope with sea monsters, Nazi invasions, running away from an unknown terror. But this?

Was she condemned to revisit this for the rest of her life? The water biting into her ankles like shards of ice cutting her to the bone; running through parched fields weighed down by the sodden leather of her shoes, water sloshing under her soaked socks, knowing as she ran – as she had known then – that it was too late. Nothing to be done. Alfie was dead. Her twin brother was gone and life would never be the same.

She woke, bathed in sweat, gasping for breath as though she had run across those empty, sun-scorched, Indian fields again. Rolling onto her side, she wiped her forehead and took deep gulps of air as her heart thumped against her ribs.

If Roger had been here he would have held her in his arms until her breathing returned to normal. Gwen had never been able to tell him what she dreamed about, so he would say, 'Another bad dream, darling?' and stroke her hair until she calmed. But Roger wasn't here. Something inside made her believe he wouldn't ever come back. Not this time. This time his departure had felt final. That was why she had not wanted to linger saying goodbye in the station forecourt, unwilling for him to recognise the fear, not wanting to transfer that fear to him. Behaving as though she was seeing him off to London from the station on a normal day – a charade to convince herself that he would come back to her.

Gwen dragged herself up the bed and leaned back against the pillows, drawing her knees up in front of her. If only she had been able to tell her husband how she really felt, to open herself up to him. She couldn't afford to be so exposed: to take such a risk, to allow the possibility of feeling such pain again. Instead she wore a carapace of cheerfulness and smiled through the pain. There was going to be all the more need for that now if Roger wasn't coming back. She would have to make a life for herself, scrape a future out of this mess. Smile through her tears at the world. Put on a brave face. Be practical. Try to make a difference. Until the need for that had passed and she could swallow down the codeine or jump off the top of Beachy Head and join Alfie again.

The telephone was ringing as Gwen came downstairs. She picked it up with a sense of dread, fearing a summons to attend the aftermath of another bombing. But there had been no sign of planes overhead and she'd heard no explosions.

It was Roger's mother. Maud Collingwood was a kind-hearted contrast to Gwen's own mother, dead for more than twenty years, and Gwen was fond of her mother-in-law. Now in her early sixties she had lost her husband to the last war. A stalwart of the Women's Institute and, since war broke out, the WVS, she was perennially cheerful and bursting with energy.

'Darling, thank heavens you've answered. How are you? I've been worried. When are you coming to Biddington? Everything's ready – I'm putting you in the little room at the back as it's cosier and gets the morning sun. Quieter there too so you won't hear the milkman. Do you know, darling, he's joined the LDV and he's doing his round at four in the morning to make more time for his duties. Terribly patriotic but I do hate being woken by all that rattling.'

As she took a breath, Gwen managed to get a greeting in at last.

'When are you coming? I've been anxious about you all on your own over there. Is it true what I read in the paper that they've been bombing Eastbourne? Do you think it was a mistake? Surely they can't have meant to drop bombs there? I thought the seaside would be safe.'

Gwen swallowed and said, 'It was probably a one-off. A practice run. No need to worry. Look, I can't get away, Maud, much as I'd love to see you.'

'Why ever not? Roger told me I was to be most insistent. The paper didn't give any details about the bombs so I've been ringing and ringing all morning and when there was no answer you can imagine I was worried sick. Miss Brown at the telephone exchange is fed up with me trying your line all morning.'

'I'm perfectly fine, Maud. Quite safe up here at the top of the town. I saw all the damage though. Houses flattened. An elderly man died. Another is in the Princess Alice and it doesn't look good for him. And so many injured.'

'Shocking. Then you absolutely must get out.'

Gwen twirled the telephone cord around her finger. 'I can't leave. I'm needed here. We're already short-handed and after what happened yesterday we'll probably be even shorter as more people leave town.'

'But why you? Someone else could do it. Roger was emphatic that I try to persuade you.'

Gwen smiled. 'Try to persuade me? So he realised I wasn't going to budge.'

'Do be sensible, darling.'

'It's easier for me to stay than it is for the women with children. Besides, Maud, I *want* to stay.'

The operator's voice broke into the call. 'Still on the line, Mrs Collingwood?'

'Yes, I am,' said Maud. 'And I don't like to be interrupted. This is an important call.'

'Just doing my job. Need to keep the lines open.'

'I think we're done now. I do have to dash, Maud,' said Gwen. 'Need to get some supper on.'

'Can't Mrs Woods do that?'

'She's gone. Back to her son's in Hailsham.'

There was a long sigh at the other end of the line. 'But, Gwen, darling, you're surely not thinking of cooking for yourself?'

Gwen bristled. 'I'm not completely helpless, Maud. Please let's close the subject. I'm staying put.'

'But I promised Roger.'

'Don't worry. I'll tell him you did your best but I dug my heels in. He won't blame you. He knows what I'm like. We have been married for fifteen years!'

'Perhaps I should come and join you there. I could help out too.'

Gwen didn't want that. Having Maud to stay for a few days was always a pleasure but to have her mother-in-law under the same roof for an indefinite period was not an enticing prospect. 'Out of the question, I'm afraid.' She searched around for a reason. 'The town is off limits. You need a permit to come and go now as it's classified as a garrison town.'

'Surely not?'

'I don't make the rules, Maud. Anyway, you're much better off at home in Biddington, What would the WVS there do without you to organise them? Please don't worry about me. This place is a ghost town. I'll write every few days.'

'Have you had any news of Roger?' Maud's tone was light – trying not to convey anxiety about her son.

'No, but he warned me not to expect any. It's all very hush-hush. I don't even know where they've sent him or what he's doing there.' She twiddled the telephone cord again, weary of putting on a brave face, tired of trying to be strong. She wanted to yell, Don't you think I don't worry? Every minute of every day? She breathed in slowly and said in her chirpiest voice, 'Roger will be fine, wherever he is. I try not to let myself wonder about what he might be doing. He's a strong man and he's always been able to look after himself. He told me not to worry and that he'd come home safely. Roger never breaks a promise.' She said the words, knowing them to be a white lie and remembering how at the station he had feared he might not survive the war. She hoped Maud couldn't hear the tremor in her voice.

'You're a strong woman yourself, Gwen, darling. Remember if things get too much and you change your mind there's always a welcome for you here.'

When she'd replaced the receiver, Gwen sank into a chair. Anxiety about Roger mixed with relief that she had got the conversation with Maud out of the way and managed to hold her ground. She would never admit to her mother-in-law that she worried all the time about him. It was the not knowing that was so hard. Listening to the wireless and reading the newspaper she was unable to know if the triumphs or setbacks reported were connected to him. He had prepared her – warning her it would be a long time before she would hear from him, possibly the entire duration of the war, but that made it no easier. It didn't stop the pain. If she were to be with Maud they would each reinforce the other's anxieties. Here alone, she hoped she would be occupied with war-work.

JOINING UP

TORONTO

The queue at the recruiting office was already lengthy when Jim arrived soon after it opened. Nearly a year into the war, he'd expected to be one of only a few.

There were forms to be completed, a doctor's examination, a physical fitness test and an interview with a recruiting panel. Filling in his personal details on one of the forms, Jim's hand hesitated at the section on next of kin. The overhead fan twirled slowly, ineffective against the stuffiness of the room. For a moment he thought of writing "None", then pictured his mother, strained and thin with worry. He couldn't protect her from pain that may lie ahead and she had a right to know if her son were to die. Besides, there'd be a payment if he were killed. It would be selfish of him to let that windfall go to waste. He pictured her opening the telegram, reading it, then letting it fall onto the table, tears welling. His father would jump up to comfort her, wrapping her in his arms, before turning, his face disfigured by anger and grief, upon Walt. "This is all your fault," he'd shout, and Walt would hang his head in shame. Jim held his breath, moved his pen across the paper, wrote his mother's name and signed his own at the bottom of the page. It was done now.

Perhaps it was because of the events of the past few days, but the nerves Jim would normally have felt at the prospect of being grilled by men in uniform were replaced by fatalism. He no longer gave a damn what happened to him.

Many of the would-be recruits were desperate for the King's shilling – or in this case the dollar-a-day pay and three square meals, but the army wasn't greeting everyone with open arms. Many fell by the wayside after the medical once-over. The man in front of Jim, a smoker with a hacking cough, was shown the door. Flat feet and bad teeth saw off a few more and the fitness tests ruled out a large number of pale-faced weaklings accustomed only to desk work, or coming from the ranks of the unemployed and under-nourished.

Jim's muscular body, height and the strength honed by years of labouring on the family farm, meant he sailed through the physical tests. The interview which followed took less than a minute.

'Why do you want to join up?' a man with stripes on his sleeve barked at Jim.

'I want to serve King and country.'

'We need farmers more than we need soldiers.'

Jim said nothing.

'Any soldiers in the family?'

'My father served in the last war.'

'And he expects you to serve in this one?'

Before Jim could answer, the man stamped his form, handed it back to Jim, and shouted, 'Next!'

Jim looked at the piece of paper as he left the office. He'd passed. The following morning he was to report to barracks, where he would be issued with uniform and become a serving member of the Second Canadian Infantry Division. Feeling numb, he was unable to care that he'd signed his life away. He doubted he would care about anything again after what Walt and Alice had done to him. His emotions had been eviscerated like ripping the guts from a slaughtered chicken.

Jim's last evening as a civilian was spent in a picture house, away from the beverage rooms and brothels of Toronto. In the dark of the cinema he slumped deep in his seat, eyes fixed on the screen as the newsreels played. The images flowed together: a collage of ships and planes, falling bombs and shattered buildings, English people gathered in the London Underground, singing as bombs rained down upon the city above them, and the brave young pilots of the RAF battled the Luftwaffe over the fields of southern England. Images of war and destruction were played out against an accompanying soundtrack of chirpy music and a commentary voiced by an upbeat American who spoke of the war as if it were the World Series.

The main feature began. At the ticket booth he'd hesitated, torn between *My Favourite Wife* and *The Grapes of Wrath*, but had decided the travails of itinerant farm workers were too close to home. The antics of Cary Grant, Irene Dunne and Randolph Scott were causing great hilarity among the audience but did little to raise Jim's spirits. Grant was playing a man who had accidentally ended up with two wives, while Jim had failed spectacularly in his efforts to acquire just one. He stared at the screen, defying the actors to make him crack a smile. But such is the power of moving pictures that by the time the characters lined up in front of a judge, trying to untangle the mess they had woven, Jim heard laughter and realised it was coming from him.

As he left the movie theatre, a weight descended on him again, and yet underneath it something had lifted in his chest. Life would go on. Life must go on... unless the war had other plans for him. He even hoped it had. In the meantime he determined that Walt and Alice would no longer inhabit all his waking thoughts. He would not let them. They had stolen his future and tainted his past but the present would be his alone.

~

THE FOLLOWING WEEKS passed in a blur of drilling, eating and sleeping. Jim kept himself to himself, answering when spoken to but making little effort to ingratiate himself with his fellow recruits. He liked wearing uniform, liked the anonymity it granted him, liked the way he could become almost invisible.

Not long after he'd signed up, he found himself on a troop carrier, due to sail from Halifax, Nova Scotia to Liverpool, England. Before the war, the ship had been a luxury transatlantic liner, comfortably housing around a thousand passengers, but now it was crammed to the gunwales with five thousand troops.

As they left port the deck was crowded, everyone wanting to catch a last glimpse of Canada, knowing they might never see home again.

Regardless of what happened in the war, he swore he would never return. If the Germans didn't get him he'd stay in England – or move to the United States. He'd had enough of Canada.

Jim found out he was bunking side-by-side with other soldiers on the bottom of the now-drained swimming pool. Every available corner of the ship had been used to squeeze in sleeping space. The men were squashed, pressed up against each other so that Jim, if he were able to sleep at all, was often woken when the man next to him rolled over in his sleep. The dormitory smelled stale and sweaty, undercut with a lingering whiff of chlorine. Meals were no better. With so many mouths to feed, the strain on the kitchens was such that the troops were limited to two meals a day on short rations and were obliged to stand queuing for long periods.

Jim leaned against the ship's railings, puffing experimentally on a cigarette. Everyone in the army seemed to smoke, but so far Jim hadn't taken to it. The sea air was bitterly cold. Jim shivered. But you didn't grow up in Southern Ontario without being used to extremes of temperature. He stared out across the empty expanse of the North Atlantic, picturing the acres of wheat on the day he had left, golden, ripe and ready. Walt and his father would have long finished the harvesting. The seeds he had bought before he left the farm would be sown by now. The dark earth, tilled and brown, would be planted with winter wheat and root vegetables. He thought of the creek that ran along the bottom of the slope behind the farmhouse: the old rope dangling from the branches of the cottonwood tree. Walt and he had played there as boys, swinging from the rope, sweeping out over the creek, whooping and laughing, hanging on as long as they could before letting go and screeching as they hit the cold water. That spot had been special, almost sacred. It was there that he'd asked Alice to marry him and now he knew that it was there she had first betrayed him with his brother.

He pushed away the image of Walt and Alice kissing under the tree and imagined his mother, hands covered in flour, the muscles on her arms tense as she kneaded dough. He saw her eyes, red and puffy, the narrow ridges running down the middle of her forehead, the down-turned mouth. Jim knew he'd caused her pain by disappearing without saying goodbye – he wished he hadn't – wished he hadn't needed to. He pictured his father, rocking slowly in his chair in front of the empty hearth, pretending to read the newspaper but looking over the top of it, anxious for his wife.

Then there was Walt, bag packed and slung over his shoulder, kissing his mother goodbye, hesitating beside his father's chair, then having elicited no response, slinking silently out of the door. Jim had imagined so many variations of this scene, but they always ended with Walt leaving. He couldn't bear to think of the alternative – Alice arriving. He couldn't face the prospect of the four of them seated around the kitchen table, chatting about the weather, selling the heifers, or who would win the prize for the biggest marrow in the local farm show.

'Where're you from, buddy?' The accent was unfamiliar.

'Hollowtree, Ontario,' Jim said. He was in no mood to talk but the man was not to be put off.

Stretching a hand out, the soldier said, 'Name's Greg. Greg Hooper. I'm from Regina. Saskatchewan.'

Jim tossed the cigarette butt into the sea and went to turn away. Then he remembered that these men would be his only companions for who knew how long. A man he snubbed today could be the man who'd save his life tomorrow. The enemy was Hitler. No point in making any others. He accepted Hooper's hand and told him his name.

THE FIRST KILL

EASTBOURNE

*I*n the aftermath of the Whitley Road bombing Gwen kept trying to imagine how she'd react if her own home were crushed to rubble. It wasn't the fabric of the building, the furniture or the furnishings she would miss. It was the irreplaceable things – photographs, letters, gifts, each of which bore memories and associations. She stood at the window and let her hand graze over a pottery vase in white lattice work sitting on the sill. Belleek. Bought for her by Roger on their honeymoon in Ireland. She used to fill it with roses from the garden, but had fallen out of the habit. Today she would pick some and place it on the mantelpiece. There may be a war on, but little things like that could lift the spirits.

What Churchill was calling The Battle of Britain had been raging in the skies of southern England since around the time of the bombing. Now, about a month later, Gwen heard an aircraft in the sky and looked up. Her heart always lifted when she saw the concentric rings on the wings and fuselage of the little planes and she was learning to spot the difference between Spitfires and Hurricanes. But more often than not the planes were German bombers with their big black crosses, advancing on a path of destruction. Since the attack on Whitley Road the Luftwaffe had passed overhead, their sights on more strategic targets than Eastbourne.

Gwen watched the little plane climb high into the sky, flying directly upwards, nose pointed to the clouds in a vertical ascent, only to turn and dive downwards, straight towards the white-capped waves. It was British – a Spitfire. For a moment she thought it was in trouble, then, as it pulled up short and began to ascend again, she realised the pilot was showing off – perhaps celebrating that he was still alive after his dogfight. She tried to imagine what it must feel like, the sea rushing up to meet the plane, the skill of the young pilot in knowing precisely when to turn, when to pull out of the dive. Did risking one's life in battle every day, watching one's friends plummeting earthward to their fiery deaths, make these young pilots casual? Did it make them tempt fate – constantly testing the boundaries between life and death, between winning and losing?

Carrying a suitcase filled with a couple of Roger's suits and some of her own unwanted clothing, Gwen made her way to Meads Street, grateful that she wasn't going to have to drag the full suitcase back up again. The road was steep and going downhill it was hard not to break into a run. Coming back up was always a breathless challenge.

She went into the church hall and spent the afternoon unpacking clothing from her suitcase and others that had been deposited there. People had been generous but once this lot was sorted she wondered where their next supplies would come from as so many residents had already abandoned the town. If there was more bombing there would be more clothing needed. They would have to go door to door.

Some of the things she was sorting looked as though they hadn't been worn in years. There was an overpowering smell of mothballs. She took each item, shook it out, ran a clothes brush over it, checked for stains and damage and, if it passed muster, measured the size and folded it up. There were separate sections for men and women, each grouped by estimated sizes, and piles of neatly-folded children's clothes. They tried to make it as easy as possible to match people to the right size, as there was no time or space for people to try things on. All this lot would be loaded into a van and moved to the main clothing centre in town tomorrow.

As she crossed the street and began to walk up the road to home, a high pitched scream split the air above her. A piercing whistle froze the blood in her veins. Deafening. She looked up. An aeroplane was in a steep dive, corkscrewing down towards the ground and so low in the sky that she thought it was coming at her. A plume of smoke poured from its damaged fuselage. It was going to crash. Instinctively, she ducked, crouching against the wall bordering St Andrews School, her hands over her head and her heart thumping. The pavement under her shook as the plane smashed into the ground and acrid smoke and the smell of burning fuel filled the air. Stumbling towards it, half-blinded by smoke, she was conscious only that there might be a pilot trapped inside.

The crash site was on the other side of the road in the grounds of the Aldro School. The siren of the fire engine was already sounding, as it made its way from the fire station round the corner in Meads village. The truck sped past her, the crew jumping out with hoses at the ready. Gwen ran towards the wreckage then stopped. She tried to get closer but the heat of the burning wreck beat her back. It was a fiery furnace, flames obliterating the outline of the fuselage. Her skin tightened and her breath caught in her throat. Choking, burning, the chemical stench of petrol in her nose, the taste of it in her mouth. She gagged.

Several Home Guards and air raid wardens had arrived

on the scene and gathered beside the fire truck, staring in disbelief at the blazing aeroplane. No one could possibly have survived. As the flames died back Gwen saw the pulverised mess, the once shiny carcass now a pile of tangled metal and broken wings, the wing struts laid bare and shorn of their covering. There was no sign of the crew.

Gwen turned to one of the Home Guards. His face was ashen. 'Was it one of ours?' she asked. He stared at her unable to answer. Then coming back to awareness, he broke into a grin. 'No. It was Fritz. Our boys got him. The first kill over the town.' His voice brimmed with pride as if he were the gunner responsible for shooting the plane down.

'The crew? Are they in there?' She pointed at the smouldering heap.

'Baled out – or blown out.'

'Killed?'

He shrugged. 'Put it this way, I didn't see their parachutes.'

Having established that there was nothing she could do to help, Gwen started to walk back up the hill. As she was about to turn into her own road she met another Home Guard on a bicycle. As well as his volunteer duties, he was Gwen's postman.

He pulled up beside her, braking his bike hard. 'You see that plane come down, Mrs Collingwood?'

'Right in front of me. Down there.' She pointed. 'Crashed into Aldro School – the grounds, not the building.'

'I've come from Gaudick Road. Hill Brow School. Must like our schools these Nazis. Pilot landed on the roof. Parachute didn't open. Not that it would have helped him if it had. Left it too late, poor bugger. Pardon my German, Mrs Collingwood. One less of 'em to fight for Hitler. Have a good afternoon.' He tipped his cap to her and went on his way.

TRAINING CAMP

TO ALDERSHOT

Their ship arrived on the Liverpool docks early in the morning but it took the best part of the day to get the thousands of soldiers off the boat.

Jim and Greg stood on deck, leaning over the railings watching as a never-ending procession of men trooped down the gangplank. The dockside was crowded with stevedores unloading cargo.

One of the dockers, seeing the Canadians smoking, called up to the ship. 'Any ciggies to spare, kiddas?'

In response the soldiers began showering cigarettes down upon the dockers, who downed tools and scrambled to retrieve as many as possible, stuffing them in their pockets.

'Boy, they must be desperate, eh,' said Greg. 'I'd no idea things were so bad in Merrie England. I hope they'll be able to feed us while we're here.'

'Not so merry,' said Jim, indicating the charred remains of several bomb-damaged buildings near the docks. 'Looks like these poor bastards have had it bad.'

When, in the afternoon, they eventually made it onto their waiting train, Jim was grateful that, although crowded, everyone had somewhere to sit. He settled back and fell asleep, exhausted after the discomfort of sleeping on the ice-cold floor of the ship's swimming pool.

They were heading for Aldershot, England's permanent garrison town, now housing most of the Canadian army. Their journey took them via London, and they experienced their first sight of the capital through the gloom of the black-out. Everywhere they looked were ruined buildings and great piles of rubble. Lampposts were unlit, those buildings that were undamaged were shrouded in darkness and they could see no one about on the streets.

'Everyone must go to bed as soon as it's dark,' said Jim. 'The place looks like a ghost town.'

'More like Armageddon. Poor bastards. Imagine living through this. Must have been terrifying. Going to bed and not knowing if you're going to wake up in the morning.'

Aldershot was pitch black when they arrived. Clutching each other like a platoon of blind men, the soldiers staggered out of the station onto the dark streets. They were route-marched through the deserted town as groups of men were allocated to different barracks. The whole town was a military camp, divided into North and South Camps, the Marlborough Lines to the north of the Basingstoke Canal and the Stanhope and Wellington Lines to the south. Jim and Greg were assigned to the Salamanca barracks in the Wellington lines. Their building was a Victorian red brick construction, three storeys high and girded by iron balustrades enclosing wide balconies across the front of the upper floors. The building housed six hundred men, fifty in each dorm room, on the two upper floors, while the ground floor contained the canteen, kitchens and administrative offices.

After dumping their kit in the dormitories, they were summoned to the mess hall and served with tea and sardines on toast – the first food they had eaten since leaving Liverpool.

Later, back in the dormitory, Jim was slow off the mark in establishing his territory. Greg was one of many who quickly worked out that if you were to sleep in a three-foot-high bunk bed it made sense to go for the top bunk. Jim and the other slowcoaches soon discovered that squeezing into the lower bunks that were raised a mere six inches above the floor was a challenge worthy of Houdini. The "mattresses" didn't deserve that name – indeed they were known throughout the British forces as "biscuits" and consisted of three separate shallow cushions that had to be arranged together into a vague semblance of a mattress. Once he had negotiated his passage into the bed and arranged his biscuits under him, Jim had no trouble dropping off to a deep and undisturbed sleep until woken by the bugler playing reveille next morning.

∼

WHEN JIM JOINED his fellow recruits on the parade ground, the first person he saw was Tip Howardson, his brother Walt's old school friend. Howardson watched the new arrivals as they formed themselves into a line-up in front of him, but gave no sign of recognising Jim. He wore the stripes of a corporal on his sleeve and was clearly relishing the opportunity to lord it over these raw recruits straight off the boat from the mother country.

Jim swallowed his surprise. There would be time for catching up with Tip later. Better now to toe the line and not be seen to curry favour with a senior rank. He stood to attention and stared straight ahead.

Tip Howardson walked up and down in front of them. After a few moments he barked, 'What a horrible lot you are.

Bunch of softies. Crawled out from under a haystack, have you? Well as of now you'd better sharpen up. And we'll start with you learning how to salute properly. Up, one-two-three, down. Longest way up. Shortest way down,' he shouted. 'Fingers together, palm to the front. Keep those bloody elbows back!'

He pointed to one man's feet. 'More dubbin on those boots. Spit on them too if you have to. Tomorrow I want to see my face in them.' He paused in front of Jim and knocked Jim's cap off his head. Jim bent to recover it. Howardson kicked the hat further away, a smile creasing his face as the cap was picked up by a gust of wind and blown across the tarmac, landing in a puddle.

'Hats on straight. You're in the army, not a fashion parade. Name?'

Jim wanted to tell Tip to come off it and lighten up. They'd grown up together. Same school. Tip had been glued to Walt's side when they were kids. Here he was, Jim's junior by a couple of years and now his senior officer. Instead, he said, 'Armstrong.'

'Armstrong, what?'

Jim swallowed. 'Armstrong, sir.'

Tip ignored him and addressed the whole troop. 'My name is Corporal Howardson and my job is to knock you lot into shape. You all took your time joining up, didn't you?' He walked up and down, his hands behind his back, then shouted, 'War was declared more than a year ago!' He moved close to Greg and spoke into his face so Jim could feel his breath on his face. 'Had the wind up you, did you? You a mother's boy?' He stepped away then waved his hand at them all. 'Are you all a lot of fairies?'

He turned to Greg. 'Name?'

'Hooper, sir.'

Tip jerked his head at Jim and spoke again to Greg. 'Hooper, you know this man? He a friend of yours?'

'Yes, sir.'

Howardson stepped back and addressed Jim again. 'Go and get that hat, Armstrong, before it ends up back in Canada. When I inspect you tomorrow I expect it to be as clean as it was when you were issued with it. I will be watching you, Armstrong. If you put a foot wrong I'll be there.'

Jim retrieved his wet and muddy cap. He had no idea how he was to get it back to pristine condition overnight. As he returned to the ranks he saw an officer striding over the tarmac towards them. The man turned to Howardson, acknowledged his salute and said, 'Thank you, Corporal. At ease, men.'

The officer wore the insignia of a captain on his battle-dress, was well-built and over six foot tall, making Corporal Howardson look puny beside him. He said, 'Welcome to Aldershot Camp, men. I'm your commanding officer while you are in Aldershot. I want to thank you all for volunteering to serve. Your commitment to King and country is laudable. You should be proud to serve as Canadian soldiers.'

He walked slowly along the length of the line-up, looking each man in the eye. When he reached the end he turned and walked back to the middle of the line-up and stood facing them, his hands behind his back. 'I want you all to remember that you are representing your country while you are guests here in Great Britain. You must also be mindful that some of your colleagues in the British forces are not volunteers and may have been conscripted unwillingly. The important thing is for us all to get along and act as one team. One army. One enemy. Watching each other's back. Where we come from and what we have done before matters not on the battlefield.

It's all for one and one for all as the British say and let's show Hitler that Canadians mean business.'

He glanced at Howardson and cleared his throat. 'Now, Corporal Howardson, tell these men what is the most important thing they need to remember about being in a winning army.'

Howardson barked back, 'Everything starts with the salute, sir!'

'That's right. As the United States General Pershing used to say in the last war, "Give me soldiers who can shoot well and salute well and I'll lick the enemy." And I intend my men to lick the enemy.

'I hope it won't be too long before you all get a chance to show what you're made of and make your families and friends back home proud of you. I know you're keen to take a pop at the enemy as soon as possible but in the meantime you must be patient, stay focused, and take advantage of our time in Aldershot, however long or short it might be, to work hard, and turn yourselves into a tiptop Canadian fighting machine. Corporal Howardson here will be training you hard to get you ready to take on the toughest challenges when the time comes for us to see action.'

He nodded and gave a small smile, as though weighing up the words of his speech and finding them pleasing, then with a final salute, he walked away.

Howardson turned back to face the men. 'That was Captain Bywater. You won't be seeing much of him. But I can assure you, you will be seeing a lot of me. Now, twenty times round the training ground and whoever's last to finish will do a hundred press-ups.'

~

JIM HAD BEEN in Aldershot for three weeks and all it had done was rain.

He lay on his back on his bunk in the dorm after the evening meal. Most of his colleagues had gone to the recreation room to play table tennis or listen to the radio.

He was wondering if he'd made a terrible mistake. Over rations in the canteen, a guy had told him he'd signed up the day war was declared, was one of the first to arrive in England and had been stuck in Aldershot ever since. Now, a full year into the war, there was no sign at all of any of the Canadians getting to see action.

Behind him the rain lashed at the windows. Life here had been monotonous since that first day when Howardson had them doing circuits of the training ground and then forced them to stand and watch, water dripping down the necks of their uniforms, while the poor lad who had stumbled around last struggled to do his hundred push-ups. Since then, every day had been the same, boot and button polishing, boring classroom lessons on warcraft and a non-stop diet of physical jerks under the critical eye of Howardson, who looked for any opportunity to humiliate anyone showing the slightest sign of weakness.

Jim's impressions of Britain so far were less than favourable. Aldershot was a dreary place: a huge camp, with old brick-built barracks from the last century, hastily assembled huts and concrete parade grounds. The fellow Jim had spoken to in the canteen had said British army troops came and went but the Canadians were a permanent fixture. The men in the RAF who were sent to Canada for training were hurried through then sent back again and straight into action. Many of them didn't last long up in the air – the average lifespan of an RAF pilot was measured in days – hours even, but Jim didn't care about that. He wanted war to distract him, give him a purpose, kill him even, but not leave him here in this godforsaken hole doing gymnastics and square-bashing for Tip Howardson.

'Rain still bucketing down, eh?' Greg Hooper climbed onto his bunk opposite Jim's, and sat with his legs dangling over the edge, almost scraping the ground. Greg's legs were the source of much amusement in the barracks. They were impossibly long, extremely thin and he was a shoo-in for a knobbly knees contest. When he sat in a chair, his bent legs projected far in front of him, earning him the name Grasshopper, which was then modified to GrassHooper because of his surname, but mostly now he was just Grass.

Greg rolled a cigarette. 'Want one?'

Jim shook his head. 'Thought you were listening to the radio?'

'It's depressing. Stuff about the brave British airmen, while we sit here doing nothing. I didn't join up to sit in a rainy town hearing about other people's war.'

'I know. What's the point of us being holed up here when the damned Nazis are goose-stepping their way across Europe? Why can't they let us at them?'

'Think you're ready to fight, Armstrong?' The sneering tones of Howardson cut into the conversation. 'You'd be dead in minutes. You know nothing. None of you do. Cannon fodder. By the time I've finished with you lot, you might make it onto a boat to the Continent, but right now I doubt you'd find your way to the latrines without me to show you.'

Jim said nothing; glancing at Greg he rolled his eyes and stifled his anger. He could remember picking a ten-year-old Tip up off the barn floor when he'd taken a tumble from the hayloft and grazed his knees and twisted an ankle. Tip had bawled his eyes out then and now Jim had to swallow the man lording it over him.

'I had a letter from my folks today. Very enlightening it

was about what's been going on back in my home town.' Howardson jerked his head at Greg. 'Has Armstrong cried on your shoulder yet, Hooper? Told you how his little brother's been doing his fiancée?'

Jim was off the bunk, hands grabbing at the corporal's collar.

'Take your filthy hands off me, Armstrong. You can do fifty laps of the parade ground for that. Right now.'

Hooper said, 'But it's dark, Corporal. And raining. And we're off duty.'

'You want to join him?'

Hooper's lips stretched but he said nothing.

'I said *now*, Armstrong. Waste any more time and you can make it a hundred.'

~

THE MEN WERE WOKEN in the night by the sound of sirens. The sound was distant, coming from thirty-odd miles away in London. Jim and Greg leapt out of their bunks and rushed out onto the long balcony to see what was going on. In the distance, wands of bright light streaked up from the ground to sweep the sky, searchlights seeking enemy raiders. They watched in fascination mingled with fear for what they expected to happen, but after about twenty minutes the show was over. A false alarm.

The following day, bleary eyed, they were out training. Twenty mile route marches, carrying full packs, were done once every week, walking on roads. The hard asphalt was agony after ten miles or so, especially in bad weather. Blisters were a constant trial. One of the few highlights of the dreary days of square-bashing and exercises at Aldershot was a ten minute break every hour when, as if by a miracle, tea wagons – tricycle carts – pedalled along the road to the training ground to sell them cups of tea and baked tarts. The traders made a small fortune out of the Canadians, as the men were always ravenous with hunger after training.

Jim and Greg ate apple tarts, washed down with sweet tea, while they listened to one of the lads, Scotty McDermott, performing his party piece. Scotty was able to mimic noises. His speciality was sounds of war. He was famed for his imitation of a Lancaster bomber taking off, but this morning he had added the sound of last night's air raid siren to his repertoire. It was convincing. Birdsong, crying babies, trains, farm animals – Scotty could do them all and was happy to take requests. Jim was beginning to find the novelty wearing off.

RAINING BOMBS

EASTBOURNE

Since the German plane had crashed in Meads, Eastbourne had taken a pounding, with twenty-six bombs dropped over the district of Hampden Park that night and constant air raids since. It was apparent that Germany was trying to soften up the south coast towns prior to launching an invasion.

Gwen was asked to attend fire-watch training with colleagues from the WVS and the ARP. It was taking place in one of the classrooms of the Technical College next door to the fire station. She'd expected there wouldn't be much to it. How complicated could it be to put out small fires?

There was plenty of equipment available to assist with the task. It felt strange to be sitting in a room full of women, behind desks as though they were back at school while the trainer stood at the blackboard and drew diagrams to explain the various types of bombs. To Gwen's surprise the different bombs produced different types of fire and there was a lot more to it than she'd thought.

The man explained that if you poured water on an incendiary bomb it would actually help the fire to spread – you had to use a bucket of sand or the foam in an extinguisher. For fires where you could use water, it was necessary to know how to work a stirrup pump. The women were instructed to come to the front of the class in pairs and demonstrate that they had mastered the technique, one operating the pump and the other directing the hose.

The woman paired with Gwen seemed incapable of understanding. Gwen was reminded of a classmate at her Swiss finishing school who had proved unable to master the art of threading a needle. When their turn came, the woman kept forgetting to keep her foot on the pump to hold it in place and as a result the bucket kept falling over when she pressed down on the stirrup. After refilling the bucket three times, Gwen was becoming impatient.

When it was her turn to prime the pump, the woman took over the hose and kept dropping it. The instructor rolled his eyes in sympathy at Gwen.

When she was about to pass out with boredom at the endless repetition, things started to get interesting. They donned boiler suits, then trooped up the road to the playing fields at Larkin's Field where they were told to crawl through a smoke-filled shed dragging a heavy firehose. The instructor, one of the permanent firemen, shouted at them, reminding them all to keep their heads near the ground where the air would be clearer, holding the nozzle of the hose close to their faces to take advantage of the air in the water. Gwen realised she was actually enjoying herself. It felt real, a proper physical task, the nearest thing she would ever get to fighting.

After the smoke drill, the instructor demonstrated how to use a big fire hose. Most of the women proved inadequate to the task and the exercise ended up with the uncontrolled hose sending jets of water everywhere but the direction required. Gwen watched carefully so that when it came to her turn she was forewarned, and managed to grip the front of the hose with both hands while anchoring the back end of the nozzle under her arm so the force of the water didn't drag it away. She found herself grinning like a small child when the instructor told her she was the only one who had got it right.

The combination of physical exercise and learning to do something useful, gave Gwen a rush of energy. She went home, humming a tune as she walked up the steep hill, and realised she was feeling cheerful for the first time in ages.

Back h0me, she had only an hour to get ready for a rare social event. Outraged by the Hampden Park bombing, the local newspaper had organised a drive to collect money to purchase a Spitfire in Eastbourne's name. Five thousand pounds was needed and Gwen's friend, Daphne Pringle, had invited her to a fundraiser that night at one of the seafront hotels.

The evening was a trial – a protracted event. It was all in a good cause but the auction of promises dragged on and Gwen was feeling tired.

She stood in front of the mirror in the hotel powder room, took her compact out of her handbag and, flicking it open, began to powder her nose. The case was gold and monogrammed with the initials GB on the top with an inscription on the back. It was the first gift she had received from Roger.

The powder was sweet and cloying. She made a mental note to change the brand when she next refilled it, then remembered that she'd have to make do with whatever was available. There was hardly likely to be a glut of cosmetics in the shops while the war was on.

Daphne Pringle came in to the room and stood beside her. 'So glad you could come tonight, Gwen. It must be hard for you without Roger but we need to keep up some semblance of normality.'

Gwen gave her a weak smile, snapped her compact closed and dropped it into her handbag.

Daphne, who had been rooting in the depths of her own handbag, placed a hand on her arm. 'Do us a favour, darling, and let me borrow your face powder. I appear to have come out without mine.'

Gwen handed the compact over and her friend applied powder to her nose and cheeks. Before returning it, Daphne twirled it in her hands, examining it. 'Pretty. Who's GB?'

'I am. My maiden name was Brooke.'

Daphne flipped the compact over. The back was also engraved. Gwen reached for it but Daphne held it away from her as she studied the wording.

'B-r-u-c-h, I presume?' said Daphne, as she continued to study the compact. Her voice was frosty. 'I had no idea you were German.'

'I'm not.'

'Then why do you have a powder compact with a German inscription on it? And what does *"Glücklich allen, Ist die Seele, die libel"* mean?' Her pronunciation made Gwen squirm.

'It means *The soul is only happy when it loves*. It's from a poem by Goethe. Seeing Daphne's eyes narrow, she added, 'It was a gift from Roger.'

'From Roger?' Daphne's hand went to her mouth. 'Good Lord, is he German?'

'Neither of us is German. We happened to meet there. In '23. I was at finishing school in Switzerland and Roger was working for The Reparations Commission. We met at a party at the British embassy in Berlin. I was a friend of the daughter of one of the attachés there.'

'You speak German?'

'Yes.' Gwen felt herself bristling.

'I see.'

'As far as I'm aware, Daphne, it's not a crime. I speak French as well.'

'But why did Roger have your compact inscribed with a German poem when you're both English?'

Gwen looked at her incredulously. 'Why on earth not? It may surprise you to know it, but my husband is a hopeless romantic. He intended it as a reminder of where we met. The last war had just finished and neither of us expected there would be another one. As she snapped the words out in annoyance, she felt a rush of tenderness for Roger. She did miss him terribly. Having him here tonight beside her would have made the evening less tedious.

'You never mentioned being in Germany before.'

'As far as I know I never mentioned being in Nairobi either. I spent five years there when I was a small child before we went to India. And boarding school in Yorkshire. Oh, and Roger and I spent our honeymoon in Ireland. Rained all the time. Anything else I need to fill you in on?'

Daphne laughed and handed the compact back. 'Sorry, old girl. You are a hoot! But we can't be too careful these days. Now, come on, let's get back to the fray; I want to make sure Sandy puts a bid on the dinner for two at the Grand – exactly what I have in mind for our wedding anniversary.'

Later, in bed, Gwen thought of the night she first met Roger. Tall, loose-limbed and smiling, with thick brown hair, he'd stood out in the crowd of colourless officials and middle-aged matrons. He'd behaved as though she were the only person in the room. The moment he looked at her across the crowded dance floor, she knew he would ask her for a dance. She had been captivated. He swept her up into the waltz, holding her closer to him than she felt comfortable with. But deep down she had liked it – the way he held her so confidently, as though it were the most natural thing in the world for him to hold her in his arms and she knew at once that she would fall in love with him, that she would marry him. Yet she had been absolutely fearful at the prospect.

As she came to know him, the fear grew stronger rather than abating. Loving him terrified her. She was afraid of showing anyone love, scared of making herself vulnerable, of opening herself up to the possibility of loss. Not again. Not ever.

If Roger was disturbed by her reticence, he didn't show it. It seemed to be enough that she allowed him to court her, then that she eventually agreed to marry him, despite the distance she tried to keep between them. It was as if he knew she loved him, even though she was incapable of telling him, of showing him.

Gwen lay open-eyed and unseeing in her bedroom in the dark of the blackout, remembering those first weeks of marriage, the honeymoon in rain-sodden Ireland. She loved Roger but she didn't know how to make him happy. She wouldn't or couldn't let him please her, even though she knew that would be the way to pleasing him. She felt there was something undignified about all that. Sex was something animals did. Other people. Common people. She and Roger should be above it. Love should have a higher purpose, a dignity that sex undermined. When he came to her in the dark, in their bed, touched her in places no one had touched her before, she shrank away, suppressing the part of her that welcomed it, was excited by it and wanted to give in to it – instead holding back, fighting to keep herself apart, to stop herself falling over the edge. Whenever they made love – he at first with enthusiasm, optimism, tenderness, then with a growing self-consciousness, she with passive acceptance – Gwen had felt only emptiness and despair. It was as if she sensed they would never be able to make a baby. She told herself that conceiving a child took belief and hope – a blind faith that their two bodies could combine and make another. But when his seed was inside her she imagined her body melting it away, dissolving it, absorbing it into the emptiness within her.

~

THE OMINOUS DATE of Friday 13th September 1940 marked the beginning of a terrible weekend of destruction in Eastbourne. The Friday afternoon bombings began soon before four o'clock in the heart of the town centre when three aircraft dropped a series of bombs in the main business area and to the east, where the damage included a junior school which was gutted by fire.

Gwen spent an exhausting day rushing from site to site on her bicycle, offering assistance wherever it was needed. The hospital was struggling to cope with the injured. Three people lost their lives in the attack. By the time she got home it was almost midnight and she fell gratefully into her bed.

The following morning she was due to report for fire watch duty at the Civil Defence headquarters. Before leaving for the town she stood on her bedroom balcony, looking out over the sea. The horizon was sharp-edged, separating the sea from a pale sky. The water was chalky grey, its monotony broken by a stripe of mint green, like a slash across the surface.

Out of the distance a lone plane appeared, its wings carrying the ugly black swastika. Gwen was about to go back inside when she saw a pair of Spitfires swoop over the Downs in pursuit, racing to engage with the German aircraft over the sea. Gwen looked up at the sky, her nerves on edge as the two little planes harried the larger German one. She could hear the sound of the gunfire and suppressed a cheer as the British planes shot the German Dornier down into the sea. Though she was joyful that they had succeeded, she couldn't help feeling a pang of sadness for the dead German pilot. It could only be hoped that his death was quick as the burning plane plummeted to the waves. She shuddered, imagining the young man realising he was trapped and doomed.

When she arrived at the civil defence HQ she said, 'We've zapped a German plane. Two Spitfires downed it over the sea.'

Her news was met with cheers and applause.

The local head of the WVS, Val Robson, said, 'Let's hope that means we've avoided another attack today. Maybe they'll leave us alone for a while.'

'Gosh, let's hope so. We need a bit of a respite to clear up after what happened yesterday,' said one of the helpers.

'Talking of which, we need to get our skates on.' Val Robson picked up her clipboard. Before the woman could issue her instructions, they heard the scream of the air raid sirens. They scrambled down the stairs to take shelter in the cellar of the building where they crouched down on the floor, waiting.

Gwen sat, legs crossed in front of her, on a blanket on the cold floor, a couple of wardens and three other WVS women alongside her, all listening intently. They heard the sound of explosions nearby.

'That sounds close.'

'They're going for the town centre again, the filthy rotters,' said Mrs Robson.

There was a brief period of silence, after the departure of what sounded like two planes, and they waited anxiously for the all-clear to sound. But instead of the siren they heard the noise of low flying aeroplanes again and counted as more bombs exploded. The noise seemed to go on for ever. The walls above them shook with the vibrations and the sound of the bombs was deafening.

'That's more than twenty by my count,' said Gwen.

The woman sitting beside her began to whimper. Gwen looked at her – she couldn't have been more than eighteen. Gwen reached for her hand and squeezed it. 'Don't worry. It'll be over soon. We're safe down here.'

The woman, Gwen remembered her name was Susan, said, 'I'm not scared for me. It's my mum and dad. They have a jeweller's shop in Cornfield Road. They're both in there. The bombs yesterday caused a lot of damage and they're sorting out their stock. They'll be right in the thick of it again today.'

There was nothing Gwen could say. What was the point of reassurances when she was in no position to give them? She put an arm around the young woman's shoulder and drew her towards her. Feeling the heat of the other body against her felt strange. Gwen had rarely experienced physical closeness with other people. She had always kept herself apart, distant, remote. Yet now she gained some comfort in this intimate contact with a near stranger. War was changing everything.

They waited in silence. Gwen glanced at her watch, two thirty. It must be over now. But it wasn't. This time the bombs were a little further away, but probably still within a few hundred yards. Gwen counted a total of seven explosions as Susan wept into her shoulder.

Surely they must sound the all-clear now? Three consecutive air raids. That must be it. But the enemy wasn't done with them yet. At a quarter past three they heard more explosions, this time to the south. Susan's weeping was now uncontrollable. Big jerky sobs. Shaking and shivering. The shoulder of Gwen's dress was soaked.

Gwen was surprised to realise she wasn't afraid. She

didn't want to die, to be crushed to death under the weight of the building, but she didn't believe she would be. And if it happened it happened. Rather than fear, she felt an adrenaline rush, heart beating, throat catching, almost excitement.

When the siren finally sounded the all-clear, the group emerged from the bowels of the building to a scene of devastation. The almost continuous afternoon of bombing had taken its toll on the town. Trees were uprooted and lying across what was normally a busy thoroughfare, their branches tangled with bricks, broken glass, roof tiles, rubble and lampposts. The building opposite, its facade blasted off, revealed its shattered interior, like someone surprised in their underwear. Susan gave a strangled cry and ran, scrambling over the piles of debris, rushing to find out the fate of her parents. Gwen closed her eyes, shaken, and filled with dread at what the young woman might find.

Doing her rounds on the Sunday morning, Gwen was relieved to find out that Susan's family had been unhurt in the previous day's attack. That night the bombers returned to drop another eighteen bombs and a number of incendiary devices on the town. The heavy bombardment fortunately produced no casualties.

LETTER FROM HOME

ALDERSHOT

*J*im had been in Aldershot for three months when he received a letter. It was dated a month earlier – all the Canadians complained about the unreliability of mail from home – it had to negotiate the dangers of the Atlantic with the risk of torpedo attacks, but the men believed torpor on behalf of the military contributed to the delays.

The envelope bore his mother's familiar scrawled handwriting. She'd tracked him down as he should have guessed she would. He was ashamed for not writing to her first and overwhelmed by homesickness as he read the letter. Helga wrote first about the farm, the progress of the winter wheat, the heifers that were ready to calf, her worsening rheumatism, the forecasts of an exceptionally cold winter. It was as though she were writing a report for the local newspaper, not sending a letter to her elder son who had left for war without so much as a farewell. He turned the page and the tone changed:

I AM NOT GOING to beat about the bush any longer, son. I'm disappointed that you have not been touch with your father and me. I had to find out where you were from Amy Howardson. How do you think that made me feel? When she mentioned you were in the same regiment as Tip over in England my jaw nearly hit the floor as you hadn't even dropped us a line to say you had joined up, let alone that you were already overseas.

I know you must be hurting, Jimmy, but it isn't right to take things out on your pa and me. We knew nothing of what was going on between your brother and Alice. I can tell you I was as angry as you were when I found out. I don't take well to being played for a fool. Nor does your pa. You should have heard him yelling at Walter. At first he didn't want Alice in the house. Called her all kinds of names. But then we agreed we had to make the best of things and accept that what will be will be.

Walter and Alice were married last week and have taken a few days as a honeymoon visiting Alice's grandmother in Toronto. It was a quiet ceremony. No fuss. Only the priest and us and Alice's parents. We didn't put it in the local paper. It didn't feel right in the circumstances. When it comes up, people can know, but we don't want to go round making a noise about it. And your pa told Walter and Alice they had to be respectful of you and your feelings.

THE WORDS SWAM on the page in front of Jim's eyes and he put the letter down, catching his breath. It was inevitable that Walt and Alice would marry some time, he'd just not reckoned on it being so soon. His stomach felt hollow and the blood pounded in his ears. He forced himself to read on.

ONE DAY SOON, when the war is over, you will come back to the farm. This place will always be your home. Time is a great healer and I know eventually you will find it in your heart to forgive

Walter and Alice. Remember, there are plenty more fish in the sea. I know it's a corny old saying but it's true. I've never spoken of this before and never will again and will be grateful if you don't let on either, but your pa was not my first choice for a husband. I was engaged to a fellow who died of tuberculosis. I thought I'd never get over it but then your pa came along and I have never regretted a moment of our life together.

I pray for you every night, Jimmy. Your pa says my knees are going to wear a hole in the rug by the bed, but I can't stop worrying about you. Mrs Howardson says none of the Canadian boys have seen any action and the government and the British want to keep it that way, specially with you all being volunteers. It must be nice for you to have Tip around – someone familiar who shares the same memories of home. I pray you'll all be safe and come home to your mothers soon.

Well that's all, son. I've been up early writing this while your pa is doing the milking so I need to get on and get the bread in the oven or there'll be none for his breakfast. Your pa sends his love. He's not angry with you. He understands why you felt you had to leave. He's still mad at your brother though, but that will pass I'm sure.

Your loving mother.

P.S. That dog of yours is pining for you. It's breaking my heart, son.

JIM FOLDED up the letter and stuffed it back into the envelope and put it in his pocket. His hands were shaking. Bile rose in his throat and he tried to swallow, but his mouth was too parched.

JIM WAS CONFINED TO BARRACKS. It was the third time this

month and, as usual, it was for a minor infraction. This time he had been reprimanded by Corporal Howardson because his bed-making didn't pass muster. There was no point railing against the injustice of Howardson's constant pettiness. Jim's bed was as neatly made up as all the others in the dormitory but there was no way to prove that was the case once the corporal had kicked the blankets to demonstrate his point. Jim wouldn't have cared normally, but it was Mitch Johnson's birthday and Mitch had promised to stand everyone drinks. There had also been talk of a darts match. The Canucks had acquired a taste for the classic English pub sport and Jim had become something of a star among them.

Howardson appeared at the side of Jim's bed while he was lying on his stomach reading a book.

'You think you're so clever, don't you, Armstrong? You've always thought yourself superior. But you're a snivelling coward. You took your time to volunteer and that brother of yours took even longer. You're both chicken.' Tip's face was disfigured by a sneer.

Jim rolled onto his back, his stomach lurching. Tip had been Walt's friend. Now he appeared to have turned against him too. But it wasn't possible that Walt had joined up. What did Howardson mean?

'Did you want something, sir?' he said. It was always difficult having to address this jumped-up, small-minded bully respectfully. It stuck in Jim's craw. Especially as most of the Canadian officers and NCOs were happy to be addressed by their first names.

'Stand up when you're addressing an officer.'

Jim swung his legs off the bed and scrambled out – not easy to do in a hurry from the narrow gap of the lower bunks. He dug his fingernails into his palms and forced himself to take a deep breath.

'I wanted to give you some good news.'

Jim was alarmed. His idea of good news and Tip's were bound to be different.

The corporal moved towards him, pushing his face up close so that Jim could smell a mixture of tobacco and onions overlaid with peppermint. Jim held his breath and tried not to wrinkle his nose.

'Your brother is on his way to Aldershot. Maybe he was feeling bad about stealing big brother's girlfriend and thought he ought to make it up with you. What do you think?' His lip curled in contempt.

Jim said nothing. His hands felt sweaty and he rubbed one down his leg. It wasn't true. It couldn't be true.

'There's five hundred rookies arriving tomorrow and Walter Armstrong is one of them. Of course it's always possible there's another Walter Armstrong in Ontario, but I'm pretty damned sure there's only one who comes from Hollowtree.'

He stepped away from Jim, a malevolent smile on his face. 'Going to be interesting round here. I'm looking forward to seeing Walt again.'

Tip Howardson left the room and Jim punched the wall in a rush of anger and frustration. What the hell was Walt thinking? He'd just got married. Why the hell did he want to go to war? Why had he chosen to follow Jim and leave Alice on her own? His rage built up inside like molten lava. His body felt hot, despite the cool of the draughty barrack room. He jerked his shirt collar away from his neck and punched the wall again. The pain made him look at his knuckles. Bloody. He wanted to go out, to walk, to get away from this building and keep on walking until he was miles from Aldershot, but he wasn't even allowed to step outside. He leaned his forehead against the cold glass of the windowpane and tried to breathe his way back to calmness.

It was typical of Walt to follow him into the army. Walt

had always tried to compete with him. When they were children, if he and Jim each got a toy to play with, Walt would break his own then purloin Jim's. When Jim did well in school, Walt wouldn't rest until he did better. If Jim made the baseball team Walt would have to be captain. If Jim broke a record, Walt would beat that record before the ink was dry on the page. Jim had always tolerated this with amusement. It was a kind of hero worship. Little brother wanting to emulate big brother. But stealing a sports record was one thing. Stealing a woman was another. And now the possibility that Jim could return to Canada a hero like their father must have proved too much for Walt to bear. He had to get in on the act too.

There was always the possibility that this was Tip trying to wind him up. Perhaps he wanted to make Jim's life a misery of anticipation at the prospective arrival of his brother. Tip could sit back and enjoy the days of dread until the recruits arrived and Walt's absence would enable Jim to breathe again. But he knew it was a forlorn hope. This was exactly what Walt would do. It was completely in character. Walt would have dressed it up as being a tribute to his older brother, when in reality he wouldn't have been able to bear the idea that in the eyes of the family he might be considered less noble, less brave. And he wouldn't want to risk Jim being lionised by Alice as a war hero, while Walt stayed at home and ploughed fields. No, it made perfect sense. Walt was coming and Jim was going to have to look at his brother every day on the parade ground or on exercise. Every day that would chafe at the still raw wound that was the loss of Alice, keeping it open, preventing any possibility of it healing.

Jim pulled his holdall out from under the bed and rummaged inside for the bottle of cheap whisky he had won in a darts match. He unscrewed the top and drank deeply.

The only hope he had of getting any sleep that night would be to get blind drunk. Drunk as a skunk as Grass would put it. He swigged down another mouthful and lay back on the bed.

~

THE TERRAIN around Aldershot was rough heathland – gorse and bracken growing on thin sandy soil. The soil was too poor to make good arable land. It was however ideal for the produce of war and the British army had bought up a large tract of land in the nineteenth century at a low cost per acre to create a permanent training ground for the military. Firing ranges were scattered across the landscape. Soldiers from the garrison dug slit trenches all over the countryside, only for officers to decide they were in the wrong place and they had to fill them in and start all over again. The men were not slow to recognise the pointlessness of these exercises and began to feel disillusioned about their role in this war.

Jim took an instant dislike to the countryside. It was so different from the fertile farmland of his home in Ontario. Not for the first time he questioned why he had given up a life he loved for this miserable existence in these ugly surroundings.

He had always been lean and fit, with muscles built on the daily routine of farming, but nothing had prepared him for the exercises he faced every day in Aldershot Camp. The gymnastics routines alone were exhausting, their strenuous physical regimen included lifting logs over their heads and star jumping for what seemed like hours on end. Cross-country runs were spiced up by having to crawl on their bellies though mud under barbed wire fences, tramping through ditches and ponds with full kit on their backs until their feet were like sponges, swinging between trees on rope walks or negotiating minefields. They learnt to manoeuvre tanks across rough terrain and became skilled in the operation of machine guns.

Experts came to the garrison to lecture them on the art of camouflage and why it was so critical to a soldier's survival in battle. What battle? they all wanted to ask. It was followed by day after day of putting the training into practice as Jim and his cohorts transformed into mobile bushes, covering their tin hats with sacking and weaving leaves and branches into their webbing. It seemed pointless to be spending hours polishing buttons and belts until they gleamed, only to dull their glinting helmets with camouflage so the elusive enemy would be unable to spot them.

While Jim performed all these exercises as well as any man in his unit, nothing he did was ever deemed good enough by Tip Howardson. The way the corporal singled Jim out for criticism had been noticed by the rest of the squad. Night after night when his friends went out dancing, to watch a movie or to swell the coffers of the local pubs, Jim would be confined to barracks. Howardson had him running circuits around the parade ground, doing extra duties in the canteen or the laundry and, no matter how hard he tried to stay out of trouble and perform his tasks perfectly, his corporal managed to find fault.

'I think you should make a formal complaint to the RSM,' said Mitch one day, when Jim eventually returned to the dormitory after performing fifty circuits of the parade ground in full kit at the end of a day of exercises. 'It's obvious he's picking on you, bud.'

Jim shrugged. He knew there was no point.

PART II

1941

These are not dark days; these are great days—the greatest days our country has ever lived;

Winston Churchill 1941

A NEW JOB

EASTBOURNE

*G*wen was on the terrace checking on her pots of onion plants when the telephone rang. She ran inside. It was Daphne's husband, Sandy Pringle.

'I say, Gwen, could you come and see me this morning? I'd like to discuss something with you.'

'What's it about, Sandy?' She felt uneasy. There was something about Major Pringle that always made her feel as though she were being reprimanded.

'All good stuff, nothing to worry about. Ten sharp at HQ.'

He hung up. Gwen looked at her watch. Already almost nine. Better step on it. She decided to wear her WVS uniform. She wanted to meet Sandy on her own terms and not as Roger's wife, which was how she sensed Sandy usually saw her – a less interesting and rather insignificant adjunct to her husband.

Sandy Pringle had had a distinguished career in the last war, serving at Gallipoli. After the war, there had been a spell at Sandhurst, then he had been a staff officer for the War Office and was now coordinating military activities in the Sussex region and acting as a liaison between the allied forces and the Home Guard. Sandy had gone to school with Roger and the two had reconnected when the Pringles moved to Eastbourne before war was declared. Gwen wasn't entirely sure about his exact remit, as he appeared to have a finger in many pies. His rank was Major and he had a tendency to bark rather than speak. He spoke to Daphne as though she were an insubordinate private and Gwen wondered how she stood it.

As she waited to be shown into his hallowed presence she felt nervous. Was the summons to do with Daphne's discovery at the fundraiser that she spoke German? She hadn't seen Sandy for months but perhaps Daphne had only just told him. Was he going to give her the third degree as his wife had done?

'Enter!'

Sandy's voice boomed through the door and Gwen looked around to reassure herself that she was the only person waiting in the anteroom, before opening the heavy oak door. Pringle looked at her through narrowed eyes and ran a finger over his moustache before rising to greet her.

'Sit down, sit down, Gwen.' He waved his hand at the empty chair in front of his desk. This was clearly official business, whatever it was.

'I've a job for you, Gwen. Mrs Robson tells me you're a capable and trustworthy officer and a real asset to the WVS.' He gave a slight roll of his eyes as though dismissing that anything the WVS did was of any real value.

Gwen felt a rush of excitement, tempered with irritation that he was speaking to her in such a condescending way. Was she at last to be given something to do that amounted to more than making cups of tea and sorting clothing?

'My wife tells me you speak German.' He frowned at her and again his eyes narrowed.

He *did* suspect she was a fifth columnist. 'Look, I already told Daphne that I was at school in Switzerland in the '20s. Speaking German doesn't make me a sympathiser. For heaven's sake, Sandy, er, Major Pringle, I'm as British as you are.' She paused, then added quietly, 'You know that.'

'Of course you are, my dear. Above reproach. Roger's one of my oldest friends.' The formal military demeanour softened. 'Whatever made you think you were under suspicion?' He began to laugh. 'Was it old Daffers putting the wind up you? Two left feet that woman. I'm always telling her she needs to show a bit more tact. Doesn't listen to me though. No, Gwen, it's quite the opposite. I want to put your skills to work. I'm seconding you to work on a special project. You prepared for that?'

Gwen sat up taller in her chair and swallowed. She felt a mix of nerves and excitement. 'Of course, San...I mean, sir. What would you like me to do?'

'It's hush-hush. You'll find out in good time. Need to be tested first. Got to check your German's up to scratch. And we'll need to do a security vetting. We'll do all that right away. Then you'll have to be fully briefed and trained.'

Gwen shivered with excitement. She would be doing something useful. Something that could help the war effort. Something that might make a difference.

'I must stress again the vital importance of maintaining absolute secrecy.' He tapped his chubby fingers on the desk. 'Now that Hitler has called off the invasion he's doubtless hoping we'll all sit back on our laurels. Not going to happen. The bally war may well drag on for years and it's all the more important to be on our mettle. Secrecy is everything. Sealed lips.'

'Of course.' Gwen nodded. Her mouth was dry and she had difficulty swallowing.

'Not even my wife can know what you'll be doing. Especially not my wife. Not a word. Val Robson doesn't know what you'll be doing either, so keep it that way. We operate entirely on a need to know basis. Not a word to anyone. Even Roger, if you hear from him. You can say you're doing secretarial work for the regional HQ.'

'Righto, sir.' She hesitated then said, 'I don't suppose you have any news of Roger?'

'Why would I? Haven't you heard from him?'

She shook her head and felt herself shivering. 'He did warn me I might not.'

'Well then. That's your answer.' He looked down then his mouth stretched into a grim smile. 'War's not easy for any of us but it must be tough for the two of you, being apart. My old Daffers drives me up the wall at times but I couldn't even begin to imagine what life would be like without the old girl.'

He coughed loudly as though to draw a line under the sentiment he had shown. 'Right then. Where were we? Ah yes, all this is subject to you managing to get through the training. We're taking a risk using a woman. It's demanding work. You'll need to be on the ball.'

Gwen swallowed her annoyance. It was Sandy's manner. At least she wasn't married to the old duffer like poor Daphne.

The interview seemed to be over and she was about to get up, when she realised he had told her virtually nothing. 'Will I be working here, sir? And won't I need to be in one of the services?'

'Wear your WVS uniform. That will do. No time to get other people involved. Flight Sergeant Carrington will fill you in on all the details. Decent chap. RAF. Wait outside and he'll come and get you. Dismissed.' He had already picked up a sheet of paper from the pile on his desk and was reading it.

Gwen jumped to her feet and went back out to the ante-room. Flight Sergeant Carrington, a short man with a finely clipped moustache, was already waiting for her. He led her through a maze of corridors into a windowless office. There was a woman sitting behind a desk waiting for them. She motioned Gwen to take a seat. The interview was entirely in German. At first Gwen, taken by surprise, found herself stumbling over her words. The woman told her to take a deep breath. The breathing calmed her and she managed to get through the rest of the short test with growing confidence. As well as testing her oral skills, she was asked to translate several sentences printed on a card from German into English, then several more the other way round.

Eventually the woman sat back, nodded to Sergeant Carrington and said, 'She'll do.' She stretched out a hand to shake Gwen's.

The security vetting was next. Gwen had imagined this would take days, weeks even, but things evidently happened faster in wartime. She was asked to provide the names of some references and then was left alone at a desk in an empty classroom while Carrington took the list and disappeared. After an hour a young Wren brought her a welcome cup of tea.

All must have been satisfactory as after another nail-biting hour, Carrington reappeared, perched on top of one of the desks in front of hers and began to explain her new job.

'We have a number of radio operators at work here in the town and its surrounds. All along the coast in fact. Top secret, of course. Listening in. Picking up Morse code messages from the enemy. There's a shortage of German language skills and while most of the messages are in code and are sent off to a secret destination for decrypting we need someone to translate the uncoded messages and any voice traffic before the messages are passed on for analysis. A lot of it's routine stuff. Weather reports and suchlike. Airmen reporting their coordinates. The important stuff is all encrypted, but the enemy could get careless now and then and we need to be ready for them.'

Gwen nodded, her heart thumping. Finally she was going to have a job to do that might make a difference. Even if it didn't, using her language skills and being entrusted with secrets had to be better than serving tea and compiling lists.

After a period of classroom training with a couple of Wrens and three WAAFs in a building in what had been one of the many public schools in the town, Gwen understood the basic principles of operating a radio receiver and was competent in Morse code. She was assigned to a listening post near to the main radar station on Beachy Head. Each of the women would be working in a pair with an airman or naval signaller. The decision to extend the remit to women did not go as far as entrusting them to operate without a man alongside.

GWEN WAS COLD. Colder than she'd ever been – despite her heavy coat and thick gloves. She leaned against the wall and rubbed her hands up and down her arms and tried to stop shivering. The roof was leaking and the rain was beating a tattoo on the tin covering. A drip ran down her neck so she edged sideways. Every night for the past week she'd spent sitting on a canvas folding chair in this cramped space with a young air force warrant officer who had acne and bad breath. He had made it clear to Gwen, without saying as much, that being here in a repurposed railway container on a clifftop with a middle-aged woman was not the assignment he'd been hoping for. Gwen tried to make conversation, but Warrant Officer Irving shrugged or answered her questions with monosyllables so she eventually settled for an uncomfortable silence.

Her job was to listen into the German VHF voice transmissions and log everything she heard. It was one thing to sit happily twiddling the dials of the wireless equipment in a comfortable classroom and another to be doing it with icy cold hands in a tin box on top of Beachy Head.

Most of the time it was Luftwaffe pilots talking to their controllers. As she became accustomed to listening she began to recognise different regional accents. Occasionally she recognised some of the individual voices.

The radio traffic had been quiet tonight. It meant she had plenty of time to translate the messages she had logged before they were picked up by a motorcycle rider and whisked away to a destination unknown, referred to only as Station X.

At first, on busy nights she had tended to translate as she listened, writing the messages down in English. That approach earned her a reprimand – the powers-that-be wanted both the verbatim German and her translation. It was irritating. If they didn't trust her translation skills why not just get her to transcribe the verbatim German? It was not up to her to question though, and in a war maybe it was necessary to check everything and trust no one. Gwen told herself the important thing was that she was directly involved in the war effort.

Listening to these young German pilots informing their base stations that they were headed for home made her feel close to the action, playing a vital role, even though it was hard to imagine what use her work would be put to. Much of it was reportage of things that had already happened and by the time her transcriptions reached the mythical Station X it was probably far too late to do anything about them. Maybe they were looking for patterns though? Perhaps there was significance in things that she couldn't see? It was like a giant jigsaw puzzle and she was collecting pieces with no sight of the bigger picture.

Sometimes the intercepts involved the Germans reporting sighting of British convoys. Whenever this happened she would alert Warrant Officer Irving as she listened and scribbled and he would jump into life and immediately send messages to alert the RAF to scramble to protect the ships involved. The convoys were carrying supplies of essentials – food and armaments – so her work was indeed making a difference. At last she was in the thick of things.

THE NEW RECRUIT

ALDERSHOT

*J*im was finishing his breakfast in the canteen one morning when Walt slipped into the seat opposite him. Jim stared at him without speaking, then carried on eating his porridge.

'Aint you going to say anything, Jim? Not even hello?'

Jim continued to eat in silence.

'So, you're still mad at me. I suppose I can understand that.'

Jim kept his eyes down, conscious that somewhere in the room Corporal Howardson would be watching this encounter.

Walt reached a hand to grip Jim's arm, halting the progress of spoon to mouth. 'I didn't mean to hurt you, Jim. It's the last thing I wanted. You weren't meant to find out that way. We never expected you to walk in on us like that. We reckoned we'd find the right time and place to tell you. Break it to you gently. But you didn't give us a chance.'

Jim put his spoon down, his appetite gone. He couldn't believe what he was hearing. The blood rushed to his head and his fists clenched under the table.

Walt continued. 'I've always looked up to you, Jim. Don't you think I would have avoided it happening if I could? It's upset Ma and Pa. And Alice had to go through hell at home when her folks found out what was going on. If I could have prevented all that I would have done.'

Jim looked at Walt, unable to reconcile this stranger across the table with the little brother he had always loved.

Walt leaned forward. 'Look, we didn't mean to fall in love. It just happened. One of those things. It's been hard on Alice. Folks have taken against her. Every time she's in town she says she can sense people talking about her, pointing fingers. She can hardly bear to go work in the library.' He picked up a knife and began to tap it nervously against the tabletop. 'If the two of you hadn't rushed into getting engaged practically as soon as she finished school, she would have had time to recognise her real feelings.'

Jim pushed his bowl away and got to his feet. 'You're telling me it's my fault, are you?'

'No need to put it like that. All I'm saying is if you'd waited a bit, given her some more time–'

'You're saying I pushed her into agreeing to marry me? Is that what she told you?'

Walt looked away. 'Not exactly. But you know what I mean.'

'No. I don't know what you mean at all.'

'You take everything for granted. You think it's all yours for the taking. Everything comes easy to you. You were top of your class at school. Could have gone to university if you hadn't wanted to stay on the farm. You got the best looking girl in the town. You were always Ma's favourite. Pa gave you more responsibility on the farm than me. I'm always left to run behind in your shadow. But Alice sees me in a different way. She sees me, not a paler version of you.'

Jim shook his head. 'Ma had no favourite. Pa gave me

more responsibility because I did more of the work. I did well at school because I studied hard. When will you stop thinking the whole world owes you a living, Walt? When are you going to grow up and take responsibility for your own actions?'

Jim started to walk out of the mess room but Walt was on his feet and moving after him.

Jim turned to his brother. 'Shove off and leave me alone, Walt. I joined up so I wouldn't have to look at your self-satisfied face any more. I don't know why the hell you joined up, unless it's because it's yet another thing you couldn't bear for me to have without trying to have it too. Now get out of my way.'

~

THEY WERE on an all-day regimental exercise. It was freezing cold and, late in the afternoon, the gorse was still laced with a thin dusting of frost. Six men from another company were holed up in a deserted farmhouse somewhere, playing the part of a group of Germans, and Jim and his cohort were expected to track them down, ambush the building and take them prisoner. They were at the top of a slope, looking down on the derelict farmhouse, figuring out how to take its occupants by surprise.

Greg Hooper was lying on his stomach beside Jim, looking through binoculars. 'We'll need some kind of diversion at the front of the farm so we can sneak round the back way.'

'How the hell are we going to do that?' Scotty McDermott looked doubtful.

'There's no chance,' said Mitch Johnson. 'There's no cover in front of the building. The bastards have got us.'

'Come on. We can't give up,' Jim said. 'Remember what

the corporal said. Extra chocolate rations if we capture them and an extra five miles on the route march if we don't.' He tried to inject some enthusiasm into his voice. 'Couldn't we get round the back and surprise them that way?'

'There's ten foot of barbed wire on one side and a sheer cliff on the other.'

'We could abseil down the cliff.'

'With what? Where's the rope?'

'Hell. Should have thought of that.'

They flung around more ideas but none were seen to have any merit.

'We need a distraction to lure them out of the building.' Jim frowned in concentration.

'We could get one and torture him,' said Mitch, a big grin on his face.

The others started laughing.

'Shut up you idiots, they'll hear us.' Greg sounded impatient. 'And be serious. We can't torture anyone.'

'They're supposed to be Germans. Fair game.'

'Haven't you heard of the Geneva Convention?'

'Yeah but we could say they were Gestapo, then anything goes, Grass.'

'For Pete's sake, guys, this is getting us nowhere.' Jim was losing patience.

'I've got an idea.' Mitch jumped to his feet, squatting down on his haunches in front of them. 'It's getting dark and cloudy. It'll be hard for them to see exactly what's going on. How about we start firing, then get Scotty to imitate the sound of a woman screaming and a baby crying. They'll think a civilian's wandered on to the range and got shot up. They won't be able to avoid coming out to help an injured woman and a baby in distress.'

'But there is no woman and baby.'

'That's the best bit,' said Mitch. 'We dress Scotty up as a woman with a bundle that will look like a baby.'

'Oh no! No bloody way!' said Scotty.

'Where do we get women's clothes out here?'

'We don't. We have to create the illusion. Scotty takes his battle dress and trousers off and flashes his lovely bare legs. We can make something that looks like a skirt using some canvas. Come on, guys, it's worth a try.'

There was silence for a moment while they mulled over Mitch's idea.

Fists pumping, they sprang into action.

It took a few minutes to transform Scotty into a vague semblance of a woman. The finishing touch was a couple of handkerchiefs knotted together to form a headscarf and conceal his short back and sides. Not enough to fool anyone close up but at a distance in the fading afternoon light they might have a chance of convincing someone.

Greg set the plan in motion by hurling a grenade against a rock over the brow of the hill so the occupants of the farmhouse could hear it but not see the explosion. They were always being warned of the danger of unexploded ordinance and the risk of civilians wandering onto the ranges so there was some vague logic to their flimsy plan. Scotty began to scream and wail in a high pitched voice that was a convincing imitation of a distressed or dying woman. He interspersed the screams with wails from the baby that was a bundle of gorse swaddled in bandages from the first aid kit, and began to stumble down the slope towards the building.

Two men emerged from the farmhouse and looked about cautiously. Scotty screamed again and then, flinging the baby to the ground, collapsed face down. The two men ran towards him as Mitch and Greg moved down one side of the slope using gorse bushes as cover, while Jim and the two others made their way down the other side. As the "Germans" reached the dying woman, Scotty leapt to his feet and Mitch and Greg and one of the others rushed in to help over-power them. Jim ran on down the slope, gun at the ready and hurled a grenade against a water tank outside, producing a gratifying explosion. The door of the house burst open and four men came out, looking around in confusion. Jim slipped behind them, then shouted, 'Hands up, Schweinhunds!' while his two companions each pointed their guns at the men.

'You bastards. You bunch of cheats!' one of the captives cried out. 'That's not fair play.'

'All's fair in love and war,' said Mitch. 'We've got you.'

One of the captives turned, attempting to run back into the house. Jim stuck out a leg and tripped him up, sending him flying onto his hands and knees on the gravel. Jim moved towards him, hand stretched out to pull him to his feet, saying, 'Come on, pal. It's all over. You have to know when to quit.' Realising it was his brother, he dropped his hand and stepped back.

'You did that deliberately. You cheated. You wanted to humiliate me.' Walt's voice was half-whine half-whisper.

Over the top of the slope Tip Howardson was coming towards them. 'An extra five miles tomorrow for the whole bloody lot of you.'

'But we got them, Corporal,' said Scotty.

'Where's your uniform, McDermott? What the hell do you think you're playing at? What's that on your head?'

Scotty McDermott started to explain their elaborate ruse, but it served only to madden the corporal further. 'You and Armstrong can do one hundred press-ups as soon as we get back to camp. And the whole damn lot of you are doing a fifteen miler tomorrow. Full kit. The forecast is for rain.'

As he finished speaking, they realised there was someone standing in the shadow of a gorse bush beside them. Captain Bywater emerged from the gloom. Tip Howardson turned to the officer, saluted and said, 'Captain, sir, I was reprimanding these men for making an exhibition of themselves. They've turned a serious exercise into a farce.'

'At ease, men.' Addressing the corporal, Captain Bywater said, 'I was about to congratulate them. I was watching from behind the brow of that hill. Saw the whole thing. Damned clever. I'd like to congratulate you men for your ingenuity. The screaming baby was a stroke of genius. The attacking team deserve extra rations. And if you happen to pass by the Dog and Duck I'll stand each of you a pint tonight.'

He turned to look at the captive "Germans".

'You lot are pathetic. Fancy being conned by this ugly fellow.' He pointed at Scotty. 'If that's your idea of a young woman, no one in Aldershot is safe.'

The men hung their heads, humiliated. Bywater slapped Scotty on the back. 'Damned resourceful. That's what we need. A bit of nous and imagination. See to it that they get those extra chocolate rations, Corporal.' He saluted and went back over the top of the hill.

Howardson turned to the men. 'I suppose you think you're clever. Well I'm watching you lot. One step wrong and you'll all suffer for it.' He turned to the captured "enemy". 'Looks like you'll be running your extra five miles on your own this time. Now back to base.'

As they trudged back to the main road for the five mile walk back to the garrison, Jim was near the front of the group. He turned his head to look behind him and saw Walt was watching him, his eyes filled with undisguised hatred.

BOMBED OUT

EASTBOURNE

*T*here had been no bombs since before Christmas. The people of Eastbourne were heaving a collective sigh of relief and crossing their fingers that the worst days of the town being used as target practice by the Luftwaffe were now gone. Then the bombing began again.

Gwen was doing a morning shift for the WVS in the town centre. There were just two of them, Gwen reading a book and her companion doing a crossword puzzle. Gwen wished she was on duty up on Beachy Head – at least she felt she was doing something useful instead of this sitting around and waiting for nothing to happen.

Four bombs were dropped that morning from a single plane, which swept over the town at around five hundred feet. The bombs landed in the part of the town known as the Archery, hitting houses in and around Churchdale Road.

As soon as the all-clear sounded, Gwen grabbed her bicycle and set off for the scene. The surface of Churchdale Road had been ploughed up into a deep crater where the bomb had bounced before destroying a series of houses.

A wide swathe had been cut through the row of houses,

like a scythe through corn. Gwen left her bike against a wall and made her way into the thick of the scene of destruction. No matter how many times she attended the aftermath of a bomb attack it didn't lessen the horror. Helmeted ARP men were scrambling over a mountain of debris – bricks, plaster-work, roofing tiles, wooden beams, all piled across the road in the gap where the houses had stood. The air was thick with dust. Suffocating. Choking. Stinging the eyes. Blocking the throat. This was what hell must be. Gwen covered her mouth with a handkerchief, then unfastened the silk scarf from around her neck and tied it across her face bandanna style. She moved forward, picking her way through the detritus, towards the survivors.

Further up the road, a little girl sat on what was left of the kerb clutching a teddy bear to her chest, whispering words of comfort to the bear, as her mother beside her nursed a baby. The mother was apparently oblivious to the gash across her forehead and the blood dripping down her temple. Gwen hurried over with her first aid kit and began to clean the wound, removing shards of glass, but relieved that, despite the blood, it was not too deep.

'I'd been in the back kitchen washing up the breakfast things just before the bombs dropped,' the young woman told Gwen. 'I heard the sound and grabbed the baby and ran out into the yard. Sally here was playing outside. Thank God she was all right. But my grandfather – he was upstairs. Bed-ridden. His heart. Name's Mr Arthur Moffat. Can you get someone to go over and check on him?' She looked up at Gwen, squinting against the sunlight and the dust. 'The wardens wouldn't let me go back to look for him. The noise will have terrified him. He's in the little front bedroom. Number 15'

Gwen went to check with the ARP warden who jerked his head in the direction of the gaping hole where number 15 had been. 'No one inside would have stood a chance. They've dug an old fellow out from under the rubble but I'm afraid he was dead. At least it would have been instant. If you have the man's name, go and tell that fellow over there with the clipboard.'

Once she'd informed the officials, Gwen made her way back to the woman and her two children, her heart heavy. She'd never had to break news like this to anyone before. There wasn't even time to prepare, to find the right words. She felt hopelessly inadequate.

Mrs Simmonds' eyes filled with tears. 'How am I going to tell my granny? She's in a nursing home. We lost my mother to pneumonia last year. Now this. How will I break the news that Grandpa's gone?' She choked back a sob. 'I can't believe it. He was sitting up in bed reading the *News of the World*, smoking his Woodbines and now he's gone. Poor devil.' She put an arm around her daughter, pulling her in towards herself and the baby. 'But thank God it were Grandpa and not these two.'

'You know the children shouldn't still be in Eastbourne, Mrs Simmonds. They should have been evacuated months ago.'

The woman looked up at her, eyes narrowed. 'Got any children yourself, have you? – I thought not. I'm without my husband, my mum's dead, my grandpa's just been killed in his bed and now you want to take my girls away from me?'

Gwen swallowed. 'It's not safe here.'

'Am I daft?' Mrs Simmonds waved her hands at the scene of desecration in front of them. 'But I don't want my girls being cared for by a bunch of strangers. And I'm not leaving while my granny's here. She's in an old folks' home. Can't look after herself. She lives for visits from me and the kids. Now Grandpa's gone I'm all she's got. If we're going to cop it we'll all cop it together and that's final.' She turned away and focused her attention on the child in her arms.

By the time she got back to Meads that evening, Gwen was exhausted. Too tired to cook anything. She had been living on a diet of toast, tinned pilchards and baked potatoes, and all too often forgetting to eat at all. Never having had to cook she lacked the skills to rustle up meals from her meagre rations and there always seemed to be more pressing things to do than cook and eat. She ran her fingers under the waistband of her skirt. Hanging off her. How much weight had she lost? She couldn't go on like this.

She looked around her comfortable lounge, its generous proportions dwarfing her. Why should she have all this space when the displaced people from Churchdale Road were crowded into a rest centre?

Next morning, Gwen walked down the hill to the town. She walked to the school where the bombed-out people from the Archery were sheltering. Mrs Simmonds was sitting on the edge of a camp bed, brushing and braiding the hair of her daughter as Sally stood patiently in front of her, wedged between her knees. The baby was sleeping in a cradle made from a drawer.

Gwen marched up to them. 'Do you still want to stay in Eastbourne, Mrs Simmonds?'

The young woman looked up, surprised. 'They said last night they're going to send me and my kids to Gloucestershire. I don't even know where that is.' She scowled. 'This town's my home and I don't want to go and live in some strange place. Little Brenda's only eighteen months. But they say that as we don't have a home to go to I don't have a say.'

'Can you cook?'

'Course I can cook.'

'Then I have a proposition for you. I live up in Meads. Right at the top by the Downs. It's far from the railway and the gasworks and the town centre so less chance of a stray bomb up there. How would you and your girls like to come and live in my house? You'd have your own quarters. There's a big garden for Sally to play in. I can provide you with bed and board and two pounds ten a week in exchange for a little light housework and the cooking. What do you think?'

'And the girls wouldn't have to go away?'

'They can't force you to have them evacuated if they have a place to live.'

A wide grin broke across Mrs Simmonds face. She spun Sally round and planted a kiss on her forehead. 'Hear that, Sal? We can all be together and live in a posh house. How about that!' Then she reached for Gwen's hand and squeezed it. 'Thanks ever so, Mrs. Sorry I don't remember your name. But you can call me Pauline.'

THE STAG

ALDERSHOT

*G*reg had got a bad attack of the blues. He wasn't alone; virtually everyone in the barracks was suffering from homesickness. The fact that they were not involved in any enemy action, coupled with the miserable rainy weather, conspired to ensure that a pall of misery descended over the Canadian recruits.

Jim's misery was of a different nature. He was still overcome with loss and grief at what had happened, accompanied by shame – that he had not been good enough to hold onto his girl, that he was lacking something that his younger brother had, that he had been so self-absorbed that he had failed to have even an inkling of what was going on.

The constant sneering and bullying of Tip Howardson made matters worse. Howardson lost no opportunity to goad him about Alice and Walt, trying to push Jim to lose his self-control and lash out. That would give the corporal the perfect excuse to punish and humiliate him. Jim was determined not to let that happen. Howardson had even tried to make capital from Jim's mother being of German origin. If he had hoped this would turn the other men against Jim, Tip was disappointed.

There was also the odd encounter with Walt. Jim did everything he could to avoid it but Aldershot was a small town and it was inevitable they would run into each other occasionally, especially in training exercises. Walt's attitude was surly, still smarting from being out-manoeuvred in the ambush of the ruined farmhouse. Jim sensed that Walt was regretting the decision to join up and blamed him for it. He was seeing aspects of his brother he had not noticed before – or perhaps had chosen not to acknowledge.

Being stuck in a bleak barrack room with a morose Greg Hooper was not helping Jim's own morale. In an effort to raise Greg's spirits, Jim suggested they go out into the town one evening, but Greg was unmoved, preferring to lie on his bunk and stare at the ceiling. The dark mood was beginning to infect Jim too. If he was to get through this war – or get through this training period and into battle – he had to keep some sense of equilibrium. Losing patience with Greg, he grabbed hold of his friend's ankle and yanked him off his bunk bed.

'Get up, you miserable bastard. Stop feeling so darn sorry for yourself.'

Greg, taken completely unaware, sat on the dorm floor, looking up at Jim, eyes wide. He shook his shoulders, as though shaking something off, then picked himself up off the floor. Jim's action was the shot in the arm he had evidently been waiting for. He grinned at his friend and said, 'Okay, pal, let's go. You win.'

Rather than going to the nearest public house to the barracks, their usual drinking hole, the men ventured further into the town. The Stag was a large ugly building straddling a street corner and neither of them had visited it before. Once they had penetrated the protective blackout curtains inside the door, they found the interior of the establishment unexpectedly welcoming and cheery – a marked contrast to the spartan facilities of the beverage rooms they had known back in Canada. There was beer on tap, music from a piano livening one of the bars, and – the biggest difference – women on both sides of the bar.

The noise was deafening. Men were singing along to the piano; voices were raised in conversation as everyone struggled to be heard. Jim and Greg pushed their way through the throng and then, to avoid the crush, retreated from the scrum in the public and saloon bars to a small room marked "Snug" at the back of the pub. Inside, it was anything but snug, the fire in the grate being little more than dying embers. The coal scuttle beside the hearth was empty, evidence of rationing. But at least the room had the advantage of being quiet and there were a few seats available. The rest were occupied by civilians: a group of older men playing cards, an elderly couple sitting side by side in total silence, half-empty glasses of stout in front of them. Greg was about to pull Jim back into the more convivial atmosphere of the main bar when they spotted a pair of young women at a table in the corner. Greg nodded to Jim and pulled him by the sleeve towards the pair.

'Good evening, ladies,' said Greg, with a friendly smile. He offered to buy the two of them a drink and when they thanked him, headed over to an open hatch in the wall which gave on to the central bar area.

One of the women motioned to Jim to sit down and join them. He hesitated a moment. What kind of women hung out in a drinking house? Back home, women weren't even allowed in the refreshment rooms and, had they been permitted entry, he thought it likely only prostitutes would take advantage of the opportunity. But these women didn't look like prostitutes. One of them was wearing uniform for a start. He sat down, nervous and self-conscious and waited for Greg to return while the women ignored him and continued their conversation.

Greg came back with the requested lemonade shandies and a couple of pints of beer. Jim had been avoiding drinking beer since his experience in Toronto but he decided it was time to put that behind him. Besides, this was English beer. He took a mouthful of the unfamiliar drink: flatter, more bitter than back home and served at room temperature. His first thought was that it was disgusting, but he was thirsty and a few more mouthfuls convinced him he actually liked it. It was rich, earthy and hoppy, a quickly acquired taste.

Meanwhile Greg was busy with introductions and had established that one woman was in the ATS and called Joan, while the other, Ethel, worked in a munitions factory and spent her days packing bullets into boxes. Both were good-looking but Ethel was the prettier of the two. She was blonde and that made Jim think of Alice. He pushed the thought away. Joan's dark hair was cut in a long glossy bob which she kept pushing back behind her ears. While Jim drank his pint in silence, Grass soon established that Joan was engaged to be married and from that point on he evidently felt no longer obliged to make conversation with her, fixing his attention on Ethel, leaving Jim to entertain Joan.

The evening passed quickly as Joan proved to need little encouragement to talk and seemed unconcerned whether her words elicited any response from him. He looked over the top of his third pint and saw that Greg and Ethel were already holding hands.

'Why do you call your friend Grass when his name is Greg?' Joan asked.

Jim had grown used to her keeping up a monologue and it was only when she repeated the question that he realised she was asking him something that required a response.

He explained.

'A pretty stupid name if you ask me,' she said.

Jim wanted to say that he hadn't asked her, but instead gave a noncommittal nod.

'And why do Canadians keep saying "eh" all the time. Specially him.' She nodded in Greg's direction.

Jim looked at his watch and shrugged. 'Do we?'

'Yes. But you don't, come to think of it. But then you don't say much at all.'

Jim suddenly felt ashamed. It wasn't Joan's fault that they had been stuck with each other. She was probably enjoying the evening no more than he was. He decided to be more friendly. As he was trying to think of a topic of conversation the bell for last orders rang and Joan jumped to her feet. She dug Ethel in the ribs. 'Come on, I promised Aunty Vi we'd be home before eleven.'

A reluctant Ethel pulled on her coat and the two Canadians accompanied the women through the blackout to a nearby bus stop. Jim and Joan shuffled their feet and shivered in the cold evening while Grass and Ethel kissed against the wall of the bus shelter.

'Your friend doesn't waste much time, does she?' Jim said and immediately wished he hadn't.

'I could say the same about yours, couldn't I?'

Unable to dispute Joan's logic, he leaned against a tree, avoiding looking back through the gloom to the bus shelter, where, as well as Ethel and Grass, at least half a dozen other Canadian soldiers were kissing women they had met in the pub. He wished the bus would appear and liberate him.

Joan moved towards him, pushing her body against his. 'You can kiss me if you want. I don't mind.'

Surprised, he said, 'I thought you said you were getting married.'

'So what? A kiss isn't a promise.' She looked up at him. In

the faint moonlight she looked pretty and Jim was tempted. What harm was there? – it was only a kiss. Maybe the war made people behave differently. Or maybe English girls weren't so fussy about kissing strangers. He hesitated for a moment then bent his head to kiss her. Her lips were soft and drew him into the kiss. He had begun to enjoy it, when she pulled away.

'That's your lot, soldier. No need to make a meal of it. The bus is coming.'

People piled onto the vehicle, but Ethel and Grass were showing no sign of ending their embrace. The bus conductress rang the bell and called out, 'You getting on or walking home?' Joan grabbed her friend by the sleeve and hauled her onto the platform as the bus began to move away.

Greg slapped an arm around Jim's shoulder. 'That was a great night, eh?'

Jim grunted in response. He'd enjoyed the beer and the friendly atmosphere of the pub but he wasn't exactly champing at the bit to meet the women again. The kiss with Joan had been enjoyable but kissing another man's fiancée was not something he was keen to repeat. Besides, the kiss was a reminder of what he had lost. He felt the anger about Walt and Alice rising in him again and kicked out pointlessly at a tree as they passed it.

Greg was exuberant and didn't pick up on Jim's darker mood. 'I've met the girl I'm going to marry,' he said, triumphantly. 'I'll take her back home to Regina after the war. The future Mrs Ethel Hooper, eh.'

Jim roared with laughter, his dark mood forgotten. 'You're kidding me!'

Greg grabbed his friend by the front of his battledress jacket. 'I mean it, Jim. I'm not being funny.'

'You've only known her an hour or so.'

Greg slung an arm over Jim's shoulders and they moved

on, walking as steadily as they could in the dark and after the beers. 'That's all it took. Not even that. I knew it the moment I saw her.'

Jim shook his head, still disbelieving. 'So you're seeing her again? Did you even get her address?'

'You bet I did. And we're going there for tea a week on Sunday, Sunny Jim.'

'We?'

'You're invited too.'

'Oh no! You're on your own.'

'You have to come too. Her mother will be there. Ethel says they want to pull out the stops for the brave volunteers who've come to help them win the war. There'll be cake. They're going to pool their rations specially. I don't know if I'll be able to wait that long till I see her.'

'When did you sort all this out?' Jim was astounded.

'While you were eating the face off Joanie, you bad boy.'

Jim was grateful for the blackout so his friend couldn't see his embarrassment.

THE NEW HOUSEKEEPER

EASTBOURNE

*T*he Simmondses were waiting for Pauline outside the Rest Centre. Sally was sucking her thumb, her teddy bear dangling from the other hand, and the baby was asleep in her mother's arms. Their sparse belongings were on the pavement: a small battered suitcase containing a few pieces of clothing provided by the WVS and a straw bag with items for baby Brenda. Sally, excited to be inside a motor car for the first time, scrambled onto the back seat and arranged her teddy beside her. Mrs Simmonds sat in the front with the baby in her arms.

'You don't have a lot of things,' said Gwen when they arrived back at the house. 'Will you be able to manage?'

'I've only got four nappies for the baby. There's no time to get them washed and dry before I need to change her again. I had to borrow an iron this morning and run that over them to dry them out.'

Gwen swallowed. A painful memory surfaced. A short period of joy in late September 1933 when she had rushed around the shops buying layette for a baby that a few weeks later was no longer there. A memory of pain and blood and tears and shock. Another loss she had buried deep inside her, never to be mentioned. Roger had been away in Geneva, working behind the scenes at the World Disarmament Conference. On his return when the conference fell apart in October, she kept what had happened to herself, so he neither knew she had been pregnant nor that they had lost the baby. She had meant to tell him but he was so dispirited about the failed conference, full of frustration about the intransigence of both France and Germany, the deep-rooted self-interest that appeared to govern all the parties and fear about the potential threat of Adolf Hitler, who had ordered Dr Goebbels to withdraw Germany from the discussions. Gwen had sat, legs drawn up under her and hands around her knees, listening as her husband talked, behaving in a way she had seen her mother behave before. Grief was something to be buried, locked away. It was not to be acknowledged.

She turned to Mrs Simmonds. 'I can help you with that.' She gestured towards the drawing room. 'Make yourselves comfortable. I'll only be a minute.' She ran up to a box room on the top floor. It was kept locked and was used to store unwanted furniture. There, inside a dusty trunk, she found a neatly folded pile of nappies, as well as a small collection of baby's clothes, unworn but too small for Brenda. She stifled her pain.

Mrs Simmonds was waiting in the hallway, holding the baby over one arm and clutching Sally's hand.

'Here. Nappies, a shawl and a cot blanket,' Gwen said. 'All brand new.'

Mrs Simmonds looked at her with curiosity, but evidently thought better than to ask how Gwen had acquired them.

'Come on. I'll show you your room,' said Gwen. 'I thought

you'd all prefer being in one room together since the surroundings will be strange to Sally. But if she'd like her own room we can sort that out.'

'In together's perfect.'

The room was large and on the lower ground floor of the house, with French windows opening onto a paved terrace at the side of the building.

'My housekeeper used to live down here. I thought it would suit you as there's a little sitting room next door and the kitchen beyond. There's a terrace through here which is a safe place for Sally to play and you can see what's she's up to from the kitchen.'

'Mrs Collingwood, you've done us proud. I can't thank you enough. It's like a dream.' Pauline Simmonds ran her hand along the rail of the cot that was beside the bed and threw another glance at Gwen.

Anticipating the question, Gwen said, 'My friend Daphne found the cot for you in her attic. Her children are all grown up and gone away now. It's old but it should serve the purpose. And the single bed should do Sally. The double is quite springy.' She pushed at the mattress with her open palms. 'My housekeeper, Mrs Woods, always said she got a good night's sleep here.'

Mrs Simmonds grinned and placed the baby down on the bed so she could fling her arms around an astonished Gwen. 'Thank you so much. I can't tell you how grateful I am. To do all this for us. Opening up your beautiful home like this.' Her eyes glistened with tears.

'Nonsense,' said Gwen, uncertain what to do as the woman hugged her. 'Anyone would have done the same. And I'm glad of the company. This house is far too big for me.'

'Your husband away fighting?'

Gwen nodded.

'Which service?'

'Army.' She decided not to say that she didn't actually know. She didn't want to use the term Roger himself used – The Inter-Services Bureau – whatever that was supposed to mean.

'My Brian is on the convoys,' said Pauline. 'It's hard, isn't it? Them being away, 'specially at night. No one to snuggle up to in bed!' She winked.

Gwen, embarrassed, gave her a weak smile. 'Let me show you the kitchen,' she said, moving out of the room and cutting off the conversation.

∼

PAULINE SIMMONDS WAS STANDING at the drawing room window when Gwen came into the room.

'You're so lucky living up here, Mrs Collingwood. I'd love to be able to see the sea from my house. It's only ten minutes' walk away but all we look onto is other houses.' Her voice trembled and she added, 'I mean that was all we used to see. Past tense.'

Gwen felt a rush of pity for the woman. Pauline had never complained. To lose her grandfather as well as her home and everything in it must be a terrible cross to bear, yet she was perennially cheerful.

Pauline nodded towards the paved area below them. 'We seem to have made our mark already.' She indicated the chalked numbers on the flagstones. 'Sally loves her hopscotch. She usually does it on the pavement in the street but it's all fancy brickwork up this end of town. I'll scrub it off tomorrow.'

'No, don't. She's not done any harm. Let her have her fun.'

They were side-be-side at the window. 'The sea looks

beautiful today,' said Pauline. 'It looks like there's a light under the water, shining up from the deep.' Her voice was soft. 'From a secret shining place.'

Gwen looked at her, surprised.

'I wonder how many poor souls are down there,' said Pauline, her voice quiet and dreamlike. 'Sucked under the waves over all the centuries, lying there on the bottom. Maybe that's where heaven is. Not up in the sky but under the sea. My Brian's out there somewhere on his ship.'

'Do you have any idea where he is?'

Pauline shook her head. 'Probably crossing the Atlantic, but it could be anywhere. Every day I used to go in the library to check the newspapers to make sure his ship wasn't mentioned. Then I stopped. If it's bad news I'd rather read it in a telegram than find out in the middle of the public library. And reading about all those lads like him, blasted into pieces by torpedoes, made me feel low. I know one day it could be Brian but I'm not going to think about it. Better to hope for the best.'

Gwen laid a hand on Pauline's arm then, surprised at herself, drew it back quickly. 'It's awful. The not knowing. I don't know where my husband is either. I have no idea what he's doing or where he's gone. You're right, Mrs Simmonds, there's no point thinking about it. We only imagine the worst. Much better to hope for the best and get on with it.'

'Mummy, Mummy, can I play outside?' Sally ran into the room, her plaits flying out behind her.

Pauline threw a look of resignation at Gwen and took hold of her child's hand. 'Come on then, Sal. I'll throw a ball to you.' She got as far as the door then turned back to Gwen. 'And I've told you before, Mrs C. Please call me Pauline.'

Gwen remained at the window watching mother and daughter playing in the garden, Sally's shrieks of delight rising up to her on the afternoon air. Her own child would have been six now. Gwen would never know if it had been a boy or a girl. Funny that. She'd thought as an expectant mother, no matter for how briefly, she would have been able to tell. Even though her baby had never been bigger than a prawn she thought she ought to have been able to tell its gender – that some innate sense would have given her the certainty of who the person was whom she had lost.

Most of the time she didn't allow herself the luxury and pain of thinking of her or him but occasionally she found herself choosing a name or picturing a face, working out how old the child would be now. How might motherhood have changed her? Would it have softened her or dulled her? Would she have been caught up in a round of mindless tasks and daily planning that centred around her child? Choosing a school, buying clothes, picking up toys from the bedroom floor, brushing hair, checking that teeth were cleaned and shoes polished. And how might having a child have changed Roger? Would he have been prepared to risk life and limb on whatever foolhardy mission he was undertaking now if there was a child waiting here at home for him instead of only her?

Outside in the garden, Sally had tripped on an uneven paving stone and grazed her knee. Pauline was holding her close, stroking her hair to comfort the little girl. Gwen felt a stab of envy. As the tears pricked at her eyes, she pulled away from the window. It was already nearly ten o'clock. She had to walk down to the village and get to the butchers. Then there was a huge pile of clothing waiting in the church hall for her to sort through for the WVS.

She thought again of Pauline. Her intent in bringing her here was as a replacement for Mrs Woods, but she struggled to think of Pauline as a servant. The woman had already got under her skin and Gwen was drawn to her. She'd never known anyone like her before and found her refreshing, full of life and energy.

One morning when Pauline offered to style her hair for her, Gwen was reluctant, but Pauline insisted and Gwen had to admit the results were flattering. It was some time since she had taken the trouble to experiment and she acknowledged that she had perhaps become stuck in her ways.

THE TEA PARTY

ALDERSHOT

The air in the barracks was stale and fuggy. No one ever opened a window.

Greg was impatient. 'Come on, Jimbo,' he said with a groan. 'There'll be cake. And it'll be good to be inside a proper home for once after this dump, eh?'

Jim had to acknowledge that anywhere would be a pleasant change after being holed up in the garrison. It was Sunday and he knew it was time to face up to the task he had been putting off for days – writing to his mother.

Greg wasn't having it. 'You can write home any time.' He stretched his foot out and tapped with his boot against Jim's knee. 'Please. Do it for me, pal. You know I can't wait to see Ethel again. She told me I have to bring you. She doesn't want her mother to know we're going out together yet.'

'You've only met her once, Grass. I'd hardly call that going out.'

'I've told you. She's the one. I'm deadly serious about her.'

Jim sighed. He might as well resign himself to his fate, so he swung his legs off the bed, got to his feet and was rewarded with a thump on the back from a jubilant Greg.

When they arrived at Ethel's house, a narrow redbrick terrace, they were not the only guests. Apparently Mrs Underwood had a habit of throwing her doors open to servicemen for a bit of home comfort once a month on a Sunday afternoon, saving up her rations.

'We have to do our bit for all you boys. Especially those like you so far from home.'

Jim threw a look at Greg who shrugged.

There were six or seven soldiers already crammed into the tiny parlour, sitting on the arms as well as the seats of the chairs, and a couple were cross-legged on the floor. Jim looked around. He didn't know any of them and felt a moment of relief that Walt wasn't one of them. He seemed to spend his life trying to keep out of sight of his brother. But he rather suspected Walt was doing the same with him.

So this was a typical British home? Small. Apart from the seating, the only furniture was a side table displaying a large wooden crystal radio set – or wireless as the Brits insisted on calling them. Above an ugly tiled fireplace, a mirror hung on a chain from the picture rail, evidently placed for decorative purposes only, as it was too high for any of the women of the house to have a chance of using it – Jim would have needed to stand on his toes and he wasn't short. Maybe Ethel's late father had been as tall as Grass.

Jim squeezed into a space under the window, sitting on the linoleum floor, his back against the wall. Grass had disappeared, presumably in search of his sweetheart.

The air in the room was heavy with smoke and Jim's eyes stung. He had never got the hang of smoking. Never had time for it on the farm. Since joining up he'd been obliged to have the odd cigarette but he hadn't enjoyed them and always passed his ration on to others in the platoon.

'Legs out of the way, lads! Tea's up!' A plump woman came into the room bearing a tray. She was wearing a frilly blouse that was probably her Sunday best, under an apron. Ethel was standing behind her in the doorway. Two of the men jumped to their feet and took the tray from Mrs Underwood and another vacated his seat.

'Not for me, boys. I'll let you young ones enjoy yourselves. I'm off to see to the old fellow next door. Nearly ninety he is and I always pop in and get him his supper ready. Make yourselves at home, boys. No nonsense though or I'll be back here, quick as a flash. These walls are thin as paper!'

The woman left. Jim was touched by her generosity in opening her doors to strangers and using up her precious rations to bake for them. He took a mouthful of the tiny slice of ginger sponge cake which Mrs Underwood had proudly told them was made without eggs and sandwiched with something she described as mock cream. He wouldn't be longing for a second helping, but at least it was edible, even though the cream had a weird crunchy texture and the sponge was dense and solid. The other men polished their portions off with gusto and copious quantities of tea were consumed.

Ethel had taken up the offer of a chair and Greg perched on the arm beside her, already deep in conversation. His eyes smarting, Jim got up, intending to stand outside for a while and get some air. He didn't want to wait in the street and risk being seen by his hostess and thought ungrateful, so he went down the narrow hallway to what he supposed must be the kitchen, guessing that it would lead on to a backyard.

He didn't see Joan at first. She was standing looking through the glass panel of the back door, her slender body partly concealed by the blackout curtain that hung over the doorway. She turned round and gave him a sly smile.

'You following me, soldier? After another kiss?'

Jim felt the blood rush to his face. 'Sorry. I didn't know

there was anyone in here. I wanted a bit of air. It's thick with smoke in there.' He jerked his head towards the front of the house.

She turned around to face him, a cigarette in her hand. Putting it to her lips, she inhaled then blew a slow curl of smoke into his face.

Jim tried not to cough, and felt himself blushing again. Joan took hold of his arm. 'You're not afraid of me, are you, Armstrong?'

Her ATS uniform had been replaced by a dress, a floral print, cinched tightly at the waist. Her dark hair was scooped back at one side in a tortoiseshell clip. She held out her cigarette to him. 'Have a puff. It might relax you a bit.'

There was a red circle of lipstick around the end of the cigarette and Jim felt a sudden desire to kiss her. He pushed the thought away. She was another guy's girl. Anyway she wasn't his type. Too forward. Too sure of herself. She made him nervous.

Without waiting for him to accept or refuse the offer of a smoke, she turned away and looked through the glass panel again. It was criss-crossed with tape to stop the glass shattering in a bomb blast. Over her shoulder, Jim could see a gloomy yard, with a brick shed, its door open revealing an outside toilet. A pair of bicycles leaned against one of the walls, which was draped with blackened twine, evidence of an abandoned attempt to grow something there. The paint on the back gate was peeling. It had started to drizzle again.

'You don't have much to say, do you?' Joan said. 'I like that though. Most fellows never shut up. I wouldn't mind if they had something interesting to talk about. I think *you* might have something interesting to say. I get the sense there might be hidden depths to you.'

'This is it. Take it or leave it,' he said, lifting his hands, palms up.

'You propositioning me?' She gave him another sly smile.

'That's not what I meant.'

He swallowed. She was standing so close he could smell her perfume. The urge to take her in his arms and kiss her swept through him but she moved before he could act on the instinct, opening the kitchen door and dropping her cigarette onto the concrete of the yard. She stubbed it out with her shoe then bent down and retrieved the butt which she dropped into an empty flowerpot and closed the door quickly against the rain.

'You and Ethel are good friends then?' he said, nerves still on edge and anxious to steer himself onto safer ground.

'No.'

'But–'

'She's my cousin. We're practically sisters. I live three doors away. We're the same age and grew up together.'

Jim paused. 'You seem different.'

'How so?' Her eyes narrowed.

Jim was nervous again. Talking to Joan was like walking through a minefield. He didn't know where he was safe – everything he said seemed open to interpretation.

'I didn't mean different from Ethel. I meant different from the other night. You talked a lot then. You're much quieter now.'

She frowned. 'I had to talk to fill the silence. I could tell Ethel liked your friend and I wanted to give them a chance to get to know each other. You were hard work and made no effort at all. If you and I had sat there in total silence they'd have felt obliged to talk to us rather than each other. I was doing Ethel a favour.'

She paused, gave her head a little shake, then stepped across the narrow kitchen and took a raincoat down from a peg on the back of the door. 'But there's no need now.'

Before he could reply she had left the room. She hadn't even said goodbye.

~

GRASS WAS ELATED as they walked back to the garrison. Ethel had agreed to meet him in The Stag again. He had not even noticed that Jim had absented himself from the main party, reappearing from the kitchen only when he heard it breaking up. 'I need a favour, Jimbo,' he said.

'Oh no. I'm not having that again. You want me to babysit her cousin. Well, it's not on.'

'Look, it's only until Ethel can tell her mother we're going steady. I need to get to know her mother a bit first. Need her to understand I'm trustworthy and with honourable intentions. Unless she's with Joan, Mrs Underwood won't let her go out in the evening.'

'Can't she find an excuse? Say she's going round to Joan's house and meet you instead? She is an adult, for Pete's sake.'

'Don't be daft, she's not the sort who'd lie to her mother. And anyway they all live in each other's pockets. They're a close family. She'd find out right away.'

'That Joan is more than capable of looking out for herself. She'll find someone else to talk to in the pub while you and Ethel are gazing into each other's eyes. Or she could take herself off to the pictures.'

'Come on, Jim! Please. It's only once. I'll talk to Ethel about telling her mother and then problem solved. But just this once. Do a mate a favour, eh? Joan's a good looking girl and she's clearly fallen for that Armstrong charm.'

Jim reached up and knocked Greg's cap off his head. 'Has she hell!' he said as his friend bent down to retrieve his cap.

'I'm serious. Ethel reckons Joan's got the hots for you, Jimbo.'

'What rot.'

'You can't see it, can you? Half the women in Aldershot are swooning at your feet and you're oblivious. Not still pining over that girl back home?'

'There is no girl back home. Not any more. And you're wrong about Joan. She can't stand me.'

Greg shrugged and slapped an arm over his friend's shoulders. 'I'm not going to argue with you, but please do this for me, pal. Just this once.'

The two men made their way back to the barracks via what they intended to be a quick drink in a pub in the town centre. The room was smoky and crowded and Jim was about to suggest they head back to the base, when Greg proposed a game of darts. Before long they were caught up in the competitive rush, the cheers of the onlookers and the plentiful flow of best bitter. The bell for last orders rang and after downing another quick pint they staggered out of the pub with the rest of the crowd, mostly other Canadians.

After walking a few blocks, the full moon mitigating the worst of the blackout, they heard the sound of breaking glass, followed by raised voices and a commotion. They broke into a run and, rounding the corner, came upon a small group of Canadian soldiers brawling in front of a shop whose display windows were scattered in shards over the pavement and gutter. A middle-aged couple, the owners of the damaged store, a gentlemen's outfitters, stood on the threshold in their dressing gowns, the man waving a stick in the air and shouting curses at the assailants. Jim and Greg exchanged a look before rushing into the fray to try to break up the fight. Greg wrestled one man to the ground, twisting his arms behind his back while Jim pinned another against the wall of a neighbouring shop.

'Come on, guys. Calm down!' Greg's voice was raised.

As one of the brawlers got to his feet, Jim realised it was

Walt. Leaving the man he had restrained, he turned to his brother. 'What the hell do you think you're doing? Fighting in the street? Smashing shop windows? What will the folks say if they find out? That's not how we were brought up to behave. You stupid brainless idiot.'

'Going to tell them, are you? Going to rat on me?'

There was a screech of tyres and an army vehicle pulled up and three soldiers jumped down. One of them was Tip Howardson.

Taking advantage of the commotion, Walt and the other instigators ran off, leaving Jim and Greg standing in the piles of splintered glass outside the shop. Howardson and his companions bundled them into the back of the van, oblivious to the protests of the shopkeeper, who was trying to point out that these men had actually intervened to calm the situation.

Inside the canvas-covered truck, Howardson leered at Jim. 'You're finished, Armstrong. Brawling in the streets, damaging property, disturbing the peace.' He pushed his face close to Jim's and sniffed. 'Drunk and disorderly too. Let's see you wriggle out of this one.'

'But, sir,' said Grass. 'Armstrong and I were trying to break up the fight. We'd only just arrived at the scene when you got there. Didn't you hear what the shop owner said?'

'I saw what my eyes told me, you despicable scum.'

'What are you going to do with us?' Jim's voice was calm but his heart was thumping with adrenaline from the altercation and fear about what lay ahead.

'You'll spend the night in the clink then tomorrow you'll be turned over to the mercy of the local magistrates. And I might add that the people of Aldershot are sick to death of this kind of drunken display. They'll want to make an example of you, and so they should. You've disgraced your country and the regiment.'

Jim looked at Greg and rolled his eyes. There was no point in arguing with the corporal. Better to trust to the British legal system and hope that the truth would out.

∼

AFTER A LONG COLD night in the cells, the two men were brought before the local magistrates the following day. Jim felt ashamed to be standing in the wooden dock of the courtroom, even though he knew he had nothing to be ashamed about.

Tip Howardson, as the arresting officer, was the first to make a statement, telling the bench that he had come upon the fracas while conducting a routine patrol of the city centre in an effort to prevent any disorderly conduct before it arose.

'Your worships, on behalf of the 2nd Canadian army, I'd like to express my regrets at the behaviour of these two men. They have let down the army and their nation, and abused the hospitality of the people of Aldershot. We are fully supportive of anything your worships do to make an example of them. They deserve to feel the full weight of the law.'

The lead magistrate, a man with profuse mutton chop whiskers, waved a dismissive hand at him. 'Thank you. We'll bear that in mind. Is the owner of the vandalised premises here in court?'

The man from the previous night got to his feet.

'You have sustained substantial damage to your establishment I understand?'

'Yes. I heard this morning it'll cost me upwards of six quid to mend the glass in that display window. My missus and I were up all night shifting the stock out of harm's way so no one could pilfer it. Not to mention the loss of trade while the window's boarded up. Those Canadians should be run out of town. They do more damage to this town than Hitler does. They're supposed to be over here to fight the Germans not wage war on us.'

The magistrate waved his hand again and consulted his pocket watch. 'I have received notification from the Canadian military authorities that they will put right any damage that you have incurred. Now I need you to tell us whether the individuals who were responsible for the damage are present here in this court.' He nodded in the direction of the dock.

The shopkeeper looked at Jim and Greg. 'No. I said to that chap over there last night that it weren't them.' He jerked his head in Howardson's direction. 'Told him those two lads were only trying to break the fight up. It were four other fellows who did it. They were all drunk. Came out of the Crown and Anchor and started arguing. Shouting and yelling at each other. They woke up the missus and me and I went downstairs with the poker. They were laying into each other like a pack of hyenas, then as I got to the door, one of them – looked a bit like that fellow over there but shorter.' He pointed at Jim. 'He thumped one of the others so hard he sent him flying into the shop window. Completely shattered it. I'll be picking bits of glass out of my display cabinets for months if you ask me.' He took a handkerchief from his pocket and blew his nose loudly. 'But it weren't either of them. I don't know why he arrested them instead of going after the real culprits.' He pointed a finger in Howardson's direction.

Less than ten minutes later Jim and Greg were told they were free to go.

～

THE AFTERNOON of the day they were due to meet the cousins again, Jim was reading a book in the mess when Walt appeared in front of him. It was the first time he'd been near Jim since the night of the street fight. No apology for causing Jim's wrongful arrest.

Jim lowered his head and focused on the book.

'I've heard from home, Jim.' Walt's eyes were bright and his hand was shaking as he held a letter.

'So?'

'It's from Alice.'

'Can't you see I'm trying to read? Leave me alone.'

'I have to go home, Jim. I have to leave the army.'

Jim shrugged and looked around. 'I'm not standing in your way.'

'How do I get a discharge?'

'You don't. You signed up for the duration. Only way home is in a canvas bag.'

'I can't stay here. Everything's changed. You have to help me. I've spoken to Tip and he says I need to speak to the CO. Will you talk to the CO for me? You're good at explaining things. You always know the right words to say.'

Jim slammed his book shut and got to his feet. 'Get lost, Walt. If you want to make a laughing stock of yourself, go and talk to Captain Bywater. Otherwise, shut up and forget about it. Either way you're going nowhere. They told you that when you joined up.' He started towards the door.

Walt grabbed Jim by the sleeve. 'Wait, Jim, please. It's Alice.'

Jim felt a cold stab of fear in the pit of his stomach. 'What about Alice?'

'She's having a baby.' Walt waved the letter in the air, his voice a mixture of pride and panic. 'I have to get back to the farm.'

'You should have thought about that possibility before

you joined the army,' Jim said, as the blood slowed in his veins.

'Look, I know it's hard for you, but I hope you can find it in you to be happy for us, Jim. Especially now that the baby is on the way. Isn't it time we buried the hatchet? Come on. Please, Jim. Help me. You'll be able to think of something that will convince them to let me go.' Walt's voice was a whine.

Jim shook his head. 'Don't look at me, Walt. You're on your own.' He left the room and went outside to get some air.

Leaning against the wall at the rear of the building, he realised he had been chewing the inside of his cheek and he tasted the metallic sourness of blood. His brother's naivety was infuriating. Everything was simple to Walt. When he wanted something he reached out and took it, regardless of the consequences. Jim thought about Alice being pregnant. Having the child he had dreamed he would have with her one day. And now Walt was rubbing salt into the open wound of his pride.

THE DRINKS that evening in The Stag were a welcome break for Jim after his encounter with his brother. Sitting in the Snug, Jim admitted to himself that Joan made him feel as though he was a bit daft. Slow even. He wasn't used to the company of women apart from Alice and he'd known her for most of his life. Well, he thought he'd known her. He knew now he hadn't.

Joan was completely unlike Alice, apart from being attractive on the eye. Alice had been uncomplicated, easy to be with. Joan unnerved him. Talking to her was like dancing on hot coals. He felt tongue-tied as virtually everything he said seemed ambiguous once it was out of his mouth and it felt as though she were taunting him, teasing him, like a cat with a mouse. He didn't like it. He didn't like her. Didn't like the way she unsettled him. Didn't like the way his eyes kept being drawn to her mouth. Didn't like the way he wanted to kiss her again. She was dangerous and he should keep away.

He tried silence, hoping that, like the first evening, she would fill the void. He tried to remember what she had been talking about then but he was ashamed to admit that he hadn't really listened to her. He'd allowed her to talk and interjected the odd 'yes', 'no', 'interesting' or 'really?'. There'd been a boy at school who nodded and said 'interesting' all the time so that he didn't have to think about what to say next. Jim had noticed that everyone liked the boy because they failed to realise that he had little conversation to offer and they loved the constant affirmation that their own words were interesting. Jim, naturally shy, had tried the tactic himself the first time he went to summer camp and found it guaranteed acceptance by his peers. It hadn't worked with Joan. She had seen through his insincerity, going along with it only for Ethel's sake. Now he had no choice as she was no longer playing the game.

He took a deep breath and decided to ask about her fiancé. That would serve to draw the lines between them, remind her of her own commitment and reinforce to him that she was a No Go area.

'Tell me about your fiancé.'

She shrugged. 'He's in Africa. Fighting in the desert.'

'How long since he went away?'

'Long enough.' She lit a cigarette.

'And have you known him long?'

She exhaled a plume of smoke. 'Long enough. Is this a quiz game? How many questions? And do I get a prize?'

Jim leaned back in his chair, defeated. On the other side of the table, Greg and Ethel were gazing into each other's eyes and he was stroking her hand. They were speaking barely above a whisper, lost in their own little universe. He turned back to see that Joan was watching him.

'You've stopped,' she said.

'Stopped what?'

'The quiz. Did you run out of questions?'

'There was no point. You kept giving me the same answer.'

'Maybe you need to find more interesting questions.'

He felt a rush of annoyance. 'Maybe I need to find someone more interesting to answer them.' As he said the words he wished he'd thought them and not spoken them out loud. But to his surprise Joan laughed.

'Touché.'

He smiled. 'Sorry.' Then added, 'You speak French?'

Joan rolled her eyes. 'No. I like sword fights and swash-buckling. Adventure films are rather my thing.' She held out her arm as though brandishing a sword and said, '*En garde*!' Then, sounding unsure of herself for the first time since he'd met her, she said, 'There's a new Errol Flynn on at the flicks. I don't suppose you'd like to go?'

Before Jim could answer, Ethel overheard and said, 'Did you hear that, Greg? Why don't we all go? We could go tomorrow.'

'I'm in,' said Greg. 'Come on, Sunny Jim. We can't disappoint the ladies.'

And so it was that the following evening the four of them went together to see *The Sea Hawk*. Jim thought the claim "The greatest movie in all history" on the opening titles was likely to be something of an exaggeration. The cinema was crowded and their group of four needed to split up. Greg and Ethel sat together and Jim felt ill at ease as the usherette shone her torch to show him and Joan into a pair of seats towards the back. He remembered the last time he had sat in a picture house. He'd been alone then and he wished he were now. But as in Toronto, Jim soon lost himself in the film, completely absorbed by the action unfolding in front of him. It was only as the final credits rolled that he remembered he had been worried Joan might come on to him in the dark. He was both relieved and slightly disappointed that she hadn't.

'What did you think?' he asked Joan as they came out of the foyer and stepped into the dark street. There was no sign of Greg and Ethel.

'His best yet. The fight to the death with Lord Wolfingham was so well done. No one can do a sword fight like Errol Flynn. But it doesn't feel right to see him kissing anyone other than Olivia de Havilland.'

'I'm no expert. I've only been to the movies a couple of times. The nearest picture house was miles away from us and running a farm there's never enough time.'

'For a moment I thought you meant you were no expert at kissing. I was about to correct you. You made a pretty good stab at it the other night.' She stepped in front of him so that he stumbled against her in the dark of the blackout. Her hands went up to the collar of his uniform and she pulled him towards her. Before he could think about what was happening, he found himself kissing her. Her lips were soft and he could smell the same perfume she had been wearing the previous Sunday even though she was now back in uniform. Jim pressed her up against the glass window in the recessed entry to a drapery store. Her hands were around his neck and his were around her waist. This time it was Jim who pulled back.

'I'm sorry. I shouldn't have done that.'

'Don't apologise. I started it.' She fumbled in her coat pocket and pulled out a packet of cigarettes. 'Want one?'

He declined, but took her matches from her, lit one and cupping his hand around it offered it up to her. She took a long drag on the cigarette. Then, feeling ungallant at ending the kiss she had initiated, Jim turned towards her and held her face in his hands. 'I didn't want to stop then, but I don't go around kissing women who are hooked up with a guy already. Particularly one who's stuck out in the middle of the African desert risking his life for his country.'

She turned her head away from him, drew on the cigarette and then ground it out on the pavement. 'Not supposed to be smoking in the blackout. Apparently the German planes can spot a lit ciggie from a couple of thousand feet.' She started walking, her arm stretched out sideways to feel her way along the line of shops beside them.

Jim followed her, feeling helpless.

AN UNEXPECTED GUEST

EASTBOURNE

*G*wen parked the car and crossed the road to the listening station. She was already nearly forty minutes late after waiting in vain for Irving, the taciturn RAF man, to pick her up. She hated driving in the blackout and tonight had been worse than usual as there was heavy cloud making the moon and stars invisible. She had driven at a snail's pace wondering whether she might have been better off on foot with a torch. Too late now.

The Home Guard who was on sentry duty outside the door to the hut was her old friend from the petrol station. He gave her a cheery grin and asked her what she was doing there tonight.

'Reporting for duty as usual, Mr Jenkins.'

'I think you've got the wrong night, Mrs Collingwood. There's two chaps already here. Aren't you on days this week?'

Gwen groaned. 'No! I'd completely forgotten. Wild goose chase. And it took me forever getting up here in the blackout.'

'Tell you what. I was about to put a brew on for the lads. Why don't you stay and have a cuppa with us?'

Half an hour later, refreshed by a cup of tea, she decided to leave the car and walk home following the road. Tomorrow she could take the shortcut on foot over the Downs for her shift and drive home in daylight.

Walking was not as difficult as driving would have been. And at least it was downhill all the way home. She kept close to the grass verge and used the blackout torch sparingly. At this time of night and up here on the Downs it was unlikely she would encounter a pedestrian. More likely a sheep. After a while her eyes grew accustomed to the darkness and she was able to pick up her pace. It still took her three times as long to get home as it would have done walking in daylight. She wasn't worried about getting caught in an air raid – most of them so far had taken place during daylight hours.

Closing the front door behind her, she was about to call out to Pauline, when she tripped over something on the floor. She checked the blackout was in place before fumbling for the light switch. A navy blue, man's overcoat lay in a heap in the hallway where it had evidently been discarded in a hurry.

Gwen frowned. Is this what went on when she wasn't here? She didn't want to think that of Pauline. Annoyed, she moved towards the open door into the lounge, then shocked, pulled back and leaned against the hall wall.

A man was lying on the sofa, only his legs visible, his top half obscured by Pauline, who was straddling him, her dress yanked up around her waist. On the floor beside them her panties and shoes lay discarded. The man's hands were pressed around the top of her thighs, his fingers under her suspenders.

Gwen leant against the wall, feeling physically sick. Horrible – they were like a pair of animals. Afraid to move and give herself away, she stood there, frozen, listening as the couple became increasingly excited. Why was it that she felt like the guilty party? Why did she feel consumed by shame?

The man spoke, 'Oh yes, yes. Give it to me, baby.' Pauline responded with loud gasping noises that served to increase the intensity of the man's grunts and moans. Gwen was mortified. Then the embarrassment gave way to anger. This was her home and Pauline was using it as if it were a bordello.

For a moment she was tempted to interrupt them. She wanted to throw the man out of her home. She would have liked to throw Pauline out too. But the prospect of confronting them was too embarrassing to contemplate. She crept up the stairs to her bedroom, undressed and slipped into bed. Tomorrow she would tell Pauline she had to leave. It was immoral to be having sexual intercourse with strange men while her children slept downstairs. How dare Pauline take advantage of her absence this way? How long had this kind of thing been going on?

Gwen felt as if her home had been despoiled, corrupted, stained. She had taken Pauline and the children in, encouraging them to feel at home, only to have her hospitality thrown back in her face. It would have been bad enough if the woman were entertaining men in her bedroom, but to be doing it so brazenly in the drawing room was beyond the pale. And yet it seemed out of character and didn't sit with the woman who had spoken of how much she loved and missed her husband. But what did she know anyway? She and Pauline came from different worlds.

Pauline had lacked any restraint. There was a wild abandon in her lovemaking and Gwen couldn't imagine behaving that way, feeling that amount of passion. There was no doubt that Pauline was not only a willing partner but was probably the instigator. Gwen felt herself blushing in the dark. The woman was a tart. No two ways about it. Yet she felt something akin to envy. How would it feel to be like that, so consumed by pleasure, so caught up in it that the rest of the world disappeared? No. It was unconscionable. She closed her eyes and turned on her side and willed herself to go to sleep, but her body was accustomed to being awake after her month-long stint of all-nighters at the listening post. Sleep eluded her. She tried to imagine herself on top of Roger on that sofa, but it was too ridiculous to contemplate. So undignified. So carnal. Horrible.

Maybe it was only possible to be that way with a total stranger? Anonymity cancelling inhibition. But where had Pauline picked the man up? She could hardly have gone to the pub or dancing at the Winter Garden, not with the children asleep in bed. It must have been a prearranged assignation. A man she had met in the street? On a bus? Doing her shopping? Had they agreed in advance to have sex? Or had she invited him to keep her company and listen to music and one thing had led to another? Then Gwen remembered the discarded coat in the hallway. The man, whoever he was, had been so overcome with desire that he hadn't even bothered to hang it up.

Lying there in the dark she wished that Roger was there beside her. She wanted the comfort of his bulk on the other side of the bed, to know that he was there to hold her if she woke from a bad dream. Tears threatened as she realised how much she missed having him around, seeing him reading the paper over breakfast on a Sunday morning, watching him pottering about in the garden, listening as he told her about his day and asked about hers.

Next morning Gwen overslept. When she entered the dining room, to her horror the man from the night before was sitting at the table with Pauline and Sally. He was feeding little Brenda from a spoon, while she perched beside him in her highchair. Gwen froze in the doorway, shocked at the tableau in front of her, anger bubbling up inside like a rumbling volcano. The woman was letting her children meet her lover.

Pauline turned round, saw her and jumped to her feet. 'Mrs C, meet my Brian! He's got twenty-four hours shore leave before he goes off on his next trip. Such a surprise. He turned up on the doorstep last night. Isn't it marvellous?' She stretched a hand out and stroked her husband's hair then planted a kiss on the top of his head.

Gwen was lost for words for a moment, then moved into the room her hand extended to shake Brian Simmonds's. Sally was bouncing up and down on her chair repeating 'Dadda' in an excited voice.

'How was your shift?' asked Pauline.

Gwen leaned against the doorjamb, reluctant to join the happy family reunion at the table. 'My shift changed. I'm on days this week. I had an early night last night.' Hoping that Pauline wouldn't put two and two together and realise that she and Brian had been observed the previous night, she blurted, 'In fact I need to get a move on. I don't want to be late.' Ignoring Pauline's quizzical look, she grabbed her coat from the hall and headed out of the house.

As she hurried up the hill, her embarrassment turned to indignation. Why should she have to pretend in her own home? Skulk up to bed to hide? Why should she have to be exposed to the private intimacies of Pauline Simmonds's marriage? This bloody war had changed everything.

～

GWEN SIPPED her sherry and looked at Daphne. 'What do you mean I'm too straight-laced?'

'Give the poor girl a break. She hadn't seen her husband

for months. She's been through a traumatic bombing. She's lost her home. She's lost her grandfather.'

'That doesn't excuse her for turning my drawing room into a bordello.'

'For heaven's sake, Gwen. It was her husband!'

'You didn't see what they were doing.'

'No, but do tell. I might get some tips.'

'Daphne!'

'Come on, Gwen. Don't be such a prude!'

Gwen took another sip of sherry and felt herself blushing. 'She was on top of him, half naked and riding him like a horse. They were both making a racket. Moaning and groaning and panting. It was all frightfully sordid. They'd obviously jumped on each other the moment he came through the door. He'd left his coat on the hall floor and they were doing it on the sofa, with her underwear all over the carpet. Since he's her husband I can hardly prevent them from being together but they should at least have had the decency to retire to the privacy of her own bedroom.'

Daphne rolled her eyes. 'Doesn't she share a room with her children?'

Gwen leaned back in her chair. 'Yes, she does.' She frowned. 'I am a prude, aren't I?'

'Well… I can't see what the poor kid's done wrong. She's given her husband a warm welcome home and you can't blame her for assuming you'd be out on duty all night.'

Gwen hesitated, swallowed then said, 'But you and Sandy wouldn't behave like that. It was so…undignified. I know Roger and I would never…'

Again the eyebrows arched and Daphne leaned forward and took Gwen's hand. 'I've never told anyone about this but I know I can rely on your discretion and you are a dear friend.'

Gwen waited for the revelation, but Daphne was taking

her time. She got up and went to check that the door was fully closed. 'I don't want my maid to hear.' She winked at Gwen. 'Sandy had an...' Her voice was lowered and her lip movement exaggerated as she mouthed the word. '...affair. He had a mistress.' Ignoring Gwen's gasp she carried on. 'To be honest, Gwen, it was the best tonic to revive our rather moribund marriage. Don't look so shocked.'

Gwen was rooted to the spot, lost for words. Fortunately Daphne wasn't.

'I caught them at it. Not actually having sex but kissing. It was when he was captain of the golf club. She used to go into the club a few times a week to do secretarial work: typing up minutes and match notifications for the notice board, that sort of thing. Tarty little creature. Bottle blonde. Not very bright. Much younger of course. They always are, aren't they?'

'I wouldn't know. I am stunned. I'd never have thought Sandy would do that to you.'

Daphne shrugged. 'Maybe Roger's different. He worships the ground you walk on, of course. But he is exceptional. Most men given half a chance would stray. So it's important not to give them a chance.'

'What did you do?'

'I told her to get her coat and go home and start looking for another job. Then I asked Sandy how long it had been going on and whether it was a full blown affair. He tried to pretend it was a spur of the moment kiss but he's a hopeless liar. I told him that I didn't give a fig about the scandal and I wanted a divorce. The poor wretch was beside himself. Absolutely terrified. The army doesn't look kindly on that sort of thing from their senior officers and he was due for a promotion. And I like to think that it was a moment of madness, a midlife crisis. Men can be such vain creatures. So I made him pay. I got myself a new fur coat out of it and my favourite pearls – you know the three strand ones you always admire? Don't look like that! Sandy had to realise that bad behaviour carries consequences. And anyway he likes buying me things. Why shouldn't I profit? He was after all a very naughty boy!'

'Why are you telling me all this? It's none of my business.'

'I'm telling you because it was a clarion call for me. Our...' –again the words were mouthed rather spoken – '...sex life was a bit stale. Once a fortnight in the missionary position. The usual. You know.'

Gwen was tempted to say no she didn't and once a fortnight sounded quite a lot, but she kept her lip buttoned, fascinated by her friend's confession.

'First of all I exiled him to the guest room. Wouldn't let him near me for a few weeks until he was absolutely abject. Putty in my hands. Then I thought if he wanted an affair he could jolly well have one – as long as it was with me! I decided we could add a little spice to things by going away. We acted as if we weren't married and were having an affair. The classic dirty weekend. I booked us a suite at the Ritz. Nothing but the best, darling. We went at it as though we were newlyweds again. After that we met up regularly in hotel rooms, pretended to be other people. Sometimes he'd pretend to pick me up in the hotel bar. Role play, I suppose you'd call it. And goodness me, my dear, it was like a tonic, a breath of fresh air in a stale marriage. I've learned a few new tricks I can tell you! Trouble with this damn war is we're both too jolly busy to do weekends away any more. I can't wait until it's over!'

'Please don't!' said Gwen, laughing. 'I think you've told me more than I needed to know already.'

'Food for thought, Gwen. Food for thought!'

'Well, even if I wanted to, I can hardly act on your advice. I don't even have a clue where Roger is, much less when or whether I will even see him again.' Her voice made a little choking sound.

Daphne leaned forward and patted her on the knee. 'Don't worry, my dear. I'm sure Roger is more than capable of looking after himself. This war is a bloody pain. Wretched. If I could be in the same room as Hitler I'd poke his damn eyes out with a knitting needle. And that's just for starters.'

As Gwen walked home she thought about what Daphne had told her. She had always assumed her friend had similar views on marriage to her. The last twenty-four hours had proved to be a revelation and she was beginning to realise her own marriage was not as typical as she had believed.

SUNDAY ROAST WITH THE UNDERWOODS

ALDERSHOT

*M*rs Underwood and Ethel had invited Jim, Greg, Mitch, Scotty and Pete to share a Sunday lunch with them to celebrate Jim's birthday. In the weeks since Greg Hooper and Ethel had met, he had not only charmed Ethel but had her mother eating out of his hand.

'I can't promise you a feast, boys. There's nothing much to be had in the way of a good joint. It will have to be mutton but I've saved up some coupons and the butcher owes me a few favours so there'll be plenty for all of us. Ethel and I will do our best to make it a real family occasion for you boys. You must be missing home. Sunday dinner here has to be a bit cosier than eating it in a great big canteen.'

'We can't have you using up your rations on us when we get much more food than you civilians,' said Jim. 'We'll make sure we do our bit, won't we, buddies? You work in the stores, Scotty – any chance of liberating anything tasty?'

'There's a delivery of chocolate bars due this week. I have a funny feeling it will be short one or two boxes. And tinned pears. And I'm pretty sure a bottle or two of spirits will have got broken in transit.'

They all laughed, then Greg leaned forward and said, 'I've never been too keen on mutton and I have an idea how we can lay our hands on some poultry. I think we can rustle up a couple of chickens, Mrs Underwood.' He reached his hand out to hold Ethel's.

Ethel threw him a mock frown. 'I hope you're not going to do anything that will get you into trouble, Greg. I don't want you to miss the meal because you've been locked up!'

Greg winked at her. 'Nothing's going to keep me away from you, doll.'

~

GREG, Jim and Mitch left the camp on bicycles at ten o'clock in the evening, and headed through the dark streets away from the town towards a nearby farm. Their bikes were fitted with blackout lamps but the half-light was barely enough to show where the kerbs were. Fortunately there were no cars or lorries on the roads they cycled along. After a couple of miles, they left the bikes at the side of the road, climbed through a hole in a hedge and scrambled down a slope towards the dark bulk of some farm buildings.

'I spotted this place when we were doing that cross-country run last week. There were hens running around everywhere,' said Grass.

'They're bound to lock them up at night to keep them safe from foxes,' said Mitch. 'We'll never get in.'

'Don't be chicken!'

Jim shushed them and signalled for them to stop. They squatted down beside a pile of logs. 'Aren't the birds going to make a racket if we do manage to break in? And how the hell are we going to carry them away?'

'Thought of that.' Greg waved a pillow case.

'Hey, Grass, put that down. It shows up in the dark.' Mitch was starting to laugh.

'What the hell are we doing here anyway?' Jim was having an attack of conscience. 'It's stealing, whichever way you look at it – and we should have worked out a proper plan.'

'I've got it all worked out.' Greg started to move forward and Jim and Mitch reluctantly went after him.

They were within a few feet of the large shed when Mitch tripped over a metal bucket and sent it clattering across the stone-paved yard. The clanging was amplified by the darkness of the night. Instantly a pair of dogs began barking, so loud that the three men imagined it could be heard back in Aldershot. Without another word, all three turned on their heels and ran, stumbling and tripping back towards the road.

A deep voice boomed, 'Who's there?'

Jim tripped over and rolled on his side against the hedge to ensure the farmer couldn't make out his shape in the darkness. He could hear Greg and Mitch on the other side of the hedge, crawling along the path towards the bicycles. Afraid of being spotted, Jim lay motionless and waited.

A woman's voice came from the doorway of the farm. 'What's going on?'

The farmer called back. 'Can't see a thing. Must have been foxes. Knocked a bucket over and set the bloody dogs off. Go back to bed. I'll check the barn.'

The door closed and Jim crawled along the side of the hedge until he found the gap. He ducked through, cursing as he scratched his cheek on some thorns, and ran along the road to where his bike was lying on the verge. There was no sign of Mitch and Greg. 'Rotten bastards!' he muttered to himself.

The next afternoon Jim was lying on his bunk reading a comic book someone had left in the mess room when Grass burst into the dorm, a huge grin creasing his face. He slung a sack down on the floor. Jim raised his brows then laughed as he saw the scrawny necks of a couple of chickens sticking out of the burlap.

'You crafty bastard! How the hell did you pull that off?'

'Doing it in broad daylight on my own, when the chickens were scratching around in the open. I waited till I heard the old woman call the farmer in for his dinner then I pounced. A quick snip with the wire cutters, hand in, grabbed one, a quick wring of the neck then I grabbed another. They never knew what had hit them. I even took the trouble to join the wire back up. I bet the old fool doesn't notice they're gone for days.'

'I can tell you're no farmer, Grass,' said Jim, shaking his head. 'Every farmer worth his salt knows his stock. Specially with a war on. And you do know it's theft?'

'Not theft. More like fair exchange. I left the old boy a couple of chocolate bars, a tin of peaches and an orange under a bucket. Reckon he got a good deal, eh.'

~

THE UNDERWOODS WERE OVERJOYED when the Canadians arrived with the pair of chickens. Although the birds looked a tad scrawny and undernourished, Mrs Underwood managed to stretch them into a decent meal with the accompaniment of stuffing, a few sausages and plenty of roast potatoes and carrots. The sausages seemed to be made principally of breadcrumbs but they tasted well enough. Ethel had made a trifle with the tinned pears Mitch had provided. The meal was washed down with beer and a tot of brandy to accompany the pudding. While far from feeling replete, the men hadn't enjoyed a meal so much since arriving in England.

Jim was happy not to be spending the day in the camp. But the homely setting made him feel nostalgic for

Ontario. Mrs Underwood reminded him of his mother, who always made a big effort on special occasions such as birthdays and Christmas and spent days baking, stirring and chopping. He looked round the table. Greg and Ethel were side-by-side, opposite him. He couldn't imagine looking at a woman again the way that Hooper was looking at his girl now. Alice had destroyed his ability to trust, killed his capacity to love, stamped on his belief that he would ever have a future like the one he had once hoped for.

'What's up with you, pal? You look miserable as sin. Grass slapped him on the back. 'Come on, my friend. Let's have a smile, eh.'

They cleared the table and carried the dishes back to the kitchen, where Mrs Underwood insisted on being left to herself to wash them up.

'I'm not letting you lot loose on my best wedding china. Not likely. Now get yourselves out of my kitchen. You're making it look untidier than it already is!'

They returned to the small front parlour and as it was starting to get dark, made sure the blackout was in place. Mitch sat down at the piano and they gathered around to sing. Their harmonies were interrupted when they heard the front door open and Joan walked into the room and flung her coat onto the sofa. She had on the floral dress she'd been wearing on the day of the tea party.

'What a racket!' she said. 'I bet they can hear you in Berlin.'

Jim hung back, embarrassed. He should have realised she would be turning up at some point. She and Ethel were as inseparable as Mutt and Jeff.

Joan walked towards the piano and Jim wondered what kind of mood she'd be in today. He moved away from the group and went to sit down on the sofa but Joan stepped in front of him, grabbed him by the lapels pulled him towards her and planted a kiss square on his lips. 'Happy birthday!'

The other men began to wolf-whistle and Jim pulled away, aware that his cheeks were reddening. Joan narrowed her eyes and pushed her lips together. Had he hurt her feelings? But she shouldn't have kissed him like that in front of the others as if she were trying to humiliate him. He looked at his watch and wondered if he could make his excuses and go. He could plead feeling unwell. Too much brandy?

Before he could make a move, Mitch pulled a pack of cards out of his pocket and suggested a game of rummy, which was greeted with enthusiasm by Ethel, and Jim found himself sitting at the table as Greg dealt out the cards.

As they played, he tried to study Joan without her noticing, but every time he glanced at her she lifted her eyes and met his so he looked away. What was it about her that intrigued him so much, scared him so much? It wasn't even as if he was attracted to her. Yes, she was pretty, but not as much as Alice and not as much as Ethel. He didn't know her well enough to be sure if he even liked her. Their conversations had been one-sided in the pub that first time and he hadn't paid much attention to what she was saying. Since then they had been brief and unsatisfactory, merely fragments. He could write what he knew about her on the back of his hand.

He examined his cards. He only needed the ten of hearts. He raised his eyes and then dropped them again when he saw Joan was watching him. Why did he let her get under his skin like that? And he was still puzzled why she was doing this to him when she was engaged to marry another guy. He began to wonder if this fellow existed.

As he was mulling this over, Ethel screamed, 'Rummy!' and slapped her cards onto the table.

Joan got to her feet. 'I'm feeling a bit stuffy. I'm going for a walk.' She pulled her coat on. 'Coming with me, Jim? Make sure I don't get lost in the blackout?'

Mitch made another wolf-whistle. Jim hesitated, then Greg said, 'Go on, Jimbo. The lady needs an escort.'

He followed Joan into the narrow hallway and grabbed his greatcoat from the hook on the wall. When they were out in the street she took his arm. They walked in silence for a few minutes until she said, 'Why don't you like me, Jim?'

He stopped. Her arm slipped from his. 'I don't know what you mean. Of course I don't dislike you. I barely know you.'

She made a snorting sound.

'And it feels all the time as though you're trying to get a rise out of me. Making fun. It makes me nervous around you. That's all,' he said.

He heard her give a half-laugh. 'I make you nervous?' she said. 'You must know it's the other way around.'

'Please, Joan. Stop it. You're doing it again and I don't like it. I'm not in the mood. And I bet that soldier you're engaged to wouldn't like it either. If you were my girl I'd be mad as hell if I caught you flirting with another guy.'

'But I'm not your girl and he's not here, so what harm is there?'

Jim sighed. 'You're acting like a spoilt child, Joan. Stop it for goodness' sake. Let's talk properly for once.'

'All right,' she said. 'What shall we talk about?'

Jim thought for a moment, searching for a safe topic. 'You can tell me about the ATS. Why did you join? What's it like?'

She sighed. 'I joined because I couldn't get into the Wrens. I wanted to do something for the war and my step-father reckons they'll bring in conscription for women before much longer and I thought I might as well get started instead of waiting until I had no choice. And I was working in a shop and hated it. A fish and chip shop. I always stunk of it. But there's nothing much doing in a town that is basically just a garrison. It's the army, shop-work or nothing.'

'How long have you been in?'

'Six months.'

Jim realised her arm was looped through his again. This time he didn't object. 'You like it?'

'Hate it. I nearly left when I started off. All they wanted to do was humiliate us. They bullied us until we were too broken to stand up to them. That's what the army's about – well the British army. I don't know about you Canadians. By the end of the first three weeks I wanted to run away. I hated the uniform. I hated the drills. I hated the blooming awful things they made us do. I had five solid days of cleaning toilets. Men's toilets. Then down on my hands and knees scrubbing floors. The posh girls too. Not that there are that many of them – they all go in the Wrens or the WAAF. Better husband material there, they reckon. And better uniforms. Yes, it's no wonder the squaddies call us scrubbers.' She gave a dry laugh. 'How's that supposed to help us beat Hitler? The only job I'm going to be qualified for when this war's over is as a cleaning lady. Come back, fish 'n' chips – all is forgiven!'

The streets were silent as they walked. It was late – and Sunday. Most people would be tucked away in their homes. They walked past the Ritz cinema. It was dark thanks to the blackout, as were all the pubs they passed.

In a sudden change of subject, Joan said, 'Do you think Greg's in love with my cousin?'

Jim smiled. 'Head over heels. He told me he was going to marry her the first night he met her.' Realising he had given away what Grass had probably intended as a confidence, he added, 'Don't tell Ethel that, please. I shouldn't have said.'

'Don't worry. I think she knows. She feels the same. She wouldn't shut up all the way home that night and she hasn't stopped talking about him since.'

'Do you think they'll get married?'

'If he asks her she'll say yes.'

'But when the war's over he'll be going back to Canada.'

'So? She'll go with him.'

'What about her mother?'

'Aunty Vi won't stand in their way. All she wants is for Ethel to be happy. Who knows? – she may move out there herself one day. There's nothing to keep her here. Except my mum, I suppose. They're close.'

They had reached Manor Park and Jim nodded towards a wooden bench. 'You want to sit down for a bit?'

'Okay.' She sat down, stuffing her hands into her pockets. 'What about you? How do you like the army?'

'It's much the same for us. Bullying, shaming, abuse, insults!' He laughed. 'Actually you get used to all that quickly enough. It's the boredom that gets you. We came over here to fight the war and we're left cooling our heels in Aldershot. I wouldn't mind but every other damn country in the British Empire is getting stuck in. But we're treated like little tin soldiers.'

Joan was silent for a while, then said, 'There was a murder in this park. Over there.' She pointed.

'Really? When?'

'About twenty years ago. A woman working in a bank in the town got engaged to marry a clerk in the same branch. He was a fair bit younger than her. She jilted him and agreed to marry someone else. About a week before the wedding was to take place, the jilted bank clerk followed the couple to the park and shot her in the back of the head. Splattered her brains out. Then he shot himself.'

'What a cheerful story.'

'Hell hath no fury like a bank clerk scorned.'

She lit a cigarette and Jim watched the embers glow

brighter as she drew on it. She cupped her hand over the top to hide the red glow.

'If a fire warden sees you, there'll be a fine to pay,' said Jim and wished at once he hadn't.

'You think I don't know that?'

'Sorry.'

She took a long drag and then ground it out. 'Spoilsport.'

Jim felt her shivering and without thinking put an arm around her shoulders. Joan didn't push him away as he half expected her to do, but rested her head against his shoulder and slipped her hand into the pocket of his greatcoat where he could feel it resting against his thigh. They sat in silence for a few minutes, then Jim bent his head towards her and searched for her lips in the darkness. There was a faint smell of cigarette smoke on her mouth but her lips were soft when his touched them and kissing her felt natural. She returned the kiss. It was gentle, without passion but full of a tenderness that surprised Jim. He allowed himself to luxuriate in it, pushing away the thought that they shouldn't be doing this.

Eventually they broke off and Joan leaned back into the bench. 'This does keep happening, doesn't it?'

'I'm sorry. I didn't mean to.'

'Well, thanks a lot.' Her tone was tetchy.

'I didn't mean it that way.'

'I know exactly what you meant.'

'I meant I wanted to kiss you and I let myself kiss you but I shouldn't. I got carried away.'

'For heaven's sake, Jim. Don't run a post mortem. It was only a blooming kiss. Why do you have to dissect everything?' She got up and turned up the collar of her coat, pushing her hands back into her pockets. 'I want to go home.'

He trudged along beside her. They were walking faster now. Moving with purpose unlike the slow meander of earlier. Jim cursed inwardly at his stupidity. Why did he keep putting his foot in it? But it felt as if she were always wrong-footing him. He told himself he needed to keep away from Joan. The kiss tonight had felt different and he was aware that he was in danger of falling for her. A pointless mission.

When they reached her house she opened the door and wished him a brusque goodnight. The door was already closing as he was saying goodbye.

On the way back to the barracks he tried to examine his feelings. Was it all a reaction to what had happened with Alice? He had been rejected and maybe the flirtation with Joan was a subconscious ploy to prove he was still attractive to women. But what he needed was a girl who was free of complications. A nice unattached girl who would be happy to be taken dancing and to the pictures. The truth was that what he'd like more than anything was to be given orders to do what he came here to do. If only he could be sent overseas. Do his bit for the Empire and probably take a bullet in the process. But as he imagined it he realised he didn't want to die any more.

JITTERBUGGING

EASTBOURNE

*P*auline went twice a week to visit her grandmother in her old folks' home. Usually she took the girls with her, keen to keep the elderly lady connected to the family. She worried that the war with its bombing raids, and the death of Pauline's mother and grandfather had confused and disturbed the old lady. Today she asked Gwen if she would mind taking care of the little girls, as the baby had a cold and she was anxious not to expose the frail old woman to germs.

Gwen was unsure. She had no experience of small children. Nervous that something might go wrong or that the children would cry for their mother, she hesitated, then caught the anxious look on Pauline's face and nodded.

'You're the bee's knees, Mrs C. I don't want to disappoint Granny.' She turned to Sally. 'Now you be good for Mrs Collingwood, Sal. And make sure you help her with Brenda.'

Five minutes later and she was gone. Little Brenda was playing happily in her playpen on the floor of the drawing room, but Sally sat, thumb in mouth, scowling at Gwen from the armchair where she was perched.

'What would you like to do, Sally?'

The child stared back at her, her expression resentful.

'It's raining so you can't go outside. Are there any toys you want to play with?'

Sally continued to suck her thumb, but her lip had begun to tremble.

Panic rose in Gwen. What to do? A large tear trickled down the little girl's cheek and she whispered, 'I want my mummy.'

Gwen looked about her, uncertain what to do. 'Why not play with Brenda?' The three-year-old was sitting in her playpen piling wooden bricks into a precarious tower.'

'She's just a baby.' Then the tears bubbled up and were accompanied by big breathless sobs. Brenda looked at her sister and began crying herself. Gwen cursed under her breath. What was she going to do? Pauline would be gone for at least an hour and a half.

She scooped Brenda out of the playpen and sat her on her knee. 'Shall we have a story, girls? What's your favourite?' She looked at Sally desperately. Sally just stared back at her while the tears coursed down her cheeks.

Gwen knew there were children's books in the girls' bedroom but she didn't want to go downstairs to fetch one. 'How about if I tell you a made-up story?'

Sally looked up. 'What about?'

'About a little girl who lived in a land faraway across the oceans.' Gwen had no idea what the story would be nor if she would be able to retain the child's interest. 'The little girl had a magical power.'

'What was her name?'

'Polly.'

'What was her magical power?'

'She could fly.'

'That's silly. Girls can't fly.'

'Over the seas in India they can. But only if they have a magic carpet. All Polly had to do was sit on the carpet, say Abracadabra, close her eyes and the carpet would rise up into the air and take her where she wanted to go.'

Sally was now watching Gwen intently, so she carried on, weaving a story that involved a snake charmer and a talking tiger cub as well as a cache of buried treasure. As she told the tale, Brenda's head was pressed tightly against her breast and she felt the warmth of the little girl's body against her. After a few minutes, Sally got out of her armchair and came to sit beside her, leaning her head against Gwen's arm, then her small hand reached out and took Gwen's and the three of them sat there, curled together on the sofa as Gwen finished the tale.

So absorbed was she in weaving the story, that she didn't hear Pauline come back into the room and was only aware of her presence when she said the words "The End" and Pauline began to clap. 'I think you've got yourself a job, Mrs C. I've never seen the pair of them listen like that. And certainly not to my stories.'

Pauline reached out and took Brenda in her arms. 'Time for a bath, girls. And I'll tell you how Granny was.' She threw a look of gratitude at Gwen and left the room. A moment later, Sally ran back in and reached up to plant a kiss on Gwen's cheek.

Gwen sat on the couch, touched by the spontaneous show of affection and already missing the warmth of the children's bodies against her. Their simple acceptance and trust in her had moved her. A surge of emotion rose inside her – a mixture of sadness and joy.

∼

PAULINE NEVER TIRED TELLING Gwen about the joys of dancing. 'You'd love it, Mrs C. There's nothing like being carried away by the music. You forget everything else. The war. Everything. You should try it.'

'I used to dance with my husband. Waltzes mostly. I wouldn't like to dance with anyone else.'

'I don't mean that stuff. I mean real dancing. Jitterbugging. It's such good fun. There's nothing like it. So exciting.'

'Jitterbugging?' Gwen's voice was scornful. 'I don't think so. That doesn't sound very dignified.'

'Dignified? Who wants to be dignified? It's all about having fun. Letting your hair down. I tell you it's the best buzz you can possibly have.'

'What is it?'

'It's an American dance. The Canadians do it. My friend Sue got really good when one of them taught her. She goes to the dances at the Winter Garden and sometimes when you're out on the night shifts she comes round here and shows me the moves. Why don't I teach you?'

Gwen jerked her head back. 'Oh, no. Absolutely not. No thank you.'

'Come on. Don't be a spoilsport, Mrs C. No one's going to see you. Give it a try! You don't have to do it in public… not unless you want to.'

Gwen rolled her eyes, then on impulse said, 'Very well. Just a few minutes and I want you to promise that as soon as I want to stop, you won't argue with me.'

'Deal!'

They stood side-by-side as Pauline demonstrated the basic steps, counting aloud as she did it. Gwen followed, catching the rhythm quickly. Once they'd got the basic beat down, they added some twists and turns and joined the individual step sequences up, Pauline taking the part of the man and swinging Gwen around the room. Gwen found herself laughing, then bending over for a few moments when she got a stitch. Before long, the two of them were twirling round the drawing room, the furniture pushed back to the walls and the rug rolled up and one of Pauline's records blaring from the gramophone.

By the time an exhausted Gwen collapsed backwards onto the settee, perspiration dampening her hair, they had spent over an hour perfecting the steps and putting them together in a routine. The dance culminated in a back-to-back manoeuvre that involved Gwen going over Pauline's shoulders in a backward roll.

'You've got that six beat stomp off perfect now, Mrs C – and the back-to-back. I reckon you could burn up the floor of the Winter Garden if you wanted to.'

Gwen wiped the sweat from her brow. She'd never done anything like it before and she was exhilarated. Pauline was an adept teacher and an agile dancer and Gwen hadn't enjoyed herself so much in a long time.

'You've picked it up so quickly. Let's go dancing together! Come on, Mrs C. I can get Mrs Prentice next door to babysit the girls. It'll be a laugh. We could go next weekend.'

Gwen leaned against the cushions of the sofa, catching her breath.

'It was fun, Pauline. But that's enough. My dancing days are over.'

Pauline let out a groan of derision. 'Don't be daft. You're really good at it.'

Gwen got up. 'Thanks. I enjoyed it but I won't be doing it again. And certainly not in the Winter Garden. Now, I must get to bed.'

Later, up in her room, she applied cold cream to her face and acknowledged that she hadn't had so much fun in years.

In fact she couldn't remember when she'd ever let herself get so caught up in the moment. Pauline Simmonds knew how to enjoy herself. But was it right to discard one's dignity like that? And during a war? One thing was clear. Pauline and her daughters were opening up new experiences to her and she felt the better for it.

LONDON TOWN

LONDON

*G*reg waited until the day before their furlough before telling Jim his plans. Slinging an arm round his friend's shoulder he said, 'Boy, do I have a treat in store for us, Jimbo. I've managed to bag us a pair of rail warrants and you and I are going to have us a good time in London Town.'

'For real?' Jim felt excited for the first time in months.

'Little hotel in Bayswater then it's Big Ben, Buckingham Palace and the Tower of London for us. Not forgetting the Beaver Club. And we have some serious drinking to do, my friend.'

Jim grinned. He wasn't so sure about the serious drinking but the prospect of getting out of Aldershot was appealing and he'd wanted to see the sights of London ever since he was a schoolboy, but he'd never expected it to happen.

The other factor heightening the appeal of the trip was that it meant he wouldn't have to risk running into Joan again for a while. Grass had not recently attempted to drag him along on his assignations with Ethel. Jim hadn't told his friend about what had passed between him and Joan but suspected that it had reached Grass via Ethel. He felt relieved at first but found himself thinking about her with a pang of regret. After what had happened with Alice he was in no hurry to go out with anyone seriously – especially not someone in a place he was only passing through and who was already committed to another man. He knew for many of his colleagues such a relationship would be seen as perfect – no strings attached – but Jim didn't want to be with the kind of woman who thought that was all right.

The sun was shining when they left Aldershot. The train was packed. It appeared that most of the regiment had been granted leave and were heading to London. Greg had fixed up a shared room in a little hotel in Bayswater. It was clean enough but spartan – little different from the dormitory at the garrison, apart from the two single beds instead of their bunks and a rug on the linoleum floor between the beds. In the corner was a small table and a wooden chair. A picture of the King and Queen hung over the unlit fireplace.

They dumped their kitbags and went downstairs. Jim headed for the street door, eager to make the most of their brief stay in the capital. Greg hung back, reading the notices pinned to a board at the bottom of the stairs and checking his watch.

'Come on, Grass, we've lots to see. Get a move on.'

'Hold your horses. I'm trying to work out where we are on this map.'

As he spoke there was a sound of clattering shoes on the stairs and Ethel emerged into the hall, Joan a few steps behind her. Ethel was about to hurl herself at Greg but the Canadian moved his head to signal that the old crone who manned the reception desk was watching, so Ethel and Joan walked past the men and out into the street.

Jim grabbed his friend's arm. 'You son of a bitch. You set this up without telling me because you knew I'd never agree.'

Greg jerked his arm free. 'Look, bud, you're here now. Make the most of it.' He started to move towards the door but Jim grabbed him again and held him back.

'I'm not playing ball. Not any more. I'm sick of being your stooge. If you want to see your girl, make your own plans. If Joan has to be part of them that's your problem.' He let go of his friend's arm and went out to the street, breaking into a run as soon as he hit the pavement, leaving the two women staring after him.

Jim spent the day wandering the streets, trailing along the Embankment as the dirty river moved along beside him, watching the pigeons in Trafalgar Square, witnessing wherever he went the damage wrought by the Luftwaffe on the capital city.

Walking alone through the bomb-damaged city, he felt ashamed. Running away like that and leaving Joan and Ethel standing on the pavement. Jim tried to imagine how he might feel were the circumstances reversed. His anger should have been directed at Greg not at the women, and he cringed as he thought how Joan must have felt. After all, she was only helping out her cousin. He remembered how she had chided him over his behaviour in the pub the night they met. Jim felt bad. Very bad.

By chance as he walked away from Trafalgar Square he discovered the famed Beaver Club, the haunt of the Canadian services and, suddenly hungry, went inside. The place was thronged with his countrymen as well as men from the other allied nations and Jim wolfed down a hearty stew before sinking into an armchair and reading the Canadian newspapers with a beer at his side. Maybe the day wasn't turning out so badly after all.

After stopping off in a few pubs on the way, it was late when he reached their shabby hotel and he felt tired but strangely happy. How his life had changed in so little time.

Back on the farm, one day ran into another, marked only by the changing seasons, the rotation of the crops and the birth and death of livestock. The only times he'd ventured beyond the farm had been the odd trip into town or over to Alice's place. He had never expected to see anything of the rest of the world but he had sailed across an ocean, been inside an English family home, learned to fire a Bren gun and scale up a vertical surface on a rope, and now at last he had seen the city that was the still-beating heart of the Empire. He wondered whether Greg was already asleep and what he had done to amuse the women all day. Greg would not have been pleased to have Joan trailing along with them. He doubted Joan would have been too thrilled about it either. He felt a pang of guilt but pushed it away. Joan was a grown-up. She made her own choices and if she wanted to drag along behind her cousin that was up to her.

He opened the door and the dim glow from the nightlight on the landing showed the dark silhouette of Greg in the bed so he didn't switch on the light. It was after midnight and Greg appeared to be fast asleep. Jim yawned, stripped off quickly, tiptoed over the cold lino, feeling his way along the side of his bed as his eyes slowly adjusted to the pitch dark of the blackout, then jumped under the sheets. There was only a thin blanket and an eiderdown that kept sliding off onto the floor. It was going to be hard getting to sleep. He turned over and looked in the direction of the other bed and whispered, 'You awake, Grass?'

'You'll have to go down the landing if you want to find out.' The voice was Joan's.

Jim shot upright. 'What the hell!'

'Come on. What do you expect? Give them a break. They're in love. And don't shoot me. I'm only the messenger. If it were up to me I'd be back home in my own bed. It'd be a bloody sight warmer.'

'It is freezing, isn't it?' His tone softened.

'I've been cold all day.'

'What did you do?'

'I walked. I didn't want to play gooseberry. I had hoped you might have kept me company while they were canoodling with each other. But you couldn't get away fast enough. Thanks a lot. So I went to the pictures. Saw *The Sea Hawk* again.' Her voice softened. 'I didn't enjoy it so much the second time.'

'Why's that? I'd have happily watched it again.'

'That's why.'

'What do you mean?'

'I kept thinking how much nicer it would have been if you'd been there too.'

'Really?'

'Yes.'

Jim didn't know what to say to that. He was uncertain whether to be pleased or annoyed. Was she toying with him again? He was still sitting upright against the pillow and was shivering, so slid down under the covers again.

'Are you as cold as I am?' Her voice disembodied in the dark.

'It's like the Arctic Circle in here.'

'Can I come in with you? To keep warm. Body heat. I won't touch you, I promise.'

'I don't think that's a good idea.'

'Right. We can both freeze to death then. Goodnight.'

He could hear her rolling on her side, turning her back to him. He looked across the pitch black room, his eyes barely making out the shape of her. He was wearing his shorts and a singlet. He didn't have any pyjamas with him. If he worked his way back along the side of the bed he could find the chair where he'd dumped his shirt and put that on to keep the cold at bay.

As he was mulling this over, Joan flung back her bedclothes and said, 'Bugger this! If an air raid doesn't get us the cold will. Budge up, soldier.' Dragging the blanket and eiderdown off her own bed she slipped in beside him and curled her body against his back. 'Goodnight again,' she said.

Jim lay there for a moment, welcoming the warmth from the extra bedding and the heat of Joan's body as it curved into his back. He could feel the softness of her breasts through her nightgown, pressed up against him. The bed was narrow and she moved her arm over his waist to anchor herself against him. Instinctively he placed his hand over hers. Her breath was warm on his neck and the change in her breathing signalled that she was already asleep. Drinking in the faint traces of her familiar perfume, Jim relaxed and fell into a deep and welcome sleep too.

He couldn't say how it started or who had initiated it, but early next morning, in what seemed a seamless transition, they were making love. Her body was entwined with his when he came into consciousness and they began to move together in a silent choreographed ballet. Joan eased herself under him, pulling him on top of her and moving her mouth up to join his in a slow and sensuous kiss.

As he raised himself above her she whispered, 'Have you done this before?'

He shook his head.

She cried out as he entered her, then with a long sigh her arms encircled his back and she held on to him tightly as he moved inside her.

When they were done, they lay wrapped in each other's arms. She touched his face, laying her palm against his cheek and then ran her fingers slowly downwards, to trace the shape of his mouth.

Jim stroked her hair and said, 'Thank you. It was…'

Joan placed her fingers on his lips to stop him speaking.

'I'm glad we did it and I enjoyed it but I don't want to hear one of your post mortems, Jim.'

Jim laughed, then feeling uncertain, frowned. 'What do you mean?'

'That it was nice but it won't happen again.'

Her words pierced him like ice and the room felt cold again. He turned to face her, propped up on his elbows. 'But surely this changes things, doesn't it?'

'Don't be silly, Armstrong.'

She had assumed that brittle tone that made him nervous, unsettled. It was as though there were two different Joans. She was playing games again. The ground was shifting under him and he felt disorientated and confused.

'You've known from the beginning that I'm engaged to someone else. What happened was nice and I don't regret it but it isn't going to happen again. We were thrown together by circumstances and what took place between us was just one of those things.'

'One of those things? I've never made love to a woman before. Not even my fiancée. I don't go jumping into bed with women.'

'You have a fiancée? You kept that quiet, soldier. But that makes things easier. The sin is equal on both sides. We've both cheated on our intendeds. Put it down to the war. People do crazy things in a war. And it was bloody cold. We were practically forced to have sex. I mean, it was natural under the circumstances.'

'Are you so cold-hearted? Are you telling me that it meant absolutely nothing to you? That you didn't feel that it mattered, that it was different?'

She turned towards him and rolled her eyes. 'It was only sex!'

Jim stared at her in horror. Just when he thought he had

unveiled the real Joan she had turned the tables on him again.

'You and I will each go back to our fiancés and forget it ever happened,' she said, swinging her legs out of the bed.

He reached out and took her arm. 'I don't have a fiancée any more. She left me for my brother.' He let his hand drop back onto the bed.

She walked across to the window and opened the blackout curtain to let some daylight into the room, then turned to look at him. For a moment he thought he saw the expression he had seen in her eyes when they were making love. 'I'm sorry to hear that. But it makes no difference. I told you from the start that I'm going to marry Pete.'

'Pete? So he has a name?' Jim hated himself as he heard the sardonic tone of his voice.

'Of course he has a name – but I didn't choose to tell you what it was.'

Jim put his head in his hands. How had it come to this? As he was beginning to get over the loss of Alice, he was getting slapped in the face again. Were all women such treacherous creatures? Or did he pick the wrong ones?

Eventually he raised his head and said, 'I'm sorry I read the situation wrong. I thought you felt something. I certainly feel something for you.' He realised he was using the present tense.

Joan sat down beside him. She took his hand in hers and lifted it up and kissed the inside of his wrist. 'I'm sorry, Jim. I didn't mean to hurt you. I thought you'd be like all the other guys. Kiss 'em and leave 'em. But I meant what I said. We can't let it happen again.'

Her words were like tiny stabs. All the other guys? What was she trying to tell him? Was he one of many?

'I'm going to marry Pete so that's that. I've known him since we were nippers and our families always expected us to marry eventually and I've never been good at letting people down.' She paused then added, 'Except you. I seem to have been spectacularly good at letting you down.' She looked up at him and he thought for a moment she was about to cry.

Jim wrapped her hands in his. 'But do you love him?'

'Yes, I love him.' She sighed then said, 'Just not the way I... I mean it's more of a friendship. I don't feel passion or excitement with him.'

Jim's face was a mask of bewilderment. 'Then don't marry him.'

'Passion fades. It's the other kind of love that lasts. I know that because of my mum and dad. They were madly in love, crazy for each other, but it didn't last. Dad upped sticks and left when I was six. He broke her heart. Killed her spark and her spirit. She married my stepfather when I was eleven. I don't think passion or desire are words that my stepdad would recognise. But he's made Mum happy. He's looked after her. Treats her like a queen. Worships the ground she walks on. Pete is like that with me. I think I'm a better person with him. More restrained. More grown-up. I know he'll be there for me through thick and thin and that matters. No, Jim, I can't let him down. I won't let him down. And I won't break my promise.'

~

JIM TRAVELLED BACK to Aldershot alone. He couldn't face being with what he knew would be a blissful Ethel and Grass, and Joan had already left. He had gone along the corridor to use the bathroom and when he got back to the bedroom there was no sign of her. Rather than risk running into Ethel and Greg at breakfast he had left the hotel and gone to *Maison Lyons* at Marble Arch.

As the train made its short journey back to the military

town, he told himself he'd been played for a fool. Joan had probably planned the whole thing. When they first arrived in Aldershot they'd been told to beware of the loose morals of English women and the dangers of venereal disease. The regimental medical officer had suggested that some women viewed Canadian soldiers like cigarette cards and aimed to collect as many as possible. His stomach lurched and he began to sweat. What if she'd given him an infection? Was he another notch on her bedpost?

He looked out of the steamed-up window as the train flew past rows of suburban houses. It was raining. Why had he thought it a good idea to come to this godforsaken country? He felt his face reddening and his skin prickled as the implications of what had happened dawned on him. He might as well have "sucker" tattooed across his forehead. All he wanted now was for the long-rumoured second front to open and give him a chance to fight the war. Now that the Yanks were in the frame, would Canada be even further down the pecking order?

LOST CHILDREN

EASTBOURNE

*E*ver since the dancing lesson, Pauline had increased her efforts to persuade Gwen to accompany her on a night out to the Winter Garden.

'You're so good at it, Mrs C. The men would all be queuing up for a chance to swing you around.'

'Thank you for the offer, but being swung round a room by strange men is not something I'd relish. Sorry.' She smiled.

Pauline shook her head, her expression wistful. She told Gwen about her friend, Sue, who had met and fallen in love with one of the many Canadian soldiers stationed in the town. Pauline was excited at news of Sue's engagement.

'You mean your friend is actually going to marry this chap?' Gwen was incredulous. 'Someone she met at a dance?'

"Why on earth not?' Pauline was defiant. 'Where did you meet Mr Collingwood then?'

Gwen's felt herself blushing. She pursed her lips. 'At a party at the British Embassy in Berlin.'

'Well what's the difference? Did he ask you to dance?'

Gwen smiled and conceded defeat. 'Yes he did.'

'Pots and kettles, Mrs C.'

'Fair enough, Pauline, but does your friend realise that marrying a Canadian soldier will mean that once the war's over she'll have to go and live in Canada with him?'

'I wouldn't mind that. I'm sure Canada's very nice.'

'It's a long way away. She'll be giving up her friends and family – it takes a week to get there so it's hardly like taking a train to London.'

'Yes but if you love someone.' Pauline looked wistful. 'I'd have gone to Canada to be with my Brian. Yes I'd have missed my family but love's more important.'

Gwen arched her eyebrows and sighed.

'Not convinced, Mrs C?'

'It's just that your friend can't really know this fellow. A few twirls around the Winter Garden is hardly the basis for a lifetime partnership.'

'And a few swirls round the British Embassy is?'

'That's completely different. I had plenty of time to get to know my husband. And we're both British.'

'I don't see any difference. Sue has seen her Stan every day since they met – and not just at the Winter Garden. They go to the flicks and for walks in Gildredge Park. She says he's terribly romantic. Her mum and dad have invited him round for supper loads of times. He's already part of the family.'

'But there's a war on. Everything is different in wartime. We'll all feel different about everything when peace comes.'

'If it comes. Isn't that the point? We could all die tomorrow so we may as well make the most of life now.' Pauline sat down in the chair opposite Gwen's and leaned forward, her elbows on her knees. 'We need to grab what little happiness life sends our way.'

Gwen stared at her. Pauline never ceased to surprise her. But her bubbling optimism was probably unwarranted. 'All very well, Pauline, but war makes people behave differently. Your friend is probably beguiled by a daring young man in uniform. Does she even know what he does in civilian life? The peacetime reality may be much less glamorous.'

Pauline shrugged. 'Who cares?'

Gwen suggested all manner of occupations Sue's Stan could be engaged in, from factory worker to dustman, none of which involved the wearing of a smart uniform and a constant supply of government-issue cigarettes and chocolates.

'I met Stan last week and a very nice chap he is too.' Pauline jerked her chin forward. 'I told Sue she could do a lot worse than hitch her wagon to his train. He's not bad looking, he's the best dancer she's ever partnered, he's kind and generous and he adores her. Maybe he's a bit on the short side – but so's Sue.'

Gwen sniffed. 'Let's hope he's as good a man as you paint him and doesn't have a wife and children back home on the prairies.'

'Do you always have to think the worst of people, Mrs C?' Pauline shook her head and left the room.

Gwen sat alone as the afternoon light faded. A weight of melancholy descended on her shoulders. It had been cruel to crush Pauline's optimism about her friend's future. Why had she done it? Why not play along with her? It would have been no skin off Gwen's nose. Yet she had chosen to dampen the mood. Now Pauline had gone off and things would be tense between them. All for something that didn't even matter to Gwen. Was it just a desire to be right? To know better? Or was she jealous of someone else's happiness?

Later that evening Pauline came to stand beside her on the upper terrace outside the drawing room.

'Penny for them?'

'I was...'

'It's all right. You don't have to tell me. I always get annoyed when someone asks me what I'm thinking. My

Brian did it all the time. But I'd give a boxful of bananas to have him here now asking me.'

'Bananas?' said Gwen. 'I've forgotten what they look like, let alone how they taste.' She paused. 'Pauline, I'm sorry.'

"What for?'

'I was rude about your friend this morning. Cynical. I don't what made me say what I said.'

'Forget it. I already had.'

Gwen smiled. 'Thank you. That's very gracious of you. Are the children asleep?'

'Brenda is. She'll go through till morning. Sally's pretending. I told her I'd take her to the park tomorrow but only if she went straight off to sleep. Knowing her, she'll be awake until I go to bed, talking to her toy rabbit. She's a good girl but I'm afraid the bombing has terrified her. Can't imagine how I'd have felt as a four-year-old if I was blasted out of my own home. And she misses her dad. And her grandpop.'

'I'm sorry.'

'It isn't your fault. You've been our guardian angel.'

They fell into a companionable silence for a few minutes, leaning on the balustrade of the terrace, looking out over the garden towards the sea as the light faded.

Pauline lit a cigarette and inhaled slowly. 'I lost a baby too, you know. My first. I didn't think I'd ever get over it. It used to wriggle about and kick like a donkey but one morning it stopped moving and I knew something was wrong.'

Gwen stood motionless, horrified that Pauline had guessed what had happened to her, but wanting to hear her story.

'The worst part was having to go through labour knowing the baby was dead. Cried for weeks I did. It was a little boy. I wasn't allowed to see him. I had to picture him in my imagination.' Pauline drew deeply on her cigarette. 'Brian was working in the aircraft factory then. He was a fitter. It hit him bad too, but at least he had his job to help take his mind off it. My mum had just died and I'd never been so alone in all my life. There was my granny but she was beginning to go doolally. She didn't understand why I kept bawling. She stroked my hand and I sat and stared at the wallpaper all day. Then I fell pregnant with our Sally. I was scared stiff the same thing was going to happen.' She stared ahead at the horizon.

Gwen didn't know what to say. She was torn between anguish that someone had knowledge of her private pain and relief that at last there was someone who shared it.

Pauline continued to avoid her eyes. 'Me and my big mouth. You don't have to talk about it. I wanted you to know that if you did, I'm someone who'll understand.'

At last Gwen spoke, her voice barely a whisper. 'I miscarried at ten weeks. My husband was away in Switzerland. I didn't tell him. We'd been trying for a baby for so long and I'd never managed to conceive, then when at last I did, I was so excited.' Gwen's eyes filled with tears as she remembered. 'I couldn't wait to tell Roger: I wanted to tell him face-to-face, but he was gone for weeks. I miscarried two weeks before he returned and I couldn't bear to talk to him about it. I kept putting it off. I didn't want him to suffer what I had been suffering. So I decided it was better for him not to know. And then later, I tried to tell him, but I never managed to get it out, so I shut it away.' She took a handkerchief from the pocket of her dress and dried her eyes. 'And please don't tell me that he had a right to know. I couldn't do it.'

'I wasn't going to say that. I feel so sorry for you. Going through that all alone. You poor soul.'

'That baby had been my only chance and I'd lost it. I don't know why I believed that but I was right. I never conceived again. So I made up my mind to put on a brave face and jolly well get on with life.' She took a deep breath, willing herself not to cry again.

Pauline turned sideways, hip against the parapet and looked at Gwen. 'You can't bottle something like that up forever without something giving way. You do know that, don't you?'

Gwen turned to face her. 'I haven't thought about it in years. It was getting those nappies out that reminded me. And you bringing it up of course.' Her voice turned cold and brisk. 'Now I must get on. I have letters to write.'

~

THAT NIGHT IN BED, Gwen reflected on her conversation with Pauline. It was the most intimate she had ever had with anyone. There was something about Pauline that had encouraged her to open up. On the surface the woman was brash, brisk and no nonsense, but there was a sensitivity and warmth in her that Gwen couldn't help responding to. And Pauline's love for her daughters was self-evident. Sally was a boisterous child but respectful and polite and had clearly been well brought up.

She thought about what Pauline had said about not being able to bottle up pain and sorrow for ever. But that wasn't true. Her own mother had proved that. Mary Brook had not shown a trace of emotion after the loss of her son. Gwen hadn't seen her shed a single tear. Her mother had never spoken of Alfie again after that terrible day. She didn't forbid Gwen from mentioning him, but she didn't have to – her own behaviour set the example. Gwen's mother shrouded herself in a terrible silence that refused to acknowledge Alfie's very existence, making it unthinkable for Gwen to do otherwise. It was as if her brother had never been born. Every photograph of him had been removed from the house, every childish drawing, his toys, his clothes, every trace of his all too short life. Gwen had been left utterly alone, a giant gash in her heart where her love for her brother had been. Not only had she lost her twin, her soulmate and best friend, but she had lost both her parents too. Her father had stayed on in India, sending Gwen and her mother back to England and Mary had retired into a world of religious devotion that left no room for her only remaining child. Gwen had grown up with the belief that emotions were a sign of weakness and love and affection only led to pain and loss.

Roger was unaware that his wife had been a twin and lost her brother when they were twelve. So many times Gwen had come close to telling him, but she always held back in the end, fearful that she might place a jinx on Roger, that he too might one day abandon her as Alfie had done. She believed that she carried some kind of curse and didn't want to unleash it upon her husband.

No one told Gwen directly that she was to blame for Alfie dying. They didn't have to. Wasn't it she who had suggested tying a rope from an overhanging branch of the catalpa tree by the stream so they could swing across? If it was such a good idea why hadn't she climbed up there herself and done it, instead of leaving it to Alfie? Why had she stood by and watched as he crawled along the branch on his stomach, the end of the rope tied to his belt, clinging to the thick branch like a caterpillar as he struggled to wrap the rope around it? Couldn't she have tried to persuade him to come down as he stretched his arms around the girth of the branch, trying to pass the end of the rope from one hand to the other? Or climbed after him and anchored his legs as he struggled to reach? But no. She had called him a scaredy-cat when he suggested giving up; she had stood by and watched as he lost his balance, slid sideways around the fat branch and dropped like a stone into the stream below, the rope snaking after him.

At first Gwen thought he was play-acting. She expected him to leap to his feet and make a scary noise at her. Until she saw that his head was resting on a rock and the stream around him was running red with his blood. Still she thought that any moment now he would stagger upright and she would help him make his way back to the bungalow where their ayah would dress his wounds. But Alfie made no sound and the stream flowed red, staining and scarring Gwen's life for ever after.

THE BRAWL

ALDERSHOT

*G*reg burst into the mess room. Jim was playing a
game of snooker with Mitch Johnson.

'I'm getting married, guys! Bought the ring
today and she said yes. Even her mother approves. Whad-
daya say?' He leaned across the table and tapped the black
into the corner pocket with the flat of his palm.

Jim and Mitch groaned in unison. Unperturbed, Greg
pulled himself up onto the edge of the table, his long thin
legs dangling over the edge, touching the floor. 'You'll be my
best man, Jimbo, eh?'

Jim nodded and stretched out a hand to shake his friend's.

'Come on, buddies, show a bit of enthusiasm. It's not
every day a man gets a girl to agree to getting hitched.'

'I'll tell you what, Grass,' said Mitch. 'It's a darned good
excuse for getting hammered tonight. And the drinks are
on you.'

'My pleasure, boys. It's already arranged.'

'When's the wedding?'

'Mrs Underwood wants us to wait till the war's over and
Ethel's brother's back from the navy.' He gave a woeful smile.

'But Ethel's going to work on her. God knows how long it's going to go on for.'

Jim frowned. It felt foolhardy to marry in the middle of a war. 'What if we get sent into action?'

'Fat chance the way things are going,' said Mitch. 'We're here so McKenzie King can save face. He doesn't want bad news back home so we're left to stew in this dump of a town.'

'It may be a dump but it's where I met my girl so it will always be special to me.' Grass pulled a sentimental face, clasping his hands over his chest in a parody of a romantic hero.

'Cut it out, you sentimental bastard, Grass. What we want to know is does she…' and Mitch began to move his hips frantically.

At that moment they realised Tip Howardson had entered the room and was leaning against the wall watching. Jim bent over the table, replaced the black ball and teed up his shot.

'Don't let me stop the conversation, lads,' said the corporal. He turned to Greg. 'I think what Johnson was trying to ask you, Hooper, is does your little tart go at it like the clappers, when you get her in the sack.'

Jim abandoned the shot and leaned against the table, cue in hand, waiting for Greg's response, aware that Howardson was trying to provoke a fight and ready to leap in to defend his friend. But Greg's joy at his engagement made him immune to Howardson's taunting.

'Lay off, Corporal, give a man a break. I've just got engaged to be married. We're having a bit of a party tonight in the main bar at The Stag if you'd care to join us?'

'Not tonight you're not. You're on guard duty for the rest of the week.'

'But it's not my turn, Corporal.' Greg got down from his perch on the edge of the table. 'I've told everyone in the squad I'll stand them a drink and my girl's coming along to meet them. Her mother's baked a cake and I've ordered sand-wiches. It's cost me a fortune.'

'Unless you want to do next week too, you'll shut your mouth and get on with it.'

'I'll do guard for Grass, sir,' said Jim. 'Let him have his celebrations. It's all arranged. He can cover for me the week after.'

'So you're in charge of the rota now are you, Armstrong?'

'No.'

'No, what?'

'No, sir.'

'Well shut your mouth.' He moved towards the door then turned back. 'You'll be missing the party too, Armstrong. The kit room is a bloody disgrace. You're sorting it out tonight and I'll be round to inspect.'

When he was gone, Jim flung the cue on the table. Greg was slumped on the floor against the wall, staring up at the ceiling.

'What was that about?' said Mitch. 'I mean we all know he's a miserable bastard, but that went too far.'

'I'm sorry, pal,' said Jim to Grass.

'Why are you apologising? It's not your fault.'

'He's got it in for me. That's why he's taking it out on Greg.'

'What the hell for?'

Jim shrugged. 'I knew him back home. He was in class with my brother. I don't know why he can't stand me. I guess some people don't a need a reason to hate someone.'

'Chip on the shoulder,' said Mitch, knowingly. 'Thinks the world's against him and can't stand to see others happy. He's a useless piece of shit. A bloody admiral of the Swiss navy.'

'What you going to do about tonight, Grass?' said Jim. 'Can you get a message to Ethel?'

'I'll go and tell her,' said Mitch. 'If it's too late to cancel the party we'll go ahead without you, pal, and drink your health and your girl's. Then I'll make sure the guys club together and throw another bash next week in your honour and you can be there for that.'

~

JIM WAS QUEUING in the canteen when Tip Howardson came up behind him. Jim felt Tip's breath hot behind his ear. The corporal's voice was low so that no one other than Jim could hear what he said.

'I hear Walt has got that little tramp pregnant, eh? More than you ever managed, Armstrong. I bet she fucked both of you, then decided he was better.'

Jim didn't stop to think. The non-stop drip of venom from his corporal had gone on too long and too far. Rage flared inside him and he turned, sending his tray flying and scattering mashed potato and gravy on the floor. He landed a heavy punch on Howardson's chin and rained rapid punches down on the head and shoulders of the corporal as Tip tried to protect himself with his arms. Jim was blind. He felt nothing. A dam had burst, flooding, rushing, sweeping him away. Hurt him. Kill him. Punch after punch. Blindness. Fury. End it. End it.

Grass and Mitch grabbed onto Jim and pinned down his arms as he struggled to break free. Tip's fist rammed into his chest. Winded, Jim slumped forward, Greg and Mitch still holding him. He heard the sound of glass shattering then he heard and saw nothing more.

~

WHEN JIM CAME to it was dark. Immediately he wished he hadn't woken as the pain was like nothing he'd ever experienced before. He tried to focus but the room was blurred as if he were looking through the bottom of a glass. What was he doing here?

A nurse emerged from the gloom to stand beside his bed. 'Woken up at last, soldier?' she said. 'Quite a pasting you took.'

'What happened? I can't remember.'

'You were in a fight. But never mind that now.'

The memory of Tip Howardson and his crude insults about Alice, his taunting about Walt returned. The anger rose in Jim again and he tried to sit up, but was unable to move.

The nurse took his wrist and cocked her head to look at the watch pinned above her breast. 'Better,' she pronounced, letting his arm fall back to the bed. She pushed a thermometer between his lips and then consulted a chart at the bottom of the bed.

Jim tried to speak but the thermometer made his words unclear. The nurse shook her head at him, read his temperature and returned to stand beside him. 'I'm not allowed to talk to you. You're in big trouble.'

Then she was gone, leaving Jim to stare at the shadowy ceiling and grit his teeth against the pain.

WHEN JIM WOKE AGAIN, Mitch Johnson was sitting at the end of his bed, his cap clutched in his hand.

'I can only stay a few minutes, Jim. You're meant to be off limits. But someone has to tell you.'

'Tell me what?' Jim tried to roll over onto his side as a prelude to sitting up but an arrow of sharp pain shot through his chest and he slumped back against the pillow.

'Grass is dead.'

Jim didn't think he had heard properly. 'What?'

'He had a brain haemorrhage.'

'A what?'

'The doc said it was a massive bleeding in his brain.'

Still the words made no sense. How could Grass be dead? He shook his head. 'Stop kidding, Mitch. It's not funny.'

'I wish I was kidding. But it's true. I'm sorry, pal.'

Jim closed his eyes. He would wake up in a moment and everything would be all right. But when he opened them again Mitch was still sitting beside the bed nervously twirling his cap around in his hands.

'He can't be dead. He's getting married.'

Mitch looked away.

'How did it happen?'

'Punched in the head by the corporal. Howardson took a broken bottle to your head and knocked you out and then he started stamping on you, kicking the shit out of you while you were passed out on the ground. A real frenzy. When Grass tried to restrain him he landed a hell of a punch to his head and Grass fell over like a tree. He hit the deck and never got up again.'

Jim tried to picture it but his imagination failed him. How was it possible that the long-legged, gentle giant was dead? Just like that – and because he had tried to come to Jim's defence.

Mitch winced. 'Christ, Armstrong, you look a sight. You're going to be scarred for life I reckon. You should see your ugly face. Your eyes look like a cross between a panda and a frog.' He turned his cap over in his hands and appeared to be absorbed in examining the inside. 'That Howardson is crazy. Never seen anything like it. It was as if he was trying to kill you. What the hell did you do to get him so mad at you?'

Jim looked at him blankly then shook his head.

'There's rumours going round the camp that he's mental.

Had a punch-up over a girl in town a few months ago and managed to keep it hushed up. There's also talk he attacked a woman in the park but she screamed her head off and he got the wind up and ran away. Joe Toupin saw it happen. He was going to report it but Howardson threatened him and he decided it was better to stay out of it. Turns out half the garrison had a reason for being afraid of him. Once the shit hit the fan they all started talking. The bastard was running a little scam with the quartermaster and selling stuff on the black market.'

'What's happened to him?'

'Court-martialled. Dishonourable discharge and sent back to Canada. I think they might court-martial you too. When you're well enough that is. What the hell did you go and punch him for, mate? You knew he was a crazy bastard.'

Jim let out a long sigh and closed his eyes, ignoring the question. 'I can't believe Grass is dead. What are they going to tell his folks? Killed by one of his own?'

'The docs reckon he could have died any time. They did a post mortem and it turns out he had an extremely thin skull. Could have done it banging his head getting out of bed. He was unlucky.'

Jim kept his eyes closed. He could barely see out of them anyway. He wanted Mitch to go away and leave him alone. Sensing he had outstayed his welcome, Johnson got to his feet, slapped a hand on the lump in the bed that was Jim's legs and said goodbye.

Left alone, Jim thought about Grass. Dead without having fired a shot or had sight of the enemy. He had been so full of life. Only the night before the fight happened they had sat in The Stag, moaning to each other about the warmth of the beer and talking about his plans for marrying Ethel. Poor Ethel. Jim felt sick, a heavy weight of guilt pressing down on him. If he'd kept his temper in check

Grass would still be here. How could he expect Ethel to forgive him?

And what of Greg's family? He'd told Jim he had a couple of sisters. Jim tried to remember what else his friend had told him about his life before the war. How was it possible that he had made so little effort to find out more about this man – the only person so far in the army with whom he had much in common?

There was a dull throbbing in his head and a sharp pain in his ribs. Probably broken. It was all his fault. He should have controlled his temper. Reined himself in instead of rising to the bait Tip had dangled in front of him. Tip was a maniac. Had probably always been. A bitter, angry little boy since grade school. The kind who would pinch a kid in a crowd then run away so he couldn't be blamed. The vicious streak that had characterised him as a child had festered and grown in the adult. Jim couldn't comprehend what bitterness could cause a man to be so filled with hate for so little reason.

His thoughts were interrupted by the arrival of a man in a white coat who introduced himself as Medical Officer Allison. After glancing at the charts at the end of the bed, he pulled up a chair.

'Quite a fight you got yourself into, Private Armstrong. Five broken ribs, a deep cut to the face, severe bruising to the thoracic region and four broken fingers. You're lucky your spleen wasn't damaged. How's the pain?'

Jim winced. 'Hurts like hell.'

'Yes, it will do. Your CO said to go easy on the painkillers and make you suffer a bit, but I think now you're conscious we'll show a little mercy, eh, Private?'

Jim nodded, grateful.

'Less pain you're in, the faster the body will heal. Can't think what you did to upset that chap so much. He practically kicked a hole in you. But you'll survive.' The MO took off his spectacles and polished them on the white coat that covered his khaki uniform. 'More than I can say for one of the other fellows. Private Hooper. Sad case. Friend of yours?'

Jim nodded.

'At least he wouldn't have known what hit him. Knocked out cold, poor chap. Just finished writing the report. The CO has written to his family. His war never even got started.' He scribbled something on Jim's chart. 'I'll get the nurse to give you a jab and that should ease the pain for a while. You'll be on your feet in a week or so.' He nodded and turned to leave. He looked back when he got to the doorway and said, 'Try and stay out of trouble in future, Armstrong. We don't like patching people up when their injuries are self-inflicted. There's a war to fight.'

~

IT WAS a week before Jim was fit enough to leave the infirmary and two weeks before being summoned before the court martial, still in severe pain from his broken ribs. The gash on his face was beginning to heal and the stitches had been removed.

Tip Howardson had been stripped of his rank and sent to the Non Effective Transit Depot at nearby Thursley Common to await repatriation to Canada, in disgrace for brawling with junior ranks, black marketeering and failure to set an example. The NETD was the way station for a rag bag of Canada's reprobates – drunks, misfits, crooks and black marketeers. A more serious charge of manslaughter for Howardson's part in the death of Greg Hooper was not submitted, because of the coroner's report – although there were those who believed it was to avoid the case being handled by the British courts which would have had jurisdiction.

In front of the court martial, Jim was unable to deny that he had struck the first blow, but the eyewitnesses testified that he had been provoked by Howardson. While no one had heard what Howardson said in the mess line-up, several had seen him approach Armstrong and whisper in his ear. To his amazement Captain Bywater spoke in his favour and Jim had the impression the CO had been no fan of Howardson. Mitch Johnson spoke on Jim's behalf, citing the example of Howardson's conduct towards both Hooper and Armstrong to indicate that the man had a clear if inexplicable grudge. Jim was confined to barracks for five weeks, a sentence he was only too happy to serve as it meant delaying the inevitable moment when he would have to face Ethel.

One evening he was alone in the mess, when he was visited by Walt. He'd seen nothing of his brother since the street brawl. Walt flung himself into the chair opposite Jim's, legs sprawled out in front of him.

'They turned me down.'

Jim said nothing.

'They don't care that Alice is having a baby. Told me thousands of men are in the same situation.' He thumped the arm of the chair in fury.

Jim looked at him, struggling to believe that his brother had offered no apology for being the cause of his night in jail, no condolences for the death of Grass and hadn't even bothered to visit him in the infirmary.

'Grow up, Walt,' he said at last. 'The world doesn't revolve round you.'

~

WHEN HE WAS ABLE, if unwilling, to leave the sanctuary of the barracks and venture into the town, Jim made his way with a heavy heart to the street where Ethel lived and knocked on the door. It was a Saturday afternoon and hence probable that Ethel or her mother would be at home. He had thought of bringing a bunch of flowers but no one grew flowers for sale any more and it didn't seem right to steal them from a park or garden – and most of those were now given over to growing vegetables. Chocolate bars seemed inappropriate so he settled on a few tins of peaches and corned beef bought from the commissary.

It took a while before the door was answered and Jim's heart skipped a beat when Joan appeared on the threshold.

'I've come to see Ethel. To give her my condolences.'

'You took your time,' she said bluntly. 'Too little too late. Sling your hook, Armstrong. Ethel doesn't want to see you.'

'I couldn't come any sooner. I was in the infirmary and then confined to barracks.'

She crossed her arms and looked at him with something nearing contempt. 'I wish we hadn't met either of you. The word is that you started that fight and Greg got caught in the crossfire. Well, I hope you're happy. It's cost the poor bugger his life and my cousin her future. You Canadians are every bit as bad as most of the people in this town paint you. Brawling at any opportunity. My aunty Vi and Ethel won't be holding open house any more, that's for sure. Now bugger off.' As she turned to go back into the house, she noticed the tins in his hand. 'And take your tinned fruit with you. Ethel won't want it.' The door slammed shut behind her.

Jim turned away and went back to the barracks where he borrowed a motorbike and set off on the ten miles or so to the military cemetery at Brookwood, where Greg was buried, along with other Canadians who had died since arriving in Britain. He was surprised how many graves there were, even though the ground force had seen no action. He wandered past the graves of airmen, his cap held in front of him. There were also army servicemen like Greg who had passed away without seeing a whisker of the enemy. Many were victims of road accidents, often caused in the blackout. What a bloody waste. Why cross the Atlantic only to be run over or ride your motorcycle into a tree? He had nothing to place on the grave. For a moment he wished he'd brought the tins of peaches. Greg would have thought that funny. When he located the grave, which had a temporary marker, he stood with his head bowed and tried to pray, but he wasn't a regular churchgoer and nothing he could think of seemed appropriate. So he spoke to his dead friend.

'It should be me under there, not you, Grass. You should have let that bastard finish me off. Who do you think you are? Bloody Popeye? I'm going to miss you, buddy.'

He would write to Greg's widowed mother and sisters in Saskatchewan and to Ethel as well if Joan was going to stop him seeing her in person. What the hell to say? Nothing he could say could possibly make it any better. Turning from his friend's grave, he made his way past the ranks of dead Canadians from the previous war. So many. Maybe his father had known some of them.

PART III

1942

Men may make mistakes, and learn from their mistakes.
Men may have bad luck, and their luck may change.

Winston Churchill, 2 July 1942

TRANSFER TO EASTBOURNE

'Oh I do like to be beside the seaside, oh I do like to be beside the sea.' Mitch Johnson was singing the old music hall song. One of the local girls had played it on the piano in The Stag the previous night and Mitch had been whistling and singing the tune ever since. Their regiment was about to relocate from Aldershot to the Sussex coast to take on the defence of the coastline. Jim suspected it would be more of the same – far away from the action and he was not enthused by the prospect of babysitting a coastal town. The threat of invasion had faded and it felt as though the powers that be were using the Canadian army in a sham exercise. The sneering commentary that they were a "tin pot army" smarted.

When he heard news of their pending departure from Aldershot, Jim decided to go and say goodbye to Joan. What had passed between them had troubled him since. He wasn't the kind of guy who felt comfortable sleeping with a woman and then never having anything more to do with her. He understood that a romantic relationship would not be going any further, and if he were wholly honest with himself he was more than a little relieved. The last thing he wanted was to marry an English girl. He had no firm plans for after the war – apart from being certain he didn't want to go back to Hollowtree and the farm.

Nerves almost held him back from knocking on Joan's front door. The door opened and a thin woman wearing hair curlers under a headscarf, stockings rolled around her ankles, appeared. There was a resemblance to Joan around the eyes, but the woman looked careworn and prematurely old. Her mouth turned down at the corners.

When she saw Jim standing there she retreated back behind the door, leaving just the side of her head visible. 'Whoever you are, you've caught me on the hop,' she said. 'I was finishing the housework. Wasn't expecting a caller. Thought you were the insurance man.' She waved a small cardboard-covered book at him.

'I came to see Joan.'

The woman opened the door wider and looked him up and down. 'She's not here. You a friend of Pete's?'

'No. I'm a friend of Greg Hooper who was engaged to marry Joan's cousin.'

'Yes. Poor bugger. Ethel was cut up about it. Still is. But what's that got to do with my Joan?'

'We met a few times and became friends.' The words sounded weak and unconvincing as he said them. 'I came to say goodbye as we're leaving town.'

The woman's eyes narrowed and she moved to close the door. 'Joan's never mentioned you. And while you may want to say goodbye to her she can't have wanted to say goodbye to you as she left Aldershot two weeks ago.'

Jim was stunned. 'She's left? Where's she gone?'

'If she'd wanted you to know she'd have told you, wouldn't she? Now I've work to do.' The door closed in front of him.

Jim stood in the street, his cap clutched in his hand, not knowing what to do next. He started to walk away when he saw Ethel Underwood walking towards him.

'I thought it was you, Jim,' she said. 'I had hoped you might have come to see me.' Her expression was wistful and he noticed her eyes were red. 'Can we walk together? I'm on my way into town. It's Mum's birthday next week and I want to try and find her something to wear.'

Jim nodded. 'Didn't Joan tell you? I called round to your house as soon as I got out of the sick bay but she told you didn't want to see me.'

Ethel nodded and sighed. 'She always tries to protect me, does our Joan. But you can't protect someone from their own feelings.' She smiled up at him. 'It's a kind of comfort to see you. Greg loved you like a brother, Jim. I would never turn you away.'

'But...don't you blame me for what happened?'

'It wasn't your fault. They said it could have happened any time. I'm grateful that we had a little bit of time together. It may not have been long but it was long enough to feel truly loved and I hope I had a chance to make him happy for his last days.'

'He was the happiest man in the camp. Did you know he told me that first night in The Stag that he'd met the girl he was going to marry? Love at first sight.'

'Me too.' She smiled and her eyes brimmed with unshed tears.

'What will you do now, Ethel?'

She shook her head. 'I've done with crying. Had to change the pillowcases every night. Couldn't get out of bed. Didn't want to go on. But you know, Jim, you have to get on with life. I tell myself that it's what Greg would have wanted. He said the thing he loved most about me was my smile and I keep telling myself that he's looking down on me from up there and he'll want to see that smile.' She turned to look at him. 'Do you believe in heaven, Jim? Do you think he's up there waiting for me?'

Jim shuffled his cap in his hands. 'I'm not a religious man myself. Church on Christmas. That's about it. But if there is a heaven you can be sure Greg Hooper's in it.'

'I can't believe I only knew him for such a short time. It felt as if I'd known him my whole life. I can't blame the war for taking him. I'm grateful that it brought us together. Does that sound terrible?'

Jim shook his head.

'So many people are losing loved ones every day. I'm not unusual. If they can keep going then so can I. There's a woman down the street has already lost two of her sons. One at Dunkirk and the other shot down over the Channel.'

They walked on in silence for a few minutes. Eventually, Jim said, 'I hear Joan's left town.'

'She told you?' Ethel sounded surprised.

'Her mother told me. But she wouldn't say where she's gone.'

'She's moved to another camp – over on Salisbury Plain. She's going to be working in the NAAFI there. She'll hate that. Serving up food to soldiers – she'll feel like she's back in the chippy.'

'Have you heard from her?'

'I got a letter. Told me she was stuck in the middle of nowhere. But to be honest, Jim, I think she was glad to be transferred.'

Jim nodded. 'Maybe she fancied a change of scenery. She wasn't too happy cleaning the latrines here.'

'I think she wanted to get away from you.'

Jim stopped walking. 'From me?'

'Come on. You know even better than I do. She had a big thing for you.'

The blood rushed to his face and he struggled to find words.

'Joan never talked about it, but I could tell. She knew you weren't interested. Especially when you ran down the street to get away from her in London. That was cruel of you.'

His head dropped and he felt ashamed.

'I wanted to spend the day with her. So did Greg. We both felt bad for her. But she wouldn't hear of it. We set off together to have a cup of tea in Lyon's Corner House and while we were queuing for a table she disappeared. We turned around and she was gone.'

'I'm sorry. I didn't mean to behave that way. I was actually angry with Greg, not her. He hadn't told me you were both coming to London. And it wasn't that I wasn't interested in Joan. It's that I didn't want to get tangled up with someone engaged to another guy.'

'I said the same thing to her. Told her I could tell she was soft on you and that maybe she should break it off with Pete, but she wouldn't have it. Told me she was in love with Pete and had been having a flirt with you to pass the time.'

'I think that's right. She was playing with me.'

'Look, Jim, it's not up to me to interfere but I don't believe that. I know my cousin and even if she did her damnedest to convince me otherwise, I think she had feelings for you.'

Jim didn't know what to say. They walked on in silence, then he said, 'We're leaving town too. Being sent to Sussex. By the sea.' He grinned at her. 'Oops. I wasn't supposed to tell anybody that.'

Ethel nodded. 'I won't breathe a word. But the whole town knows anyway. You'll like it more than Aldershot. It's supposed to be a nice place. I hope I'll see you again one day, Jim. Maybe when this horrible war is over and you get sent home they'll send you back via Aldershot. If so, please come and see me and Mum.'

'Of course I will. If you hear from Joan, tell her...No never mind. Better not to say we met and we talked.'

'I'll say nothing. She'd have a fit if she knew I'd been telling you all this.' They had reached the centre of the town. Ethel pointed towards a store on the other side of the street. 'That's where I'm headed.' She stood on tiptoe and kissed Jim on the cheek. 'Bye bye, Jim. Don't ever forget Greg, will you?' She hurried across the road and disappeared into a drapery store.

~

IT WAS CRAMPED and uncomfortable in the back of the truck but the men's spirits were high. Anywhere but "Aldershit" had been the consensus. The CO told them they would be billeted in houses around the small coastal town of East-bourne and they relished that prospect. The old Victorian dormitories of the Aldershot garrison had been draughty, spartan and overcrowded. The institutional food was barely edible and although they would be eating in a regimental canteen in Eastbourne too, they were convinced that it couldn't be as bad as the mass catering at Aldershot. They drove into the town with the truck stopping at intervals to drop men off at their billets.

The truck climbed up a long road from the centre of the town, through tree-lined roads with big houses. The men couldn't fail but be impressed by the grandeur of some of the residences, several of which had formerly been exclusive private schools, but the majority were substantial, architect-designed family homes. It was a marked contrast to the shabby streets of Aldershot with its lines of brick barracks. The Regimental Sergeant Major had issued them all with detailed guidelines about how they were to conduct themselves in their new accommodation, with particular regard to the preservation of hardwood parquet floors, rationing of bath water and the avoidance of drunken carousing in the streets.

Jim, Mitch and a lad called Gordon were assigned a billet in a house with civilian occupants. They groaned when they heard the news. How much better to have the unfettered run of a house left empty after its occupants had been evacuated, than to be tiptoeing around trying not to upset their hosts.

'There aren't enough empty buildings to house the whole unit so you fellows are going to have to move in with the householders. I know you don't like it, but rest assured the home owners like it even less,' said the RSM. 'Imagine how your wives or mothers would feel about horrible people like you invading their homes. I expect you to behave the way you'd want British soldiers to behave if they were staying in your place back home. Clear?'

'Yes, sir.' They spoke as one.

LODGERS

EASTBOURNE

The news of a new inflow of Canadian soldiers into the town news had reached Gwen a day before they arrived. There was a knock on the door. It was Daphne.

'Now don't say I didn't warn you, old girl, but it's finally happened.'

'What's happened?' Gwen frowned. She hated it when Daphne tried to be enigmatic.

'The Canadians.'

'What about them?'

'Some of them are being billeted up here in Meads. Handier for the Downs which they are apparently intent on totally destroying with their guns and tanks.' She consulted the clipboard in her hand. 'You're getting three of them. They're not officers, I'm afraid.' She rolled her eyes at Gwen. 'Rank and file. I tried. Sorry!'

'I don't care what rank they are. But why do I have to take them?'

'Desperate times. Desperate measures. We all have to do our bit. Most of them are crammed in together in empty houses but there's only so many available and we need to get people like you to take the last few in.'

'And how many are *you* taking in?'

Daphne tilted her head on one side. 'Come on, Gwen, you know that wouldn't do at all. Not with Sandy being in charge of all the home forces for the area. Apart from his position as Group Commander there's also the security implications.'

'But I've already taken in Mrs Simmonds and her children. I'm already doing my bit.'

'I thought Mrs Simmonds had taken on the job of Mrs Woods. That's hardly taking her in without strings.'

'But the baby crying at night will disturb the soldiers. And if the men roll in late at night they will wake the children.'

'You'll have to find a way round it. They only need one bedroom and the use of a bathroom. You don't even need to provide furniture or bedding – they'll have camp beds. It won't be for long and they'll get all their meals in their canteen.' She tapped her pencil against the clipboard. 'Would you like to know their names?'

'No, thank you. I'll save that pleasure until they arrive and can introduce themselves,' Gwen said, her voice full of sarcasm. She was beginning to find Daphne's smugness unbearable.

'Righty-ho. They'll be here later this afternoon.' Daphne was already moving down the drive.

'But I have to clear a room out–'

'Don't worry. The boys can move the stuff out themselves. All you have to do is tell them where to put it.'

Gwen had a good idea of where she would like to tell them – or better still Daphne – to put it. She closed the door.

'Three soldiers? That will be interesting.' Pauline was standing at the top of the stairs that led down to the lower ground floor, where she and the children had their room. 'I hope they're good looking!' She did a little wiggling movement with her upper body.

'Don't be vulgar,' said Gwen, trying to suppress her amusement.

Pauline grinned. 'Come on, Mrs C. I'm only having a bit of fun. I wouldn't look at another man. I'm happy with my Brian.'

Gwen suddenly felt tired. 'I know that, Pauline. I'm sorry. It's just that I don't want three strange men tramping through the house.'

'I'm sure they won't be doing that. They'll be up on the Downs firing those big guns all day. Then I expect they'll be painting the town red of an evening.' She sighed, then smiled. 'If you stick them up on the top floor they'll be out of your way. Since there's another bathroom on that floor you won't have the risk of them busting in on you when you're taking a bath!' She started to laugh. 'Mind you, I wouldn't like to imagine what would happen to any bloke that tried that on with you!'

Gwen decided to ignore the comment. 'But the children?'

'They won't care,' said Pauline. 'I doubt they'll see much of them. Sal should be in bed by the time they get in and the baby's too small to notice. Now, you do need to lay down some rules. No more than one bath a week and no more than five inches of water.'

Gwen frowned. She felt like a seaside landlady. Oh God, she'd become a seaside landlady.

'What about meals?' asked Pauline.

'They'll go to their canteen for all their meals.'

'But not breakfast? I could sort that for them.'

'We can't feed them. We don't have the rations for three adult men.'

Pauline sighed. 'Hmm, I can at least make them a nice cup

of tea before they head off in the morning. Do you think they drink tea?'

'Of course they drink tea.'

'I meant them being Canadians. You never know, do you? They may have different ways over there. Do you think they're going to be the French ones or our ones?'

'What are you talking about, Pauline?' Gwen sighed. 'I doubt they're French-speaking. The French Canadians are over at Pevensey Bay apparently. But I don't think they'll want to be described as being "ours".'

'I'd better break the news to Sal. I don't want her getting excited and thinking her dad's back when she hears men's voices.' She hurried down the stairs.

Gwen wandered into the drawing room and stood looking out of the window. The sea was a light blue, cloudy with chalk, flat and darkening towards the fuzzy line where it met the sky. The Downs, the houses and the school playing fields were washed in soft sunlight.

Why had she been so snappy? Pauline had clearly thought she was being critical. It had taken Gwen a while to get used to Pauline's flippancy but she knew now it was her way of coping. And why should she resent taking in soldiers? She silently castigated herself for being ungrateful. These poor fellows were probably as thrilled at the prospect of staying here as she was at hosting them. The Canadians were all volunteers and had signed up at risk of their lives to help Britain in a war they didn't actually need to get involved with. She bit her lip and told herself to be more welcoming. And she needed to be kinder with Pauline.

There was a loud knock at the front door.

'I'll let them in,' said Gwen, as she met Pauline in the hall.

There were three of them, all looking exceedingly young. They stood in a line across the pathway. It was bitterly cold and the men hopped around trying to get warm. They filed into the house in silence behind Gwen and followed her into the drawing room where she introduced them to Pauline, explaining that Pauline did the cooking and helped out around the house but stressing she was not a servant. She didn't want these lads getting ideas and presuming on Pauline's good nature. They were to take their meals in the canteen which had been set up in a nearby school hall so Gwen hoped to see as little as possible of them. They would be out on exercises all day and no doubt would be haunting the bars of The Ship or The Pilot by night.

It was only four o'clock and she usually didn't light a fire in the drawing room until after supper, to save on the coal rations. But it was their first night and they were obviously in need of warming up. Pauline knelt down and lit the kindling in the grate she had laid that morning. The fire sprang into life and Gwen urged the men to sit close to the hearth while she went to make the tea. She brushed aside Pauline's offer to make it, eager to escape from the need to make polite conversation.

When she returned with the tray, one of the soldiers was showing Sally how to play jacks while Pauline was perched on the arm of the sofa next to the other two, regaling them with the story of the destruction of her home.

'You've had a lot of bombing here?' The man speaking had a shock of red hair.

'We've had a right old clobbering. Through the second half of '40 it was bomb after ruddy bomb.' Pauline was enjoying having a captive audience.

'We had no idea you'd had so many raids here. It wasn't that bad in Aldershot, was it, guys?'

'Four civilians killed in 1940. None since.'

'We've had loads more than that killed, haven't we, Mrs C?'

Gwen passed out the cups of tea and said, 'Thirty-five dead.'

The men all whistled.

'But it's not a competition.' Gwen glanced at Pauline.

'One of them was my grandfather,' said Pauline, suddenly serious.

'Sorry to hear that, Pauline,' said the redhead.

Pauline blushed and looked away, her smile fading. Her cheerful facade masked a lot of pain. Gwen marvelled that she had only been out of the room a few minutes and the guests were all on first name terms with Pauline.

Pauline moved to stand against the door, eyeing the men up and down in frank appraisal. She had a developed a habit, whenever there were men in the vicinity, of tossing her hair and pouting her lips, like a Hollywood star. Although amused, Gwen thought it made her look faintly ridiculous but would not have dreamed of passing comment.

'Tea for everyone? I'm afraid we have no coffee,' said Gwen.

One of the Canadians, a tall man with a shock of blonde hair gave her a broad smile. 'Tea's great. But I think we can probably remedy the coffee situation, Ma'am. We'll bring you a couple of tins tomorrow.'

'I'm sorry; I wasn't hinting. You don't need to bring us anything.'

'Our pleasure, Ma'am. And do let us know if there's anything else you need and we can try and get hold of it for you. We know you folks have to manage on slim rations.'

Gwen gave him a weak smile and they lapsed into silence again, which was accentuated by the clock ticking on the mantelpiece. As the men were drinking their tea, the baby started crying downstairs and Pauline excused herself, taking Sally with her and leaving Gwen to face her guests alone.

She took a deep breath and forced a smile to her lips. 'You haven't told me your names.'

They each intoned their first names – Gordon, Mitch and Jim. Gordon was the lad with the red hair, Mitch had a crewcut and a heavy lantern jaw like a cartoon thug. Jim was the tall blond one who had offered the coffee. Gwen hoped she was going to remember them.

The tea was scalding hot, so there was no hope of swigging it down and excusing herself. Why did she find it so hard to make conversation? Perhaps it was the evident solidarity of the men, sitting side by side in a human wall on the sofa? Or their accents? Or the incongruity of three young soldiers sitting here in her drawing room. Suddenly she wanted to laugh and had to suppress a giggle.

'What part of Canada do you come from?'

They all started to answer at once, then stopped to give way to each other, then started again simultaneously, stopping as quickly with awkward grins.

Gwen smiled and said, 'Why don't we start with you, Gordon?'

When they had each told her the names of their home towns and established that no, Gwen had never heard of them, she asked them what they had done before the war. Gordon told her he was an apprentice in an engineering works. Mitch looked embarrassed and said he'd been out of work for a time and that was why he'd joined the army. 'It's terribly hard, Ma'am. Work's thin on the ground, you know.' Finally Jim spoke, telling her he had been a farmer in Ontario.

'Isn't farming a protected occupation?' she asked. 'I thought it would exempt you from military service.'

'We're all exempt, Ma'am. There's no conscription in Canada. We're all volunteers.'

Gwen blushed at her mistake. 'I'm sorry. Of course. I

should have known. And we are all extremely grateful here in Britain that you have come to our aid.'

Gordon and Mitch sniggered and exchanged glances. Gwen blushed again, self-conscious and wondering whether she had committed another faux pas.

Jim elbowed Mitch in the ribs and muttered something to him, then said, 'I'm sorry, Ma'am, but we're all getting twitchy. Some of the boys have been over here in England since the end of '39 and we've not seen any action. We're going stir crazy. Can't wait for a chance to come to Britain's aid as you put it, but mostly we've been sitting around in barrack rooms and crawling through mud on our stomachs in exercises. All we want is to take a crack at the enemy.'

His voice was melodic, softer than the American accent she knew from the cinema. He was a good-looking man. She noticed his eyes were blue and there was a sadness in them. In fact as she looked at his face she thought there was something melancholic about him generally. He had a scar running from his hairline to the corner of his eye. Rather than detracting from his appearance it seemed to highlight the handsomeness of his face. His features were strong with a long straight aquiline nose and he reminded her of the Greek statues in The Victoria and Albert Museum. There was an openness about him and, despite the sad eyes, he gave off a warmth that made her feel drawn to him. The other two men clearly looked up to him. He exuded a quiet authority.

'And you, Ma'am? How has the war been for you so far?'

Gwen smoothed out her skirt and lowered her eyes. 'I've got off lightly. Poor Mrs Simmonds lost her home to the first bombing of the town. Her grandfather was killed in his bed, poor soul. She and her children were lucky to escape. Their house was flattened. They were supposed to be evacuated but she was determined to stay in Eastbourne so I invited her to stay with me. Her husband is serving in the navy.'

'You're good friends then?'

'I only met her after she was bombed out. I work for the Women's Voluntary Service. I was helping in the clear up. She lived at the other end of town.' As she said the words "other end of town" she wondered if she sounded snobby. Then in a flash of self-knowledge she acknowledged that she was indeed a snob. She would never have so much as exchanged the time of day with a woman like Pauline Simmonds before the war – unless Pauline had been serving her in a shop or a restaurant. But she had been much the poorer for that.

'That was kind of you. To take her in I mean.'

'Not at all.' She looked up at him and felt obliged to be straight. She shot him a smile. 'Entirely self-interest. My cook had left and I haven't a clue in the kitchen.' She hesitated then added, 'But we have now become friends. Pauline has been a tremendous help to me and I enjoy her company. She makes me laugh. Cheers me up.'

'Anyone who can make a person laugh has to be good to have around. And her children?'

Gwen nodded. 'The baby is very quiet if that's what you're worried about. Sally is a character but she's a good girl. They shouldn't disturb you boys too much. They are delightful children and a credit to their mother.'

'I don't doubt it, Ma'am. And I'm not worried at all. We've been shut away with other fellas for so long it will be nice to hear children's voices again.'

'Do you have a family yourself, Private Armstrong?'

'I'm not married, Ma'am.' He smiled and added, 'But I have a dog. He's called Swee'Pea. After Popeye's baby. You know – in the comic books.'

'He must miss you.'

Jim shook his head, his eyes sorrowful. 'I doubt he'll be there when I get back to the farm. He's old. Ma said she feared he wouldn't last the winter. Miracle he's gone this far.' He rotated his cap in his hands and looked down at the floor.

Gwen felt a rush of sympathy for him. 'I had a dog once. When I returned from living in India. After my…' Her voice dried up. 'A long time ago. She died while I was away at boarding school so I know how you feel.'

Gordon and Mitch were now engaged in a side conversation. Jim got up from the sofa and took up a seat in the chair next to Gwen's, turning his body to face her.

'What was your dog called?' he said, leaning in towards her.

She could see the outline of his legs straining at the fabric of his uniform. They were long but muscular, and reminded her of Roger's. That was Roger's chair he was sitting in too.

'I don't remember,' she said, trying to mask her sudden irritation. 'It was so long ago and I was a child.'

They lapsed into silence and Gwen wished he hadn't come to sit next to her, forcing her to sustain a conversation. She struggled to think what to say next but then he spoke. 'Before Mrs Simmonds moved in did you live here alone apart from the cook?' he asked.

Gwen bristled. She hated discussing her personal affairs with strangers. And she didn't like the way he had created this side conversation. She wanted to keep him grouped with the other two – three anonymous soldiers billeted here. Injecting some frost into her tone, she said, 'No. My husband is in the army.'

Jim nodded. 'Overseas?'

'I haven't the faintest idea.' She paused. 'I mean yes, I think so, but I'm not allowed to know where.'

Feeling uncomfortable, she got up before he had a chance to reply. 'Now I need to get on. Please feel free to come and go as you wish. The front door is never locked. I'd appreciate it if you were as quiet as possible when you come in at night as there are two small children sleeping. I don't want any drunken carousing in the small hours. Follow me and I'll show you where you will be sleeping.' Without giving the men a further glance she moved to the door and out of the room, leaving them to follow.

OUT OF A JOB

EASTBOURNE

Over the coming weeks, Gwen saw little of her Canadian house guests. Her shifts at the signal listening post were often overnight and on any free days she was occupied with WVS duties, including ambulance driving and as a back-up fire warden. The Canadians took their meals in their mess a few roads away and it was not hard for Gwen to imagine that they were not actually staying in her house at all. The men shared a bedroom and bathroom out of the way on the top floor of the house and were quiet in their comings and goings.

Sometimes Gwen felt bad for the young men, being so far from home, in unfamiliar surroundings and waiting on a possible call to a more active role in the war with its attendant risks. But mostly it was not difficult for her to think of the soldiers as a collective entity, thus avoiding the need for her to distinguish one from the other and get to know them as individuals. After all, it wasn't her job. She'd allowed these strangers into her home. That was enough. No one said she had to treat them as part of her family. Pauline and the girls were one thing, a bunch of soldiers passing through another.

So she referred to her lodgers collectively as The Canadians and didn't bother to differentiate between them as individuals after that first day.

~

ONE MORNING IN MAY, a couple of months after the Canadians had arrived, Gwen had been working a night shift at the listening station and on returning home at around six in the morning, tumbled gratefully into bed and into a deep undisturbed sleep. It was lunchtime before she woke but she wasn't hungry. When she went to make herself a cup of tea, the sun was streaming through the kitchen windows. Swallowing the tea quickly, she dressed and on impulse went out for a walk. The heavy sleep had left her feeling groggy and a good tramp over the Downs might clear her head. She climbed up the hill, the soft turf bouncy under her feet. These days she needed to skirt around the slope making a longer, less direct ascent, as the main footpaths were in an area that was marked out of bounds. In the distance, she could see a group of Canadian soldiers crawling up the hill on their stomachs, heavy packs on their backs and rifles tightly gripped. They looked like giant spiders working their way up the steep slope. They must be weary of these endless exercises. She tried to make out whether any of the men staying with her were among them.

The previous week she had been having a cup of tea with Daphne in the Oak Room and they had overheard some Canadian boys – for they were mere boys – moaning about the way they were cooped up in this little town and given no chance to see action. Their wives and mothers back in Canada were doubtless grateful that the only sight of the enemy they'd had was when they looked up at the sky.

Gwen thought of Roger, bit her lip and tasted blood. A

wave of emotion swept through her and she sank to her knees on the thin springy turf. Why hadn't he explained fully what he was about to face? And why had she given him such a cold send-off? It had been so selfish. All she had thought of was protecting herself, reining back what she really thought, putting on a brave face. So she had sent him away to what may well prove to be his death without a word of love, a sign of affection, a touch to remember when he was alone and afraid. And he would surely be afraid. How could he not be? It was now almost two years since they'd parted at the railway station.

She stumbled up the hill and sat down at the top of the slope. The grass was slightly damp but the need for a rest was greater than the need for a dry bottom. It was so peaceful up here, yet the signs of war were inescapable. Barbed wire curled along the top of the cliffs, tanks had churned up the turf in places and below her in Whitbread Hollow was a Canadian firing range, silent at the moment. She could see the anti-aircraft gun emplacement on the footpath at the end of the seafront below Beachy Head. The cries of seagulls and jackdaws broke the silence as they flew over the Downs, swooping back down towards the town. Gwen picked a buttercup.

She had walked here with Roger when they first came to Eastbourne – he had bent down as they were strolling on the downs, plucked a buttercup and held it under her chin. She had pushed him away. Told him not to be silly. It was a child's game. But he had refused to let go and had gathered her into him, bent his head and kissed her. She had given in to the kiss, enjoyed it, returned it. A rare moment in their marriage when she had allowed herself to be carried away. Stop it, Gwen. Stop remembering. Stop tormenting yourself. Live in the present. That's all you have.

It was just before two. She had promised to look after the

girls that afternoon while Pauline went into town. One of the greengrocers had some oranges coming in and he'd said he would save two for the children. Gwen scrambled to her feet. At full height now she was able to see the sea and her heart almost stopped beating. Coming in low, barely skimming the tops of the waves, was a group of enemy aeroplanes. She counted them. Nine. All Messerschmitts. If she remembered her training correctly they were 109s. They swooped in low over the town and Gwen could hear the distant sound of machine gun and cannon fire. The planes, in perfect formation, roared upwards, flying towards where she was standing on top of Beachy Head. Instinctively she flung herself to the ground. Was this how she would die? Strafed by enemy aircraft on top of a cliff in the English countryside?

But the planes had more pressing and important targets than a lone woman lying on her belly in the grass, for they screamed into a steep-banked turn and headed back over the town. In shock, Gwen heard the explosions. Close below her in Meads she could see flames rising and then further across the town towards the flat meadowlands of the Willingdon Levels, a huge explosion lit up the afternoon sky. The gasworks? The thud of munitions filled the air. In seconds, the town was hidden in a pall of smoke and Gwen heard the whine of the retreating planes as they turned back towards the Channel.

For several minutes she was rooted to the spot. How many times had she stood here before, looking down at the town spread out before her? It had always been a beautiful sight, the sea peppermint green under a blue sky, the pier stretching out into the water like a slender finger, the elegant Edwardian hotels lined up along the front, the town houses in their neatly regimented boulevard-like roads and the flat stretch of grassy fields dotted with cows and sheep stretching out to meet the marshes around Pevensey. Today she looked out over an unfamiliar, dystopian world. Meads, the area where she lived, was on fire. The spire of St John's church, a familiar landmark, was a flaming beacon, the roof below it already collapsed. Through the thick cloud of smoke over the town, fires blazed everywhere. In a matter of moments her peaceful seaside home had been transformed into a battleground.

The fear she'd felt was replaced by anger. Fury that Hitler could turn his Luftwaffe on a small coastal town. The attack on Whitley Road, and the almost daily bomb raids that had followed it, was nearly two years ago and the townspeople had begun to think they could relax again. Several evacuees had returned to Eastbourne, believing it safe. The Messerschmitts that had attacked today were smaller faster planes than the Dorniers that had been the main aggressors in 1940. They were more frightening – the big bombers flew over, dropped their load and went home again, but these little single-pilot fighter planes somehow made it more personal – especially when they opened their machine guns and fired on civilians in the streets.

Gwen began to run down the grassy slope, tripping and stumbling over the tussocks of grass and the ridged ground that had been churned up by tanks on practice manoeuvres. Her heart was thumping but it wasn't fear now. It was rage. Twenty minutes later, when she reached the house, mercifully undamaged, Pauline was waiting for her.

'Dear God, Mrs Collingwood, don't tell me it's starting again.'

'I watched it happen,' said Gwen. 'They targeted us deliberately. They weren't going or coming from somewhere else. They intended to hit Eastbourne.'

Pauline reached into the pocket of her apron, brought out a packet of cigarettes. Gwen noticed the usually calm Pauline's hands were shaking.

'Hells bells, Mrs C, the Jerries can nip across the Channel and here we are like sitting ducks.' She shook her head and exhaled a plume of smoke.

Gwen stretched out a hand and laid it on her arm and gave it a squeeze. Then in an unplanned gesture she flung her arms around Pauline and hugged her. Afterwards she was as surprised as Pauline was.

That day was the first of what were to be regular "tip and run" raids on the town. The raid had lasted less than four minutes. As well as St John's church, the gasworks, railway sheds, a brewery and a lot of houses, a large chunk was blown off the end of the Cavendish Hotel on the promenade. The death toll included two Canadian soldiers, two RAF airmen, five civilians and thirty-six injured. The airmen had died in the Cavendish Hotel where hundreds of RAF crew were stationed. Their colleagues had a lucky escape as they were out of the town participating in a sports day.

As the planes had turned back over the sea to head home, they spotted a fishing boat at Langney Point to the east of the town, and attacked it, badly injuring the two fishermen on board. That night Lord Haw-Haw described the little fishing boat as a heavily-armed trawler. If the radio propagandist hoped to demoralise the townspeople, the attack and his words had the opposite effect. Eastbourne was angry.

∾

A FEW DAYS after the tip and run attack, Gwen was lying on her bed, notebook and pencil in hand, sleep eluding her. Instead she was drawing up a list. All her life she had resorted to lists as a way to fortify herself with order, not always successfully. Now with the inescapable impact of the war, the long absence of her husband and the presence in her home and her life of Pauline and her daughters and the

Canadian soldiers, the act of compiling and curating her daily to-do lists was a means of anchoring herself. She was exerting a small but significant control over the circumstances that, since war had begun in earnest, had thrown her world into chaos and torn control away from her.

Writing the list was also a distraction. There was the usual anxiety about Roger – always there in the background and often moving centre stage, prompted by bad news on the radio, a familiar song that reminded her of him, or by one of the regular monthly telephone calls from his mother. But today her worry was more immediate and was not for Roger.

Sandy Pringle had asked her to come to his office. Gwen was anxious about the out-of-the-blue summons and decided it could only be bad news. The radio traffic had been quieter lately and she had overheard Warrant Officer Irving, her uncongenial RAF colleague, discussing rumours that all the listening posts were to be consolidated into the south-eastern control centre at Hell Fire Corner in Kent. The hours she spent in the cramped and uncomfortable little hut on the Downs had given meaning to her life, had made her feel that she was at last doing something useful, something that might in some small way make a difference to the progress of the war or the saving of a life. Her duties with the WVS were of course important, but they didn't offer her the same satisfaction. Being valued for her knowledge of German was a source of satisfaction that dressing wounds, driving ambulances and making tea could not compete with.

The following day, she made her way to HMS Marlborough – she would never get used to calling it that – to her it would always be The College – for the meeting with Sandy Pringle. She stood outside the heavy oak door of Sandy's office and knocked tentatively. Her palms were sweating and there was a hollow ache in the pit of her stomach. He was going to tell her they were shutting down Beachy Head. She was sure of it. Not the main radar station up there. Just her little leaky-roofed hut with its single wireless. She swallowed and entered.

Sandy didn't even look up. He waved a hand to signal her to sit down and continued to shuffle his papers, signing his name to documents with a flourish of his tortoiseshell fountain pen. Gwen wondered why she was so nervous. She'd known Sandy for years, sat around a table with him, Roger and Daphne, playing bridge, tramped over the Downs with a bag of clubs playing mixed foursomes at the Royal Eastbourne Golf Club; damn it – she'd even seen him drunk, slumped at the end of her dinner table after he had downed enough whisky to put Falstaff to shame. She remembered what Daphne had told her about their dirty weekends and suppressed a smile. So why was she so edgy, like a small child waiting to be reprimanded by a teacher?

Eventually Sandy sighed, leaned back in his chair and screwed the top back on his fountain pen.

'No easy way to do this. Not my decision. Directive from HQ. All available forces have to be deployed efficiently. You've done a first rate job.' He coughed and looked away, staring over Gwen's shoulder out of the window.

Filling the silence, Gwen said, 'You're closing down the listening station?'

'Certainly not. It's too damned useful to do that. Some of the intelligence we have gained from your work up there has been absolutely vital.'

She heaved a sigh of relief.

He coughed again, then said, 'However, we have a town full of allied soldiers and we need to prioritise their use over that of ordinary citizens. The Royal Canadian Corps of Signals are taking over from the RAF. That wouldn't have ruled you out from continuing but several of the Canadian infantry are fluent German speakers due to family connections and it makes more sense for one of them to take on your duties. Plenty of other things for you to do, and we need to keep the Canucks happy. Restless lot. Apparently they're cheesed off that they've not seen active service yet and we have to find more for them to do than spending all day on the firing ranges.'

'I see.' Gwen bit her lip, fighting a sudden urge to cry. She wanted to point out that the Canadians could be sent overseas at any point and then she'd have to return to the job – or train another soldier up to do it. She felt resentful. It was because she was a woman and because Eastbourne was swarming with redundant Canadians she was going to be forced back into making beds and pouring tea. There was no point in arguing though. It would get her nowhere – and earn her a reputation for being bolshie.

She wondered if she was dismissed and started to get up.

The Major rapped his knuckles on the desk. 'I'm not done yet.'

Gwen felt her cheeks reddening, infuriated at having to kowtow to Sandy.

'There's always a need for a smart gal like you, Gwen. We can make use of you here. Top secret stuff. Plenty of work in the typing pool and we can't take on just anybody. You've already been vetted so you'll be ideal.'

'But I can't type.'

'Can't be that hard to learn. If it was that difficult you wouldn't get so many young girls taking it up. You'll soon catch on. Remember there's a war on. All hands to the pump. I'd rather have a reliable trustworthy gal like you who may be a bit slower bashing the keys than a qualified typist who doesn't know when to keep her trap shut.'

Gwen fiddled with the cuff of her jacket, struggling to find the right words. She was angry. Feeling patronised, used, humiliated. Her work up at the listening post had been good. She had given no cause for complaint and it was ungrateful and unfair of the military to dispense with her because there were spare men around. Why weren't the Canadians being sent to the front? There were enough of them. Surely there was a way Mr Churchill could use them for what they had been trained. But what was the point in arguing? Eventually she breathed in slowly and said, 'When do you want me to start?'

'Couple of days. Need you to train up the Canadian chap who will be taking over from you. The man is a competent Morse decoder and has had basic training in using the radio equipment. All you have to do is show him how to transcribe. Make sure he knows how to fill in the damned forms. You know how HQ get the wind up if they're not completed correctly.'

Pringle got to his feet and began pacing in front of the window. Outside, a group of naval cadets were playing an impromptu game of cricket.

'Instil in him the need for speed and accuracy. Make sure he knows about the pickups and what to do if the motorcycle rider doesn't turn up. You know the drill.'

'Yes, sir,' she said, wishing she could add; so why not let me carry on doing it?

'He'll be sitting alongside you at the station. You show him the ropes tonight. Tomorrow get him to do it while you supervise and then, unless he makes a pig's breakfast of it, he'll be on his own the night after. You can start here Monday morning in the typing pool.'

So – she was not only to be deprived of her role, she was to train up the man who was to take her place. The unfairness and pointlessness enraged her. It was like the last war. Women had been in demand to drive ambulances, had risked their lives to tend the wounded, taken on jobs in factories to make armaments, only to be cast aside and sent back to the kitchen as soon as the surviving men came home from the front. This war was to be no different. Smarting with anger, she left Sandy's office and strode down the long school corridor and out into the flagged courtyard where she had left her bicycle. Cycling back up the hill she channelled her anger into the energy needed to tackle the steep gradient.

That evening when Gwen arrived at Beachy Head there was no sign of her replacement. Her spirits lifted. Perhaps they'd had a change of heart and found another job for him. She took up her usual place next to Warrant Officer Irving and accepted a cup of tea brought over to them from the next door radar station by the Home Guard sentry. It was a warm evening, still light even though it was nearly ten o'clock.

Gwen liked the night watch. The shift was six hours and it meant going to bed at five in the morning but, apart from negotiating the blackout on the way home, it was nice to be awake and working while the rest of the town was sleeping, doing her bit to protect them, helping in a small way to bring about the end the war.

The outgoing listeners handed over the logs to Gwen and Warrant Officer Irving and told them it had been a quiet evening so far with very little chatter from the Channel. Gwen adjusted her headphones and smiled. Back to business as usual.

After about twenty minutes the door opened and the Canadian soldier walked in. Gwen sighed. Not only was she to lose her job after all but lose it to a man who couldn't even be bothered to turn up on time. She didn't look at him, leaving her RAF colleague to reprimand him for his late arrival.

'Sorry. I had trouble finding the place. I went to the chain home station next door.'

Gwen turned to look at him. It was one of the three chaps

she had received into her home. The good-looking one with the elderly dog. The one who had been over-familiar.

He recognised her at the same moment. 'Mrs Collingwood! I didn't expect to meet you up here. They told me there was a woman who'd been seconded from the Women's Voluntary Service but I never guessed it would be you.'

She nodded, and seeing the puzzled look on the airman's face, explained that the Canadian was billeted in her house. She turned back to him. 'I'm sorry. I can't remember your name.'

'It's Jim,' he said quickly.

Irving rolled his eyes. The informality of the Canadian army was legendary. 'Evening, Private Jim,' he said.

Jim looked abashed. 'It's Armstrong. Private Jim Armstrong.'

The RAF officer extended a hand. 'I'm Irving. Now I'll leave you to Collingwood's mercy.'

Jim looked nervous. Gwen gestured to him to take a seat at the small metal table and began to explain the procedure and how she and Warrant Officer Irving worked together. She took him through the paperwork, explained how the transcripts were prepared in both German and English and went through the handover procedure with the riders from HQ. She was seething with resentment and raced through her explanations so quickly that Jim had to ask her to repeat some of the points. In the corner Irving twiddled his dials, headphones on, absorbed in his task.

'Okay, Collingwood. Jump on board,' said Irving.

Gwen grabbed her headset, listening in to the VHF radio and transcribing the Morse as the transmission progressed, leaving Jim to sit and watch, until Irving threw him another pair of headphones. 'May as well listen in, even if Collingwood's still in charge tonight, Armstrong.'

The intercept was between a Luftwaffe pilot and his

control station. When Gwen had first started the transcriptions she had been puzzled by the strange terminology the Germans used such as references to *kirchtum* – church towers. By now she had worked out that it was merely a reference to the altitude of the plane. She was not supposed to remember what she heard and what she transcribed and the forms were whisked away by the motorcycle riders to some unknown destination for analysis. She doubted if there was much of real interest. Anything important would be encrypted and relayed in a more secure way than these brief verbal exchanges between airmen and their controllers. She took a strange satisfaction in recognising the voices of some of the individual Luftwaffe pilots though. It didn't happen often, as most of the air traffic frequencies were monitored further along the coast in Kent and at Hastings, but there were occasions when she picked them up and often wondered about the identity of these men, whether they were married, had children, which towns or cities they came from.

Frequently Gwen heard derogatory comments about Germans from people in the town. While sharing their anger at what the war was putting them through, Gwen resented the way friends and neighbours lumped every citizen of Germany into the same pot. Though she acknowledged the evil of Hitler and his henchmen, Gwen stopped short of tarring the entire population of Germany with the same brush. She remembered German classmates from her school in Switzerland, a family she lodged with one summer in Munich when she was trying to improve her German, the shopkeepers who had served her, the waitresses in the *Kaffeehaus* who had brought her sachertorte and coffee. She remembered the laughing eyes of the tram conductor who held his tram up for her when she was running down the road, the fat dimple-cheeked cook who had ladled her extra dumplings with her soup. It was impossible to think of these people as the enemy. Impossible to feel hatred, to wish them dead, to believe them all culpable of the crimes of their leader.

When the brief transmission was over, Gwen took off her headphones and turned to Jim. 'Did you get that?'

He held out a piece of paper. She read what he had written down – a word perfect transcription of the brief exchange between the pilot and his control tower. Gwen sighed, disappointed at his competence.

'Good,' she said, grudgingly. 'Now translate it.'

Armstrong scribbled with his pencil and returned the paper to her. There was nothing she could quarrel with in his work.

Suppressing her annoyance, she said, 'I'll show you how to fill in the forms ready for the dispatch rider.'

The night passed quickly and when their shift ended Gwen had to acknowledge that Jim was going to be a competent operator. 'I've been allocated two days to show you the ropes, but I don't think that will be necessary. You seem to have got the hang of it so I'll let you get on.' She was aware that her voice had a caustic tone.

Armstrong frowned. 'Aren't you coming tomorrow? But what If I have questions or am unsure what to do?'

She gave him a withering look. 'You know as well as I do, Private Armstrong, that is extremely unlikely.'

'Unlikely but possible.' He gave her a broad grin and she had to admit that he was likeable even though she was trying her hardest not to like him. He was also attractive with those blue eyes and long legs. She brushed the thought away as if it were a stray fly.

THE BEACH AT HOLYWELL

The day after she'd been forced to hand over her headset to Private Armstrong, Gwen went down to the beach. Near Holywell there was a break in the barbed wire and while the foreshore was out of bounds and still heavily mined, the promenade was accessible. Gwen liked to walk along to the bottom of the cliff below the now neglected Italian Gardens, past the Edwardian beach chalets and the closed up Holywell tea room. The area was effectively the end of the line before the beach gave way to the vertical chalk cliffs that became Beachy Head. Before the construction of the gardens and the promenade, the area had once been home to lime kilns and chalk pits where the local fishermen worked to supplement their income from the sea.

The late afternoon was mild but overcast and the sea more grey-green than peppermint. Shallow waves lapped at the shore and beyond them the water stretched out, calm and flat like unfurled silk cloth. It was going to get dark soon but she had her blackout torch and there would be a full moon tonight. Moonlight on the sea always created a silvery light which illuminated the path.

Gwen sat on the wall in front of the chalets. At one time she and Roger had thought of renting one, but the idea was dropped as he was travelling so much with his job and once it became clear, if unsaid, that they were not going to have children. Like the tea room, the beach chalets were closed up, not just for the winter but for the war. Gwen tried to remember what it used to be like here on a peacetime summer day, the promenade scattered with people strolling, children playing in the shallows or fishing in the rock pools under the cliff for shrimps. Ice cream and cups of tea, teacakes and scones. Buckets and spades – although the sand was accessible only at low tide on the shingle-dominated beaches.

This was the time of year she loved best down here. The time when she was rarely disturbed and was free to sit and think, or walk, mulling over problems, indulging memories. It was rare she ran into anyone now that the war had made the seafront virtually out of bounds and most of the town's children had gone away. She usually saw a couple of soldiers or Home Guards in charge of the Bofors gun under the cliff but othèrwise the place was deserted and she revelled in her solitude.

She pulled her thick Arran cardigan around her and stared at the sea, losing track of time. On evenings such as this, she would talk to Alfie. After all those years since her brother's death, Gwen still felt his presence. It was torture, knowing he was not there yet feeling he was. Not physically – there was no ghostly hand to touch her – but his spirit was still in her, around her. They used to finish each other's sentences and often communicated without speaking. A favourite game was to think of an object and have the other guess what it was. It was their party trick.

Alfie was the only person she had told about her lost baby, apart from the doctor and now Pauline. When she had discovered she was pregnant she had whispered the secret news that he was to be an uncle. After the miscarriage happened she had sat in this same spot on the wall of the promenade and wept as she told him what happened. She had heard no words in response from Alfie but telling him was a small comfort, a burden shared.

This evening she wanted to tell him how mixed up and confused she felt, how her normal restraint was crumbling, how she worried constantly about Roger, how much she missed him. Yet undercutting all this was fear. Fear that she was a hollow shell, a husk of a person, incapable of expressing the feelings that came so naturally to other people. Gwen thought of Daphne and her dirty weekends with her husband in hotel rooms. She thought of Pauline Simmonds and her passion for her husband. She and Roger had never known anything like that together. And yet she loved him. She really loved him. She had no doubt of that.

What held her back? What stopped her feeling the desire that was second nature to other people? Was it Roger himself? Was it that she didn't find him attractive? She explored the thought and then dismissed it. As soon as she'd seen him across that dance floor in Berlin she had been drawn to him. No, it wasn't him. It was the act itself. It seemed wrong to allow oneself to lose control in that way. To abandon dignity, to let go. Were she to do so she feared she would be lost forever, made vulnerable, exposed. And that meant confronting the possibility of losing Roger too. After Alfie, she didn't think she could bear it. And she cared too much for Roger to expose him to the possibility of being jinxed by her love. Better to do as her mother had done and keep her emotions strictly reined in. Get through life as if it were a series of tasks to be ticked off a list, until one day she would be free of it all and be united with Alfie again.

This evening was quiet. Just the occasional cries of gulls and jackdaws and the gentle murmur of the waves.

Gwen didn't notice Jim Armstrong until he was right beside her, so lost in thought was she. He pulled himself up onto the wall next to her.

'I wanted to say sorry,' he said.

'What for?' She was annoyed at the interruption.

'Taking your job.'

Gwen shrugged. 'It wasn't your decision. You don't need to apologise.'

'I know – but I wanted you to know that I do understand how annoyed you must be about it.'

'Thank you.' She continued to stare out to sea.

'I didn't ask to do it.'

'I know.'

'They did a skills audit and it came out that I understood German. I mean I told them. My mother is German. Well, she's Canadian but born in Germany and she grew up with German as her first language. I had no idea you were doing the work before me.'

'Look, Private Armstrong, I've told you, there's no need to apologise or explain.'

'Call me Jim,' he said. 'But I saw how you looked at me and I wanted to... you know... acknowledge that.'

Gwen sighed and turned to face him. 'All right. Yes I was annoyed. I still am. I was doing a good job. They had no cause to replace me. They need to find work for you lot and yes, that makes me angry. How do you think it feels to be sidelined because you're a woman? Used when they have no alternative, and then flung aside like a piece of seaweed. And to add insult to injury they expected me to show you what to do.'

Jim nodded. 'I'd feel the same in your shoes. I can understand, because I've spent months training to fight this war.

That's what I joined up for, only to be sent here to do exercises and target practice. So, I do know how you feel. It seems to me that Allied Command has as little respect for Canadians as they do for women.'

Gwen smiled, then sighed and offered him her hand to shake. He took it and his grip was firm, his hands warm. She looked up at his face. His eyes were a brilliant blue, intense, sad. The scar down on his face was paler than the rest of his skin. She had a sudden urge to raise a finger and run it down the ridge. She pushed the thought away. Her stomach gave a little lurch as she realised again she found him attractive. Squeezing her lips together tightly she turned and looked back at the sea.

'Are you married, Private Armstrong?'

'It's Jim. No. I was engaged but not any more.'

His tone told her not to ask any more questions but her curiosity overcame her caution. 'Why not?'

'I found out she preferred my brother.'

She hadn't been expecting that and was lost for words for a moment, then said, 'How dreadful. That can't have been easy. And I didn't mean to pry. It's none of my business.'

Jim shook his head. 'It hasn't been easy. It still isn't.'

'Did you love her?' Why was she asking him this?

'Still do. But I hate her at the same time.' He paused for a moment then looked at her. 'Can you understand that?'

Gwen nodded but said nothing. She didn't know what to say. The conversation was running away from her like a spool of thread.

'We would have been married by now if it hadn't happened. She married my brother pretty much as soon as I'd left. She's knocked up now.' Seeing her puzzled frown, he said, 'Sorry, you don't use that expression over here, do you? I checked into a hotel on a trip to London and they asked me if I wanted to be knocked up. They meant an early morning call. We use it to mean becoming pregnant.'

Gwen smiled. 'Yes, I can see how that might prove awkward.' She hesitated before asking, 'And it wasn't your child?'

Jim shook his head and picked up a pebble and hurled it at the sea. 'Absolutely sure it wasn't my child. We never... Hell, I don't know why I'm telling you all this.'

She didn't know either, but she said, 'Maybe it helps to unburden yourself with someone you barely know, who won't judge you.'

'Maybe you're right. Anyway that's why I joined up. Couldn't wait to get away from the pair of them. I was humiliated. We live in a small community. Everyone knew Alice and I were getting married. We'd been sweet on each other since we were in school. You can imagine the gossip I'd have had to face as soon as people heard she was leaving me for my little brother.'

He threw another stone into the water. 'Maybe they already knew. Perhaps the whole damn town knew. I might have been the last to find out that they'd been making out under my nose. Anyway, I wasn't going to stick around to discover.'

Gwen shivered and buttoned up her cardigan. She asked herself how they had got onto such personal territory so rapidly. She was not usually the sort of person to invite confidences and Jim Armstrong was a virtual stranger. Yet she felt attuned to him. Drawn to him. Comfortable with him. She wasn't even annoyed any more that he had found her here in her personal retreat.

'What about you?' he said. 'I got the impression you didn't like being asked about your husband the other day. I'm sorry if I was intrusive.'

'You weren't,' she said with a sigh. 'I was being touchy. I'm always touchy. I seem to have turned touchiness into an art form.'

Jim smiled and nodded.

'I suppose I avoid talking about Roger as it would force me to think about what I feel. It's easier for me to bottle it up and keep it hidden.'

'I can understand that, Mrs Collingwood.'

'Call me Gwen.' She was abandoning her habitual caution now. 'I have no idea if he's behind enemy lines – although I think he must be, otherwise he would have written to me. He could be in the Far East, in Africa, in France.' She shook her head. 'The Balkans, Norway. Germany even. I lie awake at night trying to imagine what he's doing. All the time terrified that if he were taken prisoner I might not even find out about it. If he were dead I wouldn't even know.' She choked back a sob. 'I'm sorry. I didn't intend to become emotional. I never do usually. I hate to be soppy.'

'Soppy? You've every right to be emotional about it.' He laid a hand on her arm.

Gwen looked down as he gave her arm a slight squeeze and she thought how nice his hands were. She always noticed men's hands. Roger had nice hands too. Sandy Pringle had little fat hands with short stubby fingers. She often wondered how Daphne could bear to be touched by hands like that.

What on earth was she doing, sitting here on a wall by the beach with a complete stranger, thinking about men's hands? Get this conversation back onto a safer keel, she thought. Talk about him. Stop talking about Roger.

'You'll meet someone else,' she said at last. 'You'll forget all about this Alice. It sounds to me as though she wasn't worthy of you.'

Residual loyalty to the woman he'd intended to spend his

life with made him say, 'Alice is a wonderful person. Beautiful, calm, warm and friendly.'

'A bit too warm and friendly by the sound of it.' Before the words were out of her mouth she regretted them. Why was she being so waspish?

He took his hand away from her arm. 'You have no right to say that.' Hadn't he told himself the same thing many times over the past months? But hearing it from a stranger was different.

Suddenly reckless, she said, 'Look, Jim, she was sleeping with your brother. I barely know you but it's clear to me that you're worth more than that.'

'That's right, you do barely know me. In fact, you don't know me at all and you certainly don't know Alice.'

'I'm sorry.' She paused a moment and then said, 'But I do know that if I were engaged to be married I wouldn't jump into bed with my fiancé's brother. It's a terrible thing to do.'

'Alice must have loved Walt a whole lot for her to do what she did. Or else Walt forced her. She's not the kind of girl who would have done it otherwise. She's not cheap.' His words sounded hollow.

'Forced her?' said Gwen, horrified.

'Not like that.' He looked at her aghast. 'I meant he must have exerted pressure on her.'

'Is she a bit dim, this Alice?'

'Why are you being like this? Why are you saying these awful things?'

'I'm trying to get you to see that she's not the innocent you're portraying her as. I'm trying to get you to acknowledge that what you had was probably not worth having.' As the words came out of her mouth she was shocked at what she was saying, but she was angry. Not with Jim, but with that girl far away who had so casually caused him pain and taken his feelings so lightly.

'What right do you have to say that?' Jim jumped off the wall and moved in front of her. 'You don't know her. And I loved her.'

'Good. Past tense.'

'Still love her.' The words were lame and without conviction.

'It was an infatuation, Jim.' She paused, then decided she'd said enough. She barely knew Jim Armstrong but there was something about him that she was drawn to. It was not just his charisma and good looks but her recognition of the same self-hate that was in herself. This Alice had caused him to feel diminished and she didn't want him to feel like that.

Jim turned from her and walked towards the edge of the promenade where he picked up another stone and hurled it across the beach and into the water.

Suddenly determined to make him see the truth she said, 'When did you first know you were in love with her?' Why was she asking him this? She'd die rather than reveal such intimacies about herself.

He hesitated, dropped his hand as he was about to hurl another stone. 'I can't think of one moment.'

'Well, pick a few. What was it about her that made you think, I'm going to marry that girl?'

He turned back to her, his face puzzled. 'How do I know? It crept up on me. I guess I always loved her. Since we were kids.'

'What did you talk to her about?' Gwen could barely believe what she was saying but felt compelled to keep going.

'What do you mean?'

'What kind of things did you talk about?'

Jim pondered a moment, then shrugged. 'Everything and nothing. The farm. Her job at the library. Hell, I don't know.'

'What makes her so special? Come on, tell me.'

He moved back towards her. 'Why? If you're so smart tell me what made you fall in love with your husband.'

'That's private.'

'You have the cheek of the devil, Mrs Collingwood. Who the hell do you think you are?'

'It's completely different. My husband hasn't slept with another woman.'

Jim gasped then said, 'How do you know? He could be making out with some French woman right now.'

Gwen heard the crack of her hand across his face, before she realised what she had done. Jim stood, rooted to the spot, then grabbed her by her shoulders.

His eyes burned into her then he dropped his hands and let her go. 'I'm sorry. I asked for that,' he said.

Before Gwen could answer, he was walking away, striding back along the promenade towards the town. She watched him disappear into the gloom, her heart pounding, her breath uneven. All she could think about was that when he grabbed her by the shoulders she had wanted his hands to move down and pull her against him. She had wanted to know what it would be like to be crushed against him, to feel his breath hot against her face, to feel his mouth on hers.

Gwen had never in her life behaved like this before. She had deliberately provoked him, determined to get him to acknowledge that this Alice was nothing but a slut, determined to push him over the edge so that she could engage his emotions.

With a sudden flash of self-knowledge she realised it was her own emotions she was trying to engage. What was wrong with her? Why was she behaving this way? Her desire had taken her by surprise. Where had this overwhelming surge of longing for a man she had met a few days ago come from? Was it because she missed Roger?

Gwen began to walk back slowly towards the series of

steps that led up the cliffside back to the roadway, her feet dragging as she went up. It would take her twenty minutes to walk back to the house and all she wanted was to be safe at home in her bed. Guilt and shame washed over her. She'd had no right to do what she did to that young man. To taunt him and push him like that. And to want him to kiss her – when she loved her husband, when he was facing God knows what.

I am the worst kind of wife, she thought. The very worst.

~

IT WAS three days before she saw Private Armstrong again. Gwen didn't know whether he had gone out of his way to avoid her – and she could hardly blame him if he had. Each day the two other Canadians stuck their heads around the dining room door as she ate her breakfast to wish her good morning before heading off, but there was no sign of Jim. Wondering if something had happened to him that night and he had not returned to the house, she mentioned his absence casually to Pauline when they were in the kitchen washing the dishes.

'He gets up earlier than the other two. I saw him first thing this morning. He told me he was on duty later today up Beachy Head.'

Gwen smiled. 'That's all right then. I thought for a moment he'd gone AWOL!'

'Nice lad, that one,' said Pauline. 'He's got lovely eyes. Makes you think you're drowning in them when you look at him. Come-to-bed eyes my friend Betty calls them.'

Gwen felt herself blushing and reached for the teapot, emptying the tea leaves on to a sheet of newspaper, ready to throw away.

'Don't throw the tea leaves out, Mrs C. Let them dry then

put them on the fire. They burn beautifully and every little helps. Now what was I saying? Yes, that Jim. He's such a handsome chap. Shame about the scar, but I can tell you if I wasn't married to my Brian I'd have my eyes on him.' She gave a dirty laugh. 'Ooh no, I wouldn't be chucking him out of bed for eating cream crackers.'

'All right, Pauline. I think you've made your point.'

Pauline laughed. 'Come on, Mrs C, ease up a bit. I'm only having a giggle. There's little enough to laugh about these days.'

PAULINE'S NIGHT OUT

EASTBOURNE

Gwen wasn't thrilled about her new role in the typing pool. She didn't mind the typing itself, but the sheer tedium of the stuff she had to transcribe was beyond boring. Far from the military secrets she had hoped to be party to, it was mostly reports from Canadian officers for the Canadian Military HQ in London and, as the troops evidently had little meaningful to do, the reports were extremely dull. Her main task was compiling an up-to-date address and telephone list with map references for all operational units in the town and its surroundings. This was a job of mind-numbing boredom, but one that required maximum attention to detail. As she walked along the corridor each day, she wished there was a role for her behind the closed doors with blacked-out windows where WRENs were hard at work on something too important for the likes of Gwen to know about. She kept telling herself to grin and bear it as it was all for the war, but it was hard not to feel that her capabilities were being wasted.

Sitting at home one evening Gwen realised it was the third week running that Pauline had asked her to babysit while she went out dancing with the Canadians. 'They're lonely and bored, those lads and they want a bit of fun,' she'd said. 'And there's not enough women left in the town to go round. I'm doing my bit for the war effort.'

Gwen had asked her if it was right to be out enjoying herself with other men while her husband faced all manner of dangers on the Atlantic convoys.

'I'd like to think that if my Brian was lonely and in port a nice girl would be happy to have a dance with him. Brian and I love dancing. I'd never do anything I'd be ashamed to tell him about. No harm in a bit of dancing. You should give it a try. I could ask the lady next door to babysit the girls and we could go together. We'd have a laugh. Loosen up!'

'I don't need loosening up thank you, Pauline.' But she couldn't help smiling. She probably did.

When Gwen had been to the hairdressers, earlier in the week, she overheard a conversation on the topic of loose morals. The women in the salon had been talking about a woman whose husband was in the air force, and who was allegedly having an affair with a Canadian soldier.

'Soldier?' one of the women had said. 'More like soldiers. Lots of them. Little more than a prostitute, if you ask me. She may not take money for it but in my mind it's as bad. She's having fun while her husband is risking his life. It's a different fellow every night of the week. Morals of an alley cat.'

'As for those Canadians, don't get me started,' said the hairdresser as she dabbed setting lotion onto the woman's hair. 'They're good for absolutely nothing. All they do is get drunk, play at target practice and churn up the Downs with their blasted tanks.'

'You're right about that,' the first woman replied. 'My husband was talking to one of the Home Guard who said there's almost nothing left of the lighthouse at Belle Tout.

They've blown it to bits. No respect. Goodness knows what Sir James will say when the war's over and he finds out his house has been blown up for no reason at all. They'll probably blame it on the Germans. Those Canadians are a bunch of shirkers, if you ask me. If they were any good as soldiers Mr Churchill would have used them by now.'

Gwen debated whether to jump into the conversation in the Canadians' defence. Certainly she'd seen no examples of drunken behaviour among the men billeted with her, and it was hardly their fault if the army had yet to deploy them. In the end she'd stayed silent and carried on reading her book.

Tonight she planned to say something to Pauline about her dancing expedition. It wasn't that she minded babysitting for the little girls. There was never a peep out either of them once Pauline got them down, and Gwen rarely went out in the evenings anyway so it was no inconvenience. But there was something about Pauline's casual attitude that riled her. She flirted with the soldiers, in particular with that Mitch fellow and Gwen couldn't help remembering the night she had walked in on Pauline and her husband. It still made her blush with embarrassment. A woman who clearly enjoyed conjugal relations as much as that might well find it difficult to stop herself getting involved with another man.

If she tries it on in this house that will be the end of it. Gwen dug her fingernails into her palms. She would ask her to leave. Never mind the cooking. Then she remembered Sally and baby Brenda. How could she possibly expel them from what had become their home? And she couldn't deny how devoted a mother Pauline was. How much she loved her husband as well. Everyone had different ways of getting through the war. Maybe she did need to loosen up a bit. What was wrong with a bit of harmless flirting? It was wrong to assume Pauline was guilty of anything more.

It was almost midnight when Gwen heard the front door

open and whispering voices in the hallway, followed by the sound of boots being removed and muffled footsteps on the stairs as the Canadians went up. She waited in the drawing room for Pauline to come in to say goodnight, but there was silence. She got up and moved towards the door, opened it and found Pauline wrapped in the arms of Mitch Johnson, kissing him with enthusiasm.

Gwen coughed and the pair jumped apart. Mitch's face turned a deep beetroot and even Pauline had the grace to look ashamed.

'It's not what you think, Mrs C,' said Pauline. 'I was demonstrating what a French kiss is.' She giggled. 'For Mr Johnson's education. He's led a sheltered life back in Canada. He wanted a practice run before he tries it out on the girl he fancies.'

Gwen remained silent.

Mitch pulled his cap off and bowed his head slightly. 'That's right, Mrs Collingwood. I asked Pauline, er, Mrs Simmonds, for some advice as I don't seem to be having much luck with the ladies.'

'Maybe if you concentrated on the lady you are interested in and not on Mrs Simmonds your luck might improve.' Gwen could hear the sarcasm in her own voice and felt ashamed. Mitch Johnson was barely a man. Eighteen or nineteen at most. It wasn't fair to blame him. The fault lay with Pauline.

'All right, Mrs C. So I fancied a kiss. Shoot me! Guilty as charged, m'lud. I'd have thought you'd understand, what with your husband being away too.' Her eyes were defiant. 'What's so wrong with having a little kiss? I know my Brian wouldn't worry. He knows I'd never go with another man, and he wouldn't begrudge me showing a little kindness to a lonely young soldier.'

All Gwen's frustration and anger at the loss of her job, the absence of her husband and the way she'd let herself be drawn into that intimate conversation with Armstrong at the beach, came to the surface. 'Show some self-respect, Pauline. I won't tolerate that kind of behaviour under my roof.'

Pauline whirled round, her face furious. 'You might understand my *behaviour* if you weren't all dried up and bitter like a bag of old currants.'

Gwen leaned back against the wall, feeling her legs weaken under her.

Pauline jerked her head at Mitch. 'Go to bed, Mitch.'

The soldier looked relieved at his reprieve and bounded up the stairs.

'I'm sorry,' said Pauline. 'I shouldn't have said that. It was uncalled for and I didn't mean it. If you want me to leave I'll have our bags packed tomorrow.'

'Go to bed.' Gwen walked back into the drawing room, shutting the door behind her.

She sat on the couch and bent down, head in her hands. Dried up and bitter like a bag of currants. Pauline was right. She was.

TWO WHISKIES

EASTBOURNE

*J*im was confused and depressed. He had loved Alice, hadn't he? If he hadn't, if he had never truly loved her, then his whole life had been a sham. Yet the things Gwen Collingwood had said the other night had unsettled him. She had been insistent in her questioning. It was none of her damned business and yet what she said had bothered him. If he had loved Alice shouldn't he have been able to say why?

In a corner of The Ship he sat and nursed his pint. He'd been avoiding Gwen for the past few days, angry with her but even more angry with himself. The pub wasn't as crowded as usual and he was left in peace while a small contingent of his countrymen gathered around the piano, singing along as one of their number played the tunes.

Jim tried again to find the right words to describe Alice. He kept coming back to the words beautiful, warm and friendly he'd used to describe her to Gwen. Instead of calm he decided on serene – then remembered that terrible night in the barn when Alice had appeared anything but serene. Wanton, passionate, hungry were better ways to describe what he had seen in her that night. She had never looked that way with him. It must be his fault. He was incapable of arousing passion in her. Jim realised with a jolt that their relationship had been built on friendship, familiarity and fondness. Maybe that would have been enough? But it evidently wasn't.

The pianist was treating the pub to a rendition of I've got Sixpence. The Canucks were singing along, drowning out all conversation. Jim downed the rest of his pint and went to the bar to buy another.

A couple of Canadian soldiers that Jim didn't recognise were buying drinks for two women. Port and lemon, Joan's favourite drink. That and lemonade shandy. He thought about the night he had spent with her in that London hotel room. That hadn't exactly been a night of passion – more a half-awake accident. A fumble at dawn. And yet there had been an intensity about it. Perhaps he only thought that because it was his first time? His only time.

How would he have described Joan if Gwen Collingwood had asked him? Annoying, elusive, unexpected, inconsistent, interesting, disconcerting? Mysterious, mocking, manipulative, stubborn, fascinating, infuriating. He took his beer back to his quiet corner, wishing Joan was with him now. She couldn't hold a light to Alice in the looks department and he had never known where he stood with her. Even if she hadn't been engaged to another guy he doubted he would have asked her on a date. She wasn't his kind of girl. They came from different worlds. He couldn't imagine her raking hay or helping to round up a stray calf. Alice had happily done those all those things. And yet there had been something about Joan that made him feel excited and unsure of himself. But there was no point wasting time thinking about her. She'd well and truly given him the brush off.

Women were a mystery. Jim wondered if he would feel

differently if he'd had sisters. He doubted it somehow. Take Gwen Collingwood. She was a piece of work. All those questions. She'd been relentless. Why should she care about what he felt for Alice? He studied his pint, looking into its cloudy depths as if hoping to find an answer there. Gwen was a beautiful woman. Not in the same way as Alice – all pure and shining and blonde. No, Gwen had a cold beauty. Aloof and distant and yet somehow fragile. Brittle. Her voice was hard-edged, clipped, upper class – so different from the way Joan and Ethel spoke. Buttoned-up, that was what she was, she surrounded herself with a barrier to keep everyone at a distance. Stiff upper lip, they said about the British – but she had revealed something else the other evening – a pent up anger when she spoke about having to relinquish her job to him. And who could blame her? She had made him angry too. She had goaded him about Alice, got right under his skin until he had retaliated and she lost all that control and slapped his face, revealing another woman, one capable of raw emotion. Jim reluctantly admitted he had wanted to pull her into his arms and kiss her. He tried to suppress the thought. It was ridiculous. She was at least ten years older than him, and married. He had deserved to have his face slapped for what he'd said about her husband. He still didn't know why he'd said it. Maybe because she'd hurt him and he wanted to hit back?

The men around the piano had been joined by the two women with their port and lemons and had moved on to singing 'Doing What Comes Naturally'. Trouble with me, he thought, is nothing comes naturally.

The door swung open and half a dozen men came into the pub, laughing. One of them was Walt. He hadn't expected to see him in his local. Walt's company were billeted in Old Town and Jim knew that most of them frequented the Tally Ho! pub there. He slugged down the remains of his beer and made his way to the other exit before his brother had a chance to spot him.

When he got back to the house, the drawing room door was open and he noticed the French door to the stone-paved upper terrace was ajar and the light from a lamp in the hallway would be breaking the blackout regulations. He walked out onto the terrace which ran across the width of the back of the house. The terrace was higher than the level of the garden as the house was built on a slope. Underneath it and to the side was another paved area which was accessed via the rooms occupied by Mrs Simmonds and the children. The terrace was bathed in moonlight. He leaned against the wall, resting his hands on the cold red brick. The sea looked beautiful, the moonlight turning it into molten metal, bare skeletal trees outlined against it like dark veins.

'Peace offering?' Gwen Collingwood appeared beside him, holding out a glass tumbler. 'It's whisky. I never drank the stuff until the war but I've developed a taste for it.'

He hesitated a moment then took the glass from her. She chinked hers against it. 'I had no right to put you through such a cross-examination. It was none of my business and I overstepped the mark,' she said.

'It wasn't you who was out of line. I shouldn't have said what I did about your husband. It was unforgivable. I'm sorry.'

'Then we shall both have to pretend it never happened.' She smiled and sipped her scotch.

Jim nodded in the direction of the sea. 'It's beautiful tonight.'

'The sea is always different,' she said. 'Every day, every hour. Always changing. That's why we bought this house. My husband wasn't sure, with it being so far out of the town and so high up, but I fell in love with the view.'

Jim winced, uncomfortable that she had mentioned her

husband again, still feeling guilty for what he had said about him. 'You must miss him.'

Gwen sighed. 'I think about him all the time. I worry about him.' She swirled the whisky around her glass. 'I'm not sure about anything any more. This war has made the world we lived in before seem unreal and strange. It's as if we were living in a false construct. Playing at living. What's happening now is the reality. Being hungry, making do, listening all the time for the planes, clearing up debris, putting out fires. I can't imagine going back to the life I had before.'

'You make it sound as though you prefer things now.'

'Perhaps I do in a way. I have a purpose. A reason to get out of bed each day.'

'Until I took that away from you,' he said ruefully.

She waved a finger at him. 'No more apologies. Besides even if I can't work at the listening post any more I still have more to do now than I did before the war. Whether it's fire watching, typing, or making tea for people who've been bombed out, it has to be better than the futile life I lived before. I make a difference, however small, to people's lives.'

'Funny that,' Jim said. 'It's the other way around for me. The war has been a waiting game. Back on the farm I used to love my life and the way the work followed the seasons. Every day there were so many jobs to be done. My folks depended on me. Mind you, they must be getting by somehow without me and Walt.'

'Walt?'

'My brother.'

'The brother who…'

'The one and only. He followed me over here. He's in the same regiment. His company are in Eastbourne too. He walked into The Ship tonight – that's why I came back here early. I spend my life trying to engineer things to avoid having anything to do with him. I volunteer for stuff that I know he won't be involved in. Anything that requires a single volunteer, no matter what, I'm the man.'

'Why did he join up? I thought you said...' She hesitated to mention Alice again, then said, 'Aren't they expecting a child?'

Jim shook his head. 'He didn't know she was pregnant when he signed up. Once he found out he tried to get sent home, the idiot.' He swirled his whisky round the glass. 'I don't know why he joined up. Said he felt guilty not serving. Our father did his bit in the last war and I was already here.'

She was looking at him, expecting him to go on.

'Walt's always been competitive. Can't bear to feel he's left behind in anything. We did everything together but the more I've thought about it the more I've realised he must have resented me. Even now he's got Alice he's still trying to outdo me, or match me or however his twisted brain justifies it. I cared for him but it turns out he's only ever seen me as a rival.'

Gwen was silent.

'Do you have any brothers or sisters, Mrs Collingwood, Gwen?'

Gwen sighed, closed her eyes and then said, 'I had a brother. He died.'

Jim turned sideways, elbow on the balustrade and looked at her. 'I'm sorry.'

'He was my twin. We were twelve when it happened.'

'That must have been hard to bear.' He laid a hand on her sleeve.

Her voice was barely a whisper. 'I don't know why I'm telling you this. Not even my husband knows.'

Jim's hand moved down her arm and rested on her hand. He left it there.

'It was my fault Alfie died. We were playing. We used to

dare each other to go further all the time, to take stupid risks. Our family was living in India although we were sent back here to England to separate boarding schools. We hated being apart and when we went home to India for the summer holidays we became wild children, undisciplined, spending our days climbing trees and swimming in the river. Doing anything and everything we weren't supposed to do. It was paradise. We loved it. And we loved being together again.'

'Your folks? Didn't they know what you were up to?'

'Too preoccupied. Theirs was not a happy marriage. My father was absorbed in his work. He was a district officer, travelled a lot. My mother was caught up in the British expatriate social life. She spent her days playing cards and tennis. Alfie and I were left to the care of our ayah – an Indian lady who had more or less raised us. But we knew how to get around her and how to get away. We believed we were invincible, indestructible.'

She stopped, and Jim was uncertain whether she would continue. He waited, his hand still on hers. His thumb began to move slowly, involuntarily, making little circles between her thumb and first finger.

'Alfie fell from a tree while he was trying to make a rope swing. He would have got down when he realised the branch was too thick to reach around with the rope, but I told him he was chicken.' She stared out to the sea. 'He overbalanced and fell into the stream. I thought he was play acting at first, but he'd cracked his head open on a rock. Died instantly.'

Gwen's voice was steady, dispassionate, as though she were describing the weather, but Jim felt her hand trembling under his. He continued to stroke it.

'My mother never forgave me. Or herself. After Alfie was buried she never mentioned his name. We returned to England without my father and Mother found religion.

When I was fifteen she got cancer and died. My father remarried and sent me away to school in Switzerland. I met my husband Roger in Germany. He was working there and I was visiting friends. Daddy didn't come to the wedding. I never heard from him apart from a card at Christmas, written by his new wife. Then a few weeks before the war started I got a letter from her to say he'd died. Heart attack.'

Jim could see her face in profile, lit up by the light of the moon. He felt strangely moved, protective, touched. She had shown him her vulnerability and he was overwhelmed with the urge to hold her. He pulled her towards him and took her in his arms, holding her against his chest, feeling her warm breath through the wool of his battledress. Gwen stood motionless, letting him hold her. Jim stroked her hair, then bent and kissed the top of her head. She moved back to look up at him and as she did, knocked her empty whisky glass off the balustrade. They heard it crash into pieces on the paving below.

They jumped apart as a voice rose up from underneath them. 'Is that you, Mrs C? You all right up there?'

'Dropped a glass, Pauline. I hope the children haven't woken. Don't let Sally out there in the morning until I've had a chance to clear up the pieces. Good night.'

Jim looked at Gwen Collingwood and saw that she had reassumed her formal and distant demeanour. It was like a curtain closing. The moment had passed. She didn't look at him as she opened the French door and went into the house. 'Goodnight, Private Armstrong,' she said.

Left alone in the darkness of the terrace, Jim was puzzled. Had he imagined it or had she been about to kiss him on the terrace? Had he misread the signals? What the hell was he doing? First an engaged woman and now a married one. Was it all a reaction to what Alice had done to him? Pull yourself together, man.

Gwen was a beautiful woman and, in spite of her brittle exterior, Jim was drawn to her. He felt he could tell her things he would have never dreamt of telling anyone else and she had been equally open with him. They barely knew each other. They were years apart. And yet…

Stop it. She's married. It must have been the whisky. Otherwise why would she have gone inside and cut him off like that? Don't think about her.

But it was no good. No matter how hard he tried not to think about Gwen he wanted her with an intensity of desire he had never known before.

THE CAKE QUEUE

*I*n the sanctuary of her bedroom, Gwen was sitting at her dressing table, brushing her hair. She frowned at her reflection in the mirror. Jim Armstrong's pale blond hair and blue eyes with the brightness of cornflowers, reminded her of a German boy she thought she had forgotten long ago. She had gone for a weekend to Bavaria with one of her school friends, not long before she met Roger. The young man had asked her to dance at a party, sweeping her around the room with his eyes locked onto hers until she felt herself blushing but was unable to look away. When the music ended he nodded at her, clicked his heels in that funny Bavarian way, and left the room. She never saw him again. He was probably up there somewhere in the sky now, diving and swooping and dropping bombs, or falling from a burning plane into the sea, like one of the men whose plane crashed in the Aldro school a couple of years ago. Perhaps he was one of the young Luftwaffe pilots she had listened into on the VHF radio. What a strange world they were living in, where total strangers tried to exterminate each other, solely because they had been ordered to do so.

She studied her reflection in the mirror, with a critical eye. There were fine wrinkles around her mouth and at the corner of her eyes. Her age was starting to show. That had never bothered her before. She was not in the least bit vain. But now she wished she were ten years younger. There was no doubt about it – Jim Armstrong had been about to kiss her. And she had been about to let him. If she hadn't knocked her glass off the balustrade and disturbed Pauline the kiss would have happened. But that would have been unthinkable. Wouldn't it?

What was happening to her? Almost kissing a Canadian soldier. A virtual stranger. A man at least ten years younger. Probably nearer fifteen. He had an excuse. He had been abandoned, betrayed, treated cruelly by his brother and his girlfriend and now far from home, probably bored, possibly afraid, certainly lonely. There was no excuse for her. She was a married woman and loved her husband. And she was a hypocrite. Hadn't she had a row with Pauline about kissing that Mitch fellow? She still felt guilty about the way she had behaved towards Pauline and now here she was herself. Allowing herself to participate in a pointless flirtation was out of the question. No, it was never going to happen.

Gwen put down the hairbrush and sighed. She had so wanted it to happen. She had positively ached for it to happen. Were he to walk into her bedroom now she would rush into his arms and take him into her bed.

But Jim didn't appear at her door.

Gwen lay on her back, sleep eluding her, letting herself imagine what it would be like to have Jim with her now. The memory of Pauline and her husband making love came to her and she thought of herself straddling Jim Armstrong. She gave a little gasp and allowed herself to indulge the fantasy, in the knowledge that the reality was never going to happen. Her hands ran over her body, feeling her nipples harden through the satin of her nightgown. She sighed and arched her back, then the voice in her head told her to stop, to pull herself together, to show some self-control, some self-respect. Propping up the pillows behind her, she reached out to switch on the lamp, picked up the book on the bedside table and began to read.

~

THE FOLLOWING MORNING Gwen parked the car on the seafront, a few yards down from the Wish Tower, the martello tower that had stood guard over the front since the wars against Napoleon, its original defensive purpose pointless now in the face of fighter-bombers. It would probably get hit itself before long, she thought.

The rain-drenched seafront was deserted and drab. The floral displays in the Carpet Gardens between the Wish Tower and the pier had been sacrificed to the war effort, the colourful flowers displaced by onions. Everything looked ugly. Barbed wire snaked along the edge of the promenade, rising about six feet high and preventing entry to the heavily mined beaches. While the fear of invasion had faded since 1940, Gwen could feel the proximity of the enemy. The Channel was such a narrow strip – surely too inconsequential to keep out Hitler's armies if they decided to cross?

The rain sounded a dull drumbeat on the roof of the car. The sky had been blue when she'd got up this morning, with the sea shining like a pearl. Now, a few hours later, the clouds hung like thick smoke and the little palm trees on the lawns next to the tower looked like bedraggled hedgehogs. She had come so close to letting Jim Armstrong kiss her last night. No – that wasn't true – it wasn't right to say she had almost let him kiss her – the truth was that it was she that had wanted to kiss him, to initiate it. In fact, she wanted to kiss him now. Wanted it with a hunger that she'd never known before. She closed her eyes and let out a deep breath, imagining what his lips would feel like on hers, how she would feel enfolded in his arms. There had been a charge between them. Unmistakeable. So why had he hesitated? What made him behave like an honourable man? Maybe it was a soldiers' code of honour – not to touch another man's wife.

Why was she feeling like this? Behaving like this? She didn't love Jim Armstrong. She was certain of that. At least she didn't love him the way she loved Roger. But she couldn't possibly let herself think about Roger right now. It was all too complicated. What had happened between her and Jim was inexplicable. She was like a teenage girl with a crush. Pull yourself together. You're a happily married woman. You're more than ten years older than him. He's a stranger. He's a soldier. He's barely more than a boy. He could be dead before long. Hell! We could all be dead before long. What does it matter?

Over and over in her head the thoughts whirled. Rational, buttoned-up Gwen tried to hold the line as this new wanton Gwen ached to break through it. She had never known desire like this. Never let herself know it. On that wet Irish honeymoon she had felt desire for Roger but had shut it away, let the fear take over. So why now was she struggling so badly not to give in to the temptation that was Jim? It was as if her body had taken over her mind, pushed it into subjugation. Desire was making her a stranger to herself.

She thumped her fist into the centre of the steering wheel, jumping with shock as the horn sounded shrilly.

How was she going to face Jim again? How, after the way

they had talked, the undeniability of that almost-kiss, could she look him in the eyes?

Gwen's agonising was interrupted by loud rapping on the passenger window and then the door was wrenched open and Daphne Pringle climbed inside the car.

'What on earth are you doing sitting here in the pouring rain, woman? Have you run out of petrol?'

It took a moment for Gwen to reorient herself to the present moment. 'I – I was on my way into town. I thought I'd get in the cake queue.'

'So what are you doing sitting here on the seafront?'

'Waiting to see if the rain might ease off in a bit. I didn't fancy standing in a queue in a downpour. You know what the cake queue can be like.'

Daphne frowned. 'No, I don't actually. I send Mrs Elliott. I thought you had that girl. Shouldn't she be the one waiting in line for cakes?'

'The baby isn't well.' Gwen was surprised how easily the lies flowed – then asked herself why she was lying at all. What was wrong with telling Daphne she'd come here to be alone with her thoughts?

'But why sit here in a cold car? Honestly, Gwen, when I saw you through the window I thought something terrible had happened. You looked as though you'd received bad news. I thought you might have heard something about Roger.'

'Of course it's not Roger.' She realised she sounded snappy, irritated. 'I mean, it's nothing. No bad news. Nothing to report. I'm sitting here in the rain minding my own business.'

Daphne reached for the door handle. 'There's no need to be like that. I was worried. That's all. I hope you'd do the same.'

Gwen reached her hand out and stopped Daphne. 'I'm

sorry. There truly is nothing wrong. I was sitting here wishing the damn rain would stop. Now can I drop you off anywhere?'

They drove in silence to the Hydro Hotel, where Daphne was meeting Sandy for a drink after he had finished a briefing there. Gwen swung the car into the car park and Daphne mumbled her thanks, still clearly offended. Once she had disappeared into the building Gwen burst into tears.

THE TELEGRAM

A telegraph boy from the post office was standing on the step when Gwen answered the door. Seeing the buff envelope she knew at once what it was and her knees buckled. Slumped in a chair in the hallway she saw it wasn't addressed to her. Relief rapidly switched to sorrow for Pauline and she went downstairs with the telegram in her shaking hands.

Pauline was sitting beside Brenda's high chair feeding stewed apple to the baby. She was laughing when Gwen entered the kitchen. Sally was sitting on a rug on the floor next to her mother; her teddy, a doll and a stuffed penguin that she had been given for Christmas were lined up in front of her. The child appeared to be telling them all a story. Pauline called out, 'Kettle's boiled. I'll make you a cuppa in a jiff.'

Gwen hesitated in the doorway. She didn't know what to do. It seemed wrong to have Pauline read what could only be bad news in front of her children and risk distressing them, but she could hardly take the children away and leave her alone to absorb the news.

Pauline turned to look at her and her grin vanished when she saw Gwen's face and the brown envelope in her hands. She put the spoon down, swallowed, and got to her feet. 'For me, is it?' she said and stretched out her hand for the telegram. 'Watch the girls a while, will you?'

Gwen nodded. She sat down in the chair vacated by Pauline and began spooning fruit into Brenda's open mouth while watching Pauline walk to the bottom of the garden.

Sally scrambled to her feet. 'I'm going to Mummy,' she said.

'No, darling. Please. Give Mummy a few minutes on her own. She'll be back in a moment.'

Sally, evidently sensing something, moved over to Gwen, who pulled her up onto her lap. Stroking Sally's hair, she suggested they play the aeroplane feeding game with Brenda, hoping to distract Sally, while at the same time trying to look out on the garden.

Pauline was sitting motionless on the wooden bench under the beech tree at the bottom of the garden. The telegram was in her hands and her head was lowered over it. She appeared to be reading and rereading it.

Gwen hadn't known what to expect. Pauline usually wore her heart on her sleeve and was an emotional woman, but she was also a strong one. She was staring at the flimsy beige paper with its strips of white carrying the words every wife most feared and dreaded. Gwen didn't want to leave her there like that, alone under the tree. She tried to imagine how it would feel if it were she reading the missive from the War Office and what Pauline would have done for her, but her imagination let her down.

Indecision gripped her. Was it better to take the children out to Pauline and hope that she would find comfort in their presence or did that risk causing more distress? Pauline would want some time to prepare herself to break the news to Sally.

The kitchen door opened and Private Armstrong stuck his head around. His face registered surprise and pleasure at seeing Gwen here in the kitchen. 'Sorry, Mrs Collingwood, I stopped by for a cup of tea. Pauline usually makes a pot around this time. I can come back later.'

'No. Can you watch the girls for a few minutes,' she said, giving him a meaningful look. She reached out a hand to Sally and said, 'Mummy's had some news and she's feeling sad. Soon she's going to want a big cuddle from you. But I need to speak to her first so I'd like you to be a good girl for Mummy and stay here with this nice gentleman and help him take care of Brenda. Can you do that, Sally?'

Sally's brown eyes fixed on Gwen and the little girl nodded, solemnly. 'Jimmy can read me a story,' she said, to Gwen's surprise. 'And then I'll kiss Mummy better.'

Gwen stood, poured the kettle into the teapot, then ran upstairs and returned with a bottle of whisky and added some to the cup before pouring the tea. She smiled in thanks to Private Armstrong, and went out into the garden. She sat beside Pauline on the bench and reached for her hand.

Pauline turned to face her, her eyes wet with tears. 'The navy regrets to inform me that Brian Henry Simmonds has been killed in action. I thought they'd say "Missing. Feared dead". Isn't that what they're meant to say? Aren't they supposed to leave you with a bit of hope? He might have got picked up out of the water. Mightn't he? It's possible, isn't it? Or had time to get in a lifeboat?'

Gwen put an arm around her and held out the cup, holding it for her to drink as though she were a small child.

'I only had a letter from Brian last week. He was due for a bit of shore leave. I was looking forward to seeing him. Dear God, what am I going to do? How am I going to tell our Sal?

What the hell am I going to do without him?' She kicked at the ground with the heel of her left foot. 'And what a bloody awful way to die. In the freezing waters of the Atlantic... or blown to smithereens by a torpedo.'

Gwen laid her hand on Pauline's arm.

'Do you think he'd have known? Had time to panic? If he's got to be dead I want it to have been quick. The worst would be if he it was a slow death. Trapped below decks in a burning ship. Drifting in the water and slowly freezing.'

'Don't do this, Pauline.'

'Which do you think's worse? They say drowning is a good way to die, but I can't believe that would be true if it's so bloody cold.'

Her voice broke and she began to sob. Gwen held out a handkerchief but Pauline ignored it. She spun round and faced her, anger now in her voice. 'It's not fair. My Brian was a good man. He didn't deserve to die. What's wrong with this world? I'm so sick of the bloody war. He was only thirty. His whole life in front of him. What have I got left to live for? I loved that man. I really loved him.' Pauline's voice was now a wail and she began to keen backwards and forwards on the bench. 'If I'd known what was going to happen, I'd never have kissed that lad. It were only a bit of fun. It didn't mean nothing.'

'Of course it didn't.'

'You looked at me like I was a cheap tart.'

Gwen closed her eyes and squeezed Pauline's hand again. 'I'd never think that of you, Pauline, and I'm sorry if I looked at you like that. I was tired. I know you loved your husband. It has always been plain to see. And Brian must have known that too.'

They sat in silence, broken only by the sound of Pauline's sobs. Eventually she said, 'Give us that hankie.' She took the handkerchief, wiped her eyes and blew her nose and then stood up, smoothed down her dress and walked towards the house.

She turned back to look at Gwen. 'I'm going to tell Sally about her daddy and then tonight when I've put them to bed maybe you and I can share some more of that bottle of whisky.' She walked into the kitchen, head high.

~

'IT'S SO BLOODY SAD. My Brian barely even knew our Brenda. She was born the day war was declared; 5th September. Brian left for his ship two weeks later. We used to say she was his goodbye gift to me. Now she'll never get to know her dad.' Pauline plucked at the sleeve of her cardigan, gathering up bobbles of wool fluff.

'How did Sally take the news?'

'Cried her little eyes out. But ten minutes later she had her head in a book. I don't think it's sunk in. She's got used to him not being around. I think she cried more because she knew I was upset, even though I tried not to show it. Put on a brave face. You'd have been proud of me.' She gave Gwen a wry smile.

'I'm beginning to think it's better not to smother one's emotions,' Gwen said. 'Remember what you told me when you talked to me about losing my baby? Better not to bottle things up, you said.'

'Oh I did, did I? Giving out advice freely as usual. I'm sorry. And I barely even knew you.' Pauline sighed. 'Any chance of another tot of scotch?' She held out her glass.

When Gwen had replenished their glasses, Pauline sipped her whisky and said, 'I met him when I was fourteen and had my eye on him right away. He asked me out when I was sixteen. He was an apprentice then – two years older than me. Ever so handsome. Once we started courting neither of us looked at anyone else.

'Course my old man wasn't keen on him at first. Thought I'd be better off with an office clerk. Someone who didn't get his hands dirty in a factory. He wanted me to better myself, what with me working in Bobby's then.'

'I didn't know you worked there,' said Gwen. 'You might have served me – which department?'

'I wasn't on the counters. I worked in accounts. I was good at arithmetic at school. I think Dad rather hoped I'd catch the eye of one of the managers or accountants there, but once he got to know Brian he came round. Everyone loved my Brian.' She sighed again. 'Specially me.' The emotion sounded in her voice and she turned away, pretending to cough, but Gwen wasn't fooled.

'How long were you married?'

'Ten years. We got wed when I was eighteen. A big do. At Our Lady of Ransom. We're both Catholic, though neither of us have been good about going to Mass, apart from getting the girls christened and the big feast days and that. Mostly to keep my mum happy before she and my dad died.' She got up and walked across the room then came back and flung herself back down on the sofa. 'I loved him to bits. Brian was special. He was a one-off. There'll never be anyone else like him. I'll have to find someone else but I'll never be able to love them like him.'

Gwen looked at her in surprise. 'Why will you have to remarry?'

'I can't have my girls growing up without a father. And how would we manage financially? I don't mean right now – I can't even bear to think about another man yet, but in time. Besides, I'm not the type to be a widow. I like to have someone to look after, fuss over. But whoever it is will always be a poor second to my Brian.'

She sipped her whisky and leaned back in the chair looking up at the ceiling. 'But one thing's clear. I'm not getting hitched to anyone in the services. I can't go through this again. I'll have to wait till the bloody war's over. We're never going to win though. Bloody Hitler's going to get us in the end. And I hope it's sooner rather than later now. I can't take much more of this.'

Gwen gasped. 'You don't mean that, Pauline. You don't actually believe we'll lose the war? Not after all this?'

'I'm sick and tired of it. I think lots of people are. There's only so much we can take.'

'But all the sacrifices we've made? All the men like Brian who've given up their lives? You can't want that to be in vain?'

'My Brenda's never known anything except wartime. I want her to have a normal life. A proper childhood. Not quake in terror when she hears the sirens going. Sally's old enough to remember what it was like to have her dad sat at the end of the table eating his tea every evening, and what it was like to be able to play in the street without being afraid a German pilot's going to blow her to bits. No, I want it to be over, even if it does mean we have to be under the rule of Adolf Bloody Hitler. It can't be worse than this.'

Gwen realised Pauline's defeatism owed more to bereavement than to a genuine conviction that the war would be lost. 'I think you should try to get some sleep now, Pauline. You must be shattered.'

'That's an understatement. I expect I'll cry myself to sleep tonight. But then that's it. Over. Got to get on with it. I'm no different from thousands of others who've lost their husbands in this war.

'It's my girls that'll keep me going. You can't give in to grief when you've kiddies to bring up. If it weren't for them I don't know what I'd do. I'd probably wait for the next air raid and stand in the middle of Terminus Road and let the blasted Jerries machine gun me.' She gave a dry laugh. 'Though knowing my luck, they'd miss.'

Gwen stretched out a hand and squeezed Pauline's. When Pauline had gone, she sat on, nursing her whisky in the gloom and listening to the ticking of the clock.

A LETTER FROM ALDERSHOT

TO ALDERSHOT

he handwriting was unfamiliar, but the postmark was Aldershot. Wondering who might be writing to him from there now that the regiment had transferred to Sussex, Jim opened the envelope. Flicking the page over to see the signature, he was surprised to see it was from Ethel.

Dear Jim

I hope this will reach you. They told me to write care of your regiment and it would find you.

I thought you ought to know that Joan is back in Aldershot and living again at her mum's. She has left the ATS. Can't go into the reasons why in a letter and anyway it's not my place to tell you and she'd murder me if she knew I was writing to you. The thing is she heard this morning that Pete was killed in the western desert. I think you should get in touch with her. I can't say any more.

With kindest wishes

Ethel

THAT WAS IT. A few short lines penned in a schoolgirlish handwriting. Jim screwed the paper into a ball and hurled it at the waste basket. If Joan thought he was going to drop everything and chase after her now that she was free, he wasn't going to do it. Then he realised he was being uncharitable. It wasn't Joan who was asking him. And the poor woman was probably beside herself with grief over her man getting killed. Spare a thought for poor Pete too. Jim had never met the man but couldn't help but feel sorry for a fellow who had copped it out in the desert, so far from home. He'd seen the newsreels and he didn't envy those buggers stuck there in the blistering heat.

Jim lay back on the bed. Joan hadn't entered his thoughts in months. He hadn't allowed himself to think about her. There was no point mooning over a woman who was going to marry another man. When he thought of her he felt ashamed at what had happened between them. It had been so pointless, desperate even, seeking comfort in sex to avoid being cold. He'd assumed Joan was a good-time girl, ready to jump into bed with anyone who took her fancy but set on marrying her fiancé.

What if she wasn't the woman he thought she had been? Could she have been a virgin after all? But why then would she have let him make love to her? It didn't make sense. But then nothing made sense to him any more.

He swung his legs over the side of the bed and went to retrieve Ethel's letter from the basket. Reading it again he wondered why she had written it. Why had she been so vague about Joan leaving the ATS? No, not vague, deliberately enigmatic. And how would she have been able to get out? Conscription for unmarried women under thirty had been in force since the end of 1941, so the army wouldn't have let her go. Unless she'd done something wrong that justified her dismissal? But in that case surely she would have been punished not discharged. If it was something really bad she wouldn't be back home in Aldershot, but banged up in prison awaiting trial. For God's sake, Jim, stop inventing things. Ridiculous things! If he wanted to know what happened he'd have to ask her. But why would he want to know?

~

TWO DAYS later Jim set off for Aldershot, having secured a day's leave and a travel warrant.

The train pulled into Aldershot on time. Jim never ceased to marvel at the efficiency of the British railway system. The trains may have been tiny compared with the behemoths they had back in Canada, but they ran on time and they were a darn sight faster. When the express trains whistled past without stopping at a station they practically sucked you off the platform. And the high pitched whistles the station staff blew to announce the departure of a train were piercing – like having a dentist drill through your skull. But Jim acknowledged, as did most of his countrymen, the British knew how to run a railway. It augured well for their management of the war – although as Jim had never been on a German railway he wasn't well placed to judge.

He walked from the station to the street where Joan lived with her mother and stepfather. He was nervous approaching the house and prayed that her mother wouldn't be the one to answer the door. He wanted to talk to Joan alone. For a moment he contemplated calling on Ethel first and getting her to arrange the meeting but rejected that idea as being too formal and organised. He wanted Joan to believe that this was a casual thing, that he happened to be in Aldershot and thought he would drop by.

In fact, Jim still didn't know what he was doing here in

the town. Why had he allowed himself to waste a precious twenty-four hours of leave to high tail it across southern England to see Joan Kelly? He tried to convince himself it was to make sure she hadn't done something terrible to get thrown out of the army, that he wanted to pass his condolences onto her at the loss of her fiancé, but his real reason was to find out whether she would behave differently towards him now that Pete was no longer in her life.

Outside the house he hesitated, the nervous feeling that Joan always raised in him coming to the fore again. He knocked and waited, fists squeezed inside his pockets, unaccountably nervous. There was no response from inside and he was about to turn away and head back to the station when he heard a sound behind the door. A narrow crack opened.

'I thought you lot had all left town long ago,' said Joan from behind the door. 'What do you want, Jim?'

'I came to see you. I've got a day pass.'

'You should have better things to do with your time off.' She started to close the door.

Jim caught the edge with his hand and felt her pushing hard against it. 'Come on, Joan. Don't be silly. Open the door. I've come all this way to see you.'

All he could see was half of her face and he could feel the weight of her body against the door.

'Well, you've seen me now. So bugger off.' Her eyes looked puffy as though she had been crying.

'I heard what happened to Pete. I'm sorry.'

'No, you're not. You can't be. You never even met him.' There was a catch in her voice and Jim was afraid she was about to cry.

'No, but I'm sorry for you. And sorry the poor guy didn't make it. It's too bad.'

'Please. Go away, Jim. Go back to the seaside and carry on

playing soldiers with your friends and leave me be. Now take your hand off my door before I slam it on your fingers.'

He took his hand away. 'Joan…' But she had already shut the door.

Jim walked back to the station, uncertain whether he was relieved that he had got it over with and wouldn't have to think about Joan any more, or disappointed that she had been so cold to him.

On the way back to Eastbourne, he puzzled over what had happened. He sat in the draughty train, trying to figure out why she had refused to talk to him, and why Ethel had hinted that he should get in touch with Joan, when it was so evident that she wanted nothing more to do with him. He would never understand women.

As the train made its way on the home stretch between Lewes and Eastbourne his thoughts drifted to Gwen Colling-wood. She was undeniably cold, aloof and distant, and yet when he was near her there was an electric current passing between them. She was older, married, out of bounds, but he couldn't help imagining what it would be like to break through that icy exterior to the woman underneath. Why was he always attracted to women who wanted nothing to do with him?

SHARING A CONFIDENCE

EASTBOURNE

*G*wen had become friendly with one of the Wrens in the typing pool. Vicky Freeman was, like Gwen, married with her husband overseas. He was an officer, serving in Africa with the Grenadier Guards.

One afternoon they were sitting in the sunshine on the grass of the College cricket pitch, abandoned by the schoolboys, still used for the occasional match between servicemen stationed here, but today deserted. They finished their fish paste sandwiches and lay back on the grass to soak up some sunshine and enjoy what was left of their lunch break.

Vicky sat up, squinting against the sun. 'How long has your husband been gone? What do you do now he's away? You know, for you know what.'

Gwen felt herself blushing. 'Two years, and if you mean what I think you mean, I don't do anything.'

'Really?' Vicky lay back on the ground. 'But you must miss it, surely.'

'I miss *him*.'

'Come on, Gwen. Don't be coy. You must miss *it* as well?'

I suppose so,' she said, embarrassed to say that she had

never liked *it* that much. Was she the only married woman who didn't enjoy that aspect of marriage? 'What about you? What do you do?' she asked, curious.

'I have a lodger. He's married too. Wife and kids are up in Scotland. He's an engineer, seconded here for the duration to oversee reconstruction after bomb damage. Mostly gas mains and stuff like that.'

'You mean… you and he…?'

'Yes. We live as man and wife. It's an arrangement that works for both of us.' Vicky's tone was matter of fact.

'Do you love him?' Gwen sat up, her legs curled under her, fascinated.

'Yes, I do actually. But I love my husband too. And Eric – he's the engineer – loves his wife. We both know we're only together while the war lasts. But who knows how long that will be? Live in the moment, Gwen, that's my philosophy. When it's all over, Eric will go home to Scotland and Gerald will come home to me, God willing.'

'But don't you feel bad? Guilty? It may be wartime, but it's still adultery.'

'No, I don't feel bad. In my opinion when we're living with the possibility of dying at any moment, all the rules change. Eric's wife doesn't know and what she doesn't know can't hurt her. Eric will return as devoted as ever and she'll be none the wiser – Scotland's far enough away.'

'And Gerald?'

'Gerald knows.'

Gwen gasped. 'How did he find out?'

Vicky rolled onto her side and faced Gwen. 'I told him. We have no secrets. We love each other and that means we trust each other.'

'But what did he say when you told him?' Gwen was incredulous.

'He said he was happy I had someone to watch over me.

He says he can sleep easier knowing I'm not alone in the house and I have someone to care for me. He knows how much I love him and I know he loves me. But we both know we could be dead tomorrow so isn't it better that we grab a bit of happiness? I wouldn't begrudge him that and he certainly doesn't me.'

'Gosh,' said Gwen, stunned.

'I don't like to admit it, with everyone going about behaving like Mrs Miniver, but the war terrifies me. I couldn't sleep for fear of the invasion happening while I was in bed and since the air raids began I spend my life in abject terror.'

'I'd never have guessed that,' said Gwen. 'You always seem so confident.'

'I hide it well. But until Eric came into my life I was desperately lonely. I had no one to turn to and I was a blubbering wreck. A big lonely scaredy-cat! Eric is my rock and I love him dearly.'

'I see.'

'What about your husband?' Vicky rolled onto her stomach. 'Wouldn't he feel the way Gerald does? Wanting you to be happy? Wanting you to be safe?'

'Yes, of course he would want me to be happy and safe. But would he want me to be living as the wife of another man? I very much doubt it.'

'He's the jealous type, is he?'

Gwen frowned. 'I wouldn't say that, but that's because he's never had cause to be jealous. I've never given him cause.'

'If anyone laid a finger on me while Gerald was around he'd probably have flattened them, but this is different. War makes everything different.'

Gwen thought of Jim Armstrong and how she had longed to kiss him. The desire she had felt for him was so intense that she was afraid if she gave rein to it she would never be able to stop herself. Maybe that meant she didn't really love Roger? But she knew that wasn't true. She loved him very much. But had she ever desired Roger? The question was more had she ever allowed herself to desire Roger?

'You look worried. I hope I haven't offended you,' said Vicky.

'No. You've made me think.'

Vicky laughed. 'Oh dear. Have I put ideas in your head?'

'It's just that... I don't know how to explain.'

'Spit it out. My lips are sealed.'

'I was wondering... is it possible that the war can change you?'

Vicky smiled. 'A better question would be is it possible that you can get through this war without being changed! By the time we come out the other end we'll all be different people. Life's so intense. I can't even recognise the person I was before. If you'd told me in '39 I'd be living in sin with another man I'd have laughed my socks off. If you'd told me I'd be working! And in a typing pool.'

'I think the war has changed me. Back in '39 I'd never even have had a conversation like this. I'd have cut you off before you got started. I wouldn't even have lain on my back on the grass like this. Far too undignified.'

Vicky grinned. 'You and me both. Hell, I was even presented at court. It was another world.'

'Do you think it's bad of me to like this world better? Is it terrible of me? With so many people getting killed. Lives disrupted. But do you know, Vicky, I don't think I've ever felt so alive.'

'Me too.'

'Yet after that terrible night raid on Tuesday, how can I possibly justify feeling this way? The whole town took such a pounding.'

'But that's exactly what I mean, Gwen. Live for the moment because you may not even wake up tomorrow morning. I know if I cop it in an air raid I'd rather be lying in Eric's arms than shivering alone in my bed – and Gerald thinks so too.'

Before Gwen could reply, the scream of the sirens cut into the peace of the afternoon and they ran for the shelter, Vicky clutching Gwen's arm.

DIEPPE

19TH AUGUST 1942, EASTBOURNE

*J*im woke early, dressed and made his way to the kitchen to make a cup of tea.

As he waited for the kettle to boil he stood in front of the window, hoping the whistle of the kettle wouldn't waken Pauline or the children whose bedroom was next door to the kitchen in the lower ground floor of the house.

Dawn was breaking and the sea lay below a white sky like a smudged grey fingerprint. He was surprised to hear the sound of aircraft so early in the morning. Something was afoot. The Germans rarely bombed the town in the early hours, preferring broad daylight or the occasional night raid under a full moon. He opened the back door and stepped onto the terrace to look up at the sky. It was spattered with aeroplanes heading south over the Channel.

Had it started? The mythical second front? Jim forgot his tea and rushed from the house, heading for company headquarters. Something was definitely afoot. It would explain why so many units had been moved out of Eastbourne in the past days including most of his own company. Jim's unit was among the minority who had been held back, his commanding officer telling him that their current work took priority. Jim would continue at the listening post and until further notice would be reporting directly to the British, under RAF Sergeant Carrington.

He began to run, anger bubbling up inside him. All this time stuck in Britain and now, as finally Canada was to see action, he was going to miss out.

On the road he ran into his friend Scotty McDermott, now a motorcycle dispatch rider and also staying behind. More aircraft screamed overhead and Scotty had to shout to be heard, 'It's started without us. Bloody typical. The second front.'

'You're kidding?'

'I had to ride to Portsmouth yesterday. Just got back. There was a ton of men from the Second Division piling onto ships. Lucky bastards.'

Jim shook his head. 'Do you think we'll be following soon?'

Scotty shrugged. 'I sure hope so. As long as the bastards don't surrender before we get over there.' He gunned his motorcycle into life then shouted over his shoulder, 'Your brother was there. Saw him boarding.'

Jim spent the rest of the morning hanging around the mess, hoping for news. He wasn't due to be on duty at the signalling post until later that day. All morning his fellow soldiers were speculating about the action they were missing in France, while overhead the sky was dense with planes. At midday the Regimental Sergeant Major burst into the room and called a roster of men, Jim included, who were to be in full fighting order ready to get onto a waiting truck within the hour. Jim and those colleagues who'd been selected grinned with delight. At last. This was it.

The truck screamed out of the battalion headquarters and headed west from the town. 'Where we going, Sarge?' someone called out.

The RSM barked out of the side of his mouth, 'Port of Newhaven.'

A cheer went up in the truck at the word port. It meant sailing. France. Invasion. Jim wished he'd had a chance to say goodbye to Gwen. She'd have no idea where he had gone. Then he realised she'd find out soon enough once news of the invasion of France took hold. It was probably better this way. He'd be back. He knew he would.

The men were all in a state of high excitement. As they rattled along the road, they were part of a steady flow of vehicles – mostly trucks and ambulances – all speeding towards the Channel port.

Their vehicle arrived at Newhaven and parked up. Ships and landing craft were arriving and unloading men, the majority of them wounded. The realisation dawned on Jim that the war games were over and this was it – real war where soldiers got wounded, captured and died, where battles were won and lost. He looked at Mitch and Gordon. They were silent: it seemed the same thought was striking the whole unit.

The RSM got down from the lorry and headed over to a building on the dockside. The men waited in silence, overcome by excitement and anxiety. Eventually he reappeared.

'Everybody off.' He handed round clipboards. 'In pairs. One write names down, one check tags. You need to list every man returning. Get their names and make sure you double-check the tags too. Alive or dead.'

'Aren't we going over there, Sarge?' One of the soldiers jerked his head towards the horizon, where the dark grey sea met a paler grey sky, striated with drifting smoke. They could hear the distant sound of battle coming across the water from the French coast some sixty-five miles away. 'Aren't we part of the second front?'

'There is no second front. Just a commando raid this morning on the town of Dieppe. All over now.'

As he spoke, a landing craft disembarked its load of passengers – a ragtag band of weary men who looked shell-shocked, their faces blackened and bloodied and their eyes vacant. Another craft disgorged more of the same, along with a small band of German prisoners with their hands up. But this was all a prelude – what followed was boat after boat of casualties, the overwhelming majority in the uniform of the Canadian army. Jim looked out to sea where there was a queue of vessels, large and small, waiting to dock and discharge their human cargo.

Jim and his comrades moved forward to meet them. The arriving men were filthy, uniforms torn, faces bloody. Some had limbs missing. Eyes were vacant or closed, shutting out the memory of the horror they had witnessed.

One of the walking wounded was a man Jim knew from Aldershot. He stumbled towards Jim, grabbing his battledress as he said, 'We were massacred, Armstrong. They were expecting us. Sons of bitches knew we were coming. We were mown down like skittles.' His voice was shaking and his eyes were wild. 'A disaster. A goddam disaster. They sent us in like lambs to the slaughter.'

What to say? Words were inadequate. Jim nodded and wrote the soldier's name on his clipboard, then watched the man stagger over to the Red Cross lorries. He turned around to identify the next man.

The stream of dead, wounded and dying continued all day. Man after man, grateful to have survived, but harrowed by what they had witnessed. The realisation that this was not just a routine battle but a complete routing of Canadian infantry by the enemy descended on the men as the day progressed. Jim's disappointment that morning at missing out, gave way to relief. Anger too. At what the enemy had done, but most of all that so many men had been sent on a raid that was clearly ill-prepared and miscalculated.

Jim was exhausted but his tiredness was nothing in comparison to what these troops had been through. As the evening descended, the queue of ships diminished. Jim moved forward as the last craft moored. This vessel carried a payload made up almost entirely of dead men. He worked side-by-side with Mitch, lifting the bodies onto stretchers, placing them in line on the dockside, to be carried away on trucks after they had checked their dog tags and listed them on their clipboards. He recognised several faces. Men he had last seen playing darts in an Aldershot pub, crawling through undergrowth in camouflage, or joining in a singalong in The Ship.

He didn't recognise Walt at first. His brother's face had been partly blown away by shellfire, but his body was intact and the name on his tag left no doubt. Disbelieving, Jim stood beside the body, staring at Walt's broken features, trying to recognise the brother he had grown up with, loved, and recently done all he could to avoid. He'd told himself many times he hated the sight of Walt. He'd even wished him dead. As he looked at him now all he could feel was a terrible sadness, an emptiness and utter disbelief.

His emotions ricocheted back and forth between anger that Walt had got them both into this war in the first place and had now turned Alice into a grieving widow with a fatherless child, and sorrow that their brotherly love had been destroyed and even in death could not be resurrected. Intertwined with this was guilt. If Jim hadn't joined up, Walt wouldn't have done. It should have been he who had been slaughtered on that French beach. He closed his eyes, trying to invoke the memory of the little brother he had loved. The boy he'd fished with in the creek, the grinning, happy-go-lucky youth he had once been. But all he could see was the horror of Walt's damaged face.

In the lorry back to Eastbourne that night, he thought of his mother and father. Helga would be distraught, but she had an inner steel that would see her through this. He was less sure about his father. Donald Armstrong had been reso-lutely opposed to either of his sons going to war, fearful that what had happened to so many of his friends in the Great War would happen to them. Jim knew he had to write to his parents but could think of no way to lessen their pain.

He didn't want to think about Alice – how she would be getting a telegram to break the news that the child she was carrying would never know its father.

A few days later, sitting in the Tivoli picture house, Jim watched the newsreel report on the Dieppe raid. The casual-ties had been devastating – around nine hundred Canadians killed and two thousand taken prisoner. Yet the news report was upbeat. The raid was portrayed as a kind of victory, with the emphasis on the courage and fortitude of Britain's plucky Canadian allies. What would prove to have been the blood-iest day in Canadian military history was described as a successful dress rehearsal for future action against Nazi Germany. Jim bristled with anger. Nine hundred men and his brother had staggered up that beach to be butchered in a barrage of artillery fire on what could more truthfully be described as a suicide mission.

∼

JIM WAS SITTING on the garden wall, above the terrace. Today it was deserted, as Pauline had taken her children to visit her grandmother and he presumed Gwen was at her work in the military headquarters. He was so deep in thought that he didn't hear Gwen come up behind him. She laid her hand on the small of his back.

'I heard from Pauline about your brother, Jim. I'm sorry.'

He turned to look at her, then looked away again.

'We quarrelled.'

'Yes. You told me, about Alice.'

'Not just over Alice. We fell out about his wanting to go back to Canada. He asked me to help him make the case but I wouldn't help. The last time we spoke I told him to get lost.'

She placed a hand over his. 'It wouldn't have made any difference. They would never have allowed him to go home when he'd signed for the duration.'

'Maybe not, but I could have tried to help him figure out a way to get discharged.'

'You're too hard on yourself, Jim. You couldn't be expected to live your brother's life for him. And you need to stop beating yourself up. It's not your fault he's dead.'

'I didn't say that.'

'You didn't have to.'

He turned towards her and saw that her eyes were wet. He moved closer, his heart thumping. They stared into each other's eyes and he knew he was going to kiss her and that she wanted him to.

Then the kitchen door burst open and Sally Simmonds ran onto the terrace. 'I've got a lollypop!' she cried. 'But Mummy says I can't have it 'til after tea. I don't think I can wait. Come and tell her I can have it now, Aunty Gwen.'

Gwen, her face flushed, moved towards the little girl and bent over her, stroking her cheek. 'But Aunty Gwen agrees with Mummy,' she said. 'Lollipops always taste better after tea.'

Sally looked dubious but went back into the house. 'Can I have my tea now, Mummy,' she called as went inside.

The spell broken, Gwen followed her, turning to give Jim a sad smile as she went indoors.

TOGETHER

EASTBOURNE

*J*im was alone, reading a book, when Gwen came into the drawing room. Pauline had gone to spend the night at her grandmother's bedside, as the old lady was seriously ill, possibly close to death. The other Canadians were drinking in The Ship. Jim had said he'd follow them down there but was showing little inclination to do so.

'Fast asleep. Both of them,' said Gwen and sat down at the opposite end of the sofa. 'They are such good children. I love having them here in the house.'

'They're cute kids.' Jim put down his book.

There was a silence for a few minutes, then Jim said, 'Did you never want children yourself?' Then when Gwen turned her face away, he realised he had wandered into dangerous territory. 'I'm sorry. I'm always putting my big feet in it.'

Gwen sighed, then said, 'I tried for years to have a child. Month after miserable month, waiting and hoping and praying, but deep inside believing it would never happen. Can you imagine what that does to you?'

He held her eyes.

Gwen looked away, staring into the middle distance. 'Other people having babies with no effort. One after another.' She pulled the sleeves of her cardigan down over her hands. 'You start to believe it's your own fault. That you must have done something bad. That it's a punishment. I'd been responsible for my brother's death so how could I be trusted to bring another child into the world?'

Jim remained silent, still watching her face. Her mouth straightened and she pinched her lips in, then her hand moved to smooth down her skirt. She took a deep breath and turned to look at him again. 'I even thought it was my own body rejecting, refusing, blocking the possibility of a baby.'

'Don't blame yourself. There are millions of couples who can't have babies. And you were a child when your brother died. It was an accident.'

'You think it's self-pity, don't you?' She looked at him, her eyes sad.

'I never said that. Quite the opposite. You need to cut yourself some slack, Gwen.'

She took a deep breath and told him about the baby she lost when Roger was in Geneva. Jim listened intently, then said, 'Why did you never talk to him about what happened and how you felt? Didn't he have a right to know?'

'Of course he did,' she snapped. 'But what could he have done?'

'Understood what you were going through for a start. Did he never even mention the subject of you having children?'

Gwen sighed and said, 'Yes. Early on when we thought it would be easy. Then when it didn't happen Roger wanted us to go together to the doctor, but I would have hated that. Too embarrassing. I was brought up to keep things private, to take what life dealt and get on with it without complaining. And it seemed easier not to talk about it.'

She got up and moved over to the window, resting her

hands palm-down on the ledge. 'It was always there though. A dark shadow between us. I think he was as scared as I was to bring it up. He didn't want to seem as though he was disappointed; he didn't want to upset me. When there's something like that – a blockage – it becomes impossible to break through it. Unmentionable, but always there between us.'

Gwen looked so alone and so vulnerable standing there by the window. Jim got up and went to stand beside her.

'I don't know why I'm telling you all this. Maybe you should be a priest. I feel like I've been to confession.' Her smile was rueful.

'I don't feel like a priest,' he said, struggling with the desire to take her in his arms.

As though sensing what he was thinking, she moved away and sat down again on the sofa. 'I used to think I was cursed. If I let anyone get close to me something would happen to them. I used to sit here in this room, when Roger was at work, thinking about how to kill myself. Everything seemed so pointless. I didn't want to go on. I was looking for the right time but the right time didn't come. Then, since the war, I've realised that death is close to everyone. It's everywhere. It's indiscriminate. Now that it feels much harder to hold onto life, I want to go on living. Does that sound mad?'

Jim shook his head. 'I know what you mean. When I left Canada I wanted to go to war and never come back. The idea of dying as a hero appealed to me. I thought everyone would be sorry and that it would be some kind of vindication of what had happened to me. But I've not been near the enemy and wonder if I ever will. And the longer it is, the harder it's going to be if I do get my chance. I even wonder if I'm up to it. It's one thing to run over the Downs with a heavy pack on your back and another when it's real.' He leaned back against the windowsill, his eyes fixed on her. 'When my brother died in the Dieppe raid it made me question what I was doing. As well as Walt there were men I'd known at school who lost their lives in that operation. They probably started out full of hope and idealism. I never had either. Just a need to escape and find oblivion.'

'You don't feel that way now?'

'No. Like you, I don't want to die any more.'

Gwen got up and walked over to the sideboard and poured them each a whisky.

'This is getting to be a habit,' she said, as she chinked glasses with him. 'How was your trip to Aldershot the other week? I was surprised you wanted to go back there. All you Canadians seem to hate the place.' She narrowed her eyes and smiled at him. 'Did you have an ulterior motive for going?' She leant against the mantelpiece, sipping her scotch.

'Am I that transparent?' he said. 'If I had a motive it was a misguided one. I was on a fool's mission.'

She nodded. 'Go on.'

'There was this woman.'

Gwen smiled. 'There's always a woman.'

'It wasn't like that. At least not really. She was the cousin of my pal's girl. Grass, Greg I mean – Grass was his nickname – used to drag me along to keep the cousin occupied while he and his girl, Ethel, were dating. Then Grass died. Brain haemorrhage. Anyway, Joan was engaged to another fellow who was off with the Eighth army in North Africa.'

'What's she like, this girl you were babysitting?'

'A real puzzle. I never knew where I was with her. And anyway she isn't my type.'

'What is your type? – no don't tell me – beautiful, warm, calm, blonde and preferably called Alice.' She smiled.

'I suppose I asked for that. No, Joan is about as different from Alice as you could imagine. She's tough. She's unpredictable. She's... well as I said, you never know where you are with her.'

'So you're drawn to her?'

Jim took a glug of whisky. 'Hell, I don't know. I don't know what I feel about anything any more.'

'So why did you go and see her?'

'Her cousin wrote to me to say that Joan's left the army and her fiancé has been killed. I wanted to offer her my condolences.'

Gwen raised her eyebrows.

'What?' he said, defensive.

Gwen ignored him. 'Why did she leave the army?'

'That's what I wanted to find out.'

'And?'

'She wouldn't see me. Wouldn't even open the door more than a crack. Told me to bugger off and stay away.'

'That's an extreme reaction for someone who was engaged to another man and was just a casual friend. Are you sure there isn't more to this story?'

Jim drained his glass. He looked down then raised his eyes to meet hers. 'Something happened. It was an accident. We ended up in bed together.'

'When you went there the other day?'

He laughed. 'No. Months ago. Before I was stationed here.' He told her about the trip to London and how they'd ended up sharing a room. 'It was freezing. She got in with me to get warm. We found ourselves... you know... we were half asleep. Neither of us meant for it to happen.' He ran his hands through his hair, embarrassed.

'I see.'

'It was a bit of a fumble. I don't remember much about it. It was awkward next morning. She made it clear it wasn't ever going to happen again. She didn't want to cheat on the guy she was engaged to marry.'

'And what about you? What did you want?'

Jim put his head in his hands. 'I don't know. I don't know anything any more. When I was with her I thought... but then I've barely thought of her since.'

He sighed then said, 'No. That's not true. I have thought of her. But I didn't want to. She was out of bounds. And as I said, not my type.'

'And you never found out why she left the ATS?'

'Joan is one of those people who spell trouble. I expect she got into some kind of disciplinary thing and they threw her out of the army. That wouldn't surprise me. She didn't like military life. Hated it in fact.'

They lapsed into silence for a few moments. 'Do you have a cigarette?' said Gwen.

'I don't smoke.'

'You must be the only soldier in the entire allied forces who doesn't. I don't either but I have a sudden desire for one.'

Gwen got up and walked over to a table in the corner. She turned back and looked at him, smiling. 'Pauline smokes like a chimney and leaves packs all over the house – thanks to the generosity of your colleagues. Here we are.'

She took a cigarette and lit it, breathing the smoke out slowly. After a second puff she stubbed it into the ashtray. 'I don't know why I did that. I don't like the taste. The idea was better than the reality.'

'Like a lot of things.' He looked at her, keeping his eyes fixed on hers.

'Not everything,' she said. She moved over to stand in front of him. Jim reached up and pulled her down beside him. For a long moment that felt like a slow beautiful torture they looked into each other's eyes and then at last their mouths met.

All the anger, confusion and frustration that had characterised Jim's recent life exploded in that moment. He was overcome with a desire for this woman that swept over him like a tidal wave. He held her tighter, drinking in the sensation of her lips on his. She sat on his lap, her arms around his neck, her mouth hungry. Surfacing from the kiss she whispered, 'Some things are even better in reality.'

Jim loosened his tie, flinging it onto the sofa beside him and began to lift her blouse up.

'Not here,' she said. 'Come to bed.' She took his hand and led him from the room.

～

THE NEXT MORNING, Jim woke before Gwen and lay on his side watching her sleeping. She was so beautiful. Her face had a calm and a peace that it lacked when she was awake, when she was usually frowning and with a worried expression. Their lovemaking had been a revelation. The buttoned-up stiffness of the woman who had all her emotions under control – or who preferred to behave as though she had no emotions at all – had been replaced by an abandon that had surprised and delighted him. It was as if Jim had unleashed a genie from a bottle.

He traced the soft arch of her eyebrow with a finger then ran it down the length of her nose. He felt her stir slightly in her sleep, then she opened her eyes. For a moment it was as if she were questioning where she was and who he was, then her frown dissolved into a smile.

Jim bent down and kissed her slowly. 'Good morning,' he said.

'What time is it?'

'Only six o'clock. We have plenty of time,' he said, kissing her again.

'I had no idea, you know.'

'No idea about what?'

'That it could be like that.'

'Like what?' he said, moving his hands to her breasts. 'Like that?' He stroked her skin. 'Or like that?'

'Like everything.' She was smiling, then closed her eyes and gave a little gasp as his fingers moved over her body. 'I always thought I wasn't any good at making love. That I didn't even like it.'

Jim continued to touch her. 'Oh Gwen, you're very good at it. And unless I'm much mistaken, you like it very much.'

THE MINE

DECEMBER 1942, EASTBOURNE

*G*wen sat in the bath, shivering. The water had been hot when she got in but, when there was only five inches of it, the result was a hot bottom and reddened legs while the rest of her body was exposed to the chill of the unheated bathroom. She bent her knees and tried to submerge her top half, keeping her head up. It was no good. Her breasts were above the water, like two small hillocks, the skin dimpled with goose bumps. No matter what position she was in, part of her was exposed to the cold air. The only thing to do was to wash as quickly as possible.

She picked up her flannel and began to soap herself. As she moved the wet cloth over her skin, she imagined that it was Jim's hands. She shivered again, remembering how it felt to have his hands move on her body, his bare skin against her skin. Her cheeks burned and she closed her eyes.

Gwen had never expected to feel this way, never imagined that her body could respond to another's like that, never believed that she would know such pleasure. With Jim she behaved with a wantonness that shocked her. Something had been loosened inside her. When they were together she felt she was melting away, losing her boundaries, losing herself in him.

~

THE WIND WAS bitter as Gwen walked down King Edward's Parade towards the town. She had forgotten her gloves and so stuffed her hands inside her pockets. Once upon a time she would never have dreamed of doing that as it spoiled the line of a good coat and stretched the fabric out of shape, but she no longer gave a damn about such things. War changed everything. The familiar walk along the seafront took her past hotels that were boarded up, or housed airmen and soldiers where once they had welcomed holidaying families. Gun emplacements were on the hotel roofs, metal fencing and barbed wire closed off the beaches. In front of her the Cavendish Hotel had lost its east wing back in May, leaving a gaping space where she and Daphne had once stood side-by-side powdering their noses and talking about the inscription on her powder compact. A line from a poem by Yeats drifted through her mind: 'All changed, changed utterly: A terrible beauty is born.' Yes, it was all changed utterly, but there was no beauty, terrible or otherwise. On this dull wintry day it was desolate, bleak, grey.

Gwen was about to turn back when she saw a commotion in front of her. The promenade in front of the pier was crowded. People were being moved back by the police. More police were on the pier, and she could see others in a rowing boat underneath it.

'What's going on?' she asked a policeman at the edge of the crowd.

'Someone's spotted a mine floating towards the pier. But there's nothing to see and nothing to worry about, Madam. It's one of ours.'

Gwen gave a dry laugh. 'That's all right then. I presume it's some kind of intelligent mine that only explodes near Germans?'

The policeman failed to register her sarcasm and shook his head. 'As it happens, Madam, it is fitted with a safety device that prevents it from exploding at all if it breaks loose, as it evidently has. It's tied to the pier now so it'll be quite safe.' He turned to the small crowd. 'Move along now, people. Nothing to see. It's not an enemy mine. Show's over.'

Gwen walked off, heading to Bobby's to buy some hair ribbons to give Sally on her upcoming birthday. The department store was quiet. Everywhere in the town was quiet these days. At least during the day. In the evenings the streets were full of Canadian soldiers moving between the various pubs, heading to the cinema to watch a film or to the Winter Garden to go dancing. Those women still in the town were in great demand at the dances. The idea of being in a big crowd being pawed by a succession of soldiers as they whirled her around the dance floor was not appealing. But then she thought of being swept up in Jim's arms and shivered with excitement at the prospect. She wouldn't want an audience for that though. Her time with Jim was theirs alone.

She made her way slowly up the long hill towards home. As she reached the top, there was a loud dull boom followed by an echo. There'd been no aircraft noise. Gwen spun around to see an enormous column of white water rising vertically into the air around the pier, followed by a second plume of water and smoke. The pier was covered in a cloud of smoke. "One of ours" was evidently one of theirs. It was beginning to get dark so Gwen hurried on, praying that no one had been hurt in the explosion.

When she got back to the house, Jim was waiting for her in the drawing room. She ran into his arms. After they kissed she said, 'Did you hear that explosion about fifteen minutes ago? Down by the pier. It was a German mine. It–'

Jim wasn't paying attention, so she stopped. 'What's the matter?'

'I have to leave Eastbourne. I have to leave you.'

Gwen breathed in slowly, trying to calm her emotions. She swallowed and told herself she wasn't going to cry. At least not while Jim was with her. She took another breath, then said, 'We knew it would happen sooner or later, my love.' Then fear taking hold she added, 'Where?'

'Salisbury Plain. More exercises, I imagine. Who knows, Gwen? I may be back here before long. Or knowing my luck, back to Aldershot Camp.'

'When?' She hoped he wouldn't hear her voice trembling.

'Tomorrow.'

Gwen gasped. 'So soon?'

Jim put his hands on her shoulders to steady her. 'I've just heard. We're being sent to a holding camp.' He paused, then unable to dissemble, he added, 'I don't know how long we'll be there but then I'm pretty certain we'll be sent overseas soon. They haven't said where, but there are rumours it will be somewhere in the Mediterranean. Maybe North Africa. That's where all the action is.'

Gwen's lip trembled. 'I kept hoping it wouldn't happen. I prayed the war would end first and you wouldn't have to see any action.'

He shook his head. 'I've wanted to be involved for so long. I'd have bitten your hand off to go, but now it's happening all I can think about is leaving you.'

'I know.' She leaned her head against his chest.

'I can't tell you what these past few weeks have meant to me.' He stroked a hand down her hair and pulled her closer.

Gwen looked up at him. 'You've taught me to feel. It was as if until I met you I was locked up. You had the key.

You've freed me. You opened my heart.' Her voice was breaking.

Jim tried to speak but she laid a finger on his lips. 'I'm grateful to this bloody awful war for bringing us together,' she murmured. 'We would never have met in other circumstances. Our worlds collided thanks to the war. It's been one short beautiful moment in time and I'll treasure it for ever. I'll hold you in my heart always. I love you. I'll always love you. And you need to know – I've never said that to anyone before.' She brushed his lips with hers.

He sighed. 'I love you too. I hate leaving you, knowing we might never meet again.'

'It's better to accept that we'll never meet again. You'll return to Canada after the war. We each have lives that we'll pick up when it's over. I have no regrets about what happened between us and I never will, Jim, but I've always known it couldn't last forever.'

He closed his eyes in silent acknowledgement of the truth of her words. 'I'll write when I can, when I know where I'll be,' he said.

'No.' Her voice was tremulous and she shivered and eased herself away from his embrace. 'It's better we say goodbye here tomorrow and recognise what it is – a final farewell. Don't let's spoil what's been a perfect time. We have responsibilities and people who need us. You have the farm to take care of – your father will depend on you now your brother's gone. You have to go home and when the war's over Roger will return. And I will be here waiting for him.

'I was an empty shell before the war, before you. Now for the first time I feel alive. I owe you so much.' She put her arms around his neck and buried her head in his chest. 'You've made me terribly happy. You've made me want to live, to go on, even though it has to be without you. Can you understand what I'm saying?'

His hands stroked her hair and he held her tightly and kissed the top of her head. 'Yes. I wish I didn't but I do.'

'I love my husband and I'll never leave him, but it doesn't mean I don't love you and will always love you.' She drew her head back and looked up at him. 'And I think there's a girl in Aldershot who'll want to see you return safely from wherever you're going.'

'What?'

'I have a feeling.' She smiled at him. 'Call it feminine intuition if you like.'

'Joan? Come on. She wants nothing to do with me.'

'You're wrong about that, my darling. I'm certain.'

'Please, Gwen, don't talk about her. She's history. And there was never really anything between us.'

Gwen smiled at him then ran her fingers down his cheek. 'I think there was. My beautiful Jim. God, I'm going to miss you.'

'I haven't gone yet,' he said. 'We have all night so let's make the most of it.' He bent down, kissed her then gathered her into his arms.

PART IV

1943

You have to run risks. There are no certainties in war. There is a precipice on either side of you — a precipice of caution and a precipice of over-daring.

Winston Churchill, 21 September 1943

BACK IN ALDERSHOT

ALDERSHOT 1943

It felt strange to be back at the Aldershot garrison. The place was unchanged, ugly and crowded with soldiers, but the atmosphere was different. The undiluted boredom and the frustration born out of inactivity had been replaced by tension and anticipation. There were familiar faces, acquaintances renewed, absences noted. So many men had died or been captured in the Dieppe raid, and while no one mentioned their absence, everyone felt it. In a matter of days, hours even, they would be embarking on active service themselves at last.

Jim thought of Walt and how his brother had wanted to return to Canada when he found out that he was to have a child. A child who would be more than a year old now. Jim's niece. A child who would never know her father. Not so long ago, he would have considered returning to the farm, seeking a reconciliation with Alice and helping to raise Walt's daughter. Rose – that was her name, Jim's mother had said in her last letter – Rose. A pretty name. But when he thought of Alice it was with a heavy heart. He didn't want to become close to her again. After what had happened between him and Gwen he would never see Alice with the same eyes. The war had also made a difference to that. But there was a risk that if he returned he would be sucked into a role he no longer wanted to play.

What was the alternative? Gwen? Don't be a fool. He'd always known there would never be a future for them. She loved her husband and was not the kind of woman who would walk out on him. He wished she was – but knew that one of the reasons he loved her was that she was an honourable woman. He tried to push her to the back of his mind, but she remained at the front, filling his thoughts.

One thing was clear. Before much longer he and his platoon would be piling onto a ship and sailing off to face the enemy at last. The anticipation in the air was too strong to ignore. Something was up and this time Jim was certain it wasn't going to be a false alarm. Perhaps he would be mowed down by a German machine gun as soon as he faced the elusive enemy – that had been his wish when he joined up, but not any more.

He picked up a comic book that one of the men had left lying on his bunk and flipped through the pages absently. What did the future hold? Life or death? An eventual return to the farm? On the face of it he had open choices, once the war was over, supposing he survived, yet he felt the tug of responsibility. His parents would expect him to return and run the place. His father was getting on and the loss of Walt would have aged him further.

Jim flung the comic down and forced himself to think about Hollowtree Farm. He saw the wheat as it had been the day he left, ripe, yellow and ready for the combine to trawl through it. He remembered the smell: musty, dry, yet with an underlying sweetness, and the way the threshing always made him sneeze. He thought of the little creek where it ran behind the farmhouse, the water clear as crystal and cold as ice. The lowing of the cows in the barn in winter as they nuzzled at the piles of hay. The taste of the cream: golden and rich on the top of the milk, the scent of fresh-baked scones coming out of the range in the kitchen and the taste of them, warm, crumbling and melting with butter. He saw the fire crackling in the grate, sparks jumping as his father laid a fresh log on top and settled down to read the farmers' almanac. As the picture built in his mind it grew more appealing and he realised he couldn't imagine not returning one day. The farm was in his blood and he must acknowledge and embrace it. Going home didn't have to mean taking up with Alice again. He could do the right thing by her and his niece, ensure that they weren't short, but inheriting Walt's responsibilities didn't include any more than that. Alice would have to return with Rose and live at her parents' place. It was out of the question that she should remain at Hollowtree Farm. Besides she'd be entitled to a war widow's pension. Already feeling better, Jim went down to the mess room.

He was playing a game of darts when a soldier he didn't know stuck his head round the door and called, 'Anyone here called Jim Armstrong? There's a pretty gal in civvies looking for him. She's waiting outside.'

The room erupted in whistling – it was a rare event that a townie would venture into the barracks. There were several good-natured cat calls and comments. Jim brushed them off and hurried down the stairs. Could it be Joan, calling a truce?

It was Ethel.

She stood there, looking frail and nervous outside the barrack building. Her anxious expression changed to relief when she saw him.

'Thank goodness you're all right, Jim. I was worried you might have been involved in that raid to France. I know so many of you were.'

Jim clutched his cap in his hands. 'My brother died over there.'

'I'm so sorry.' Ethel's eyes were teary. 'This dreadful war.' She gave him a hug.

'It's good to see you, Ethel. Really good.' He grinned at her.

'The word is that you're going to Italy any day now.'

'How do you know that? They haven't even told us.'

'I've lived in Aldershot all my life. Word gets around. I know people who know people.' She smiled and nodded her head sideways.

They fell into an awkward silence then both started to speak at once, before each conceded to the other. It was Jim who finally spoke. 'How is Joan?'

'She's well. I think you should see her before you go.'

He gave a sardonic laugh. 'Not likely. She all but slammed the door in my face last time I tried to see her. Spoke to me through a crack.'

Ethel drew her lips into a thin line then said, 'She didn't want you to see her like that.'

'Like what?' Jim frowned, puzzled. 'She's not been hurt, has she? What exactly happened, Ethel? Why did she leave the army?'

Ethel laid a hand on his arm. 'I think you should come with me and let her tell you herself. It's not my place.'

'But if she had something to tell me she'd have told me when I called.'

Ethel sighed and said, 'She's proud and she's stubborn.'

'But what…'

'Come and see her now. Please, Jim.' She grabbed at his sleeve.

'Does she know you've come to fetch me?'

She shook her head. 'I told you she's a stubborn woman. You know that, Jim.'

Twenty minutes later they were outside the little terraced house where Joan lived with her mother and stepfather.

'You sure this is a good idea, Ethel? Joan made it pretty clear she wanted nothing more to do with me.'

'Shut up and come in. Door's never locked.' She pushed the door open and Jim followed her into the narrow hallway.

'That you, Ethel? I'm in the back kitchen.' Joan's voice.

Jim felt a little lurch in his stomach. Ethel nodded to him and he followed her into the rear of the little house.

Joan was standing at the back door, looking out into the yard in the same position she had been in all that time ago at the tea party in Ethel's house. As they came into the room, she turned and gasped in surprise.

Jim's surprise was no less. In her arms she was holding a baby, who was feeding at her breast. She jerked her cardigan over her breast and turned away.

Jim was rooted to the spot. He looked at Ethel who said nothing.

Joan said, 'Why have you brought him here? I told you not to, Ethel. I bloody well told you.'

Ethel laid a hand on Jim's arm, gave it a squeeze and slipped out of the room.

Jim stood motionless, his thoughts racing, his mouth unable to form words. He had so many questions, yet he already knew the answers.

Joan continued to stand with her back to him, holding her baby to her breast, as though waiting for him to leave.

Eventually he spoke. 'It's mine, isn't it? That night in London?'

Jim waited, but she remained silent. Suddenly he became impatient. 'For God's sake, Joan. You're one hell of a stubborn woman. I have a right to know.'

She shuddered a long sigh then turned to face him. 'I didn't want you to know. It was a mistake and I take full responsibility for it. I was the one who started it. I have only myself to blame.'

'What the hell are you talking about? It takes two to make a baby. Let me see it.'

'It's not It,' she said, 'He's He. And he has a name.' She paused for a moment and swallowed. 'He's called James, but we call him Jimmy. I named him for you,' she said, unnecessarily.

Jim's heart pounded in his chest. The baby was still buried under Joan's cardigan, sucking at her partially concealed breast.

'You should be sitting down. You might drop him and he must be heavy.'

'So you're an expert in childcare, are you now, Armstrong? And no, he's not heavy at all. He's in a sling under here. I always feed him standing up, otherwise he won't stay on the breast. He wriggles too much.'

As she spoke he saw she was blushing. Jim stood beside her feeling awkward and uncertain as the baby continued to suckle.

'Either get out of here or stick the kettle on if you're staying,' Joan said. 'Tea's in that canister over there. You know how to make a cup of tea, don't you?'

By the time he had made the brew, the baby was asleep and Joan led him to the parlour at the front of the house, where she signalled him to sit on the sofa and then placed the sleeping baby in his arms and went to stand in front of the fireplace, sipping her tea and watching them.

Jim pulled back the shawl that was partially covering Jimmy's face and looked at his son. He ran a finger over the baby's cheek, marvelling at the soft peachy down of his skin, the tiny nose and the delicate rosebud lips.

'Sit him upright. You might have to wind him.'

Jim looked at her helplessly.

'He doesn't often get wind but if he does, you'll need to rub his back until he burps it up – but he looks happy enough.'

'He's beautiful,' said Jim. As he held his son in his arms, feeling the warmth of the little body against him, listening to the little snuffling sounds of the sleeping infant, Jim was overcome with love. He looked across at Joan and smiled, then he bent his head and kissed the baby's forehead. The baby opened his eyes for a moment, long enough for Jim to see that they were bright blue, like his own. He held a finger out and Jimmy curled his own tiny ones around it. Jim gazed at him in wonder and a rush of happiness ran through him.

'Why didn't you tell me? Would you have let me go away without knowing? How could you do that? Why?' He looked at her helplessly.

She moved away from the fireplace and went to stand at the window with her back to him, folding the fabric of the net curtains through her fingers. 'I didn't want you to feel obliged to stand by me. You never wanted me. I made all the moves. You played along to be polite. It didn't seem right to trick you into getting stuck with me.'

Joan turned and went to sit in the armchair opposite, leaning forward, her elbows on her knees, looking at the floor rather than at him and the sleeping baby. 'There have been so many girls in this town that have got knocked up as you Canucks call it and forced their fellas into marrying them. I don't want to force anyone to marry me. I want to marry someone of his own free will.'

'But you didn't even give me the chance, Joan.'

'No point. I know one thing about you, Jim Armstrong, and that's that you're a decent fellow and would insist on doing the right thing. I didn't want that. I didn't want you doing the right thing, doing your duty, like I'm some kind of sacrifice.'

'That's why you wouldn't open the door when I came to call on you last year. Because I'd have seen you were pregnant.'

'And if you had, I'd planned to tell you it was Pete's.'

A cold chill went through Jim. 'You mean it could be Pete's?'

She shook her head and sighed impatiently. 'Of course it wasn't Pete's. You know damn well he was in the desert. And he and I, we never… I was a virgin until that night in London. I wanted to give you an out.'

She looked up at him as he sat holding the child. He bent his head again and kissed his son.

'I don't want an out,' he said.

'Maybe I do. I don't want to be with a man who's doing his duty or who sees me as second best.' She spoke the words harshly and the baby woke and started crying. 'Give him to me,' she said. 'I need to put him down upstairs. You'd better go, Jim. We're doing fine without you. Don't you worry. Me and little Jimmy have each other now. That's all we need. We don't want you.'

Her words were like a physical slap. Here he was again, standing on shifting ground as she ran rings around him. She took the baby from him and moved to the door. 'Let yourself out will you, Jim. And please don't come back again. It's better if you forget about us.' She left the room and he listened to her footsteps mounting the stairs.

Jim sat on the settee, motionless, in shock, his brain a tumult of emotion. After about ten minutes, he got up and went up the staircase. He stood on the landing, looking at three closed doors, uncertain which to open, listening. The house was silent but then he heard the baby breathing and snorting in his sleep. He opened a door and found Joan lying on her bed, face down, the baby fast asleep in its crib beside the bed. Any doubts left him and he moved across the narrow space, lay down beside her and took her in his arms. She gave a little sob and turned to look at him, her face wet with tears. He wiped them away with his fingers then bent over and kissed her.

'You silly goose,' he said. 'Why on earth would I want to leave you?' He took a deep breath and then spoke the words he hadn't known he wanted to say until he was saying them. 'I love you, Joan, and I want to marry you. Will you have me? Please say you will.'

She looked up at him and said, 'You silly goose, of course I will.'

SHOPPING FOR SHOES

SATURDAY 3RD APRIL 1943,
EASTBOURNE

*O*ne Saturday morning a few months after Jim and his colleagues had left Eastbourne, Gwen was sorting through household bills when Pauline came into the study with Brenda in her arms.

'Sorry to interrupt you, Mrs C, would you mind watching Brenda for a couple of hours while I take Sally into town?'

'Of course not.' Gwen smiled.

'Only she needs a new pair of shoes and I've been putting it off for ages because of the air raids.' Pauline leant against the desk. 'It'll be much quicker and easier without the baby.'

'I's not a baby,' said Brenda indignantly. 'I's free.'

'You are indeed three and getting to be a big girl. We'll have some fun while Mummy and Sally are in town, won't we?' said Gwen. She turned to Pauline. 'It's no trouble at all.'

'You get so little time off from that place, I hate to spoil your day off.'

'I'll be much happier playing with Brenda than sorting through all these bills.'

Pauline put the child down and the little girl scrambled into Gwen's open arms.

Gwen turned to Pauline. 'Be careful in town.'

'We'll only be in South Street. And we won't be long. Straight in and out. I can't put it off any longer as the soles of Sally's shoes are almost worn through and her toes are squashed. They grow so fast it's hard keeping up.'

Both women were mindful of the continuing air raids the town had suffered, many of which had concentrated on the main shopping street, but neither wanted to voice their concerns. Last Christmas German raiders had shot at people in the street as they were out doing Christmas shopping.

After reading Brenda a story, Gwen took the child into the garden to play on the swing Jim and Mitch had rigged up last summer from one of the trees.

Gwen pushed a squealing Brenda back and forth. The little girl was growing up so fast, developing her own personality and gaining in confidence each day. She had an infectious smile and a sunny temperament and was clearly a bright child – Gwen had started teaching her the alphabet and the child was a fast learner. Her blonde hair was tied in pigtails and her cheeks flushed as she puffed them out and swung her little legs back and forth.

Looking at her, Gwen felt the familiar pang of loss for the child she had never had. When the war ended and the house in Whitley Road became habitable again the Simmonds would want to return to their own home. Gwen didn't want to imagine living without the sound of the children's voices as they played in the garden and dreaded the thought of having to say goodbye. God willing, it would coincide with the return of Roger, safe from war and she tried to console herself with that thought. There would be nothing to stop Pauline and the children visiting.

Over the two years that the Simmondses had been living with her she had come to see them as an extension to her family. Were it not for the war she would never have met Pauline. Now she would trust her with her life.

The scream of air raid sirens shattered the quiet of the spring morning. Gwen swept Brenda into her arms and ran into the Anderson shelter in the garden. Brenda started to cry as the siren continued its piercing and terrifying wailing. Gwen cradled her, feeling her little heart beating against her chest. No matter how often the raids happened it became no less frightening. Powerless, she crouched in the small shelter, hoping the enemy planes would head away from the town. But their engines screamed as they descended. Please God, keep Pauline and Sally safe.

Brenda's tears turned to whimpers as the explosions echoed and boomed. Gwen tried to count the bombs but they were coming so thick and fast she was unable to distinguish between individual explosions. The ground shook under them. It was a bad one.

The two of them clung to each other until the all-clear sounded.

She took out her handkerchief and wiped Brenda's tears away. 'All over now.' She bent her head and kissed the little girl. 'Brenda, my darling, I need you to be a very good girl. I'm going to take you next door so nice Mrs Prentice can look after you for a bit, while I go into town and pick up Mummy and Sally. I'll bring them back as soon as I find them and then I'll have to go and help the poor people who might have been hurt by the bombs.'

Brenda began to cry again.

'You need to be awfully brave and grown-up. Can you do that, Brenda? Can you be a big girl for me and for Mummy?'

Brenda nodded, her little face solemn and her thumb in her mouth.

Gwen quickly changed into her WVS uniform, left the child with her next door neighbour, and drove as fast as she could towards the town centre. As she descended the hill, dust and smoke clouded the air and she could smell burning.

As she approached South Street, opposite the town hall, it was apparent that one of the many bombs had fallen nearby and her stomach clenched in fear and dread. Don't let it be them. She parked the motor car and, grabbing her tin hat and her ARP armband, began to run down the street, stumbling over the broken glass scattered across the road from blasted shop windows. Please God, let them be safe. Let them have made it to the shelter. She repeated the words over and over again in her head.

A large metal sign lying across the pavement almost tripped her up and, with a sinking heart, she recognised the familiar black tin placard emblazoned with a large white S to signify the entrance to the communal shelter. It must have been torn off the front of the shelter in the blast.

At the junction with Spencer Road, close to the church of St Saviours, Gwen gasped, her knees weakening under her. All that was left of the shelter where she had hoped Pauline would have sought refuge was a pile of rubble in the road. It had been a surface air raid shelter, made of brick walls with a concrete roof. It was not constructed to withstand direct hits – intended only as a refuge from blast damage for people who had been caught outside when the sirens sounded. Gwen froze in her tracks, too shocked and terrified to move forward, certain that Pauline and Sally would be among the dead.

Lamp posts and trees lay in the road, torn out of the pavement by the force of the blast. Clergy from St Saviours wandered between the air raid wardens, hoping to find a living soul to whom they might offer consolation. Home Guards and ARPs were digging through rubble while policemen held back onlookers. Seeing Gwen's uniform and armband one of the policemen waved her through.

'I'm looking for my friend,' she said to a warden. 'She was shopping in South Street with her little girl and I think she may have sheltered here.'

'Better hope not, love,' he said, his mouth narrowing into a thin line. 'No one in there stood a chance. Direct hit. They're taking the bodies to the mortuary. What's left of them. If you want to find out you'd better get over there.'

When she reached the hospital, Gwen sat with anxious relatives and friends, many of them injured, in a packed waiting room, where the atmosphere was febrile. It was two hours before they let her into the mortuary room. A passing hospital orderly spotted her – he knew Gwen from her WVS duties when she had often accompanied distressed relatives to identify family members. The orderly motioned her to follow him and ushered her into a room where she was horrified to see so many bodies, each covered with a sheet. As well as victims of the Spencer Road shelter there were casualties from across the town including from the main shopping street, Terminus Road.

'Looking for a family member?' he asked, his voice quiet.

'My friend and her six-year-old daughter. They live with me.'

'I'm sorry,' he said, looking away. 'What I'd like to do to that bastard Hitler. You say she had a little girl with her?'

'Yes, with blonde hair, cut in a short bob.'

The man frowned, tilting his head to one side. 'Over here.'

He pulled back the top of one of the sheets and there was Sally. Gwen's knees buckled. Sally looked perfect, her face unblemished, her hair still held back on one side by a tortoiseshell slide. The man reached out a hand and steadied Gwen. 'I'm so sorry,' he said. 'It's her, isn't it? What a bloody awful shame.'

Gwen nodded, her throat constricted, her mouth dry.

'You want to sit down a moment? If you can remember what the mother was wearing I'll see if I can find her.'

Gwen sank onto the wooden chair he offered. 'She's blonde too. Permanent wave. Pretty. About twenty-eight. A blue coat.' She thought for a moment. 'Wearing a pink dress with navy polka dots.'

'I'm going to get you a cup of tea and I want you to drink it in the office over there while I find your friend, Mrs Collingwood. Give me five or ten minutes.'

Gwen nodded. Her skin was prickling, nerves jangling. The man handed her a cup and she sipped the sweet tea. Her body was shaking and the cup rattled against the saucer as she held them. Thoughts refused to form. She tried telling herself to focus. What was she going to do? What about Brenda?

The orderly stuck his head round the door again and his mouth turned down at the corners. 'I think I've found her, Mrs Collingwood. She's in much worse shape than her daughter. We can do the identification by the clothes.'

'No.' Gwen shook her head. 'I want to see her. I need to see her.'

With his hand on her arm, he guided her towards a table and eased back the sheet.

Gwen looked down at her dead friend on the slab and gave an involuntary gasp. Pauline's crushed face was almost unrecognisable, but there was bright red lipstick still fresh on her lips. Gwen imagined her sitting in the shelter reapplying it as the bombs rained down on the town.

~

THAT APRIL SATURDAY had produced the worst casualties for a single raid of any in the entire war, with thirty-two dead and ninety-nine injured.

There was no Jim to comfort her when Gwen mourned the death of Pauline and Sally. She had never felt so alone. Grief over Pauline and her daughter was mixed with anguish over what might await Jim and an aching loss at his absence.

She would have despaired, were it not for Brenda. The little girl needed her. She remembered Pauline's words at the death of her husband – bringing up her daughters was her only reason for living. Now Gwen was all Brenda had, and she intended to devote her attention single-mindedly to the little girl. It would mean giving up her work in the typing pool and her WVS duties. In a year or so, when Brenda started school – assuming the schools were open again by then – she could return to work part-time, but now working in any form was out of the question. She was needed at home.

Not long after Pauline's death, the little girl looked up at Gwen as she helped her eat her breakfast. 'Are you my mummy now?' she asked.

Gwen gave a gasp and felt her heart stop. 'Yes, my darling. I'm your mummy now.' She scooped the small child into her arms and held her tightly, kissing the top of her head, breathing in the sweet soapy smell of her as she fought back tears.

~

'YOU'RE GOING TO WHAT?' Daphne Pringle's tone was one of horrified disbelief. 'Good Lord, Gwen, you can't be serious. Adoption?'

'I'm completely serious. As soon as the war's over I'll make it official.'

'But Roger? Doesn't he have a say in this?'

'Roger will feel exactly as I do. We will both be Brenda's

parents. We've always wanted to have children. I love Brenda and I know he will too.'

Daphne tutted and shook her head. 'She's a dear little girl but she comes from another world. And I hate to say this but breeding will out. No matter how well you bring her up, her origins will tell in the end.' She lowered her voice as though afraid of being overheard. 'I never said it when the poor Simmonds woman was alive, but I always thought her rather...common. Not her fault. She couldn't help being working class, any more than the child can. And after all she was your cook not your friend. But honestly, Gwen, even the name Brenda screams commonness. If you do persist in this hare-brained idea you must at least consider changing it.'

Gwen was speechless.

Ignoring the look of dismay on Gwen's face, Daphne pressed on. 'I know you feel some kind of obligation to Mrs Simmonds, and of course it was a terrible thing for the poor woman and her daughter to be killed, but you mustn't let that affect your judgement. Having a child is a lifelong commitment. The little girl will be better off in an orphanage where perhaps one day a family of similar background might adopt her. Perhaps someone who lost a child in the war.' She stretched out a hand and patted Gwen's sleeve. 'Do see sense, darling. It's not as if Mrs Simmonds were family. Better to get the child into a children's home sooner rather than later, before she becomes attached. After all, she'll be in good company – so many children have lost parents in this filthy war – and so many children have coped marvellously being evacuated. She'll have forgotten you in a week or so.'

Gwen stared at her in disbelief.

Daphne however was unstoppable. 'Please see sense, Gwen. Everything will seem different when Roger's home and the war is over.'

'I had no idea,' said Gwen. 'No idea you were such an

unmitigated snob. A stuck-up, self-serving, shallow individual without an ounce of compassion. Well, I know now. My friend, Pauline Simmonds, had more kindness and understanding in her little finger... and she was much better company.'

'Really!' The indignation in Daphne's voice was matched by the redness of her face and her puffed up cheeks. She jumped to her feet. 'You've lost your mind, Gwen. I've never been so insulted in all my life.'

'You'd better go – before I say something else.'

Daphne picked up her handbag and moved to the door. 'I can see now why you want to take on that little girl. You have no breeding yourself.'

'If having breeding makes me like you, then I hope I haven't.'

But the door had already slammed shut behind Daphne.

INTO BATTLE

JULY 1943, SICILY

*W*aiting in line on the crowded deck, Jim's eyes were blinded by the brilliant sunlight. It was weather for bringing in the corn, or sitting in the meadow enjoying a picnic with the sun warming and browning the skin. Instead he was in the Mediterranean, ready to leave his ship and land in Sicily. They were there to fight their way across the island as a precursor to an invasion of mainland Italy. The men stood in crocodile formation, each holding onto the bayonet scabbard of the man in front.

The signal to disembark was given, and Jim gasped at the shock of cold water up to his armpits. Together they began wading through the sea to the beach, as the enemy bombarded them with shellfire. He was caught up in a haze of smoke and foaming water, the sea churning around him like a boiling cauldron. The man beside him vomited, a mouthful of salt water causing him to succumb to the seasickness that had plagued so many of them on the voyage.

Jim scrambled out of the shallows, oblivious to the cold of the sea and the fountains of water as shells exploded around him. Adrenaline surged through his body, and he raced up the beach, staggering towards the vineyard where they had been told to seek cover, the sound of machine gun fire blasting his eardrums. Several men fell, his friend Mitch among them, some of them tripping as their feet hit the land and they lost the resistance of the water around them. Jim flung himself onto his stomach and crawled over to his friend. Sniper fire began and he rolled behind a rock, grabbing Mitch by the collar. He hauled him up the beach, bending low, ducking and zigzagging to dodge the gunfire. The sun was scorching hot and the air was dense with smoke and the stench of shellfire.

The vineyard afforded little cover, the young vines low from the ground. Jim dragged Mitch under the shade of an olive tree and examined his friend. Mitch's shirt was soaked in blood; he was unconscious, but still breathing. Jim loosened his tie but before he could ascertain the nature of the injuries, his sergeant signalled to him to move on up the vineyard to join the rest of the platoon, ready to advance with tanks towards an Italian-controlled airstrip.

'Shift your arse, Armstrong,' yelled the sergeant.

Jim had no choice. He looked back and saw the company medic had already reached Mitch and was treating him on the ground.

The Italians appeared to have little stomach for battle and as more Canadians swarmed onto the shore, the gunfire lessened and Jim and his colleagues were able to move toward the airfield with little opposition from the disheartened Italian troops. Within a matter of hours they had captured their target, along with over four hundred Italian prisoners. Fifteen Canadians were wounded and seven dead. One of the dead was Mitch Johnson.

The death of his friend touched Jim deeply. He felt hollowed out, empty and saddened by the waste of such a young life. Mitch was only twenty-one. But there was no time to dwell on loss. He had a job to do.

The early success against the Italians at the coast was no indication of what lay ahead for the Canucks. The warm Sicilian sun gave way to cold cloudless nights. As they advanced further into the island, the fighting got tougher. They were now facing the Germans who controlled the interior of the island and had no wish to relinquish their territory.

Their first, real, protracted fighting took place on a hill, above a village occupied by the enemy. Working their way down the scrubby hillside in the early morning light, looking out for snipers and dodging sporadic mortar fire, Jim was paired up with two other guys, a private and a lance corporal. Their orders were to make their way as close to the perimeter of the village as possible and report back on what they saw. As they came within sight of the first houses, the scream of machine gun fire shattered the quiet dawn and Jim reeled in horror as the lance corporal was ripped open by a sustained burst from the automatic gun. Jim and the other soldier turned back to help the man but he was already dead, his stomach a gaping hole with his guts pouring out.

Jim had never thought about the smell of battle. He had only imagined noise, colour, shapes and movement. It hadn't occurred to him that there would be a smell from a man mown down in combat. It was the same throat-closing, sickening stench that he had experienced on a visit to the abattoir. Bile rose in his throat and he gagged. He turned to speak to the other lad, a fellow named Billy Baker from Winnipeg, but before he could get his words out, Billy took a shot in the arm from a sniper. The impact of the bullet spun him around and Jim watched, helpless, as a second bullet ripped into his stomach. Jim dropped to the ground and crawled over to Billy, who was lying where he had fallen behind a thorn bush. The scrub gave them both cover so Jim crouched beside the man, pulled open his battle dress jacket and began to swab at the blood with a piece of cloth from his pack.

The man reached a hand out and grabbed Jim's wrist. 'No. I'm finished.'

Jim eased his hand away. 'No, you're not, buddy. I'm going to make you comfortable and then crawl back up the hill to get help.'

Another rattle of machine gun fire peppered the hillside above where they were lying.

Billy's voice was barely a whisper. 'Too late. I'm done for.' The man's eyes were heavy, his lids drooping. He reached a hand up and held onto Jim's. 'Say a prayer for me, will'ya?' Then with a gurgling noise, a dribble of blood bubbled up through his lips and ran down his chin and the life went out of his eyes.

Jim closed the lids over the blank staring eyes. There was no sign of anyone else from his platoon. He stayed under the thorn bushes all through the day, lying beside the dead bodies of his comrades under the blazing Sicilian sun. Every time he tried to emerge from the cover of the scrub, German gunfire pushed him back. He could not see anyone else in the platoon, but he knew they were there somewhere on the hillside as he could hear occasional bursts of gunfire. The sun beat down and the flies gathered and settled on the bodies of the dead men as their blood dried in the heat of the day. There was no way of retreating until the cover of dusk. Jim lay helpless, next to the corpses of his comrades, fighting nausea at the stench of blood and death.

As night fell he heard a distant throbbing above him and saw aircraft approaching. His heart juddered with fear. The moon was full and the planes were coming in low – the enemy-held village clearly their target. Americans, he realised with relief. As the planes swept down towards the

German-held settlement they began to strafe the hillside. Behind him Jim heard a British voice shouting, 'The sodding Yanks are firing on us. Bloody idiots. Didn't anyone tell them we were here?'

To the sound of American bombs exploding, Jim scrambled to his feet and with the rest of his platoon, now visible shadows on the hillside behind him, ran towards the village to finish the job the Americans had started. As he ran, fear and doubt left him, replaced by anger and adrenaline. An image of Joan holding Jimmy in her arms swam in front of his eyes. Nothing's going to stop me coming back for you, he said to himself and, rifle above his head, he ran down the hillside towards the village.

PART V

1945

We must work to bind up the wounds of a suffering world

Harry S Truman, 1945

AFTERMATH

JUNE 1945, EASTBOURNE

A week after the bells rang out for victory, Gwen took Brenda to the church where the child's parents had married. They had gone into the town on VE Day, and the little girl had waved her victory flag but after a while had begun to cry, tired and overwhelmed by the crowds and the noisy celebrations. Gwen had also felt constrained in her desire to celebrate the end of the war, by the tragedy that had befallen the Simmonds and the absence of Roger. Jim's absence too made the VE Day celebrations bitter-sweet. Gwen had no idea if he was alive or dead.

Today's visit to the church would be a quieter and more fitting opportunity to give thanks for the end of the long and terrible conflict, show respect for those no longer with them and pray for the safe return of Roger to her and of Jim to his family.

She helped Brenda light candles for Pauline, Brian and Sally, then remembered old Mr Simmonds, Pauline's grandfather who had died in that first raid on Whitley Road and Pauline's elderly grandmother who had passed away not long after Pauline was killed. They lit two more candles and knelt together and prayed for them all.

'My grandparents are in heaven with Mummy and Daddy and Sally. Will you go to heaven and leave me too?'

Gwen had a lump in her throat. She pulled the little girl to her, holding her tightly. 'No, my darling. I don't plan to go to heaven for a long, long time.'

'Good. If you go to heaven I want to go with you.'

Gwen ran her hands over Brenda's hair and cupped her chubby chin in her hands. 'I'm not going anywhere, my love. I'm staying right here with you.'

Brenda looked thoughtful for a moment and then said, 'At school I said all my family had died and Miss Collins said that was sad for me.'

'Not all of them,' said Gwen. 'You have me and you do have a grandmother. Now the war's over you'll get to meet Grandma Maud.'

'Is she your mummy?'

'No, my mummy's in heaven too. Grandma Maud is my husband's mummy.' As she tried to explain, Gwen wondered why it was all so complicated. She was nervous at the prospect of explaining her new grandmotherly role to Maud and of course introducing Brenda to Roger when he returned. If he returned.

Gwen had still heard nothing from Roger nor any news about his whereabouts and she was becoming more dispirited every day. Now that the war in Europe was over, there was no reason why he should not be in touch – unless he was somewhere in the Pacific, or languishing in a Japanese prisoner of war camp. She shuddered. Or he was dead. She reached for Brenda's small hand and squeezed it.

'Why are you sad, Mummy?'

'I'm thinking about all the poor people who had a bad time during the war, and who we won't see again.'

'Don't be sad. Miss Collins says heaven is lovely. Nicer than here. She says it's a big sunny garden and everyone is happy. They have sweeties and birthday cake every day.'

Gwen smiled and stroked Brenda's hair. 'That sounds nice.'

'Do you think they have lots of toys too?'

'I'm sure they do, my darling.'

~

TWO MONTHS after the end of the war, Gwen still had no news of Roger. Her repeated enquiries to the War Office went unanswered, apart from a slip of paper to advise her that someone was dealing with her enquiry and would be in touch in due course. Fear at what the silence implied, and anger at the cavalier attitude of the military, compelled her to go to see Sandy Pringle. She was nervous about facing Sandy, following her fight with his wife, but she steeled herself. Sandy was Roger's friend. It was natural that she should turn to him for help. He was the most senior person she knew in the military with all kinds of contacts in the War Office and government. He was well placed to pull strings to try and discover her husband's whereabouts.

Either Daphne hadn't told her husband about their argument or Sandy had more discretion than she had given him credit for, because he made no mention of Daphne nor Gwen's plan to adopt Brenda. He promised her he would do everything he could to expedite enquiries about Roger.

Two days later Major Pringle called her. 'I won't beat about the bush, Gwen. It's not good news.'

Standing beside the telephone table in the hall, her knees buckled and she sunk back into a chair.

'Looks like he was on a special mission behind the lines somewhere in Vichy France, organising a chain of Resistance groups. Nothing's been heard of him since we took back Paris. The Nazis were crawling all over occupied France rounding people up indiscriminately to try and flush out the Resistance and several operational circles were broken. Everyone assumed Roger had gone dark to protect his network. But it looks like the network was infiltrated and betrayed. Five of his known agents were shot but there was no news about Roger. No easy way to say this but the likelihood is that the damned Boche got him. I think the best you can hope is that he was able to pop a cyanide pill before they tried to make him talk.'

Gwen slumped forward in the chair, feeling faint. She struggled to breathe.

'Frightfully sorry, old girl. Damned savages. A cursed nation led by a criminal lunatic. Chin up, try to be brave. Shall I ask Daffers to pop over and hold your hand for a while?'

'No!' she practically yelled down the telephone. 'Please, no. I want to be alone. Thank you for your help, Sandy.'

'We'll get the whole truth before long. Special Ops will be debriefing everyone and they'll unearth the facts in the end. But it takes time and their resources are thin on the ground – there are a lot of Nazis to be brought to justice.' He paused. 'The official line on Roger is missing in action, but I don't want you nursing false hopes. I had some pretty frank discussions up the line, or I wouldn't be telling you this.'

'Thank you for being so open, Sandy. I appreciate that.'

When she hung up she put her head in her hands and gave way to the tears that were welling up. Was this divine retribution for her affair with Jim Armstrong? Was God punishing her for her infidelity? For not loving Roger enough? For never showing him what he meant to her?

But God, if he existed, was indiscriminate in who he punished in this war. This bloody, stinking, rotten war. It was all so damned unfair. How could there be a God if he allowed such horrors to happen? Innocent children blown to smithereens or crushed to death under bombed buildings. Leaving families bereaved and broken. Allowing Hitler to bring down such evil on the world.

Fishing in her skirt pocket, she pulled out her handkerchief and wiped her eyes. Pull yourself together, woman. You owe it to Roger's memory to be strong. And to be strong for Brenda. An image of Jim swam in front of her eyes and she sobbed again. She was so alone. So lost. So feeble.

As she sat rocking in the chair in the draughty hall, there was a movement behind her and she felt Brenda's small hand slip into her own. The little girl said nothing. Moving against Gwen she scrambled into her lap, resting her head against Gwen's breast.

'Don't cry, Mummy. Show me where and I kiss it better.'

Gwen wrapped her arms around the child, holding her tight and drawing strength from Brenda's trust and vulnerability. In that moment, she made a vow to herself that she would never hesitate to demonstrate the love she felt for Brenda. She wouldn't let herself become the cold, distant woman her own mother had been. The dried-up, cold, inexpressive person she had been since Alfie's death, was gone forever, banished by the privations and challenges of war, the friendship of Pauline, the passion of her love affair with Jim and now the unconditional affection of this orphaned child. She wasn't going to let that person come back.

'You've already made it better, Brenda.' She brushed her tears away with the back of her hand and smiled at the child. 'You've made me so happy, my sweet. I love you very much.' She bent her head and kissed her daughter.

~

LATER THAT DAY, Gwen decided to take advantage of the summer sunshine to take Brenda to the beach. In the weeks since the armistice, the town was shaking off the trappings of war and re-modelling itself in its former role as a holiday resort. The barbed wire that had blocked off the beaches was gone, the anti-aircraft guns dismantled and removed, and where uniforms had been everywhere now there were holidaymakers and townspeople, bare-armed and dressed in cotton shirts and dresses and once more children played happily on the town's beaches. Gwen gathered together buckets, spades and fishing nets and prepared a picnic. The continued rationing meant that it was still a frugal affair, but things were beginning to ease up a little and she was hoping the tea rooms might even have ice cream for her to treat Brenda.

The beaches at Holywell had always been quieter than those nearer the pier and the Wish Tower, being further from the town centre, accessed by steps down the cliffside and rocky at low tide. That was why Gwen loved it so much here.

The sea was calm and blue today, fading to a silvery white at the horizon. The water shuddered and twinkled with tiny diamonds where the sun touched it. Gwen turned her head and looked back towards the east, where the water was a chalky turquoise, darkening to blue towards the horizon. She looked at her watch. Another hour before it would be time to pack up and take Brenda home. Something caught her eye as she looked eastwards. A tall figure in shirtsleeves, jacket slung over his shoulder, was walking along the promenade. Although he was too far away to see properly, there was something familiar in the way he moved. Gwen squinted in the bright sunshine and then her heart jumped and she was on her feet, oblivious to everything, everything but the man who was now running towards her.

'Wait here, darling, just a moment,' she said to Brenda, barely able to form the words, and she was already stumbling up the shingle towards the steps.

He was moving quickly and before she could get to the steps he had leapt from the stone walkway down onto the beach. One stride and she was in his arms.

He held her so tightly she could barely breathe and she wept tears of joy.

'You came home. I knew you would come home. Oh my love, you've come back to me.' She clung to him, arms around his neck, head buried in the warmth of his chest, her ear pressed against the sound of his heart beating.

Roger tilted her chin and kissed her and she returned his kiss with passion.

'My darling girl,' he said at last. 'I've dreamed of this moment every day of every year since I went away, but those dreams weren't a patch on reality.' He drew her to him and kissed her again.

They were so caught up in the embrace that Gwen didn't notice that Brenda had wandered across the beach to join them and was tugging at Roger's trouser leg.

He looked down at the child, surprised.

Brenda gazed up at him.

Roger took a step back, then squatted down in front of the little girl and said, 'What's your name, then?'

'Bwenda.' She took a step sideways to Gwen and lifted her hand to grasp hers. 'Who's he, Mummy?'

Roger got to his feet and looked into Gwen's eyes, his face a mixture of puzzlement and hurt.

Gwen clutched at the front of his shirt. 'No. It's not what you think. Brenda's mother and sister died in a raid and her father was killed on the Atlantic convoys.' She took his hand and said, 'Brenda is a special girl and I love her very much.'

Brenda studied Roger for a moment then hid her head in

Gwen's skirt in a sudden fit of shyness. Gwen bent down and lifted her in her arms. 'Say hello, darling, then we'll all go and see if we can find you a treat in the tea rooms.'

Brenda turned her big eyes on Roger and then in little more than a whisper, said, 'Is he my new daddy, Mummy?'

He looked at the little girl and said, 'If you'll have me, I am. Now how about a piggy back?' He reached down and lifted the giggling child onto his shoulders. 'Let's go to the cafe and get you an ice cream.'

Gwen linked her arms through her husband's and said, 'Thank you, my love. Thank you.'

Gwen's hand cupped the back of Brenda's chubby calf as it dangled down over Roger's chest, and leaned her head against his arm.

~

THAT NIGHT, when Brenda was sleeping and they had eaten their meal, Gwen moved to the gramophone and put on a Glenn Miller record. As the music filled the room she felt Roger move behind her and stand with his body pressed up against hers. He moved her round to face him and began to dance with her. The French windows were open and they danced out onto the terrace where he kissed her again. Light spilled out onto the stone paving from the drawing room. No need for blackout any more. Gwen looked up to the sky, where what they once would have called a bomber's moon poured milky light onto the dark of the sea. A lovers' moon, that's what she would call it from now on.

The End

AFTERWORD

The impact of the second world war upon the quiet seaside resort of Eastbourne was enormous. The town was said to have been the most heavily bombed of the South East of England. The first bombing, of Whitley Road and St Philips Avenue on 7th July 1940 was two months to the day before the Blitz began in London. That first bombing, on a Sunday morning, was probably more by accident than design as the Dornier 17 which did the damage had been heading elsewhere but was turned away by anti aircraft fire so dumped a stick of ten bombs on the town as it retreated from England. There was no doubt about the intention behind the raids that followed over the course of the rest of the war.

In more than one hundred raids, the death toll was one hundred and seventy-two civilians and twenty- seven forces personnel. Four hundred and forty-three civilians were severely injured with a further four hundred and and eighty-nine slightly injured. Four hundred and seventy-five houses were completely destroyed, a thousand seriously damaged and twenty thousand slightly damaged. The bombing destroyed many notable landmarks including the town's library and fire station, Barclays Bank, Marks and Spencer and the church of St John's. As well as bombs, the population faced machine gun attacks from fighter planes as they walked the streets.

The Canadian army had a presence in Eastbourne over most of the war with units stationed there between July 1941 until they moved out of the town in 1944 to assemble and prepare for the D Day landings. I did not attach Jim to a specific regiment, as the 23rd Infantry which was based in Meads didn't leave Canada until 1943, whereas Jim, like many Canadians was based in Aldershot before Eastbourne.

All the characters in the book are entirely fictitious but all the bombing incidents are closely based on real ones.

If you would like to keep up with new publications from Clare, get early or exclusive notice of special offers please sign up for Clare's mailing list. You will get a FREE copy of Clare's short story collection *A Fine Pair of Shoes and Other Stories*. Go to www.clareflynn.co.uk to get your free book now

ACKNOWLEDGMENTS

I am so fortunate in my editor, Debi Alper. As well as being an acclaimed novelist and editor, Debi is also a highly regarded teacher of creative writing and I am grateful to have her wise counsel and editorial skills.

I am indebted to the members of my critique group – three fellow authors, Margaret Kaine, Jill Rutherford and Merryn Allingham and editor Jay Dixon, who have given great advice and feedback over many months.

Thanks to Helen Baggott my eagle-eyed proof reader – and for squeezing me in at the eleventh hour. Also to Jo Ryan, Anne-Marie Flynn, Jill Rutherford, Sue Sewell, Jenn Brown and Clare O'Brien for their feedback. Having the scrutiny of different people, each of whom notices different things is invaluable. When one lives with a book for many months it is easy to let inconsistencies slip by – and you have all been fantastic help in spotting these.

Thanks to Joan Fairbairn and June Brown for sharing their wartime memories with me and to Sue Rowe for her help with German language and suggesting the Goethe quote.

Finally to Anita Jay who was the reader who won my name-a-character contest. She came up with Scotty McDermott and wanted him to be an airman. As there are no airmen in the book he had to make do with being a soldier but he did get to be a motorcycle dispatch rider, a master mimic of noises and even got to do a bit of cross-dressing while on manoeuvres.

I have a lengthy list of sources I consulted in researching this book but would like to mention two which were particularly invaluable in understanding the bombing of Eastbourne and the Canadian presence here. They are *Wartime Eastbourne* by George Humphrey (Beckett Features 1989) and *Canucks by the Sea* by Michael Ockenden (Eastbourne Local History Society 2006)

ABOUT THE AUTHOR

Clare Flynn is the author of four other works of historical fiction and a collection of short stories.

A former Marketing Director and strategy consultant she was born in Liverpool and has lived in London, Newcastle, Paris, Milan, Brussels and Sydney and is now enjoying living in Eastbourne on the Sussex coast where she can see the sea from her windows.

When not writing she loves to travel (often for research purposes) and enjoys painting in oils and watercolours as well as making patchwork quilts.

Contact Clare -

www.clareflynn.co.uk
clare@clareflynn.co.uk